A Vision of Loveliness

Ewen kicked Ares into a gallop just as the figure in the distance rose and began to stumble forward. Though wearing some sort of breeches, the person was unmistakably female. She was tall and slight, except for her full bosom, which any red-blooded man could spy clearly in such a scandalously tight blouse. Her hair was its own wonder, with thick, white-blonde ringlets flying loose in the breeze. Ewen wondered what kind of woman would have the gall to trespass on Cameron lands.

They were upon her in seconds. She didn't even have the chance to jump out of the way. Time suddenly seemed to stop. *I'm going to be trampled by a troop of mad, hairy, dirty Scotsmen in skirts*, she thought. The impact knocked her back into unconsciousness.

Ewen reached her just as she was crumpling to the ground. The laird didn't need to slow much in order to gather her up into his saddle, featherlight as she was. Sorting out her injury without removing the peculiar blouse she wore would be an aggravation, but he wouldn't have his men eyeing this woman. He had no idea where she came from and he surely didn't trust her, but something about this lass lying still in his arms compelled his protection. Her features held him spellbound. Ewen wanted to run fingers through that wind-whipped mane and pull her to him, claiming that mouth with his own. His head was suddenly mad with images of her mouth, those full lips, sucking and biting with a passion that would surely rival his own . . .

Master
of the
Highlands

Veronica Wolff

B

BERKLEY SENSATION, NEW YORK

THE BERKLEY PUBLISHING GROUP
Published by the Penguin Group
Penguin Group (USA) Inc.
375 Hudson Street, New York, New York 10014, USA
Penguin Group (Canada), 90 Eglinton Avenue East, Suite 700, Toronto, Ontario M4P 2Y3, Canada
(a division of Pearson Penguin Canada Inc.)
Penguin Books Ltd., 80 Strand, London WC2R 0RL, England
Penguin Group Ireland, 25 St. Stephen's Green, Dublin 2, Ireland (a division of Penguin Books Ltd.)
Penguin Group (Australia), 250 Camberwell Road, Camberwell, Victoria 3124, Australia
(a division of Pearson Australia Group Pty. Ltd.)
Penguin Books India Pvt. Ltd., 11 Community Centre, Panchsheel Park, New Delhi—110 017, India
Penguin Group (NZ), 67 Apollo Drive, Rosedale, North Shore 0632, New Zealand
(a division of Pearson New Zealand Ltd.)
Penguin Books (South Africa) (Pty.) Ltd., 24 Sturdee Avenue, Rosebank, Johannesburg 2196,
South Africa

Penguin Books Ltd., Registered Offices: 80 Strand, London WC2R 0RL, England

This is a work of fiction. Names, characters, places, and incidents either are the product of the author's imagination or are used fictitiously, and any resemblance to actual persons, living or dead, business establishments, events, or locales is entirely coincidental. The publisher does not have any control over and does not assume any responsibility for author or third-party websites or their content.

MASTER OF THE HIGHLANDS

A Berkley Sensation Book / published by arrangement with the author

PRINTING HISTORY
Berkley Sensation mass-market edition / February 2008

Copyright © 2008 by Veronica Wolff.
Excerpt from *Sword of the Highlands* copyright © 2008 by Veronica Wolff.
Cover art by Aleta Rafton.
Cover design by George Long.
Hand lettering by Ron Zinn.
Interior text design by Laura K. Corless.

ISBN: 978-0-425-21899-0

BERKLEY® SENSATION
Berkley Sensation Books are published by The Berkley Publishing Group,
a division of Penguin Group (USA) Inc.,
375 Hudson Street, New York, New York 10014.
BERKLEY SENSATION and the "B" design are trademarks belonging to Penguin Group (USA) Inc.

PRINTED IN THE UNITED STATES OF AMERICA

10 9 8 7 6 5 4 3 2 1

For Adam,
my very own romantic hero.

Acknowledgments

There are so many people I'd like to thank for helping me make my first book a reality:

My editor, Cindy Hwang, for taking a chance on me, for her razor-sharp edits, and for the enthusiasm that has made my introduction to publishing such a delight.

My agent, the wonderfully supportive Stephanie Kip Rostan, whom I was so unbelievably lucky to have found.

The San Francisco Bay Area chapter of Romance Writers of America, for being so welcoming to this wide-eyed rookie and generously showing me the ropes; particularly Monica McCarty and Kalen Hughes, who have, on more than one occasion, fielded questions on everything from copyedits to cravats. And the Celtic Hearts chapter, especially Cindy Vallar and Sharron Gunn.

Diana Donovan and Liz Dunn, who cheered me on when I stared down those first blank pages.

Anna Livia Brawn, whose insightful notes, Latin skills, and well-timed glasses of wine meant so much.

Martainn Mac an t-Saoir, *ceud taing matha* for gamely proofing some very salty Gaelic. And Urmimala Sarkar, for introducing us.

Too many websites to count, especially Electric Scotland, Akerbeltz.org, and Clan Cameron Online.

Padma Kaimal, who first taught me the joy of describing what I saw.

Liz, Myra, Mo, Monica, Michael and Anna, Keri, Britton, Laura, and Erica, for all that baby rocking, preschooler parking, and just plain commiserating.

Rudolph Reyes, for Uncle Rudy Group, as well as the administration of everything from legal advice to "margarudys" at critical junctures.

Ivan Wolff, for the loving support and for always leaving behind the good wine.

Joey Wolff, for being such an enthusiastic early reader and for always looking out for us.

Mom and Dad, who thought it the most natural thing in the world that I would write a book, with a special thanks to my mother, my chief plotting partner.

And last but not least, my amazing husband and best friend, Adam, who believed before I did that I had a book in me, and for being a partner with me in this, as in all things.

Prologue

The teacup slipped from her knotted fingers and landed in the saucer with a sharp clink. Sighing, the old woman massaged her aching knuckles. There had been a day long ago when the thrill of youth had infused her like a flame burning bright, and though she was never what one would call beautiful, her head of shining honey-colored curls had framed an easy, irreverent smile and perpetually flushed cheeks.

And now she was no more than an old mystery, the subject of children's fireside tales. Kindlier folk recognized her as wise or, at worst, benignly eccentric, wielding the wisdom of her many years through the prism of an otherworldly insight.

Others called her witch, made warding signs with their fingers, and covered their children's heads at the mere mention of her name.

Her name. She didn't recall the last time she'd heard her Christian name. She doubted anyone but herself even remembered it. She speculated that she had been known only as Gormshuil for generations now. Perhaps as long as it would've taken for the children who were robbed from her to see babes of their own grown into men. *Gormshuil*, such an ugly word. Gormshuil, the blue-eyed one. Named for her ghostly eyes, pale blue like a hazy summer sky bled of its color.

Gormshuil studied the tea leaves in the bottom of her cup. They clumped into a black and glistening half moon, a portentous omen that clashed with the delicate pink roses printed on her tea service. It had been a gift when she was a new bride, a lifetime ago. Since then, she'd sold off all of her other possessions, but she still couldn't bring herself to part with the old china. To use it every day, to see the pattern that she had loved when she was just a pretty girl who liked pretty things, was to feel grief's sharp grip fresh on her throat. She vowed that she would never let that anguish soften into numb memories of sadness and regret. Her pain was what defined her now and she would have it keen, bearing it like a spike in her belly.

No woman should have to endure outliving her family. And in such a way. Her man and her boys had been suddenly cut from her life with a matter-of-fact violence that gave birth to a kernel of hatred and a dream of vengeance that for many years were the only things that got her to swing her feet over the side of the bed and plant them each agonizing morning once again on the ground.

Gormshuil studied the tiny pink blooms and remembered how Fergus had worked so hard to surprise her, away for almost a full fortnight he was, traveling all the way to Edinburgh to buy the fragile china. She had never known she could ever own something so lovely. Bearing blooms like the roses in her cheeks, he had said.

The old witch pushed the absurdly delicate cup away and silently ridiculed herself and her small indulgence. One like her could ill afford sentimentality.

Society hadn't taken kindly to a solitary woman, and after the deaths of her husband and boys, she was forced to get by as well as she could on her wits alone. A wry smile turned at the corners of her mouth. As well as she could had been well enough indeed.

Her Fergus had always lovingly mocked those "women's arts" that she had learned from her grandmother. Gormshuil had known the sexes and birth dates of all her bairns when they were no more than slugs in her belly. And she had also known how to slip the *dwamie* babe she'd known would be too weak for this earth.

Small good any of her foresight or talents did when she hadn't even been able to save her own family. Her wry smile turned bitter. An indifferent enemy claimed their lives and left her to die. But die she didn't, and all that had remained to forge her own survival were her accursed arts and a heart so weakened she could barely see the green side of winter each year.

It was when she was forced to rely on her craft as a livelihood rather than a hearthside pastime that she truly refined her skills. She was canny enough to make herself valuable to those in society who wielded power, those seeking one who understood discretion as much as sorcery. Rather than the folk remedies and fortune-telling of the old spey-wives who were likely as not to end their days on a burning stake, Gormshuil learned the divination of unseen dangers and portents. She ingratiated herself to those with the real influence in the Highlands.

And thus a mourning and destitute widow fashioned herself the Witch of Moy.

❁

As she did every day, more times a day than she could count, Gormshuil took a deep breath and willed herself to endure just a bit more. Soon she would join Fergus and her boys. But this was not the day.

She studied the cup, turning it around and around as the cold brown tea puddled in the saucer. The old woman was agitated. It was her sixth cup that day and still the leaves told her the same thing.

One comes.

Chapter 1

Lochaber, February 1654

Ewen rose before dawn to run through the series of sword poses that he had rehearsed every morning for over fifteen years. Black hair loose past his shoulders, naked but for his long linen shirt and the blade at his back, he put himself through his paces.

The claymore had belonged to his father and was too large to carry on his waist by his side. Instead, Ewen had fashioned a scabbard of leather and silver so that, when sheathed, the sword hilt rose from between his shoulder blades. Ewen raised both arms, reached behind his head to grasp the sweat- and bloodstained leather grip, and slowly withdrew his weapon. Deadly sharp, the steel blade hissed as he raised it above his head. It was a slow and deliberate dance, with a sword that most people would not be able to lift with one hand. Up on one foot, down to bended knee, he struck and parried an un-seen enemy. By the time the sun started to peek through the mottled glass of his bedroom windows, Ewen was covered in a thin sheen of sweat, his rippling muscles taut and pumped from the exertion.

A knock on his door startled Ewen out of his reverie. "Aye, come," he grunted. The heavy, brass-studded door opened a crack and Katherine, the homely, plump-cheeked housemaid, peeked in. "Would you like me to fix you a bath, m'lord?" As she spoke, she noticed the laird's state of undress. Although his shirt reached nearly to his knees, Kat's cheeks flamed. She had bathed him herself when he was just a babe and she a girl of fifteen, but Ewen was clearly a youth no more. The sight of this half-clothed six foot four inch sweating warrior was too much for even a normally prudish old maid to ignore.

Ewen, used to the assessing looks of women, spared her further discomfort with a brusque "No." In clipped tones, he added, "I must meet Donald and the men. There's water in the basin. That will do."

His voice was gravelly, deep, with a sultry heat like the crackling of a slow peat fire. It had changed at a young age, and quickly too. Kat marveled how at times the laird's voice took on an almost gentle quality, incongruous for such an otherwise fierce man.

Ewen noted the tender look that washed over the maid's face. A smile touched the corners of his eyes as he added, "Thank you, Kat." She pulled her face out of the room and quickly pulled the door shut.

Ewen removed his scabbard, peeled off his sweat-soaked shirt, and dipped his hands in the basin by his bedside. The water was bitterly cold from sitting out all night, but the icy rivulets streaming down his back and thighs were invigorating. The sensation sent a shiver up through his loins and he became hard despite the chill of the water. He smirked to himself and wondered whether it was the early hour or the coming mission that made him go erect. Ewen had all but shut women out of his mind, so he didn't imagine that would be the cause. Not that he hadn't appreciated a good tumble in his day, but after such a miserable marriage in his youth, he decided one wife per lifetime was quite enough. A clan chief needed to be discreet with his affairs, and Ewen had decided long ago that there was no place in his life for romance.

At thirty-two, Ewen Cameron, seventeenth captain and chief of Clan Cameron, was younger than most other clan leaders. Having faced the death of his father at a young age, Ewen was thrust quickly out of his childhood. His grandfather had been temporarily reinstated as chief and Ewen sent away for years of formal schooling. He returned, eager to trade his books for sword and targe, and so it was that his Uncle Donald fostered the boy until he was ready to lead the clan.

Donald trained Ewen in the Highland warrior's arts with a singular intensity, for the clan chief needed to be the strongest, the bravest, and the surest with his weapons. During battle, he would ride ahead of his clansmen, not putting his men in danger that he wouldn't himself willingly embrace. The clan chief needed to be ready to accept his own death in order to protect his people, a lesson that Donald instilled into the youth with a near-ruthless rigor.

Donald also understood that though a good warrior was skilled in the arts of war, it took a great warrior to understand honor and the needs of his people, and so impressed intellectual ideals and aspirations into his young charge. Unlike other boys in the clan, Ewen studied Latin, Greek, and French. While other youth spent their days clacking wooden training swords, Ewen's uncle insisted he help with the house accounts.

Ewen pulled a freshly laundered linen shirt from his wardrobe and dressed himself to fight. A Highland warrior lived to defend his people and his honor, and most men had certain rituals they performed before battle. Some chose the company of women, others relied on prayer. For Ewen, it was methodical preparation—cleaning his weapons to a brilliant sheen, slowly honing steel until his sword and each of his three smaller blades could as easily split the finest hair as eviscerate a grown man.

After lacing his shirt, he wrapped himself in a freshly cleaned swath of tartan, which he tightened at his waist with a brown leather belt and large silver buckle. Ewen then began the elaborate process of arming himself. He spread all of his weaponry onto the bed and systematically checked and double-checked each piece as he donned it. He concealed blades under the cuffs of each of his boots, tucked a dirk at his belt, and, finally, sheathed his prized claymore on his back.

Ewen threw what remained of the wool tartan over his shoulder, fastening it with a silver brooch. He rubbed a bit of imagined tarnish, even though the Celtic hound shone from the polish he had given it the night before. Fingering the pin,

Ewen invoked the memory of his father. The laird smiled at his almost superstitious need to wear the token to battle, invested as it was with the near-mythic significance of a father's last gift to his son.

He would submit to no man. And, as his father's before him, his men were known as the sons of the hound.

Chapter 2

Scottish Highlands, Present Day

Lily exhaled sharply as she dug her thumb along the muscle in her forearm. She hadn't done any drawing in years and she wasn't about to let a cramp stop her now. Working on her sketches consumed her; already she had spent an entire morning vigorously rubbing and blending pastels in an effort to capture the land around her.

It was a nice change from the night before, which had ended badly. It'd been a full week since she had arrived at her rented croft and, save for the occasional curious wave from a friendly passerby, her only company had been the shaggy Highland cattle who spent their days grazing on the clumps of verdant green amidst the purple heather and gray rocks of the glen. Lonely for a little fun, she'd made the drive to Inverness and decided to brave one of the local college hot spots complete with rowdy boys, heavily made-up girls, and a loud band. All in all, she thought it would be a fun place to disappear while checking out what constituted nightlife in the Highlands.

After ten minutes pressed up against the bar hoping one of the bartenders would notice her, she began to regret her decision. Annoyed, she thought she could see why the local girls got so dolled up. How else to get a little service in this joint?

She turned to leave but was stopped by a hulking and very drunk young man. What he lacked in height, the kid made up for in width. With a too-tight black T-shirt stretched over his biceps, he clearly imagined himself a buff physical specimen. *Too bad*, she thought, *he didn't pay the same attention to his stomach muscles*, which were well hidden beneath his considerable beer belly.

"Excuse me," Lily whispered, lowering her eyes and trying to dart underneath his outstretched arm.

"Oi, it's a Yank!" the kid bellowed. He stank of whisky and vomit. Lily decided it was time to get out of there. By getting to know the locals, she definitely hadn't been thinking of drunken college boys. What had she been thinking anyway? She should be back at her serene little cottage, watching a movie, with a sinful midnight snack as her company.

"Yes, um"—Lily gave a half smile in an attempt to brush off his interest and again tried to duck out—"excuse me."

"Not sso fast, lassie," the boy slurred. "Is it true what they say about Americans?"

Lily tried again to escape, definitely not wanting to know what he was referring to. The band was between sets and the bar suddenly seemed eerily quiet. Lily felt an uneasy electricity in the air—the kind, she thought, that must precede a bar brawl.

"Please let me by."

"Aye, please let me by," the boy singsonged in a falsetto voice. By that time, a couple of his buddies had sidled up next to him to watch.

She felt her temper rising. While some women might have tried to diffuse the situation, Lily fought with fire, refusing to shrink from anyone, muscle-bound or not.

"Oi," Lily mimicked. "Now let me by." She walked headlong into his chest to move him aside, but to no avail.

"Look you drunken imbecile, I'm leaving." She knew that this was the wrong way to handle the situation, but it was clear that none of his buddies were interested in cutting short that evening's entertainment, so she would have to stand up for herself.

She noticed a handful of twentysomething girls huddled at her elbow, looking on sympathetically. A flame-haired girl flashed her a lopsided smile in show of support, and Lily found new reserves of bravado.

"Cretin," she spat, and tried once again to duck out.

By that time the bar was silent and everyone had their eyes on the American who appeared to be in over her head.

Lily fumed. She had simply wanted a night out, to be left alone, to check out a local band and maybe do a little people watching.

"Come on, luvvie," the boy mumbled. The smell of his breath was starting to make Lily ill. "Just give us a quick snog, aye?"

She had only meant to slap him, but somehow her fist ended up connecting with his jaw. Some of the college girls got in on the action and, rooting Lily on, tossed their beers in the boy's face.

Beer sprayed on his friends. Then the girls were doused. Then their dates got involved. And, before Lily knew it, she'd started an all-out pub fight. She had slipped out a side door to the sound of crashing beer bottles.

Lily had always prided herself on not being one of those timid, shrinking violet types, but inciting a pub brawl was beyond the pale. Studying her sketchpad, she thought with more than a little dread that she would need to return to the bar sometime to apologize to the owner for the ruckus.

She tossed the pad aside and, knotting her unruly pale blonde hair into an impromptu braid, marveled anew at the scenery. She had always heard tales from her grandmother about the grandeur of the Highlands, but no words could capture the vastness, at once beautiful and bleak. She looked around, awed by the contrasts. Wind howled and ripped tendrils of her hair loose from her braid, yet the coarse plants that dotted the moors barely moved, hovering low to the ground in an angry tangle with the purple and white of heather and thistle. Mean, scrubby little plants pronouncing to the world, *what, this little breeze?* Much, she imagined, like the Highlanders themselves. Strong, impermeable, and quick to understate a bad situation.

In the distance there seemed to be another country altogether as birds swooped lazily over one of the Highlands' innumerable lakes, the water impossibly still. Rugged mountains stood like austere sentinels on the far shore, their jagged silhouettes appearing somewhat softened in reflections on the glassy water. Except for the flickering shadows of gray storm clouds across the surface, the water was dark blue and violet in the morning light, making Lily finally understand why folk imagined lochs could harbor such enormous monsters in their depths.

She slowly gathered her pastels back into their tattered cardboard box and wondered that before coming to Scotland, years had passed since she had done any artwork at all. She had stumbled straight from an art degree, a passion for painting, and aspirations of arts education for underprivileged kids into an eighty-hour-a-week job in Silicon Valley. No art. No kids. And certainly no underprivileged anybody.

Touring Scotland had seemed to Lily an ideal opportunity to get some thinking done. To have a little alone time to reflect on where she had been in the last few years. What the haze of late-night hours, stock options, and board meetings had meant, if anything.

Mostly she came because of Gram. Her dear grandmother who'd left her native Highlands when she was not much more than a girl, eager to see what the rest of the world held in store. Gram, who never did lose her lilting brogue or the youthful light in her eyes.

She had always said that Gram had done all the heavy lifting, raising her as she did when her biological mother took off when Lily was just in grade school. Sandra, as Lily had insisted on calling her mother, had become infatuated with some third-string minor league baseball player who'd breezed into town for training camp. When the time came for him to breeze back out, Lily's mom had her bags packed and ready, figuring she had a better shot at romance not saddled with a kid, and while she was still on what she liked to call "the right side of forty."

Sandra rambled back into town some years later. This time she had a balding sixtysomething banker by her side and was thinking to pick up where she left off, eager to fill out her new role of staid suburban wife with a ready-made child. Lily wouldn't have it, which didn't much matter anyway. By that time, Gram and her "wee bonny *bàn*"—as she had lovingly nicknamed Lily for her outrageously curly white-blonde hair—were inseparable. The old woman was fiercely protective of her granddaughter, and it was only after some cajoling that she allowed Sandra and the new husband even to see Lily.

And now Gram was gone.

It had always been easy for Lily to deny just how old Gram was because she'd been so vital, ever obsessing over her crafts and poetry and roses.

Though she was comforted by the fact that Gram had gone peacefully in her sleep, Lily found no consolation. Rather than celebrate Gram's memory, she couldn't get past a laundry list of regrets. Gram had dropped everything and made endless sacrifices to raise Lily, when she should've been playing bingo and touring the globe with her seniors' group instead.

Now that her grandmother was gone, Lily found that instead of pursuing the next big thing in her career, all she wanted to do was escape to Gram's homeland. To take that "one last trip to the Highlands" that her grandmother dreamt of before she died.

At the outset, Lily thought it'd be an opportunity for a little reflection. The landscape was so solitary, though, she found she had almost too much time to think.

Back in San Francisco, she had gotten used to not dealing with much of anything outside of her work. It had started in the 1990s, when her temp job at a small Internet magazine had spiraled into a creative director position as she reached the ripe old age of twenty-four. A number of years, thousands of hours and one soured relationship later, she found herself with nothing but a used luxury sedan, a sizeable nest egg, and a few new wrinkles. Not even laugh lines, those. Just a couple of creases developing in her usually furrowed brow.

Lily wondered what it had all been for anyway. She had been an artist. And instead of following her dreams, she had ended up arranging layouts for other people's photographs of places she'd had no time to visit.

Maybe it had all been to prove Sandra wrong, to prove that she could get an art degree and not end up panhandling in the street. All she knew was that she surprised even herself when she hit the business world. Lily's colleagues had thought she was shrewd, viewing the temper that had been a liability in her personal life as a take-no-prisoners attitude. She kept thinking, just one more year of vesting stock options and then she could quit and paint to her heart's content. But she never did quit.

Then the technology market crashed. It started out slowly at first: the occasional minor layoffs, management re-orgs. But before she knew it, she was the lone designer among tracts of empty cubicles, left to pack up the pieces of a failed online venture for an anonymous corporate parent.

All those years at work and she had never even made any real friends. The MBA types blurred together in a sea of khaki and navy blue, people distinguishable mostly by which color BMW they chose or whether they hung Stanford or Harvard pennants in their offices.

There was one guy she saw for a few months last spring— a computer programmer who was a bit on the nerdy side. It was pleasant enough, until he got transferred to the corporate headquarters in Boston. Somehow the topic of Lily putting in for her own transfer never came up, and the relationship fizzled as blandly as it had begun.

Reflecting on her career, she was left with a sour taste in her mouth. Years of denying herself a life, and for what? A pile of worthless stock options?

And she'd done it at the expense of the one person in the world whom she truly loved and who truly loved and understood her. All the sacrifices her grandmother had made, and the only way Lily had ever repaid her was to become so consumed by some meaningless job that she prioritized Gram right out of her life.

She replayed in her head all the vacations that were cut short by her demanding schedule. All the times she put off returning Gram's call for a day or two, caught up as she was in some work-related project. All of Gram's home-cooked dinners she backed out of, wanting instead to stay late and catch up on e-mail.

She had even been too busy to properly mourn her Gram's death.

At the time, Lily had a thousand ways to justify it to herself. She had been the lead on a creative pitch to the board members, asking for one last round of funding to save her company. The meeting happened to be the day after Gram's funeral. Lily rationalized that Gram would've wanted her to press on with her life, especially as this was a prized task she'd been handed.

So she hadn't even taken a day to grieve.

Now the only people Lily had left in her life were a mother and stepfather who were veritable strangers and a handful of college buddies she played phone tag with every six months or so.

❀

Lily wadded up the tartan blanket she'd brought to insulate her from the damp Scottish hillside, shoved it into her pack, and got to her feet. Spinning slowly around, she sought her next landscape subject. A shift in focus might be just the thing to clear her mind. If only one of those stately bucks that roamed the hillsides would stand still long enough for her to sketch. She'd even settle for a shaggy old Highland cow.

Spying what looked like a small footpath in the distance, Lily set off down a particularly rough hillside. Although she was headed away from her cottage, she figured that the best way to get out of her own head would be to take a brisk hike. She could do with a little adventure, and if she got lost, the mountains and the loch would serve as a reference point to get her back by dark.

She smiled when she caught herself humming a tune that she hadn't thought of since she was young. Whenever Lily had a hard time falling asleep as a child, her grandmother would stroke her hair and sing her favorite lullaby, with words that had passed down through generations of Gram's own Clan MacMartin, telling of a fairy lad mysteriously come to Lochaber and made a hero. Lily would listen in wonder to the story she knew better than any other, hearing it as if for the first time. Or sometimes she would just drift off to sleep, hearing only the mesmerizing lilt of her grandmother's voice.

She could hear that voice in her head now, Gram's rich alto brogue, as clear to her as if it had just been yesterday. Regardless that she had sung the song hundreds of times, Gram would always begin the same: "My wee bonny *bàn*, now here's a tale of a young lad, bookish but braw he was"—Lily smiled at the memory of Gram and how she'd always elongate the word *braw* into an extended crescendo—"your long-ago cousin on the MacMartin side." As if any family had existed for the elderly woman other than her own Clan MacMartin.

Then she'd always stroke Lily's hair, slowly singing,

"He was a fey lad and not so old
With hair spun from rings of gold.
Upon Letterfinlay soil he did land,
Claiming he came from a future grand.
A MacMartin lad who knew no fear,
Clan Cameron took and held him dear.

"A sidhe lad
In red and green plaid
And charming to behold.

"One day tragedy learnt his name
In a skirmish with men in coats of flame.
To protect the laird whom he called his brother,
He gave a gift he could give no other.
On a bonny hill the lad met his ruin,
When he took a bullet meant for Sir Ewen.

"A sidhe lad
In red and green plaid
Died before he was old.

"The fearsome laird and his hounds did forgive
Any trespasses the fey lad did give.
For known as but a lettered young man,
He proved himself worthy of clan.
Honored is he until this day,
For a most precious price he did pay.

"Lochaber lasses still grieve for the lad,
A MacMartin hero in Cameron plaid."

Lily took a deep breath, moved to see that very Lochaber land for herself. Tears stung her eyes as she thought of how happy it would have made Gram to stand once again on Scottish soil. Serenity washed over Lily, as if some imaginary force that had constricted her chest suddenly released. A feeling of connection overcame her. Shaking her head, she savored the paradox.

Standing on one of the loneliest spots on earth made her feel she'd come home.

Chapter 3

A solid hour had gone by and Lily still couldn't find the right spot to round out the day's drawing. She had followed the path down a steep incline, winding between large rocks, stopping every now and then to pick one of the tiny wildflowers that grew along the hills to press into her sketchbook, and worked her way along what she thought was the base of the hill that she'd perched upon all morning, the spot that had afforded her such a glorious panorama yet so many unsatisfying sketches. Stopping short, Lily looked back and realized that she had traveled much farther than the circumference of the original hill, and the valley she'd been hiking through had gradually narrowed into a deep gorge.

It was past noon and the sun was already starting to throw elongated shadows. Thanks to a rocky outcropping rising sharply above her, patches in the trail ahead were cloaked in darkness. Tenacious clumps of yellow brush forced their way up between the rocks at her feet, making the path jut out at precarious angles, while in other spots years of uncontrolled growth obscured it altogether, forcing Lily to slow her pace in order to pick her way along. She pulled her sweater tightly around her neck and told herself that it was merely a chill and not uneasiness that made her flesh shiver.

Just when she was about to curse her earlier expansive mood and all the sentimentality that had well and truly gotten her lost, Lily saw it. Just ahead on the right, set into the rock, so matter-of-fact, yet defying all logic.

A doorway.

She had been so focused on not stumbling along the uneven path, she hadn't been paying attention to the rock formation that shadowed her, reaching higher as the trail narrowed. She studied it more closely now, and what had seemed like solid granite resolved into a pattern of hundreds of individual quarried rocks, stacked tightly, each unique shape wedged perfectly along the next to form a massive man-made wall reaching two stories high, and likely once as solid as bricks and mortar.

Blooms of lichen and moss that had seemed to protect it in a curtain of white and green were actually ravaging the ancient stone, working in tandem with gravity to wear down carefully ordered slabs of masonry into crumbling ruins. The mottled colors blended into the lush, dark greenery that was visible just within the doorway, and had camouflaged the entrance when viewed from afar.

Closer now, she saw it clearly. Its presence was announced by a massive lintel bisecting the rock. A disembodied breeze rustled the leaves of whatever plant life grew within, making the gateway seem to hum with a life of its own.

She knew the sensible thing would be to turn around while she could still backtrack along her original trail, but the artist in Lily clamored to discover something beyond the ordinary. A unique subject to inspire her long-neglected creative energies. Ignoring her better judgment, she veered from the path.

The doorway was wide but low, and Lily was forced to stoop as she carefully pushed her way through the ferns that shrouded the entry. The walls were staggeringly thick, and it took two steps to walk through the entrance. Although there was no roof overhead, it took Lily's eyes a moment to adjust to the gray filtered light that illuminated the space in a surreal haze. The walls were actually curved to form a massive circular structure, and she wondered if she hadn't stumbled upon the remains of a great tower or ancient broch.

The greenery that had been visible through the doorway was in fact an immense hedge. It clung close to the stone, curving to echo the shape of the rounded enclosure. Towering close to seven feet overhead, it filled Lily's line of vision.

At first glance, the plant beckoned to her. Dark berries the size of cherries bobbed gently among bushy leaves fluttering lazily in the breeze. Flowers dotted the branches and the plant appeared decorated with small purple bells. Smiling, Lily stepped closer, thinking to pluck one of the happy blooms to press in her sketchbook.

Her hand froze in midair as nasty little aspects of the plant revealed themselves. The flowers, though purple, were a dingy shade like the color of a day-old bruise. The leaves were also drab, and laced with dark veins that eerily suggested a life force beyond that of a simple plant. But for the fruit that shone a deep black, the entire hedge was dulled by short, bristly down that only furthered the sensation that an otherworldly spirit pulsed within.

Lily tried to look through the greenery, but the plant was dense with immoveable gnarled branches, ancient and woody at the base, growing into fleshy outer limbs the color of rotten eggplant.

A thin path wound its way to her right and left, matted with loamy brown moss and remarkably clear of roots or other debris. A few steps in, Lily noticed a gap in the plant. She had almost missed it, as the opening merely revealed more of the same unending green shrubbery. She leaned on one foot to look in and caught her breath. Long corridors split off to either side, off of which were more openings, which she assumed led to even more corridors, like a colossal labyrinth. She had seen pictures of garden mazes when she'd studied European architecture in college, but the quaint, whimsical topiaries found in London gardens weren't anything like this. She had the fleeting sensation that this maze had a life of its own. It had clearly been neglected for years, and she fancied it was a sort of malevolent force waiting to consume her.

She shook her head as if that could dispense with the fear that suddenly gripped her. Lily wanted to prove to herself that she wasn't afraid. If she were to make a fresh start in her personal life, she would need to embrace a little adventure. Besides, she figured, what better sketching opportunity than the bizarre Escher-esque maze right in front of her?

Lily passed through the opening and was thrust into a complete and shocking silence. She fought the sensation of being swallowed up, becoming one with the plant itself. She hadn't noticed the birdsong that had ridden along the rustling breeze until its sudden absence left only the sound of her own breath echoing around her.

She was standing in a small room, with those hairy green leaves, dark fruits, and flowers forming the walls around her. Three passages offered themselves, each showing glimpses of dark green hallways forking into more green rooms offering more passageways.

Momentarily hypnotized by the effect, Lily took a tentative step through one of the passages. Alarms sounded in her head, but she gulped back the now-consistent throb of unease with the thought that she'd go just a few feet to grab a peek around the first corner or two and then turn immediately back, retracing her steps exactly.

She took her first left and then her first left again—just enough to be completely surrounded by the massive plant. It was dizzying. Everywhere she looked there were shades of green and openings into more green and darker green shadows.

Abruptly, claustrophobia seized Lily's chest and she decided it was time to get out immediately. She took a quick mental snapshot for the drawing that she would dash off once back outside the labyrinth, then confidently took her first right, then first right again. But instead of taking her back to where she started, that placed her in another green alcove, which opened up to three other intersecting corridors.

Fighting back a wave of panic, Lily mumbled to herself, "Okaaay. No biggie," her voice comforting her in the now deafening silence. "I must've taken the wrong first right is all." Lily backtracked left and left again to return to what she thought was her first stopping point.

Now she was alarmed. She thought she'd retraced her steps exactly, but she was standing in another, larger alcove formed by the increasingly malevolent-looking shrub. She studied the space—could this have been her original starting point? Were there only three openings in the first room? She thought there had been four. She tried going left again. This time she knew she was completely lost as she peeked her head into what was to be her second left only to see a much larger rectangular space opening onto just two other passages. She jerked her head back out of the alcove—she knew she hadn't seen that room before. The last thing she needed was to get even deeper into this maze than she already was.

"Think, Lily, think." Wasn't there some sort of law of physics she could turn to in this situation? Like, a law of the universe stating that, if you keep turning left, you'll eventually get back to where you started? *Okay*, she thought, *so I'm no scientist, but there must be some other way to work through this.*

She remembered the mazes that she loved to do as a kid. This damned maze couldn't be any more difficult than one of those. How big could it be, anyway, when she hadn't even seen it from her perch on the hill? Her strategy, she decided, would be to plow bravely forward, leaving some sort of trail as she went. Surely, eventually, she would find her way back out.

Another hour passed, and Lily's mind had cleared of everything but the single-minded focus of systematically working her way through the maze. Her pattern was: head down a corridor, taking every first right until she hit a dead end, then retrace her steps and start the pattern over again taking every second right, and so on. She scuffed her heel into the path as she went to mark her trail.

Lily came to an abrupt stop. She found herself standing in what was the only entrance to the smallest alcove yet. Directly across from her was a niche cut into the wall of shrubbery, displaying a pale gray stone carving about three feet by three feet square. Lily couldn't fight the artist in her and, transfixed, slowly approached for a better look. The niche itself had long since become overgrown, so Lily had to pull some branches away to get a good look at the carving, shuddering as a clump of the plant's heavy black berries brushed against her hand.

It had been done in very hard rock, Lily thought probably granite, which surprised her since it would've taken some pretty sophisticated tools to get lines this delicate into rock that hard. Even the ancient Egyptians hadn't figured that one out. It had a surprisingly smooth surface for something continually exposed to the elements. A geometric pattern lined the outer edge of the square, reminding Lily of the chevron motif popular in ancient Greek sculpture. Every four inches or so, though, the chevron pattern was interrupted by one of many different carved markings, which Lily thought were runic characters like the kind found on Celtic knickknacks at the Glasgow airport tourist shop.

The center, though, was what really captured her attention: lines carved in rudimentary shapes, interspersed with deeply carved points. Blurring her eyes, she imagined she could see simple human and animal shapes represented in the form of the lines. If she had to hazard a guess, she would say that she had discovered an ancient star chart, but surely something of that nature would be in some museum somewhere, not all the way out here. No, this had to have once belonged to some rich, eccentric Scot who let his garden get away from him. It was just the sort of lawn ornament that she could picture being sold side by side with those silly gargoyles that had become so big in gardening stores back home.

But she couldn't get over how smooth and cold the stone was. The clean quality of the lines suggested to her that this had to be more than your average garden statue. She slowly traced her finger along each line, all the while wondering in the back of her mind what kind of tools an artisan would need to carve with this kind of precision. Smooth line. Point. Smooth line. Point.

She became transfixed. Beginning in the upper left corner, Lily ran her finger slowly over the outlining edge of the carving, feeling the chevron pattern flow into a runic character then back to the chevron pattern again. A random thought popped into the back of her head and she thought with wonder how it is that the blind can learn to read Braille. She sensed that her own finger was becoming more sensitive to the rhythm of the pattern, and that if she were only to concentrate a bit more, she too would be able to close her eyes and take in the entirety of the image with her hand alone. When her finger returned to the upper left corner of the carving, she slowly and systematically began to trace each line and each point in the center of the stone.

Lily was torn from her reverie when, upon dipping her finger in the last point at the end of the last line, the ground beneath her feet jolted. She bit back a shriek as her mind raced to make sense of what was happening. The earth heaved again. A crooked half smile somewhere between amusement and terror quirked her features as Lily's last conscious thought was how ironic it was to die in an earthquake while on vacation outside San Francisco.

Chapter 4

"I'll not understand why you're off to treat with such a man as Monk."

"Aye, and a bonny morning to you too, Uncle." Ewen flashed a smile at Donald. He well knew his uncle's querulous temperament and had expected that a meeting with the new leader of Cromwell's army would not sit well with the old warrior.

He prized his uncle's bravery and knowledge—the man had been invaluable in Ewen's early days as laird—so he often gave Donald great latitude in any disputes.

Donald continued, undaunted by Ewen's attempt at humor, "The man's a murderer who's spilt the blood of your kin. It was you who delivered more than a score of Cameron men to the Earl of Glencairn to rise against these Commonwealth whoresons, or have you forgotten so soon? He's a devil, that man is, that's why they wear those red tails on their coats."

"My uncle you may be, but you're not the laird. Sir." A roguish gleam in Ewen's eye kept the potentially volatile exchange light. "I'll never forget the destruction he and his bloody British footmen have wreaked on Highland soil. We both of us regret we weren't at the Battle of Worcester when so many Scotsmen fell, or have *you* forgotten so soon?"

"General Monk, och." Donald spat in disgust. "The man's not honorable. I vow lad, I'll redress not being by my brothers' sides at Worcester." His voice boomed with growing zealousness, echoing down the empty stone hall. "Damnable Monk. He's slow as an old merchant galley, blowing where the wind may, aye? Leaving orphans and widows in his wake. They who've luck enough to be counted among the living, that is."

"Uncle, respectfully." Ewen halted and turned, gritting his teeth so as not to lose patience with the irascible older man. "I am Lochiel, aye? And as such, I have to do what's best for the whole clan. A laggard and a scoundrel General Monk might be, but he's asked for an audience and I will hear what he's about."

"Och, if he doesn't stab you in the back first," Donald muttered under his breath.

"Aye, in my head, the man's no better than a common reiver, but if treating with him could mean peace for the Highlands, then so I shall."

After a moment, Donald gave a brisk nod. His scarred face cracked into a snarl that would look much more like the smile it was were it not missing a couple of teeth. "I suppose you have the right of it, lad." Not used to such an outburst of emotion, Donald's usually surly mien returned. "But the moment Monk shows his true colors, I'll spill his blood myself, aye?"

"Fine, uncle." Ewen clapped his hand on the other man's back. "Now can we be off, or are there other theatrics you'd have off your chest first?"

Donald was still shaking his head when they approached the courtyard where stable boys awaited them, holding the reins to three mounts. The laird prided himself on his ability with horses and although his stallion wasn't exactly easy on the eyes, he was the soundest and most courageous warhorse he had ever ridden. Ares was almost completely black but for one red sock on his right hind leg. It was the color of spilt blood, and Ewen had always felt it an auspicious mark for a battle horse. Ares's nose was thick and blunt and covered with numerous spidery black scars, shining dully, artifacts of battles past.

By the time Ewen and his companions crested the final hill

revealing Loch Garry and the rugged countryside below there were but a few hours of daylight left. The loch itself was small compared to others in the Highlands, but the view was dramatic nonetheless. The water, silver in the late afternoon light, snaked a path through countryside rough with clumps of shrubbery and thin evergreens that spiked the horizon. The low, rugged peaks of Knoydart held silent vigil in the distance, seeming all the more barren for the dense gray mist that shrouded them.

Ewen stopped, frowning. He had observed large groups of fighting men before, but the assemblage gathered in the glen below made him deeply uneasy. He had led many skirmishes in his life, fighting side by side with men of his clan or those who counted themselves allies, and they were always a reassuringly motley bunch. The larger battles against the redcoats had always been a patchwork of tartans in all colors and combinations.

Scots, both young and old, armed with musket, broadsword, pike, or bow and arrow counted themselves among his people's fighting men. Some came astride horse, others on foot. Grooming varied wildly, with some wearing crisp linen shirts and fine woolen jackets and trews, their hair well combed underneath their bonnets. Others appeared more savage, racing into battle on foot, untamed hair flying. Ewen always favored his tartan, a distinctive red and green plaid that he wore with fierce pride.

Looking now at the valley below them, though, made his blood run cold. Not for fear of the redcoats' fighting prowess, for Ewen had bested more than a few British regiments in his tenure as laird. What he found disturbing was the sight of this well-oiled machine made up of anonymous boys in red. They were overdressed and undertrained, bearing firearms that proved suicidally slow to reload when faced with a raging Highland broadsword and targe. Who were these young men who sacrificed everything, wielded as tools by British generals, to be used then discarded? To be a Highlander was to be a warrior, but that was also synonymous with clan and country, a proud and noble identity that any man would willingly give his life for. But these boys in their snow-white shirts and breeches, did they know what they fought for?

Ewen hoped he came that day to wage peace with Cromwell's own General Monk. It wasn't that he feared battle. There had been many a time in the midst of a skirmish when Ewen had said a prayer—not for courage, but rather to beg God's forgiveness, for he went to the field not just willingly, but with a zealous thirst for the fight, to see injustices that had been done to his people avenged one hundredfold.

What he did fear more than any battle was something he knew deep in his bones: no matter what passed that day, the fighting would persist. More Highland blood would be spilt, more Highland cattle and lands raided and ravaged, and more politicking by men like Monk would continue to define the fates of boys taken from their mothers to face death, be it wearing tartan or a coat of red.

And, Ewen thought, God help him but he would be there on the front lines, ecstatic battle rage writ clear on his face, claymore brutally cutting down any who stood against his Highlands.

"Aye." Ewen's voice came out as a deep growl. "It's time then."

"And which do you suppose might be the good general's tent?" The laird's foster brother, Robert, rode up beside him and eased the tension with apt sarcasm, uncharacteristic for the quietly bookish young man. Compared to the meager furnishings of the rest of the camp, General Monk's tent stood out as nothing short of a spectacle. Tall enough to accommodate a dozen standing men, it was made of fine linen cloth, soaked in paraffin to repel the Highland mist and rain. A large flap extended from the roof and was braced above the ground to create a covered entryway where Monk or his guard could stand untouched by the elements.

Ewen and his men tethered their mounts and descended into the valley encampment, drawing more than a few stares from the young redcoats doing what it was soldiers do: polishing guns, stoking cooking fires, or just sitting about in circles, drawing deeply from battered metal cups that were almost certainly filled with some sort of alcohol.

Wood smoke hung thick and gray in the air, but it couldn't banish the unmistakable smell of hundreds of men living together in close quarters. The soldiers made do with small tents arranged in tight rows, their once-stiff duck cloth now limp, mottled with spattered mud and mildew from the inexorable Highland drizzle.

By this time, most eyes were on the Camerons as they wound through the camp. The laird purposely led them on a meandering route in order to get as good a look as possible at how his enemy was encamped. He was pensive. Not seeming to notice the stares of the redcoats, Ewen distractedly worried a small stick, slowly snapping off twigs and leaves, appearing lost in his own distant thoughts, although those close to him knew that not one detail of the camp was lost on him.

A guard was posted outside Monk's tent. He was busily absorbed in an afternoon nap, eyes partially hidden by his wig, knocked askance by his bobbing head.

The laird pressed his stick into the flesh of the sleeping redcoat's neck. "I'm glad you find the accommodations comfortable," he said in a mischievous whisper as the soldier's eyes shot open. The man's ruddy cheeks quivered as he stammered "Wha—? P-please don't hurt me, sir. Wh-what do you want?"

"We're here to see the general." Ewen flung his stick aside and stepped forward to open the thin curtain that concealed the entrance to the tent. He glanced at the sentry. "I assume he's in here." It was an announcement, not a question.

The soldier's face paled and Ewen turned to see a stoutly regal figure now looming in the entrance. "What is the meaning of this?" The man directed his question to the guard, not even acknowledging the presence of the Camerons. The soldier was now standing. One of his buttons had come undone during his nap, creating a yawning gap in the too-tight red coat that strained over his belly.

"General Monk, I presume?"

The man answered with the merest of nods.

Ewen continued, "I'm Ewen Cameron, seventeenth captain and chief of Clan Cameron. This is Donald, brother to my late father. And this, my foster brother, Robert MacMartin." Each man nodded toward the general at the mention of his name.

"You requested an audience, and we've come, aye?" Ewen's nonchalance belied the tension of the moment.

The inside of the General's tent was as well appointed as any Highland cottage. A small fire burned on one side of the room, vented through the top of the tent by way of a copper stack. Two leather-backed chairs were placed in front of the fire, a half-played chess game sat on a table between them. There was a large cot in the corner, piled high with furs.

The laird slowly paced around the tent, inspecting his surroundings. "Now, shall we get down to business? I haven't the stomach to stay here longer than necessary."

Ewen paused for a moment to study the chessboard then slowly raised his head to meet Monk's gaze. "Tell me why you've summoned us and what it is you'd have of the men Cameron."

The general was smoothly elegant in a way that Ewen immediately distrusted. He dressed not as a soldier, but as a British nobleman. Ewen sized him up at once, assessing that his wig, the gold buttons on his overcoat, and the silk stockings that hugged his thick calves would cost more than what a Cameron clansman could make in one year working the land. Fine, impossibly white lace framed his face and peeked out from underneath the cuffs of a sky blue coat embroidered with whisper-thin gold threads. His aquiline nose jutted sharply from his face in counterpoint to otherwise jowly features. Although in his early fifties, Monk had a stately air and a physical confidence unusual for his otherwise stout frame. Ewen imagined that he drew the attentions of many a lady and the ire of more than a few young lords.

"Down to 'business,' as you call it. But of course, Ewen Cameron, seventeenth chief of Clan Cameron." Monk gave him a well-oiled smile.

"I see you're dressed for battle, General."

Monk's fashionable clothing was startling in the context of all the hundreds of redcoats waiting just outside his tent for imminent battle.

"Touché! And 'Monk' will do fine, thank you Ewen. You don't mind if I call you by your Christian name, do you?"

"As you wish." Ewen dropped unceremoniously into one of the general's leather chairs. "Now enough of the niceties, Monk. I'll not ask you again. Why've you called the Camerons to the middle of a redcoat camp? I'm assuming it's not for tea and biscuits, aye?"

Monk picked up a decanter from atop a side table at his

elbow and gingerly poured himself a snifter of brandy. "Ah, yes. Why indeed have I called you here. Brandy?"

Ewen's impatient glare answered for him.

"You and your tenacious Highlanders seem to be fighting a losing battle. Even now, those of your . . . farmer-warriors"—Monk bit back an affected smile, lips pursed in a tight red bow, dimpling his fleshy cheeks—"who weren't slain have been forcibly dispersed back into your savage countryside with that fellow of yours, oh"—Monk fluttered his hand in mock impatience—"what is his name . . . General Middleton! That's it. Those Highland . . . generals . . . are so difficult to keep track of, are they not?"

An unctuous smile spread across Monk's face as he eased himself into the other chair and leisurely swirled and nosed his drink. "Mmm, a noble little vintage. Only once have I enjoyed better—a fine Armagnac aged in the private cellar of some monks in Gascony. Nothing like a little monastic prayer to improve the character, eh? You know, the French call Armagnac their eau-de-vie. They believe it holds therapeutic powers, and after experiencing it, I am loath to disagree. Perhaps when these vulgar proceedings are concluded, you too might enjoy a snifter."

"I think not, Monk. *Uisge* is the true water of life. Your brandy is for men who've not the mettle for a true Highland drink. Now if you're through orating, I'll hear what you're about."

"Of course, I digress. I was saying how our fine fighting Englishmen are systematically quelling your little Highland insurrection. Indeed, other of your Highland chiefs and fellow Royalist insurgents have surrendered their arms in recognition of the supreme authority of the English Parliament. And, for my part, I have treated them with great leniency."

"Och, you mean you bought them. Well, I'm not for sale. I'm not pulled where the tides may take me. Unlike yourself, as I understand it. You were once a Royalist, is that not true? Your father spoke for the king, yet it became . . . inconvenient for you to do so. Have I the right of it?"

Monk's genteel façade momentarily flickered, and Ewen continued after only the briefest of pauses. "Now if that's all you've to say, our business here is through."

"I wouldn't be so hasty if I were you, laird. That is not all I have to say. I'm offering an end to the killing of your men and recognition of your custodianship of Cameron lands. All you need to do is order your men to desist in these skirmishes, which though potentially catastrophic for you, are for the English army no more than the harrying of midges."

"You offer me lands that I already call mine? The Highlands are not for you to give." Ewen rose abruptly. "I'll thank you to allow me and mine safe passage out of this camp."

Ewen glanced back at Monk from the tent entrance. "White queen to rook four. Mate in two."

"Very nice, I was wondering if you'd see that move." A tight smile curled the edges of the general's mouth. "I will see you again, ah, what do they call you . . . Lochiel? You will soon learn that this is only the beginning. The English Parliament is here to stay, and you have only begun to feel the might of its authority. Cromwell is its arm and I, good sir, am the gauntleted hand that imposes its will."

Monk took a slow, deliberate sip of brandy. "You will come to understand that your Highlands are merely a province of England. Your lands merely the commons. If you would keep your people safe and your lands intact, Ewen Cameron, seventeenth captain and chief of Clan Cameron, I recommend you consider my offer. For if you do not, you will be considering a premature grave in its stead."

"Till we meet again, then, General." Ewen paused before exiting the tent. "And one thing for you to think on. My people have a saying. 'A shored tree staunds lang.' It means threatened folk live long, in case you've not the Scots tongue."

This time only two redcoats caught sight of the Highlanders as they left the camp.

❋

Ewen looked up at the position of the sun in the sky. If they rode hard, they would be back at the Cameron keep in time for a late supper. He would have some good come of the day, even if that only meant ending it with a hot meal. Now they were racing the sun back to Tor Castle, and all they had to show for their meeting were empty bellies and spent mounts.

He had heard that Monk was trying to buy every chief this

side of Edinburgh, though he hadn't fully credited it until his meeting with the man. Word was, more than a few Highlanders were aligning themselves with the general, and Ewen supposed he couldn't blame them. Offers of money, land, and security were hard to snub, especially as the redcoats showed no sign of halting their trail of blood and destruction through the Highlands. The British soldiers laid waste to land and cattle as they went, cutting men down without mercy, taking others prisoner to send off as slaves to English plantations in the West Indies. If it were merely a matter of property or battles between men and men alone, it would be a different matter. But the redcoats put all villagers to the sword, regardless of age or sex, inflicting horrors dependent on their mood or the depths of their fury and resentment on any given day.

Ewen had hoped to broker peace, but he wouldn't sacrifice the integrity of his land and his people to do so.

"We are sons of the hound." He fingered the brooch his father had given him.

"And we will be on no man's leash."

Chapter 5

In her dream, Lily was sunbathing at Baker Beach back home. She was on her stomach, resting her face to one side in the sand. It was one of those rare San Francisco days where the sun was beating down. Her body was warm, languorous, and she felt as one with the rhythmic ebbing and flowing of the waves, which she felt echo through her body. Her left cheek was hot and slightly damp where it rested on the packed sand. She shifted slightly, enjoying the sensual feeling of the earth cradling her body. The warmth intensified, though, and little by little Lily's mind rose to that place between waking and sleeping. She became gradually aware that she wasn't on the beach. The warm sand cradling her face became sharp gravel digging into her cheek. She began to realize that the heat didn't emanate from the ground—it was her body that was hot, and getting hotter. Slowly, all the sensations of fever washed over her. She became aware of specific pains in odd places—her right knee, the side of her neck, her eyelids. The fever became more uncomfortable as her body seemed to consume all the heat from the ground, which now felt painfully cold against the hot ache of her limbs.

How odd, Lily thought, *to be hit by a fever like this, so out of the blue*. There had been a tremor of some sort—maybe she had fallen and hit her head. That thought got her eyelids fluttering. If she had a head injury, she needed help immediately; falling asleep could be disastrous.

The entire morning came back in total clarity. The maze, that mysterious stone carving. She must've been thrown through some break in the shrubbery, for there was sunlight all around her instead of that hideous plant. That would explain the numerous scrapes that she felt stinging the side of her cheek. She shuddered at the memory of those drab leaves and black fruit that in retrospect seemed nothing short of malevolent. As painful as her fall was, she was relieved to be free of the labyrinth. She hadn't realized till then just how terrified she had been, how trapped and lost she had felt. It was hard not to let her imagination get the better of her and she shrugged off notions of evil spirits toying with her.

Lily lay there for a moment taking a physical inventory. As acute as her fever was, it had been hard to feel anything but chills and heat gripping her body. Now she became aware of excruciating pain in her right shoulder, which she assumed must have been what had broken her fall. She wriggled fingers and toes. Nothing seemed permanently damaged, but her body was on fire, and the chills wracking her told Lily that her fever hadn't stopped rising.

She tuned back into the ground beneath her. She remembered her dream, lying on the warm sand, feeling the pulse of the waves drumming the beach around her. She opened her eyes with a start. She could feel something—a distant rumbling in the earth beneath her. She could almost hear the pounding as she felt it reverberate through her body, growing in its intensity with each passing second. She worried that the earth was sounding another coming tremor, so she gritted her teeth and pushed herself to her knees. If an earthquake was to hit again, she was determined to keep her eyes open this time.

Lily gasped as pain shot through her torso, and looked in horror at her right arm lying limp at her side. If she had a dislocated shoulder, which seemed the obvious explanation, she would need to muster all of her strength and find help immediately before she went into shock. Clutching her useless arm to her side, she slowly rose to her feet and turned around and around to get her bearings.

Lily thought it odd that she could no longer see those mean leaves and branches of the plant in the maze. Instead, she was standing in the shadow of a sheer granite face that reached ten feet above her head. The Scottish landscape was so uneven, Lily thought perhaps the maze was precipitously situated on the edge of one of the many Scottish hills and the force of the tremor had tossed her like a rag doll over the edge. That would account for the dislocated shoulder and the myriad aches that wracked her body, though it did nothing to explain her suddenly high fever.

She froze. The thundering sound she had heard was getting closer. Lily focused and thought she could hear a man's voice. Horses, it was men on horses.

❖

Ewen shot his uncle an aggravated look. "Och, I thought this day could get no darker." He kicked Ares into a gallop just as the figure in the distance rose and began to stumble forward.

Though wearing some sort of breeches, the person was unmistakably female. She was tall and slight, except for her full bosom that any red-blooded man could spy clearly in such a scandalously tight blouse. Her hair was its own wonder, with thick white-blonde ringlets flying loose in the breeze. Ewen wondered what kind of woman would have the gall to trespass on Cameron lands.

They were upon her in seconds. She didn't even have the chance to jump out of the way. Time suddenly seemed to stop. Lily had always believed that when her moment came, she would see her life flash before her eyes. Instead, absurd and highly detailed thoughts flitted through her mind. *I'm just like a deer in headlights*, she thought. She smirked. *Hairy men in skirts. I'm going to be trampled by a troop of mad, hairy, dirty Scotsmen in skirts*. The impact knocked her back into unconsciousness.

❖

Ares reached her just as she was crumpling to the ground. The laird didn't need to slow much in order to gather the lass up

into his saddle, featherlight as she was. Then they had lost a
bit of time, forced as he'd been to slip her arm back into its
socket. No good would have come from letting an injury like
that go untended. They couldn't risk the perilous amount of
blood that would surely pool at her shoulder; as it was, he felt
ill at ease not binding the arm immediately, but that would
have to wait till their return home when they had more time
and a decent healer besides. Sorting out her injury without removing the peculiar blouse she wore had been an aggravation,
but he wouldn't have his men eyeing this woman. He had no
idea where she came from and he surely didn't trust her, but
something about this lass lying still in his arms compelled his
protection. He reminded himself to remain on guard: a morning spent with General Monk didn't dispose one to think
kindly of strangers. As far as he was concerned, his people
were at war, and he had to be skeptical of every person who
set foot on Cameron land.

Ewen studied her. He had never before seen a woman in
breeches. Robert rode up alongside, blatantly studying the
mysterious woman's figure, so clearly outlined in her tight
garb. "What peculiar garments." Robert leaned in to eye her
legs more closely and continued, "These fabrics represent a
type certainly not to be procured in these Highlands. Though
the idiosyncratic cut certainly does highlight her . . . feminine
aspects . . . eh, rather, the more . . . feminine manifestations
of her person . . ." Ewen shot him a stern look, and Robert
hastily finished, "I would not have reckoned on a lass in
breeches, but she looks right bonny."

Ewen looked down and couldn't help noticing for himself.
The lass did indeed have a fine shape to her legs. But it wasn't
her legs that drew his attention.

She had the most exquisite face he had ever laid eyes on. It
wasn't that she was the comeliest lass he had ever seen, for
she wasn't. Her complexion was flushed and spoke of time
spent under the sun. The wind had made a spectacular tangle
of her hair making her appear like some demon *baobhan sith*
lass caught unawares. Her features weren't what one would
deem fine. The mouth was full, with a slightly crooked front
tooth that made the bottom lip appear uneven. Ewen imagined
it only appeared thus because she was so still; he mused that

this was the type of lass whose face wasn't often such a mask of serenity, for the set of those same features in the moments before she fainted was all raw defiance. Defiance and a hint of humor that Ewen, incredulous, thought he'd spied playing at the corners of her mouth. Her eyes had challenged the clansmen, stance claiming that she would not go down without a fight. Not what the laird typically encountered from the females who ingratiated themselves into his circle.

And yet, those same features held him spellbound. Ewen wanted to run his fingers through that wind-whipped mane and pull her to him, claiming that indelicate mouth with his own. His head was suddenly mad with images of those full lips and that crooked tooth sucking and biting with a passion that would surely rival his own. He would run his hands over the coarse fabric of her breeches and wrap her legs about his body. Seize those breasts, straining so against the buttons of her shirt, in his hands, his mouth. And perhaps finally find in this braw and peculiar lass his match.

"Lochiel!"

"Aye," Ewen's voice came out a low growl, "hold your tongue. You've no need to shout, you coarse lout."

"That he does when you're off daydreaming. The lad near bust a gut trying to get your attention."

"That so, uncle? Well then, Robbie, you'll forgive me, I was putting my mind to other matters."

"Och, Ewen, your mind . . . your mind was on that lassie you've perched on your lap." Donald's eyes twinkled scandalously. "And that's assuming you've blood left in that head of yours, and it's not all traveled south of your sporran."

"Enough, old man." Ewen's voice held an uncharacteristic threat that silenced the younger man but only seemed to further amuse his uncle. "If you've the breath to chatter on like a fishwife, then you're not riding hard enough."

The laird pulled Lily closer and kicked Ares into a canter, forcing the party to ride back to the keep in silence.

❀

Lily's eyes fluttered open. Her mind struggled to make sense of where she was and what had happened. The fever had abated, disappearing as quickly as it had hit. It had barreled violently through her, leaving only a hot, parched throat in its wake. Try as she might, she couldn't hold on to one thought for long. It was as if her head was filled with static. She deliberately blinked her eyes tightly shut then open again, attempting to focus.

She tried to remember what happened. She must have fallen. Then, were there really horses? Lily carefully began to make small movements. Her ribs were sore but she could breathe without discomfort. And, despite a pounding headache, she could move her head without trouble. A dull throb radiated out from her shoulder. Someone had clearly set it for her; the ache was nothing compared to the screeching pain that had been there when it was out of its socket. Otherwise, nothing seemed to be broken, and she just had to be thankful that help had stumbled upon her when it had. Thankful and wary too, about the situation in which she now found herself. The riders who had come upon her hadn't looked like your average Highland villagers.

She looked around. She appeared to be in the home of some local family. And it was more than a farmer's family at that, judging from the size of her room. The walls were composed of large, rough-hewn gray stones. The room itself was kept surprisingly warm by a small but steadily burning fire in an otherwise sizable hearth along the far wall. She craned her neck to take in a large tapestry hanging over the bed. Fine needlework outlined what looked like the depiction of a hunting party. Women in long dresses and small pillbox caps sitting sidesaddle, bows and arrows cocked. Men in tights with swords drawn. Hounds dotted across the countryside. Lily found it to be a charmingly odd image and one she imagined was hundreds of years old. A large, antique tapestry in mint condition—no farmer's family indeed.

She carefully shifted onto her side, turning her back to the enormous slab of dark oak that constituted the bedroom door. Facing the light full on was a shock at first, but as her eyes adjusted she could see that the entire wall was made up of a series of large windows, each pointed at the top and comprised of hundreds of tiny panes of glass. The center window featured a prominent stained glass rosette that depicted what looked like a family's coat of arms.

Lily shut her eyes and let the weak sunlight play on her face. If she concentrated, she could almost imagine the feeling of warmth on her skin. She began to feel drowsy again. Her breathing took on the languorous rhythm of near sleep. She inhaled deeply; the smells around her had an almost hypnotic effect. There was a strong note of lavender fighting to overcome an inescapable mustiness that pervaded the room. Something about it relaxed Lily, reminding her of the cloying old-woman scents that had always enveloped and reassured her when visiting her grandmother's house. She found herself humming a quiet tune: "Upon Letterfinlay soil he did land, Claiming he came from a future grand. A MacMartin lad who knew no fear, Clan Cameron took and held him dear . . ." She smiled drowsily. Of course, Gram's song had sprung into her head unbidden. She was in her Gram's domain now.

She really should get up and thank whomever it was who'd helped her and get on her way, but Lily couldn't fight the exhaustion that weighed her down, making her mind fuzzy and her body once again nearly incapable of movement. She pulled the covers up over her shoulders and shuddered as she realized in her half sleep that the blanket was no blanket at all but a large fur of some kind.

Lily thought she heard a door creak open somewhere on the edge of her hearing—the sound seemed far in the distance, as if at the end of a tunnel, though she knew it must be her own door opening. Fighting now to keep her eyes open, she used her remaining energy to turn and see who was there. All she glimpsed was a blur of red and green tartan and long black hair as a man who filled the doorway turned to go. Just like the song, she mused. Hazy impressions fought to resolve themselves into thoughts. "In red and green plaid, And charming to behold . . ." She couldn't figure out if she was comforted or unnerved by the connections that were being made somewhere in the back of her muzzy brain. Stretching out her legs, her last thought before slipping off to sleep was, why couldn't such a well-to-do family afford a less scratchy, lumpy bed?

❈

Ewen was not pleased with the arrival of the mysterious woman. Two winters past, Gormshuil had warned that another stranger would come. At the time, he did not believe the old witch. And yet, seeing this woman stumbling, lost on Lochaber soil, Gormshuil's words resonated in his memory.

Nobody knew the old woman's true name or origins, so they called her simply Gormshuil, after her blue eyes that were as faint as the winter sky. She had some peculiar habits and frightened some of the younger serving women, but Ewen welcomed her to his hearth to respect the memory of his grandfather who had treasured her as an advisor.

"Another comes," she had said.

Just as Robert had come so many years ago. A pretty lad he had been, with fine, fair features unlike the typical Highland scamps his age, when he appeared on the hills of Letterfinlay as if from a fairy tale. The MacMartin clan originally took him in, but too many questions were whispered about his origins so, as a favor to the MacMartin laird, Ewen's grandfather took Robert in as a foster son. Nobody thought to question a Cameron chief, and the inexplicable means of the lad's arrival soon became a forbidden topic.

And now another unexplained arrival.

Despite Gormshuil's warning that another would come, Ewen had certainly not expected a woman. He had no desire to devise more lies in order to cover up for another lost soul—meeting one in a single lifetime was more than enough for the laird, particularly if this one posed as many trials as Robert. He loved his foster brother and God bless him, but some days Ewen thought the lad would drive him to the grave with his ill-timed quotes, self-proclaimed scientific inquiries, and general pedantry. Ewen regarded himself as a man of letters and admired scholarly pursuits, but sometimes Robbie drove him mad with his impractical and bookish nature.

Besides, the strange appearance of a lad was easily accounted for. Boys are fostered at allied clans all the time. But an unexplained lass. The village would buzz for years with gossip and conjecture about her arrival.

The strange woman unsettled him. Something about her was more foreign than Robert had been. Her clothing was so peculiar. He had never seen a woman in breeches nor, for that matter, had he ever seen such sturdy attire. Though it didn't appear to be as waterproof as tartan, her breeches were made of the most rugged material he had ever seen. The clasp, too, was remarkable. Wanting to avoid unwelcome curiosity, he'd had Robert dispose of her belongings.

Then there was the matter of her shoulder. He had only ever seen a grown man withstand that type of injury; he knew it to be one of the most painful, save for being wounded by gunshot or sword. He was impressed that she could withstand such pain.

Who was she, and why did she have to land herself under the care of the Cameron clan?

Robert had spoken of a labyrinth, and, though years had passed since the lad's arrival, Ewen remained dreadfully uneasy about what this mysterious maze was. How it would choose a person. Or why.

And now this new stranger. The one, he suspected, whom Gormshuil had prophesied.

Ewen was a man grounded in the realm of reason. His was a world of power gained and asserted through tradition and physical prowess. He had no use for witchery, and no use for tales of years past or years to come.

Chapter 6

The first thing to pierce Lily's consciousness was the sound of another person breathing. A slow, deliberate inhaling and exhaling that spoke of one accustomed to keeping their body measured and mind in check.

She opened her eyes, and the most formidable man she had ever seen filled her vision. He sat as still as the rock of Ben Nevis itself. Shoulder-length black hair framed a face carved from stone, the sharp edges of cheeks, nose, and chin softened only by faint black stubble. He was in full traditional Highland regalia, with a crisp linen tunic tucked into red and green tartan. Laced loosely at the neck, the shirt revealed a small triangle of smooth, muscled chest. She caught a glimpse of a dagger peeking out from the top of one of his leather boots.

Lily stretched, savoring her body's reaction to such a man. Spending time in the rugged Scottish countryside must've conjured such a traditional Highland warrior in her sleeping mind. His dangerously pure and potent maleness called to some well-buried ultrafeminine aspect of herself. Her dream had painted him with such vivid detail too, all the way down to the *sgian dubh* in his boot. She didn't recall the last time she had an erotic fantasy, and this was a welcome one. Lily opened herself to that familiar warm loosening of muscles, the rhythmic pumping of blood through her veins, the sensation of her body unfurling, with mouth and legs parting to take what he would give her. A sensual smile curved the corners of her drowsy lips as she imagined nipping the salty stubble of his chin just before taking his mouth to hers.

His brow furrowed and intense blue eyes bored into her own as if he were able to take the measure of her soul with just one look. That steady gaze was met with a shriek from Lily, suddenly jolted back into reality. Waking reality. This was no dream man. He was a flesh and blood stranger sitting but an arm's length from her. She sat up faster than she knew her stomach muscles could take her, causing the thick fur cover to fall to her waist. Lily gasped as the cold air hit her body and she realized she was barely clothed in a nightgown made only of thin ivory linen, trimmed with delicate lacework around the neck and cap sleeves. She prayed that he wasn't the one who had stripped and changed her into something suitable for an antique doll.

Lily steadied herself and tried to meet this stranger eye to eye. She felt a bit like a bird that's discovered it's been unwittingly stalked by a silent—and very hungry—cat.

She took in his every detail while her heart pounded, unsure if her reaction was from the thrill of being face-to-face with a Scotsman who looked as if he had dropped right out of an old legend, a little ripple of leftover desire, or simply from pure fear. Studying the pattern of his red and green tartan, it dawned on Lily that this must be the man who'd checked on her as she slept. She was thankful that she hadn't seen him this clearly at the time or her sleep would have been fraught with nightmares.

The size of him alone was alarming enough. Lily estimated that he was well over six feet, all broad shoulders, heavily muscled arms, and powerful legs. It was his face, though, which Lily found the most unsettling of all. It wasn't his features as such that provoked fear. Looked at individually, every part of his face was actually quite handsome. Strong, square jaw; aquiline nose; broad, high cheekbones; a firmly set mouth that you couldn't quite call full; and indigo blue eyes that glittered dangerously as he looked Lily up and down in her bed. She unconsciously pulled the covers more tightly around her neck and thought that it was the sum of those stark, strong features that made this man so intense.

She couldn't figure out if he was the handsomest creature she had ever seen, or the fiercest.

"What . . . ?" That single word alone sent a shooting pain through the right side of her skull.

Lily gave a start at the sound of a cleared throat from across the room. She turned to discover a somewhat foppish man seated in the corner. He didn't look at ease with himself; the slight tilt to his chin, arrow-straight posture, and delicately crossed legs gave him an appearance that Lily could only describe as pretty. He had a full head of soft curls, lit gently by the sun that shone through the thick glass windows and made his hair glimmer in shades of yellow and gold.

The blond saw that she was paralyzed with fear, and Lily imagined he bit back a small smile to watch the hulking black-haired Highlander take advantage of her stillness to fully size her up. Her unease was rapidly becoming all-out fear, and she looked back and forth between the two as silence choked the room. These men clearly had saved her life, but just who were they and what were their intentions now?

Lily looked back to the young man in the corner, stunned by his bizarre clothing. Unlike his companion, the blond was dressed in some sort of period court costume. Wherever he found his getup, it must've cost him a fortune. He was wearing a short, fitted jacket in a mustard-colored silk or satin. Lily had never been good at fashion and could barely tell one fabric from another but she could see that these threads were the best. His sleeves were puffed out at the upper arm and patterned with rich, navy blue brocade. His perfectly matching outfit was completed by navy blue satiny silk pants, puffed and gathered at the knee, with deep vertical slashes of mustard peeking through pleats in the fabric.

Perhaps it was catching sight of the preposterous mustard-colored tights that hugged the blond's calves, but Lily managed to gulp down her panic and let her temper take over the situation. "Don't just stare at me! Where am I?"

"Sssh, hush now lass, we don't have much time." The man

at her side spoke, his voice an almost sultry Scots burr that made goose bumps ripple across Lily's arms.

The black-haired Scot shifted slightly, leaning back in his seat and crossing his arms. Though in a position that suggested relaxation, Lily felt his physical energy as if he were a leopard ready to pounce. His feet were planted on the floor with knees spread apart, and Lily couldn't help but trace her eyes up his boots and along his knee into the darkness of his kilt. She felt the blood rush to her cheeks when she realized where she had been looking. The creak of his leather chair was the only sound in the room.

His eyes never left Lily's face. She began to feel physically uncomfortable with the sensation that those eyes were boring clean through her.

She tightened her grip on the fur blanket and backed as far as she could against the bed's black oak headboard. "Who are you anyway? Why am I dressed this way? Where are my clothes?" Each question was more urgent, and louder, than the last.

It was the blond who broke the silence. "Tell us, mistress, what century is it?"

"Look, I don't have amnesia or anything. Please just give me my things and I'll be on my way."

Lily silently tried to calm herself with reassurances that, certainly by the end of the day, and with a glass of particularly strong single malt in hand, she would be able to chalk this up to some grand Scottish adventure. And so she filled the unsettling silence with an answer to his question. Anything to get dressed and get out of there.

"The twenty-first." She cursed herself the moment she said it, wishing it had sounded more like a proclamation than a question. She was still flustered, though, from the black-haired man's unwavering stare.

A distant look washed over the blond's face. If Lily didn't know any better, she would've sworn that it was awe. "So, I haven't been asleep for a hundred years like Rip Van Winkle, have I?" she croaked, trying to break the tension with a weak joke.

Neither of the men in the room got the humor. The black-haired one finally spoke. "No, lass, I don't know any Winkle. Stop nattering and listen. Were you at the labyrinth?"

"I, well, yes I was. At least that's what I think it was. Some sort of old-fashioned garden maze. The walls were high and covered with vines with black berries." Lily forced her mouth to curl into a weak smile. "Like some sort of grim Halloween version of a holly bush." She hoped a dose of feeble humor would normalize the situation. As if she always sat around in a nightie chatting about the local scenery with some menacing warrior and his costumed pal.

"Vines with black berries? Aye, lass, it wasn't holly, 'twas the devil's cherries. Those who study such things know it as deadly nightshade. It's quite rare in Scotland. Any there is would've been cultivated by the witches who claim the fruit ground into a paste helps them to fly come Samhain." His tone was scientific, and though it was clear he himself didn't fancy such notions, it struck Lily as more than a little peculiar that someone could discuss such things with a straight face. "Villagers say it's the devil himself who goes about tending it in his leisure."

Preposterous subject matter aside, Lily was mesmerized by the sound of the man's voice. If she weren't so taken aback by his fearsome presence, she imagined she would find it sexy. It was deep, resonant, and she found she listened more to the rhythm of his brogue than to the actual words he was saying.

It took her a moment to register their conversation. Lily responded, "Yes, I think . . . that's all very interesting, now if you'd just help me with my things, I will . . ."

The blond disregarded her entirely and insisted to the man in the corner, "Be it three hundred years or thirty, Ewen, this makes no sense."

Ewen raked his hand through his black hair and mused, "Och, it wouldn't be so easy as that to puzzle through now would it? The stone chart must be part of the key."

"Of course!" the blond exclaimed. "It's to do with planetary alignment, with the stone chart at the heart of the maze representing some specific configuration of the constellations."

Lily tried to keep her composure. "Could you share with the rest of the class please?"

The blond turned to her, appearing almost perplexed that Lily would speak unsolicited, and declared in a peremptory tone, "If you would but please to let us think."

The black-haired warrior whom Lily now realized was named Ewen looked at her distractedly. "Tell no one what you have just told me."

"What did I tell . . . ?"

Ewen didn't let her finish. "Hush, lass! The year is 1654."

That shut her up. Clearly she was dealing with some very unstable people. The lodgings were on the rugged side and they were wearing some peculiar costumes, but that only further proved that she was dealing with men who had only one foot in reality.

A snippet of Gram's song popped into her head, and Lily thought of that fey lad who claimed to come from a future grand. The lyrics were simple, but who knew, maybe there were people out there who would actually believe a ballad about time travel when they heard it, and she'd stumbled into a couple of frustrated historical reenactors hoping to get whisked back for real. Either way, Lily had to figure out how to get out of there.

Looking around the room, she saw no modern appointments, though she figured that much of Europe was charming old estates and stained glass anyway. She knew that unlike Americans, most people in the world didn't have forced central air and a television in every room.

The blond leaned toward her and whispered almost frantically, "That maze is a doorway of some kind. I was but fifteen when it took me."

He turned to Ewen and continued, "If you do the calculations, it's clear that the years do not map correctly. The only explanation is that traveling is based on the stars. It would stand to reason that to voyage through time is indeed to voyage through the stars. Oh truly, Lochiel, a *fronte praecipitium a tergo lupi*!"

Lily gaped at the dandily dressed man who was now spouting Latin.

He amended, "That is to say in more vulgar terms, you are betwixt a rock and a hard place, my dear foster brother, if you had harbored hopes of returning this anonymous woman to her own place and time."

Lily's nervousness blossomed into full-fledged panic.

"Och, I know the Latin, Robbie. A precipice in front and

wolves behind, aye? Don't be daft. Sometimes you can't see past the page to the life in front of you. Your Latin is of no use to me. I'd have action, not adages." Ewen paused. "Tell me, did you burn her clothes as I asked?"

Lily screeched, "You did what?" She was now terrified.

Neither man seemed to notice her, though. The blond nodded, "My apologies, Ewen, I suppose I can be a bit of a *helluo librorum*, a true glutton for books am I!"

The laird merely glared.

Robert added hastily, "The sweater and shawl were acceptable. The breeches, though"—he sighed wistfully—"those I was forced to surrender to the smithy's fire and a true shame it was. I've never laid eyes on such finely crafted material. Breeches cut for a woman—who would imagine?"

That did it. So these men thought that all women should wear only dresses. Weird historical reenactments are one thing, but burning her Levi 501s was entirely another issue. Adrenalin pumped through her. She tried to appear casual while she searched the room for clothing and an easy exit. She prayed that there were other people in the house and not just these wackos. *The nightgown must belong to someone—if there were another woman in the house,* Lily thought, *she might be sympathetic and offer help.*

She had seen a few men on horses just before she passed out and imagined in horror that she had stumbled into some sort of bizarre anachronistic Scottish man-cult with a penchant for damsels in distress.

Lily shut her eyes to fight off the wave of nausea that washed over her at that thought. *Keep it together, Lily,* she thought. *You've seen enough news magazine shows to know that you have to play along with nuts like this. You just need time to think. If only there weren't a hammer pounding away in your skull.*

She mustered her best captive-girl voice and asked sweetly, "Do you have any Advil or aspirin? My head is killing me."

Wrong question. That set Ewen off. "You silly lass! You'll be taken for either a witch or a lunatic unless you keep your mouth shut. Only three people know who you are. My grandfather took Robert as his ward after he fell through that cursed maze. And now Robbie, my uncle, and I remain the only ones who know the truth of it."

His voice held a note of admiration as he continued, "It was only the wisdom of my grandfather what spared him. A lad near grown, and a stranger at that, kything out of the sky and onto a glen in Letterfinlay."

Robert also had a run-in with that hideous maze? Gram's lullaby popped once again into her head. "Upon Letterfinlay soil he did land, Claiming he came from a future grand . . ."

She didn't understand what was going on. Did they actually know that song? For a fleeting moment, Lily thought maybe she was going crazy, or that she had found herself in the past, or had even been there all along. She shook her head—time travel was a thing of fantasy. These men were clearly deluded and apparently had the money to pursue their fetish.

"Do not disregard Gormshuil," Robert said. "She too has a comprehensive knowledge of my tale."

"Aye lad"—exasperation flickered a moment in Ewen's eyes—"the witch Gormshuil knows your story as well." He once again pinned Lily with that dark blue gaze. "Now lass, listen to me. You're no longer in your own time, and I don't know what we're to do with you, and with that strange accent."

"Look who's talking," Lily mumbled. Her joke to herself was rewarded with a viselike grip on the chin.

"Mind me," he snarled. "You must remain quiet until we can figure out how to explain you. First, where are you from? What languages do you speak?"

"Get your hand off me." Lily jerked her chin away. "Would you like a list of my hobbies and interests as well? Turn-ons: walks in the park, turn-offs: mean people." She shot him a pointed look.

"Look, I appreciate your help, but really, I'm fine now. I'd just like to get back to my cottage."

The men glowered in silence, so Lily answered the original question. "I'm from California. I studied a bit of French in high school, does that count?"

"You mean to tell me that you don't speak any other languages?"

"Surely you've studied Latin," Robert interjected.

Ewen cut him off. "You're from . . . where?"

"You know, the United States. America. The US of A."

The silence continued.

"Oh, I get it, would you rather I refer to them as the colonies?"

"Ah." Understanding registered on Ewen's face. "But I fear that won't do. You'll have to be from France, then. A horrible accident befell you on your journey and impaired your memory. That will gain us some time. And, if you run across one with the French tongue, well, we'll just have to claim you as a wee daft in the head."

Lily's fury didn't have time to manifest itself before she heard a quiet scratching at the door. He turned to her, "Quick lass, what's your name?"

"Lily. Lily Hamlin."

"No. From this day forward, you're Lily Cameron. And keep your silence."

The men regained their composure and, in his sweetest voice, the blond said, "Come." Lily could've sworn she caught Ewen rolling his eyes.

The door creaked open to reveal a small, hunched woman in a long, bibbed skirt and bonnet carrying a tray of food. Lily's stomach rejoiced at the thought of some nourishment. She didn't know how many meals she'd missed, and she would need energy if she was to figure out how to get the hell out of there.

She studied the woman with the tray. As she approached, Lily realized that she must only be in her late forties, even though at first glance she'd looked much older and more haggard. Lily hoped that she wouldn't be expected to wear a ridiculous costume like this woman's. Her long, tan-colored skirt was made of a coarse material and looked the worse for wear. A yellow and blue tartan shawl was cinched around the woman's shoulders and more than compensated for the dull color of the skirt. Lily could see bare feet peeking out from underneath and thought despairingly that it would be hard to make an escape wearing such a long skirt.

"Lochiel, Master Robert, I came to check on the miss and brought a spot of food."

So the blond's name is Robert, Lily thought. And "Lochiel" must be a term of address for the one named Ewen.

Though she spoke to Ewen, the old woman at the door seemed to be addressing Lily. The servant was looking at her expectantly, and Lily realized that she must be quite the curiosity, having been secreted up to the house unconscious. Remembering her orders to be silent, Lily merely smiled weakly at the woman. This satisfied her, for she bustled right over, put the tray down at Lily's bedside, turned to Ewen, and said, "Aye, well, you'll let me know when you need more of me."

"Thank you, Kat, you may go."

Kat bobbed deeply to Ewen and slipped out through the closing door. Lily noticed that the maid acted much more deferential to him than to Robert. Though, considering Ewen's fearsome demeanor and looks, she couldn't blame the woman.

"Well then and where are our manners?" Robert sat forward in his chair and, placing hands on knees, managed to make his already straight posture even more perfect. "Introductions are in order."

Ewen scowled at Robert's nonchalance and the suggestion that all matters were somehow settled. Lily had to admit she felt like scowling too. A lot more than introductions were in order, as far as she was concerned.

"Lily, may I present my brother—or shall I say foster brother?—the formidable Ewen Cameron, seventeenth captain and chief of Clan Cameron."

Lily wondered at their use of the word *brother*. It was clear that there was no way on earth the lithe blond in gold and blue silk by her side was related by blood to the commanding figure with wild hair and full Highland regalia. Even their accents were vastly different. Robert's accent was thick, but no worse than those of any of the men she would chat with at the pub over a dram of whisky. She found this Ewen, though, to be barely intelligible. She couldn't quite put her finger on it, but something about the burred and rounded edges of his speech was unusually stilted to her American ear. She could barely follow his extraordinarily thick brogue and would be surprised if Ewen had ever stepped foot outside of the Highlands in his life.

Lily was unsure what her approach should be. "It . . . it's nice to meet—"

Ewen turned the full force of his gaze onto her and interrupted, "Once again, lass, what can you do?"

The question felt more like an accusation from the commanding Scot. Feeling vulnerable, she tried to pull the covers up tighter below her chin, even though she was already practically strangling herself with the sheet. She spied Robert out of the corner of her eye craning his neck in interest, as if he were examining some new biology specimen, and Lily thought she understood the exasperation she sensed on the part of his elder brother.

"Wh–what?" Lily cursed herself at how feeble that had sounded.

Ewen's voice was gruff with impatience. "Lass, I said, what can you do? If you're going to stay, you need to make yourself useful. Do you cook?"

Lily felt a mingled sense of relief and then panic, first as she recognized that these two strange men had accepted her, and then that she was expected to stay on in their household.

"Well?"

"No."

"No?"

"No, I don't cook." Lily lived on burritos and pepperoni pizza. Assembling a mean ham and cheese sandwich was the extent of her culinary prowess.

The clan leader looked dumbfounded.

"Are you good with household accounts? Managing a maid staff? Sewing? Other needlework? Tending the garden? Minding the horses?"

As she shook her head in response to his litany of questions, the clan leader's frustration was becoming quite clear.

"Well dammit, lass, what are you good for? What is it you do for your husband to help mind your home?"

Lily's panic turned to anger. Was he planning on setting her up into indentured servitude? "I'm not married," she snapped.

Robert finally intervened, preventing any further escalation. He took over the interrogation loudly and slowly, as if he were translating for a child. "Now"—he stumbled for the briefest of moments on her name—"Lily, if the clan is to take you under its protection, we need to find a place for you in the Cameron household. You weren't married, ever?" She caught the condescension in his voice.

As Lily shook her head no, the two men exchanged a brief look of disbelief. By seventeenth-century standards, Lily was certainly beyond her marrying years, but it was obvious from her pale skin, unblemished hands, and lean body that she'd never had to do a day of hard labor in her life.

"So, did your father take care of you?"

Again, she shook her head no.

"Ahhh, I understand." Robert shared a knowing glance with Ewen as an almost childishly naughty smile lit on the corner of his mouth. "So, you were a, shall we say, a working woman?"

Lily began to say that, yes she was a working woman, when his insinuation finally hit home. Her face reddened, and, trying desperately to keep her temper in check, she fumed, "NO! I am most certainly not, not that!"

Robert, his mouth pursed into a tight smile, looked at her expectantly.

"I . . . I work on the Internet."

Blank stares.

"You use a net?" Robert earnestly tried to understand. "You fish for your living?"

Lily looked at him as if he were an imbecile. "You know, computers."

Blank stares turning into impatient blank stares.

She really had landed herself in the backwoods of Scotland. What the hell, she'd never see these men again. "Artist. I'm an artist."

"An actual artist?" Robert exclaimed. "Ah, *ars longa, vita brevis*. Our life, so very short, but art, art spans the ages, is that not the truth of it? An artist among us, as well as a lass. I cannot say I've ever met a female with aspirations beyond that of the needle and thread." An almost dramatically wistful expression washed over the blond's face. "I have never been so very keen on landscapes, but a good hound portrait, now there is something to buoy a man's spirits."

"Och"—Ewen shot a steely glare at his younger foster brother—"pull your mind out of the clouds, boy. All that time with your nose in a book, and you're still damp behind the ears."

Ewen turned back to Lily, who had edged as far back on the bed as possible. His jaw unclenched just a little. "Don't be afraid, lass." Ewen's gaze lingered on the thin wisps of white blonde curls that framed her neck, and the pale expanse of throat visible above her covers. He abruptly shook his head. "Don't be troubled. We'll find you a place." He sighed. "An artist, eh?"

He studied her hands, which, despite their grip on the sheets, were clearly delicate with long, graceful fingers. "Well, I don't know how it is in the future, but I'm unable to apprentice a woman to any craftsman."

His eyes brightened. "Are you interested in children?"

Lily found herself feeling curiously unsettled at the sound of his voice. Now that she had attuned herself to the cadences of his accent, she was mesmerized by its deep, gravelly tone.

She neither liked nor understood where this discussion was going. "They . . . I . . . well, someday I would like to have . . ."

"Och, no lass! You've some strange notions of conversation." A smile cracked the laird's features for a split second, and then he continued, "What I mean to say is, how do you fare with children? My son. He is a . . . a spirited lad. No governess has managed to tame him, much less tend him for more than six months at a stretch."

Lily couldn't understand it, but she felt her heart sink at the news that this startlingly intense Scot had a wife. She shook her head to clear it—surely she was still groggy from her fall.

"Yes, I . . . fare well with children." Lily was tempted to speak what was really on her mind, namely, *I won't be here long enough to even meet your child, sir*.

"And you're schooled?"

She took affront that the level of her education would be called into question. "Yes. Well."

Ewen seemed to appreciate her indignant reaction. "Then it's settled, aye?" He turned to Robert. "She'll be John's nanny."

She could've sworn she heard Robert mumble, "And good luck to you."

❂

Lily sat in the tub of hot water planning her escape. She'd been anxious to bolt, but the maid had been in constant attendance, hovering, smiling, and nodding mutely, anxious to see to Lily's every need.

The other woman had orchestrated a bath for her, an elaborate and maddeningly time-consuming operation involving a large copper basin, men in tattered period dress, and innumerable buckets of hot water. The moment Lily eased into the water, though, Kat had disappeared.

Relishing the brief moment of privacy, she hurriedly scrubbed herself. The scalding water soothed her aching body, and Lily thought it was just the respite her injured muscles needed before she made a break for it. Tears stung her eyes to see the pastel still smudged at her fingertips, but Lily vowed to pull herself together. She would get out of there. Immediately.

She wondered if the maid was trapped there as well, but thought better of bringing Kat along with her. She could always come back with the authorities to help the poor woman.

She had no idea why these people insisted on keeping her under their roof, but she was going to have nothing of it. Lily thought perhaps she should've been terrified, but she didn't get the sense that she was in any true physical danger from Ewen or Robert. Despite Ewen's fearsome looks, she somehow knew that he wouldn't harm her in any way. Instead, a peculiar inner calm infused her, enabling her to focus on the task at hand.

She stood to dry herself with a large and not-at-all absorbent square of cloth. Lily decided she'd dress quickly and sneak out in the bustle just before dinner. The castle's other occupants would likely be busy readying for supper, and it seemed like her best shot at slipping out unseen. Besides, she didn't know when, or if, she'd be left alone again.

Ewen and his brother probably belonged to some sort of historical society and the last thing she wanted was to be forced into membership. Although they seemed harmless enough, this Cameron family's insistence on their impeccably accurate historical tableau was disturbing.

Looking around the room, she thought that the two brothers had spared no expense at re-creating a laird's castle of centuries past. Lily had to admit, the results were surprisingly accommodating. Though the thick rug on the floor and furs on the bed could use a dry cleaning, they made what would otherwise be a cold stone room feel warm and inviting.

The steaming water, such a reminder of familiar comforts, had cleared her head and soothed the last of the feverish ache from her bones. Between the long walk and her fall, Lily had gotten filthy. Though she'd had only a small sliver of a cloyingly rose-scented soap, she felt as if she'd scrubbed away the mishaps of the day.

Lily figured she had no more than an hour. Although her hair was still damper than she would have liked for chilly night travel in the Highlands, the clothes that Kat had left for her were sturdy and thick. At that moment, however, she sure was missing good-old American fabrics. The tartan shawl that Kat had given her, though blessedly warm, was scratchy and held a smell that Lily hoped was just must.

She could hear distant bustling noises emanating from the floor below. As she cracked her door to check the hallway for people, the smell of some kind of roasting meat wafted into her room. She shut her eyes, feeling momentarily weak from hunger. Something about the fall that she took had left her famished, and she hadn't exactly been sated after the Spartan lunch of brown bread and hard cheese that Kat had served earlier that afternoon.

From the commotion, she realized that there were far more people staying there than just Kat and the Cameron brothers. Looking up and down the cavernous hallway, she noted that she was indeed stranded in an antiquated castle. There was no electricity to be seen. Even though dusk had fallen, the hallway was only dimly lit by a series of torches. Her sense of inner calm wavered. She really did need to get out of here. Between the Camerons' period dress, the rough accommodations, and the gamey smells rising up from the kitchen, Lily had no desire to see what other niceties these brothers had up their sleeves. For all she knew, there was a dungeon in this medieval pad of theirs.

Although her stomach disagreed, Lily knew that this was her only opportunity to make a run for it. She didn't have a plan but figured that if she could make it out, she'd be able to navigate her way back to her cottage. Tightening the shawl around her shoulders, Lily stifled a sneeze and stepped out into the dark hallway.

A dull ache crept along her shins, her bare feet revolting against the cold stone floor. She was immediately hit by a wave of uncertainty. These people, though odd, seemed kind and hospitable enough. And the strong aroma of roasting meat was becoming more appealing by the minute. What was she thinking to take on the Highland terrain, after dark, clad only in some sort of period costume that didn't even feature a decent pair of shoes? She fingered the coarse tan muslin of her skirt and thought the last time she wore something that fell to her ankles was at her senior prom, and she didn't like it much then either. Her waist was already beginning to itch from the material. The clothes were clearly hand sewn, and the only way to approximate a suitable fit was to gather the skirt tightly at the waist with a cloth belt.

Lily thought of the warm room that awaited her at her cottage. The notion of a hot meal and a dram of whisky by the fireplace seemed nothing short of nirvana. All she needed was to make it out of the castle and to the main road. From there she could flag down a passing car. Someone might even be out looking for her.

She padded down the dimly lit hallway. Enormous oil paintings lined the corridor, barely illuminated by the flickering torches, giving Lily piecemeal glimpses of grave Scottish warriors. Stern faces glared down at her—each belonging to a man in tartan and bonnet, bearing sword and shield. Though she was certain they would appear benign enough in the daylight, the portraits were ominous, with eyes that seemed to follow her in the darkness. The effect overpowered any remaining uncertainty that she might have felt about getting the hell out of there. She chastised herself—there were no such things as ghosts—but the images of formidable warriors, presumably long dead, urged her along at a faster clip just the same.

She reached the top of a massive stairway. Although the stone steps were relatively rough-hewn compared to the majestic marble staircases that she'd seen elsewhere in Europe, the grandeur took Lily's breath away. The granite stairs swept around and down, disappearing into the shadows of the landing below. The walls were also stonework, dotted with small niches holding thick, cream-colored tapers. Faint light played along the surface of the pitted stones and shimmered off long,

dense cords of cloudy wax that striped the walls, attesting to
years of spent candles.

The kitchen smells that Lily had gotten a whiff of earlier
were even stronger at the head of the stairs. She shut her eyes
and inhaled deeply, now savoring the mingled aromas of stew
and bread and ale that filled her senses. Once again she
paused, uncertain that sneaking out was the right thing to do.
The eerie feeling that Robert had been right flickered across
her mind. Perhaps like the lad in Gram's lullaby, Lily had
somehow been whisked from the future, and Robert, Ewen,
and the rest weren't pretending. Her mind toyed with the possibility for a moment then dismissed it in favor of the most
likely explanation, that the household was populated with Ren
Faire types who, Lily knew, could sometimes take their roles
reenacting history a little too seriously. She once knew an en-
gineer at work who had a Renaissance-themed wedding. He
wore a velvet doublet with slashed sleeves and put his bride in
a brocaded gown, the corset of which was so tight it pushed
the poor woman's breasts up to her chin. It was actually quite
a lovely dress, but Lily estimated the thing must have weighed
in the neighborhood of thirty pounds.

Past or not, she mused, the whole situation gave her a bad
feeling. Though, she supposed, she could at least get a good
meal in her stomach before taking her leave. Lily turned and,
looking back down the hallway, imagined how easy it would
be to scamper back to her room, stoke the fire, and sit in relative peace and warmth, waiting for the hot dinner that Kat
would surely bring to her.

Then she saw it on the wall, a forbidding image that froze
Lily where she stood, renewed panic seizing her. She hiked up
her skirt and raced down the shadowy stairs as quickly as she
could, the grim visage of Ewen Cameron looking fiercely
down on her from a massive portrait at the head of the stairs.

❀

Ewen didn't know what to make of the lass. Years had passed
before he'd truly accepted Robert's story as the truth. The
MacMartin clan had found the young man, half-starved and
freezing, on the banks of a small loch on their lands in Letterfinlay. Shortly before his death, Ewen's grandfather agreed

to foster Robert. Despite being young himself, Ewen had been immersed in preparing for his role as laird. So occupied, he hadn't been interested in the affairs of younger lads and had kept his distance from Robert. For all his tales of future wonders, the youth seemed more interested in books than battle, which was where Ewen's head lay. The two young men forged a relationship akin to true blooded brothers, and though neither would call their bond affectionate, they held each other and their differing interests in high esteem.

And now it seemed another had passed through this labyrinth. A part of Ewen had never fully embraced Robert's story. The lad had been prone to great fancies, and a garden maze with transportative powers seemed a childish fantasy. Ewen realized now how the nagging scientist in him had, in a small corner of his mind, held fast to the idea that Robert's story was merely the caprice of a scared and runaway young man. But now the lass. There was no constructing such an easy explanation for her. Robert had shown him the fine weave of her sweater. And there was her bizarre accent, and the fact that she had the same tale to tell as Robert— wandering through a labyrinth and taking a great fall.

There was something different about her as well. Something in her eyes that made her stand apart from other women he had known. Scottish lasses were strong-willed and strong-boned, but something about Lily spoke to a courageous self-reliance that he had never sensed in a woman before. First, there was the matter of her injury. Although having the shoulder knocked out wasn't a grave wound, it was a violently acute pain that pushed all other thoughts from your mind. Ewen was accustomed only to seeing men weather such a thing, with the lasses in his immediate experience suffering from no more than the occasional faint or heat spell. Yet Lily pushed the pain aside to deal with the situation at hand, just as his men put by their wounds on the battlefield. It was a thing he both recognized and could not help but respect.

Then there was the matter of her temperament. During their interview she was clearly afraid, and who wouldn't be, vulnerable and alone as she was. And yet, not only had she held her ground, but damn if the lass hadn't shown some sparks of temper. He had to bite the inside of his cheek so as not to smile when he glimpsed such spirited outrage on her part. Women were generally biddable and agreeable creatures around the laird, and he didn't know just how bored he'd been by them until he encountered this Lily and the fire crackling bright in her eyes.

As spirited as her temper was, there was something about the lass physically that made Ewen, generally wary of all strangers, feel compelled to protect her. Though a bit on the thin side for the laird's tastes, she was radiant. He'd been struck by the creamy fineness of her skin and the roses that bloomed on her cheeks as if permanently flushed. Clearly her hands had never seen a day of real work in her life, delicate as they were, untouched by sun or labor. It was easy for him to imagine how those were indeed the hands of an artist, with a gentle touch, sensitive fingertips articulating the world around her with paint or clay. Ewen found he wanted to take those hands in his and hide her in his keep away from any who would hurt her.

And the ethereal pale of her riotous hair—she was like a wild fey creature. Very few women of his acquaintance had hair that light, and fewer still wore their curls loose. Rather, they bound, braided, or bunched their hair into elaborate immovable styles. The laird got the sense that even had Lily tried to pull her hair back, just like her personality, some part of it would spring forth in challenge. He couldn't help but imagine tangling himself in the thick white blonde mass.

Her mouth too captivated him—he had never seen teeth so white. And with a single crooked front tooth. He imagined the feel of her bite on his skin and felt himself grow hard as he wondered what other marvels this woman held.

The Cameron laird shook his head, chiding himself. "What am I on about?" he grumbled to himself. "Carrying on like a schoolboy. And over such an excitable lass."

Since Mairi died, he had stayed clear of women. He should have known better than to let his traitorous mind wander, particularly over the curves of a hotheaded outsider—no matter how unusual her beauty.

Chapter 7

The bitter air was a slap in the face. The sun had set long ago, making way for a long and chill Highland night. *There's no going back now*, Lily thought, as she shut the heavy door behind her and ran down the wide path away from the Cameron estate. She was still amazed that she had managed to sneak out without drawing attention to herself and was thankful that most of the household had been occupied preparing for that evening's supper.

Lily ran. She cursed herself for not keeping up with any kind of workout regimen as very quickly the crisp air began to sear her lungs. A dull ache set in her throat, her body fighting to get enough oxygen to her unfit muscles. Small rocks bit into her feet—she wasn't used to going without shoes and the soles of her feet were already becoming raw. She tried to concentrate on the rhythm of her pumping legs, as they raced toward what she thought was the direction of the road.

Lily stumbled on a rut in the path. She struggled to regain her footing, her efforts in vain as she slipped on a patch of grass that was already glistening with dew in the moonlight. She landed hard on her hands and knees and pain shot up her arms, reigniting the searing agony in her shoulder that had only just subsided into a dull ache. Between enduring her fall, the fever, and all the panic and fear that she had been struggling to keep in check, Lily crumpled onto the ground in a flood of exhaustion and loneliness. Resting her head on the cool damp earth, Lily let the tears come.

She didn't know how much time had passed when the crying finally started to feel like it had run its course. Between shuddering sobs, Lily caught a glimpse of a road ahead of her. Though unpaved, it appeared well traveled. She'd made it. It was surely just an easy, albeit long walk back to her cottage now. "Keep it together, you dope," she mumbled aloud, wiping her eyes and nose. "You're safe now, so stop feeling so sorry for yourself."

Disregarding the cold damp that seeped through the fabric of her skirt, Lily settled cross-legged in the rocky grass to spend a moment gathering her wits. "Drama queen," Lily chided herself, as much to hear a voice in the silence as to bring her situation back to normal. Breathing deeply, she looked around, awed at the beauty around her—the sky was a velvety black, dotted with more stars than she had ever seen before. The moon hung low in the sky, a perfect crescent throwing soft light across the rough terrain. The night was gorgeous. It was brisk, but if she got going now, she could be back in time for a late, hot supper. One of those tasty Highland steaks and a tall pint of beer.

Roused by the thought, Lily stood. She shook the dirt and dampness from her skirt, and sniffling one last time, she looked to her right and left trying to decide which way to go. Not yet ready to part with the glorious moon in the sky, she took a left on the road and began to walk.

❦

Ewen ignored the knock on his door. He despised interruptions. The hour before supper was always his time to steal some much needed solitude and Kat should have known better than to disrupt his thoughts.

While Ewen had been busy doing some verbal jousting with Monk that morning, his uncle Donald had somehow managed to discreetly pilfer a manuscript from the tent of the unctuous general. It turned out to be potential attack plans from Cromwell himself, and Ewen was finding it to be a real gem.

The knock sounded again. Ewen tore himself from his reading with a low growl. "What?"

The door cracked open and Kat eased her way into the room. Head bowed, she barely made eye contact with the chief. Ewen chastised himself—the poor maid was clearly nervous. He softened his voice. "It's fine, Kat. Please. What's the urgent matter?"

"Th-the woman. She's gone."

"What woman?" Ewen had only a tenuous grip on his patience and wanted Kat to make her point and be done with it.

"The lass. With the hair. Lily. She's not to be found."

Ewen slammed his hands onto the table and Kat recoiled.

The warrior shut his eyes and took a deep breath, visibly working to keep his anger in check. "Thank you, Kat," he murmured. "I will handle this."

He cursed himself. Had he really been momentarily smitten with such a reckless woman? Beauty or no, he had no patience for outright stupidity. She had no notion of the dangers that lay outside the castle keep. The last thing the laird wanted to do that evening was leave the warmth of his whisky and private rooms to go in search of a foolish woman.

❋

Dawn was beginning to break when she heard the voices. Lily had walked for what felt like miles the night before, followed by an impromptu rest at the side of the road that had accidentally turned into an extended nap. She couldn't figure out why with all her walking she still hadn't run into any signs of civilization. Ewen and his men must have taken her much farther into the remote Highlands than she realized. No matter, she thought with groggy anticipation. Where there are voices, there's civilization. She'd ask whoever they were for a lift to the nearest phone, where she could call a taxi. All vacation she had seen buses rattling through the village, but now that she needed one of them, they were nowhere in sight.

The notion that she'd be eating a hot breakfast in as little as an hour roused Lily. Blood sausage, runny eggs, and porridge had never seemed so appealing. Positively famished, she mused that she'd even settle for some haggis.

She stood up slowly, mentally promising her aching body that tonight, instead of sleeping in cold damp grass, she would ditch her rented croft, leave the Highlands, and check herself into the best five-star hotel she could find in Edinburgh. Visions of a hot shower, cable TV, and room service featuring a good old American-style hamburger got her sore muscles working again.

The morning was clear. Lily felt she was seeing the world through new eyes. Having used her wits to escape danger made her feel empowered—as if she was now in touch with an inner strength that had lain dormant through years of computer work, commuter lanes, pizza deliveries, and the other banal facts of her life in Silicon Valley. Exulting in this newfound clarity, she took in every detail around her. The sun was rising from behind low craggy mountains, throwing shards of bright white light across the greens and browns of the glen. Distant birds called to each other, their melodic songs echoing through the serenity of the Highland morning. Lily admired a nearby patch of thistle, as yet untouched by the rays of sunlight, thick drops of nighttime dew still glistening on its spiky purple buds. Smiling, she inhaled deeply, wondering if thistle had a distinctive fragrance.

Instead, it was the stink of sour whisky that assaulted her senses. Her smile faltering, she suddenly felt the heat of someone standing close behind her. Lily spun around, and there stood the ugliest man she had ever seen.

Chapter 8

Lily liked to imagine that her grandmother had raised her right, and she prided herself on her ability to find hidden reserves of graciousness and civility in moments like these. Undeterred by the rotting teeth and pocked face glaring at her, she gathered her wits and was just about to bid the man good morning when he reached out and grabbed her hard by the arms. A sense of shocked unreality washed over her. This wasn't supposed to happen. The Scottish people were kind, hospitable to wayward tourists like her. So why did he have a death grip on her arms?

She took a good look at the person standing before her. His bloodshot eyes were large and round, framed by a notably small face. A nervous tick in his brows exaggerated a low, deeply furrowed forehead. He was breathing through his mouth, the stench of whisky panting out through brown and yellow teeth. Lily's stomach lurched when she noticed that his left ear was hanging by thin membranes of skin. From the crusty brown scabs around the wound, Lily estimated that someone had tried to rip off his ear no more than a couple of days ago.

He had been too close for Lily to notice his clothing before.

Her knees buckled at the sight of his uniform, her shoulders hunching as his grip on her arms became the primary source of support keeping her from becoming a crumpled heap on the ground. A red coat. He was wearing a red coat. Tarnished pewter buttons closed the jacket tight to the waist where it flared out and came to rest grazing just atop his knees. Deep crimson sweat stains radiated out from under his arms, while dark red, brown, and black patches mottled what was once a white cravat, attesting to days of exposure to blood and filth. White gaiters, also badly stained, covered his calves, a single pewter button by each ankle holding them in place over scuffed black leather shoes. Lily didn't know much about period costumes or battle reenactment societies, but the bloodstains on his clothing were terrifyingly authentic.

The previous night flashed before Lily's eyes. Men in traditional Highland garb, the castle, talk of Cromwell and seventeenth-century battles. Had something actually happened at that labyrinth? Panic tore through her, her breath coming in short gasps as the horror of what was happening to her began to crush down. *Just think through this, Lily*, she goaded herself. *You are a smart woman. You are a rational woman. You were born in the twentieth century, and if you can get yourself into this, you can get right back out of it.*

She systematically ran through possible circumstances. Had she injured her head when she fell at the maze? Perhaps her concussion led to some sort of brain damage akin to amnesia.

Or maybe she was lying in a hospital bed somewhere and this was all a nightmare. Lily could feel bruises blooming where the soldier's hands closed around her arms like a vise. The sheer pain of his grip ruled out dreaming as a possibility. No nightmare could hurt this much.

There was always insanity. All the evidence surrounding her pointed to 1600s Scotland. Perhaps she was of this time and this place and it was madness that made her believe that her reality was a high-tech America years in the future. No, she couldn't accept that. She had too much knowledge that would surely be farfetched by seventeenth-century standards, had too many memories that could be recalled at an instant. There was just too much Lily—vibrant and close to the surface—for her to be crazy. She had to imagine that truly insane people might have delusions, but that they just couldn't conjure up that much and that detailed a personal history.

Lily kept remembering Gram MacMartin's ballad of the boy who claimed to come from the future, and chided herself that it was just a silly song. Surely her grandmother hadn't believed the words. The echoes of Clan Cameron in its lyrics played at the edge of her mind. A lad with hair of gold, and the laird he called brother. Red and green plaid. And now men in coats of flame.

Lily's panic turned to desperate regret as she remembered the downright hospitable reception she had gotten at the Cameron castle. She longed to be back there, comparatively safe within those dank stone walls. Even if she would've had to temporarily adopt a false persona, there would've been a few who knew who she really was. Perhaps Ewen or his brother might have even helped her back to the labyrinth so that she could sort out where she was. Or when. She crushed that last thought. Either way, she needed to find her way back, and she couldn't imagine confiding anything about her true origins to this drunken lout of a soldier.

"Oi, Newsam, look what I found me!" Lily's captor spun her around, yelling in the direction of a small copse of trees just down the road. His accent was as thick as Ewen's had been, though his cadences were not as round and languorous as the clan chief's Scots brogue.

To her horror, two more soldiers materialized, stumbling drunkenly out of the trees. These two were in no better shape than the first. Their red coats were rumpled and discolored by the filth of battle and living outdoors. Their bleary eyes told Lily that, although they might not be drunk presently, chances were good that they had been drunk only a few hours past.

"What 'ave you got there, Corporal Neal? You know you're to share with your senior officer." A smile bloomed on the face of a tall soldier, revealing a missing front tooth. A pair of small, close-set eyes squinted at Lily, and she wondered if the lanky soldier needed a good pair of glasses. He was as ugly as the first, though in a different, almost comical way. He was easily a foot taller than his companion, though likely not one pound heavier. An enormous Adam's apple protruded from his grimy neck, resting atop a well-stained cravat. His dirt-colored hair was pulled into a limp ponytail at the base of his neck.

The third man was just as enthusiastic about the latest turn of events, though he didn't say as much. Instead he just grinned dumbly, head bobbing, as he walked toward Lily and the soldier. Even though he used a long musket as a walking stick, pouches of fat around his neck and cheeks flushed red with effort. The top of his head was bald and covered by a fine sheen of sweat, a fringe of frizzy orange curls encircling the sunburned skin.

The absurdity of this redcoat version of Laurel and Hardy overwhelmed her, and Lily shrieked, a quick, sharp sound somewhere between hysteria and fear. Her legs found their strength, and she began to struggle desperately to free her arms from her captor's grip.

Lily went rigid, a wave of terror chilling her, as the tall soldier got close enough for her to see the malevolence in his eyes. The lanky one who had been referred to as Newsam hovered over Lily, making no effort to disguise his appraisal of her.

Tightening his grip, Corporal Neal buried his face into Lily's curls and inhaled deeply. "Ay, isn't she a peach now? I do love Scot stock." Lily choked down a wave of revulsion feeling the hot stink of his breath on her neck.

"Ay, a ripe peach at that, Neal." Newsam's hand reached out and brutally squeezed Lily's right breast. He found her nipple and rolled it roughly between his thumb and finger. Lily's gasp provoked a smile from the fat one, his thin shiny lips peeling away to reveal a mouthful of tiny square teeth.

"And who gets to ride her first then?" The fat one's baritone voice was incongruously deep. Lily breathed deeply and rhythmically in a desperate search for those reserves of inner strength that she had been congratulating herself on just moments earlier. She tried to master her pounding heart at the sight of the orange-haired man adjusting the growing mass between his legs as he licked his lips.

"Keep it buttoned, Burton." Newsam, clearly the leader of this trio, snarled at the clown-haired man. He turned his face back to Lily, tiny eyes squinting deep in thought. He placed his hand gently on Lily's cheek, stroking lightly with his thumb. Reaching his hand back to the nape of her neck, the soldier slowly tangled his fingers in her hair. Abruptly, he tugged his hand up and back, violently exposing her neck. Lily stifled a scream as the pain shot through her neck and shoulders.

He met her stare and smirked. "There'll be no riding yet. Not this close to Cameron lands. We move on. With our pretty little bird."

❀

The soldiers secured her onto the rear of Newsam's horse. Lily was flopped on her belly, the mount's flanks punching into her stomach with each step. The length of rope they had used to tie her hands and feet cut into her skin with even the slightest movement. Dry heaves wracked her body, the waves of nausea aggravated by the stomach-turning combination of smells that filled her senses—the musk of horse and saddle, the iron tang of blood trickling down her hands from the bite of the rope, and the sourness of her own bile that she fought to choke back.

Her mind desperately tried to focus on a plan. She recalled an afternoon talk show she watched just after the layoffs at work. The topic had been survival, and the host was interviewing kidnap survivors. The number one rule, they kept repeating, was never to let strangers take you to a remote location; once they have you in their power, there is little to no chance of escape. Lily's heart sunk. Not only was she bound hand and foot atop a horse, she was definitely being whisked off to someplace remote.

They rode for hours, putting miles between them and the Cameron lands. Each step took Lily further away from any hope of assistance. The full extent of her situation dawned on her. She'd considered it from every angle, and still, everything pointed to seventeenth-century Scotland. There was no civilization for miles, and between the scene at Ewen's castle and these mounted redcoats, it was clear she had somehow ended up in a nightmarish version of Gram's song. Herself landing on Lochaber soil, herself hailing from a future grand.

Here at the end—for surely, she thought, she was facing

her end—what struck her was that she was utterly alone, not just in this past place, but in her own time as well. Closing herself off from any personal attachments, focusing only on work, Lily had also lost—what? Her twenties? And with it, any chance at love, or friendship, or fun. And for what? A meager nest egg that she'd never get to share with anybody.

She had been so pleased with herself and her string of triumphs. She had watched coworkers lose everything in that very first round of company layoffs while she escaped, with a promotion no less. She should've known then that it was the beginning of the end of the technology boom. Instead, she zipped around the city in her hot little silver sedan. She had been so thrilled with such physical proof of her successes—forget the automatic everything that her BMW came loaded with, the thing even had heated seats. Lily thought it couldn't get any better. All those accomplishments, those things that had given her pride and self-worth, rang ridiculously hollow now.

It hit her with excruciating clarity. She'd once had such ideals, gotten such simple pleasures from painting and reading. When had she lost touch with herself and what was truly important to her? She'd spent her adult years chasing shadows only to realize now that none of it mattered. All of it led to this moment in time. Stranded God knows where and God knows when, about to be brutalized by a trio of soldiers, and nobody would even notice she was gone. Correction. Aside from that formidable Ewen-Lochiel-whatever-he-called-himself and his brother, she could disappear off the face of the earth and nobody would truly miss her, not here, not back home. And Ewen would probably be relieved that the bothersome foreign . . . lass . . . as he kept calling her, had conveniently disappeared.

Her head ached from the tears that had been silently flowing almost nonstop since her capture. Exhausted, alone, lost, Lily let herself drift into unconsciousness.

❁

She was being shaken, hands jostling her, roughly moving her limbs into places they didn't want to go. Lily opened her eyes just as the horizon was spinning. She was being pulled off of the horse. Her makeshift bonds had caught on Newsam's saddlebag and the ugly soldier with the bloody ear was doing his best to wrestle her up and over the horse's haunches. Lily was now numb to the pain as the barbs of twine ate deeper into her raw and bloodied wrists with every move. The saddlebag slipped free and Lily toppled to the ground, her weight flung solidly down like a sack of flour.

"You Scot wenches are built like lads."

Lily struggled to focus and choked down another wave of nausea as Neal's ear dangled wildly from his scalp like an ornament.

Disgust inspired her anew. She would not give up. She could figure her way out of this, even if she was sapped of strength, bleeding, and tied up hand and foot. Newsam was barking orders to the fat one to gather kindling for a fire. She studied the sky, which was now steadily darkening to gunmetal gray. So twilight was upon them. Lily was no fool, and she knew what night would bring.

Her mind raced as Neal continued with his diatribe. "Not like the English ladies, mind. Now in London you'll find some right genteel ones, you will. Light and delicate-like. Not like you Scots hussies."

So, they thought she was Scottish. Of course. Lily realized that, in all the hours she had been with these men, she still hadn't uttered a single word. Her unrecognizable American accent would surely sound peculiar to them. She couldn't decide if she could use that to her advantage or if it would be a liability. She could rely on Ewen's cover story and pretend she was from France. Though, come to think of it, she wasn't quite sure if the French were all that friendly with the British in—what year did Robert say it was? 1654? No, come to think of it, didn't the French ally with Scotland in battles for independence against the British? She seemed to recall that tidbit from some Mel Gibson movie she had seen years ago. Why hadn't she listened more attentively to any of the myriad museum tours that she had taken on her vacation?

Newsam appeared over her. His lanky form cast a dramatically long shadow in the late afternoon light. Lily sucked in her breath as she noticed a rusty blade in his hand.

He saw her eyeing his old dagger and chuckled. "Don't mind this, missy. I'm not done with you yet. We just need to pry these big feet of yours apart." He gave the other redcoats a knowing smirk.

Burton, now finished lighting a small fire, knelt down at Lily's head and pinned her shoulders to the ground. Her senses piqued, Lily was overwhelmed by a heightened awareness of the ground beneath her. A large, smooth rock dug into her buttocks, with smaller rocks grinding into her right shoulder blade and a clump of foliage in the small of her back. Not soft and forgiving, but bristly, like thistle. She remembered, incongruously, that thistle was the last thing she saw before the image of that man's hideous face.

With one swift flick of his wrist, Newsam severed the rope at her ankles and began to saw at her bound hands. Adrenalin coursed through her veins at the thought that these men surely hadn't been this close to a woman in quite some time.

She started to flail madly, bucking her legs and wriggling her arms, but it was no use. They had a firm grip on her and it would be impossible to wrestle her way out of it. The orange-haired man loomed over her, the bald top of his head slick with sweat, panting and grunting like an animal. *So that's where the phrase* rutting swine *comes from*, she thought, and her stomach turned. Ignoring stabs of pain from her old injury, Lily flinched her shoulders to try to pull out from under him, her mind not accepting that this man who was so short could be so strong.

Her hands were untied now. How had they managed to pin them above her head so quickly? Newsam stood once again over her, his legs straddling her waist, and sheathed his rusty blade into a small scabbard at his waist. Lily was lying spread-eagle, her feet being crushed down hard into the rocky soil. She looked down to see Neal restraining her as he tried desperately to catch a glimpse up her torn skirt. Fury engulfed her anew, and unable to kick or to hit, Lily started spitting and screeching like a rabid cat. She might not be able to escape, but she would go down fighting.

"Who gets a go first then?"

"I'd like me a piece. I can't remember the last time I had me cock in a lass."

"Neal, the last birdie you had was your sister."

"Bugger off, Burton, you bald whelp. How would you know? I'll wager this is your first, eh?"

Newsam kicked Lily's skirt up above her knees. "You can both bugger off. I'm the senior officer and I get me a taste before you sorry lads."

"Why not try me first, gentlemen?" The voice was low, calm—and distinctly Scottish. Lily was flooded with relief at the sight of the Highland warrior. Ewen had emerged from nowhere, rising out of the fog of the hills, seemingly born of the rugged land around them as if he were a primeval Celtic spirit. While the three soldiers gave the impression of being trespassers in this landscape, the Scot stood firm and erect on a rock above them, rising from it as if he were carved from that ancient stone. Lily thought she had never seen a more beautiful sight.

The sun slipped behind the mist-shrouded peaks in the distance, sky dappled with moody grays and purples. Ewen's grave face was completely still, claymore already silently drawn, held unwavering before him. The only movement around him was his long, black hair billowing about his shoulders and his tartan flapping softly about his legs in the gentle breeze.

Lily drank in the vision of this man who was the spirit of the land incarnate—unyielding, powerful, self-possessed. It gave her strength. Her breath became rhythmic, deep. She stared hard into Ewen's eyes, hungry now for the power that he offered her.

Ewen's eyes met hers and a faint smile touched the corner of his lips. This was child's play to him.

It all happened in a split second. Newsam, still standing over her, was caught off guard. Turning to look at Ewen, his feet tangled in Lily's skirts and he tumbled to the ground like a felled tree. Trying to get out of his way, Neal momentarily loosened his grip on her feet, and that was all the opportunity Lily needed.

She felt one with Ewen, one with this hard and lonely land, and she felt herself brimming with a renewed strength. Rocking her hips back as best she could with her heavy skirt, she swung her feet up and slammed them into Neal's face. She could feel the crunch of cartilage as her heel connected with his face, and somewhere on the edge of her senses pain seared through her as his broken nose cut through the skin of her bare feet. If anything, the sensation drove her fury to a fever pitch.

Her hands were still pinned, the tiny bones in her wrist crushed under the pressure. She began to writhe madly, trying to wriggle free from Burton's grasp. He released one of her hands, a momentary triumph for her that was quashed when, just as quickly, his hand appeared at her neck, a dagger cutting into her throat. Lily stilled. She looked up into his face. His orange hair had turned a dark russet with the sweat that now drenched him. A bead of perspiration rolled slowly down the flushed fat of his neck, dangled there for a moment, and then Lily felt it drop onto her temple.

She heard Ewen's sword before she saw anything. There was a distant tonal sound, the razor-sharp blade humming as it cut through the air. The delicate whoosh belied its enormous size, and reminded Lily of a bird flying down, lightly, surely, to land. Lily averted her eyes as the claymore connected with Burton's quivering neck. She heard the hollow thunk as his head hit the ground near her shoulder.

The horror of witnessing a man's head being separated from his body was too much for her mind to wrap itself around. Instead, peculiar details filled Lily's thoughts. How odd, she thought, for Burton to stay kneeling upright for so long. Odder still that the sensation of his hand applying pressure to her wrist remained. It was the ghastly smell that tore Lily from her musing. Burton's bowels had released. She spun to her side and was up on her knees in seconds, spasms shuddering through her as her body tried to sick up its few remaining fluids.

She felt a pair of hands grab her roughly underneath the arms. For one brief moment, Lily imagined, hoped, that it was Ewen whisking her away from the gruesome scene. She was hauled upright and the stench of sour liquor and sweat hit her like a wall. Neal had recovered from the shock of his broken nose and held her tightly against him with one arm. A loaded pistol trembled outstretched in the other, as he used Lily's body as a shield to buffer himself from the maelstrom that was Ewen.

The laird's eyes sought hers. Fear lined Lily's face, the plea in her eyes clear. Ewen ran to her. She tried to shout a warning but it was all happening too fast. Newsam leapt like a feral dog onto Ewen's back and planted his rusty blade on the warrior's throat. Ewen froze in place, a thick rope of blood already running down his neck. The crimson flowed down to touch the coarse fabric of his shirt and veins of color exploded in all directions, forming an absurdly delicate red blossom on the cream-colored linen.

Ewen's gaze was distant. Lily sensed his deliberation. His enormous sword was completely ineffective at such short range. Trapped like an animal, he seemed to Lily pure instinct, sizing up his opponent, the situation, what his strategy would be. They only had moments before Newsam, shaking in anger and shock, would finish what he had started.

The warrior's eyes once again sought hers and found silent accord. Grasping the arm that was wrapped across her chest, Lily sprang up and, once again rocking her hips, used gravity and Neal's own strength against him. The knees, she thought, connecting with the knees would be her only hope against a stronger opponent. Ignoring her already injured heel, Lily slammed her feet down and back. With a sickeningly audible pop, she found her target.

Neal's arm went slack, and screeching, he crumpled to the ground. She lurched after the falling soldier, diving for his pistol. Seizing it, she was back up onto her feet in one fluid, determined motion.

She was a force to be reckoned with. Holding the gun steady in front of her, left hand supporting the right, legs planted firmly, she heard herself declare, "Let . . . him . . . go." Lily felt invincible.

Newsam's laughter came as a shock. "Isn't this rich? The bird thinks she can fire a gun. Put 'er down, woman, that's as like to kill you or your friend here as to even touch me. Birdies don't fire guns."

She had only shot a gun once in her life. Her college roommate had been writing an article for the school paper about women and guns. Lily gamely went with her to the shooting range for a lesson in how to handle a firearm. Though she wasn't shaken by the experience, Lily had never had any desire to try it again. She did take away enough from her lesson to know that guns kicked back hard. Antique pistols packed full of gunpowder surely more so.

Stiffening her elbows, she anchored her right leg firmly

behind her and reminded herself to breathe. The pistol was larger and cruder than the one she'd shot before, with a number of confusing levers along the top. Lily realized now she'd heard Neal fumbling to load it while Ewen dispatched the red-haired soldier. She hoped that it operated under the same general mechanics as its modern-day counterpart. Using her palm to pull back the long hammer, Lily cocked the gun.

Heart pounding, she did her best not to betray her fear. "We shall see about that, shan't we?"

The soldiers looked dumbfounded at the foreign sound of her voice and she smiled for effect.

Lily knew enough to understand that seventeenth-century weapons didn't shoot straight. Now that she had so boldly made her threat known, she wondered how exactly they were going to get Ewen out of the path of any bullets she might be firing that evening.

The Highlander solved that problem for her. Newsam was momentarily taken aback by Lily's apparent acquaintance with a weapon, not to mention her peculiar accent. Using that split second to his advantage, Ewen's hands shot to his neck. Sliding out from under the blade, Ewen was forced to slit his own throat in order to break free. The cut, though shallow and slight, bled even more profusely than before. Unflinching, Ewen rolled to the ground toward his fallen claymore, hands grasping the hilt midroll.

Forgetting Ewen, Newsam lunged toward Lily. Disgust disfigured the soldier's already ugly features, and Lily realized that her courage had shocked him. A woman who could pose a threat was a foreign and repugnant concept. The thought steeled her.

They locked eyes, and she saw his lust had turned murderous. She knew what she had to do. The wood handle of the pistol began to feel unsteady in her grip, palms now slick with sweat, muscles in her arms twitching from the exertion of holding such an awkward weight outstretched. The gun felt warm in her hands, like a living thing. The once cool metal of the trigger was now hot under her index finger. Lily gritted her teeth. She pulled.

The effect was devastating. The hammer sprang forward, its flint striking a nub of metal atop the weapon, sending a shower of sparks down to ignite the gunpowder. There was a deafening shot, and Lily was thrown violently backward from the force of it. Ears ringing, she shut her eyes and struggled to make her rib cage rise and fall as she tried to remember how to breathe.

Her right hand twitched involuntarily. Blistering pain shot from her fingernails up to her shoulder. Lily wondered if she had somehow fallen into the small bonfire the soldiers had set. She forced her eyes open and gasped at the sight of her index finger, scorched and bloody from the gunpowder.

Once again she felt two hands on her. This time, though, the hands lifting her off the ground were considerably gentler. She looked up to see Ewen's face only inches from her own, concern etched in his brow.

"Did I . . . ?"

"Aye, lass, he's dead. You did well. Quiet yourself now."

Cradling her firmly in his arms, he whispered, "You're a braw one aren't you, Lil'? I can't say I've seen braver."

Lily shot up in his arms, renewed terror in her eyes. "But the other one!"

In her panic, Lily's forehead butted hard against Ewen's chin. He chuckled, "I said calm yourself, lass. I dealt with the nasty-faced one. No need to rile yourself.

"Do you think you can sit a horse? We need to be away from this place before some other soldiers wonder what all the gunfire is about."

Lily nodded weakly, only to regret it when she caught sight of the warhorse Ewen called a ride. No Highland pony this one. But for one dark red sock, the horse was as black as night and barely visible in the growing twilight. His mane and tail were long, unruly masses that stood in stark counterpoint to the silky sheen of his body. Lily gaped when she noticed the patchwork of scars webbing the horse's face and shoulders.

Ewen mistook her apprehension for admiration and praised, "Aye, he's a bonny one, no? I call him Ares—like the god of war. He's seen me through many a battle, this one. Not the comeliest lad, but there's none braver."

Ewen had barely lifted her onto the saddle when he announced gravely, "Now that you're safe, lass, I'd say my mind."

"Uh-oh." She smiled, feeling at ease with him. "Here it

comes." Lily turned to face him, eyebrows raised expectantly. It wasn't every day she had a life-and-death experience and the rush left her feeling muzzy and inexplicably close to the laird.

"This is not a light matter, lass."

She was taken aback. Rather than engaging in what she thought would be a continuation of their easy rapport, Ewen seemed affronted by her good humor. He chided, "You've no place outside the castle walls. I don't ken women of your time, but you're my charge now and you must mind my word."

"Don't scold me like a child." Red blotched her cheeks as Lily felt suddenly piqued. "If you and your . . . your foster brother hadn't been so secretive and dramatic and, well, bizarre, I might have listened to you."

"Och, you *glaikit* lass." Ewen pulled Ares to an abrupt halt. "Tell me, what about this isn't dramatic and bizarre? I wonder that I even found you. If those men hadn't been such *bawheided* fools, it's your dead body I'd have slung over the saddle."

"I was just trying to get back to . . . where I was. How was I to know—" Her breath shuddered as she tried to get air into her suddenly uncooperative lungs, "How could I have known that I couldn't get back?"

"I'm just asking." Ewen's voice gentled. "I'm asking that henceforth you give a thought to your situation, aye?"

"That's just it." Tears began to spill down her face. "How can I think about it when I don't even understand what's happened to me? I . . . I just want to go home. Please," Lily sobbed, "you've got to help me get home."

Ewen tucked her head under his chin. "Hush, lass," he rasped. "I know the person who might can help you find your way. There's a woman, Gormshuil, she predicted your coming."

Lily's head bolted back up. "Predicted *I'd* come?"

"That *someone* would come, and"—he smiled—"I pray that none else has passed without my knowledge." His eyes softened as he smoothed Lily's hair from her face. "But you're best to guard your hopes, lass. Gormshuil is a canny old witch, but she's hard to track. And I've first the need to settle affairs in my own keep—I've redcoats ahead and MacKintoshes aback—but once I'm able, you'll have all the help you need." Cupping her chin, he added, "I'll see you home."

Ewen nudged Ares into a slow walk, and Lily felt his body

stiffen behind her. "But you're to trust me, lass. And part of that is the minding of me. If I'm to keep you from harm, you're not to venture far without the keep, aye?"

"I . . . of course." His controlling attitude chafed, but Lily thought she didn't have to like it. She just needed to survive it. "I understand."

Just get me home, she thought.

Chapter 9

For someone perched atop a formidable warhorse, Lily discovered she was surprisingly cozy. She'd been so wound up after their conversation, it had taken her a long time to sort out her skirts and get comfortable on the unusually hard saddle. Ewen, in a wave of frustration, finally just whisked her onto his lap, settling her in the crook of his arm, Lily's head nestled on his shoulder. Wordlessly, he'd unpinned the swath of tartan that was gathered over his shoulder and wrapped it around her for warmth.

Once again she called Gram's song to mind. Hearing it in her head, she felt a shot of alarm—and more than a little fascination—as she considered the parallels to Ewen and Robert. Especially Robert, whose claims of traveling through the labyrinth—come from "a future grand"—were all too explicitly referenced in the lyrics.

But Gram's song had been a tragic one, about the dead hero who had taken a bullet for his laird. The Robert she'd met was very much alive. Surely Ewen and Robert were common enough names in Scotland. For the words to be about the same men was outlandish. It would mean the song foretold their future, that Lily knew the near future. A prospect, she supposed grimly, no more preposterous than her having traveled back in time.

Utterly exhausted, Lily decided she had no choice but to ignore it for now. She didn't know these men or their world. She could only wait, and watch, and keep the riddle of Gram's lullaby to herself.

They rode in silence for some time. She was emotionally sapped, but somehow the knowledge that Ewen would help her find her way home—that he would take care of things just as he had taken care of those redcoats—made her feel safe. Her mind emptied itself of all the turmoil and she was left feeling tranquil and pleasantly blank.

The gentle swaying of Ares's gait lulled Lily. She let herself become aware of all of her aches and pains—her raw fingers, throbbing heel, and, not least of all, the solitude that had overwhelmed her just before Ewen rescued her from the soldiers. Mesmerized by the play of the bright Scottish moon on Ares's silken black coat, Lily forced her multiple injuries to recede into a single dull ache.

She had felt so starkly alone in the world. But for Ewen she would likely be dead now. Who was this man who now cradled her in his arms? The only person in the world who noted her disappearance and thought to find her. This man with whom she'd had such an intense connection in a moment of life or death. Who, despite being a virtual stranger to her, would do all in his power to help her find her way home.

She inhaled his scent—peat, damp wool, leather. His raw, earthy vitality both invigorated and soothed her. He was unlike any man she had ever been in contact with. Ewen's body felt as if it was hewn from stone, his stomach a wall of solid muscle, the cut of his arms hard and unyielding. But there was a warmth there, a human solidity.

Lily became aware of the fluid motion of his pelvis, back and forth, following the horse's gait as if they were a single animal, and she shivered as a long-forgotten awareness of herself as a woman—a woman's body with a woman's needs—thrilled through her. Thinking her cold, Ewen merely pulled her closer, tucking the tartan more tightly around her chest. A lock of his hair fell from behind his ear and cascaded over her forehead. The smell of him filled her even more intensely than before, a male musk sparking her body to awareness, pushing all thoughts of her injuries to the back of her mind. She let her rational mind slip away and allowed herself to enjoy this flare of sensuality, her body responding to another body in a way that she had managed to stifle all of these years. Nuzzling deeper into the crook of his arm, she let herself drift into a dreamless sleep.

❀

Ewen tried to look away, but couldn't stop his eyes from returning over and over to the sight of her exposed thigh extended over Ares's saddle. He marveled at how long and smooth it was. It looked strong and lean, yet soft to the touch. He forced himself to keep his eyes on the path ahead and cursed the woman for her recklessness.

She should count herself lucky that her absence had been noted as quickly as it was. Just a few minutes more and he would've been too late. Alone, he traveled swiftly, Lily's whereabouts simple enough to track. Three drunken redcoats and a retching lass carve as subtle a trail as would an injured bull elk in heat. Ewen shook his head. He had to allow that she was a brave one. His first instincts on that score had been correct. And a robust lassie too, for all her bonny appearance. She fought like a hellcat, unhindered by muscles weaker than a man's. Some of her moves had taken him aback. Leveraging her own weight to make battering rams of her feet against that lout's knee, that was one he'd like to try himself.

He'd wager that this Lily would be just as tempestuous with a man whom she wasn't trying to kill.

Och, but he needed to learn to censure his thoughts. She was rash, ill-tempered, and, he'd not forget, a stranger to his lands. It was too simple to find oneself enthralled by her peculiar brand of beauty, but such traitorous lapses of judgment could hold grave consequences, no mistake. He replayed in his mind what had been an uncharacteristically distracted and nearly fatal error. Damned if the lass hadn't diverted his attentions from the task of finishing those beggars off as efficiently as he could have. Just a single glance with those eyes had unmanned him, jarred as he was to see the usual fire of her gaze dampened by a look of such fearful need.

Ewen tugged at the neck of his shirt. That lapse of concentration had almost been his undoing. As it was, he had a rather deep wound on his neck to show for it, which he was currently finding to be an inconvenience.

No, he definitely did not need this woman's brand of magnetism, an attraction strong enough to drag a man down as surely as gravity itself pulls water over a cliff's edge. And anyone can see all the good that does the water. Besides, his days of succumbing to the attractions of women were done for. Best to spend his energies minimizing the damage wrought by such like this Lily.

❦

Lily's eyes fluttered open as Ewen was setting her down by the side of a lake. "Wake yourself, lass. The moon is setting, and with this rough road, we'll go no farther till daylight. I'll not risk Ares catching his hoof in a rut and going lame."

The gentleness in his voice unsettled her, the soft roll of his accent pitched to her ears alone. The unexpected intimacy of it sent a shiver over her skin, yet the heat that suffused her in its wake was as intense as any peat fire.

Mistaking her trembling for a chill, Ewen set up camp with an efficient focus that spoke of a man accustomed to living off the land. Lily merely stared wide-eyed at the vision of the Scottish warrior as he moved like a panther in the shadows, silently tidying Ares's tack, smoothing away rocks and branches, and gathering leaves for makeshift bedding.

Ewen grasped one end of his tartan and unfurled it. Yards and yards of red plaid wool billowed to the ground, leaving him standing only in his long linen shirt.

He was nothing short of beautiful. Despite his injury, despite the frost in the air, he stood tall in the darkness, moonlight silvering the taut muscles of his calves and thighs to make him appear like a primordial god standing still in the night, fortified by an inner tranquility and courage. Ewen pinned her with his gaze, unconsciously raking a hand through his long black hair, and Lily thought she would be undone.

"Aye, you're looking a bit dazed, lass. I fear the fever from your wounds is setting on you."

Lily managed a wordless nod.

He stalked toward her with a driven glint in his eyes, and she watched the scene unfold with a dreamlike detachment. His thighs were cut with the same steely muscle that she had felt in the rest of his body. His feet moved surely across the rugged terrain, like an animal approaching his prey. As he got closer, Lily noticed that his shirt had become unlaced, revealing the smooth chest beneath. He bent down, and the smell of him filled her senses, the scent of a man who had ridden hard through the day, all musk and leather. A visceral response tore through her, the flame of pure wanting licked up and through her body, as muscles leading from belly to deep into her most private self, long-clenched from reserved isolation, released in a rush of physical need.

Ewen wrapped his arm tightly around her shoulders and, cupping her buttocks with his other hand, lifted her effortlessly into his arms. She shut her eyes and gasping a slight sigh from between parted lips opened herself to him.

Lily shrieked as freezing water assaulted her senses. The pain of her wounds radiated anew, stoked by her anger and the frigid water, and white-hot agony tore up her legs and settled in her joints as Ewen dangled her feet and hands in the lake.

"What the hell are you doing?" Screaming at him, Lily made it clear that she did not appreciate this rude awakening from the trance she had been under just a moment earlier.

"Shush, Lil'."

Nobody, but nobody, had ever called her that. How dare he? Where did this man get off? And was that a smile on his face?

"I've had many a wound, lass. Trust me, the pain now is nothing compared to what you'll feel if we don't wash these now. I'd like to save this big foot of yours if I can."

Save her foot? The reality of her situation crashed down on Lily with renewed force. She was in the past. No doctors. No antibiotics. No modern medicine to prevent small wounds from festering into life-threatening injuries.

And, dammit, her feet were not big for her height.

Lily grimaced in pain as Ewen rinsed the grime from her fingers and wounded foot. Eventually the frigid water began to soothe her powder-burned hands and feeling returned to her fingertips. Although she estimated the damage to her hands wasn't permanent, the pulsing pain below her knee was pure anguish. Cartilage had torn the sole of her foot when she so savagely broke the soldier's nose and the resulting gash was deep, and still oozing blood.

She thought back in wonder to the scene earlier. How could she have sustained such a serious injury and not fully noticed it until now? A primal rage had swept through her. She had clawed, kicked, and fought for her life. And here she was. She was the survivor.

Such empowering thoughts dulled the anger she had been nursing since she so naively opened herself to what she thought was going to be a romantic interlude with Ewen. She shook her head, feeling a little embarrassed at the thought. Forcing it from her mind, Lily again thought with amazement how she had fought for her life and survived. It was surely just a combination of adrenaline and the heady power of victory and escape that had made her so lustful earlier. Any armchair psychologist could point to a connection formed between comrades in a fight as the source of her own misguided seduction fantasy.

For so many years now, she had been living as a rational mind moving through the world. Her grandmother had chided her, "You're not just a head on a pair of shoulders, Lily Hamlin—get out there, get some fresh air, and enjoy life a little." Instead she had chosen a self-imposed exile from her own physicality and creative spirit.

But now, somehow, this man and his wild, untamed terrain inflamed her long-forgotten instincts. She would wear her newly discovered physical and mental strength with pride. That deep well of desire she glimpsed, though, that she might just keep tucked away as her own personal treasure.

Ewen set her down beneath a large birch tree. She leaned back against the peeling gray bark, nestling into the leaves he had piled into makeshift bedding. Soft with rot and damp, they were surprisingly comfortable. She inhaled deeply, taking in the rich, woodsy smells around her. She couldn't remember the last time she had hiked, much less went camping. For someone who had just shot a man, she felt oddly at peace.

"We'll be sleeping under that." Ewen indicated a dense

bushy area. Though she assumed that he didn't have any tents hidden about, Lily could not see for the life of her what the *that* was that he was pointing to.

"Under what?"

"Aye," he said in mock seriousness, "I see you're unaccustomed to using the eyes God gave you."

Lily challenged him with a glare. In two large strides, he made his way toward the brush and, clearing away some of the heavy undergrowth, revealed a tidy little fort hidden underneath a fallen tree.

"Under this, lass."

She had to admit, it looked quite the cozy hideaway. There was enough room for two adults to lie down, if a bit snugly. Boughs, some still holding on to their brown leaves, fanned over and around the stump, offering protection from any rain or wind that might try to bother them that night.

"Oh. I see. Yes, I suppose that does work nicely."

Lily shivered. The freezing water had dampened her skirts and cold was settling into her bones. "Now, shall we start the fire?"

"No, Lil', we don't dare being spotted."

Her heart fell. Why, she thought, with the way things were going for her, had she thought this might approximate a pleasant outdoor experience?

"Those soldiers belonged somewhere, and soon somebody is going to notice them missing." He continued rustling about as nonchalantly as a regular man might, unpacking in a room in the Hilton.

"Nay, we'll warm ourselves as best we can without a fire." Despite her earlier vows of Amazonian strength and reserve, Lily had to blush at that last statement and was happy the darkness concealed her features.

Methodically, Ewen began to rip off long bits of fabric from the hem of his shirt, which, Lily couldn't help but note, was gradually making it shorter and shorter. Cheeks flushing anew, Lily thought that surely seventeenth-century Scotsmen had no notion of underwear, and at the rate he was shredding his top, all would soon be revealed.

He soon had a small handful of linen strips, and before she could utter any denials, he was kneeling in front of her, gently wrapping her wounded foot. She studied his hands in awe. They were large and strong, knuckles scored with scars. These hands had killed men, had been gashed during lethal sword-play, skin and bone deflecting potentially fatal slashes. And now these same hands were working gently, deftly, binding her foot just right. Ewen wrapped the linen snugly, but not un-comfortably tight. Looping it around, not one spot on the sole of her foot was left uncovered, the fabric wrapped smoothly over itself, not bunching around heel or ankle. It was clear that he had dressed many a battle wound in his time.

She just then noticed the dried blood on his neck and sucked in her breath. Leaning toward him, she pulled aside the collar of his shirt. The moon threw shimmering white light across his smooth chest. "I need to take care of this for you."

Oddly, Ewen didn't put up a fuss. Rather, he looked vaguely amused, as if a child had just offered to dress his cuts. Lily wasn't dissuaded, however. She simply snatched the re-maining linen out of his hand and hobbled down to the lake-side to wet the fabric.

She worked in silence for some time, overdelicately swab-bing the crusted blood from his neck and shoulders. If Ewen had a son, she thought, surely he was married. Lily couldn't imagine what type of woman would be married to a Highland clan chief. Did she live in fear or secretly run the household? Her curiosity got the better of her, and feeling at ease with their close physical proximity, she ventured, "So, tell me about your wife."

Ewen looked as if he had been slapped. Grabbing the end of the bandage out of her hand he snapped, "Och, enough." He stood, hastily tying the fabric in a knot at his neck. "Don't fash me, lass."

He began to move abruptly around their makeshift camp-ground, all the while grumbling unintelligibly to himself in half Gaelic, half English. Lily strained to hear but could only make out phrases like "you women . . . all the same . . . natter-ing *glaikit* lasses." She didn't know what the last bit meant, but assumed it wasn't good.

"I . . . I'm sorry, Ewen. I just assumed . . . I mean, you have a son, right? But I guess if you need a nanny maybe that means . . . oh." She hated how she always rambled when nervous. Then, under her breath, "I was just trying to make some pleasant conversation. Sorry."

An excruciating silence hung between them as Ewen continued to make camp. Gathering the tartan that he had dropped to the ground, he returned to the bank of the lake and proceeded, inexplicably, to wet the long swath of wool. Lily almost yelled at him to stop it—what was he thinking, soaking their only source of warmth? But looking at the angry set of his shoulders she quickly thought the better of it and bit back any protests.

As if he read her mind, without turning Ewen said, "Stop fretting. It makes the wool warmer. If you dampen it." Well, it wasn't much, but it was a start at communication. Deep in thought, he walked slowly back up to their camp.

"Sorry, lass. I'd not meant to get so angry. Aye, I was married once. And what a bonny lass she was. Bonny, and hellsent." They had only spent a short time together, but Lily had already noted that Ewen's brogue got thicker, with more Gaelic inflections, when speaking with emotion. Despite her desire to keep him at arm's length, Lily couldn't help but find it endearing, albeit more difficult to comprehend.

He reached out for his saddlebag and removed a small leather flagon. He drew a deep gulp and Lily could smell the tang of Scotch whisky. "Would you cock your wee finger with me?" Sprawling onto his side he offered her the leather flask.

Though at that moment she would've preferred something a bit more refreshing—a nice, cold beer perhaps—she accepted the drink readily. The adrenalin of the day had worn off and she thought her foot would explode from the pain pulsing from her toes up to her calf.

It was harder than she thought to manage the flask and more whisky than she intended rushed down her throat. She strangled a cough and forced herself to continue breathing. It was like drinking pure heat. This was no Dewar's. She supposed that the days of refined sipping whisky hadn't yet hit Scotland. She surreptitiously wiped the tears from her eyes and the whisky from her chin and whispered a choked thanks.

Ewen smiled. If he could tell the whisky was more than she bargained for, he didn't let on. He stayed reclined on the tartan and took the flagon back out of her hands. Taking one more drag on the whisky, he continued, "She died in child-birth. A sad thing, that. My John killed her, and the lad has been making my life a misery ever since.

"My grandfather had insisted on the match. My father passed when I was but a lad, so I was next in line to be laird. He said the clan needed me to marry young. His body was starting to fail him, and he knew he'd not make it another winter. My grandfather was a man of tradition, believed every clan chief needs a wife, he did. So he married me off like a horse to stud. With a wife like Mairi, though . . . Och, I could have done better marrying a MacKintosh, the battles we fought."

Brow furrowed, he was silent for a moment then continued, "She was unfaithful to me. To the clan too, you could say. No regard for honor. She lay with other men. With my tacksman. With a MacKintosh even." Lily could tell by the gravity in his voice that the last one was a real transgression. He looked into the distance. "Och, but she could drive a man to madness. Smooth like silk until she had you in her palm, then she'd laugh you right out the room."

Shaking his head, he continued, "She was such a bonny one. Long black hair, tiny white hands. Such a delicate lass. It's what killed her in the end. Not made for birthing bairns. But she had my grandfather charmed. She likely warmed his bed as well. To get what she wanted."

Lily shivered at the thought of a pretty, young girl bedding an aged Scottish laird. She never understood how people were able to use their bodies as tools to get what they wanted.

Ewen thought he understood the look that passed over her face and he explained, "I was in line to be chief and that was an exceeding good match for her. Bedding the men she did, she cleared a number of paths for herself, I see it plain now. If anything had happened to me, she'd have been like to find favor with the next man in line for Lochiel." He noted Lily's quizzical look and added, "That's what the Camerons call their clan chief, lass. Lochiel. I'm the Lochiel, as my grand-father was, and John will be after I'm gone."

Ewen adjusted the damp tartan underneath their makeshift shelter and, with a heavy sigh, shifted to a seated position. "She wanted to be a chief's wife, but her father hadn't much to offer a potential husband but his daughter's charms. Nay, all he had to offer was a sporran full of debt, I've since discovered. And so it was her charms that were offered to us tenfold." He snorted a laugh, tinged with more than a little disgust. "She wasn't worth the price. No lass is." Lily was annoyed at his poor regard for women, but curiosity won over and she let Ewen continue.

"I was just a young lad who didn't know better, and my grandfather was an old man flattered by the attentions of a comely lass. He arranged our marriage, and she wasn't the same after. A shrew to everyone, especially me. It's as well I grew to see her for what she was. A tiny black heart she had. Cruel to every living thing."

A clipped bitter laugh escaped him. "Cruel to all but her horse that is. I'll still not understand it. She'd beat the groom with her whip then stroke that mare for hours." He added as an afterthought, "We had to put the mare down last fall. Lamed herself kicking another mount. Took after her owner till the end, I suppose. I wasn't grieved to say good-bye to that one. It was the last ghost of Mairi left on Cameron lands.

"Except for our son John. His wickedness tries me as much as his mother ever did . . ." Ewen's voice trailed off.

Lily was overwhelmed. She could tell that Ewen had been hurt more deeply by this woman than he was letting on. It wasn't the agony of a lost love she heard in his voice, though. No, it was clear his feelings for his former wife could, at most, be summed up as young lust. What she did hear there was isolation. Being a leader like Ewen must mean standing alone, never allowing yourself to trust another, never letting any emotion or vulnerability show through. At a young age, he had discovered the hard lesson that when you have power, people rarely approach you with more than selfish intentions. Lily knew it was so in modern America and imagined it was no different in seventeenth-century Scotland.

"I . . . I'm so sorry, Ewen. That sounds horrible."

"Och, I had my youth and learned what lust will get me. Nay, I'll not marry again. I have my heir."

"But not all women are like that!"

"Aye, lass, some women are soft and kind." He laughed and winked roguishly at her, and Lily felt her face flame crimson to her ears.

"But when it comes to pledging my troth to a woman, aye, I've done my duty as Lochiel. John as my heir will take over when I'm gone. No need for me to marry again. Ever." He finished his diatribe as if it was the last thing to be said on the subject and quickly changed the topic.

"But what of you, lass? Why've you no husband then?"

His tone was incredulous, and Lily bridled at the implication that she was somehow aberrant not to have a man in her life. She replied, "It never came up."

"Your family did not find you a good match, is it?"

"That's not really how it goes in my time," she answered coolly. "Many women don't marry until well into their thirties, or later. Besides, my family wasn't really in the picture."

Ewen considered her intently, as if studying some foreign creature. "I don't ken your meaning . . . *in the picture.*"

"Oh, that's just a saying . . . it's that . . . well, it was mostly just my grandmother and me. My mom wasn't around much, and I never had a real father to speak of."

Ewen stared at her solemnly, and Lily fumbled to fill the uncomfortable silence. "My mom took off when I was young. She came back years later with some new husband, and I just, well, I just didn't want to have much to do with them."

"You had a choice?" He continued indignantly, " And what of your mother to disappear so? What sort of a woman quits her wean?"

Lily felt strangely defensive of the woman she'd spent a lifetime deriding. "It happens. Some women leave their children."

"Och," Ewen hissed, "not in Scotland."

"Oh, it'll happen."

"Nay in the Highlands," the laird replied dismissively.

"Lass," Ewen's affronted tone softened, as if he lamented Lily's worldview, even felt sorrow for her, "there's no other thing than family."

"I . . . the thing is"—Lily struggled for words—"it's just different, is all. In modern times. People move away from their families, husbands and wives divorce, we even have special homes for grandparents." Her cataloguing became more confident, even though deep down she wasn't so certain. "People change and move on and it's . . . okay."

Lily had never given much thought to it. Of course, she had regretted the absence of her mother. And envied her friends at school who had big, bustling holidays at home with relatives. But Gram was her only family really, and to discount her as somehow not enough felt dreadful, and traitorous.

"To . . . *move on* from your bairn, to abandon your flesh and blood, och, lass, if that's to be accepted in the future, then I'll have nothing of it.

"The whole clan is a family." He grew impassioned, nearly pleading with Lily. "Like the Camerons, aye? We call ourselves sons of the hound, and . . . *'tis* like that. With the laird at the head, faithful to kin as a hound to the pack. The laird . . . *I* . . . I take care with mine own. And I expect mine to care for theirs in turn, aye?"

The corners of his eyes wrinkled as Ewen regarded her. "Otherwise," he added with quiet compassion, "it's all for naught, lass. Otherwise, you're alone with naught but the ground at your feet and the stars in the sky for to guide you. And that's not any way to live, Lil'. I don't care what your century."

Lily was speechless, and the moment suspended in time, feeling utterly extraordinary, searing her to the quick. Ewen had laid bare all that had felt empty in her life, a wanting that she herself hadn't realized until that moment.

She had loved Gram, more than anything. But in Lily's world, family could be an afterthought, and now her biggest regret was that she'd let herself drift apart from her grandmother in those last years.

Lily scrubbed her hands over her face. She was exhausted, and the potent whisky was working its way through her veins, blunting her thoughts, numbing the agonizing throb in her foot, and sending a dull heat to unspool the muscles in her neck and back.

She would come up with an insightful rejoinder to Ewen's polemic against modern life. First, though, she would just shut her eyes and mull it over for a little while.

The next thing Lily knew, she was being gently lifted and settled into their improvised shelter. She tried to help the process, but gravity pulled down on her body and made her feel like a bag of wet sand. Utter exhaustion fogged her brain, and she gave up trying to open her eyes. She felt Ewen's light touch as he brushed the hair out of her eyes then, inexplicably, combed his fingers once through her thick curls.

Feeling safer than she had since her arrival, Lily stretched out on the tartan, savoring the scratch of wool against her skin. She became aware of the moisture in the fabric. Rather than chilling her, though, the effect was of a humid warmth enveloping her, reaching the cold in her bones. One last shiver shuddered through Lily as her body finally relaxed, and the purity of physical sensation pushed away all thought, diminishing logic into a meaningless hum at the back of her brain.

Lily welcomed the heat with a pure physical bliss that she hadn't felt in years.

❈

Ewen pulled the tartan around them tightly, offering her body his warmth. She had injured her foot badly, and was likely suffering from exhaustion as well. The lass would need a good warm rest or he would have a real problem on his hands. She had been through quite an ordeal in the last few days. He still couldn't wrap his mind around the fact that she wasn't of his time. But the same held true for Robert, and some things you just needed to accept on faith.

He had never seen such a strong-willed lass. To fire a pistol in that way took real courage—not to mention strength. He had felt a flush of pride for her in that moment. He didn't want to tell her that he could have easily dispatched the men on his own—a few drunken redcoats are no match for a Cameron—but he enjoyed the thrill of the fight with her. Felt a camaraderie that he had shared with but a few men, and those were of his clan.

It made him wonder about this mysterious lass who was so alone in her life, without meaningful relatives, much less a clan to buttress her. It saddened him, and angered him too, that Lily had nobody to rely on. What kind of world does it become, where family is for naught?

And why could she possibly have been sent to him?

Ewen had taken her under his protection and was glad of it. His mind told him not to trust her, and yet there was something about Lily that made him feel as if he knew her. That he recognized her somehow. That there was a rightness to her appearance in his life. For the time being, he chose not to disagree with whatever forces in the universe had placed her just there.

He lay awake for a long time, savoring what was his favorite part of the day. The woods—his Highland woods—offered a never-ending symphony of sounds. That he never noticed it by day always made him especially keen to savor it when the moon was high. The constant quiet settling of leaves. The occasional creak of a faraway branch. And, if he really strained, the faint lapping of the loch in the distance.

The stars lit the sky like a thousand candles shimmering overhead. He became intensely aware of how tiny a presence he was in the world and let the sensation wash over him. Some sought power, but Ewen always felt reassured when reminded of his own insignificance. It made it all easier to bear somehow. The responsibilities, the decisions, and the fighting most of all.

Night was so tranquil, and his days were usually filled with such . . . noise. A cacophony of physical and mental trials. He wasn't sure what he enjoyed most about such days—challenge itself or the utter calm that followed.

Today, though. Today was different somehow. He was unable to find the total peace that normally followed such physical exhaustion. He didn't know why he had divulged so much to the strange lass. With the exception of his uncle Donald, he confessed his thoughts to no man. To no woman, especially. He had allowed a momentary chink in his armor and had felt a glimmer of understanding between himself and Lily. Accepting the mantle of Lochiel, he had been forced to isolate himself at a very young age as someone apart from the rest. But there had been a flickering moment this day, a moment when he had felt he could confide in this strange woman, when he could savor the luxurious illusion that he was not so very alone.

And strange she was indeed. He had never met a woman that strong before. His wife, Mairi, had strength, yes, but of a different sort. Mairi had found power in her arrogance, her vanity. Lily, however, was a singular creature. He had stood alongside many men in battle and always secretly knew who would fall for him and who would think of themselves at that last crucial moment. He'd looked into her eyes during the fight and saw that she would have traded her life for his. Her honor and courage were etched clearly on her face. Hiding nothing, sparing nothing, she fought with him. Then afterward, she was so guileless in her questions of him. Demanding the truth from him. In another woman, he would think her frank interrogation an impropriety, but with Lily it was something else entirely. He speculated that she offered nothing short of truthfulness and naively demanded the same of those around her.

He shut his eyes in an effort to quiet his mind, and concentrated on the feel of the brisk night air on his skin. He had enough concerns without overly contemplating some lass. Inhaling deeply, he took in the scent of the forest. The lush aroma of damp wood and grass. The faint tinge of heather on the air. He thought the colder the night, the clearer the scents became.

Her smell filled his senses. Ewen couldn't help but relish it. It had been so long since he had lain by a woman, and many of those had worn cloying perfumes that mostly just made his head ache. Lily was different, though. She had a warm salty smell, but at its essence was the scent of her womanhood, sweet and rich. Ewen edged ever so slightly closer and found he couldn't stop himself from nuzzling her abundant hair. He imagined most people would deem her locks unruly. That they should be pulled back or up or powdered or whatever it was women did. But he was enchanted by the riot of white-blonde curls, thick rings that he could wind around his fingers. He gently took one of the long ringlets in his hand and, rubbing it to his lips, savored the faint smell of the sea.

He shut his eyes and fell asleep, hand still tangled in Lily's pale mane.

Chapter 10

Lily slowly roused herself from a dreamless sleep. She wondered for a moment where she was then, feeling Ewen's hot breath on her neck, remembered everything. He had tucked them both tightly in his tartan for the night. Struggling to release an arm from their cocoon, she felt a momentary flash of anger at his close proximity. How dare he take advantage like that? They were tangled up quite snugly in what must have been yards and yards of wool. Seeing the white fog of her breath in the dawn, though, Lily realized that it was exactly this intimacy that had meant a full—and toasty—night's sleep for her. She finally worked her arm free and confirmed her suspicions: there was a brisk chill in the air. Enjoying the contrast between the cold morning and their warm nest, Lily lay there, idly toying with a fallen leaf, running through the previous day's events in her mind.

The day had been so chaotic and she so exhausted, her rational mind had not played much a part in things. And then there was that flicker of attraction she'd felt for Ewen. She had been ready to open herself to him. If he had tried . . . well, thank God he hadn't. She only hoped that he hadn't noticed all that schoolgirl sighing and blushing. What had she been thinking? No, that's just it, she hadn't been thinking. There was a ready intellectual explanation for what she had felt. The intensity of the day's events had heightened her physical senses. She'd read about posttraumatic stress disorder—surely she was undergoing some similar phenomenon. Ergo her brief attraction to Ewen. It was that simple.

Images of his smooth chest in the moonlight and the tender strength of his hands flashed through her mind. Lily just as quickly smothered those thoughts. The crisp Highland air must be getting to her.

His gruff early-morning whisper startled Lily out of her reverie. "Time for us to move on, lass. If we leave now, we'll be back safe in the keep by midday." She had to admit, there was something remarkably masculine about his voice.

She pushed the thought out of her mind and rallied her tired muscles. Though she'd had a good night's sleep, resting on hard Highland ground wasn't exactly the way to combat stiffness. She slowly pried herself out of the layers of wool and assessed the damage. Her fingertips felt raw, as if she had taken sandpaper to them. She was thankful that the greatest concern with her hands was that a few of the fingernails had turned a foul yellowish brown color, like she had smoked about a thousand cigarettes the night before. The pain in her foot also no longer alarmed her. Although she still didn't dare put her full weight on it, the agony had reduced to a dull throb.

She quickly surmised that her outer appearance left a lot more to be desired. She tried to work her fingers through her matted hair, but she might as well have tried combing a bird's nest. Managing to pluck out a good number of brambles, she wondered what seventeenth-century fashion would say to a nice set of dreadlocks.

A glance down at her skirts had her hoping that there was some sort of back door to the castle that they could sneak in through. She hated wearing linen in the modern days of dry cleaning and pressing—she always felt like a magnet for every wrinkle and speck of dirt. Her current state, though, was beyond any magic that could be wrought by modern technology. Sleeping in a slightly damp skirt, tangled with a Scottish warrior, had rendered her a rumpled mess. She could even feel the indentations on her leg where the extensive web of wrinkles had pressed into her skin all night. As she smoothed her hands over her clothes, it was clear the crumpled fabric was the least of her worries. The hem of her skirt was black with silt where Ewen had dangled her in the lake. Rust-colored patches of dried blood speckled her clothes and she gulped back a wave of nausea at the realization that she had no idea who the blood had belonged to.

She heard a throaty chuckle behind her. "Stop your preening, lass. You're as bonny as the morning."

So, sarcasm wasn't a modern invention after all. "I'm a mess. And I don't preen."

"Sure you don't—no lass does, aye?" An accusatory grin flashed in his eyes.

"Let's just be going, *aye*?" Lily huffed. She was in no mood this morning. This might be fun and games for him, but she was a rattled wreck. Plus she could really use a bathroom and wasn't quite sure how to broach that one with a seventeenth-century laird.

"As you say, Lil'. I imagine you'll want to walk down by the loch first. There's a wee thicket to the side where you'll have a bit of privacy." He grinned again, damn him. Well, she was happy in this one instance that he read her mind before she had to figure out how to bring that one up herself.

"Thank you," she uttered, hoping that he'd mistake the blush on her cheeks for the fresh morning air.

Making her way back up from the bank of the lake, Lily was deep in thought. What she wouldn't do for a small packet of Kleenex right about now. She desperately hoped that they didn't have anything like poison ivy in Scotland, though she didn't know how she'd recognize it—she had been a miserable Girl Scout. When she'd failed to earn her cooking badge after the second try, she dropped out. And her most extensive experience camping in the great outdoors had been with a bunch of other girls in the troop leader's backyard. When they needed to go, all they'd had to do was walk inside and use the bathroom.

"Lass, quiet!"

Oh no, Lily thought, *here we go again*. She didn't understand why she was attracting so much drama of late—she led such a peacefully mundane life in California. Why was Ewen telling her to be quiet? She wasn't making a sound. "What? I didn't say—"

"Silence! Och, *màrach*, your big feet make a racket," he hissed.

Then Lily saw it. A wolf was stalking around the perimeter of their makeshift camp. Although she had seen copious photos in her time, she had never before seen a wolf up close. No picture could do such a magnificent creature justice. It was huge, but in a lanky sort of way, taller than your average dog, with thin, rangy legs. It had a feral energy, as if its long, lean muscles were tensed to strike at the slightest provocation. This animal looked considerably more menacing than any featured on the sort of save-the-wolf brochures that Lily was familiar with. Its fur was matted with a black fringe of dirt that soiled its white and gray coat. The mouth peeled into a snarl, black lips quivering almost imperceptibly to reveal glossy white fangs. It was a terrifyingly beautiful creature.

Ewen slowly unsheathed the dirk at his side.

"What are you doing? Wolves don't hunt people—he won't hurt us if we—"

"You'll hush or see us killed." Ewen shot her a deadly glare. "I don't know about your world, but we kill vermin like this in Scotland."

Lily was appalled. "You'll do no such thing!" She stepped forward, but not quickly enough. In a single fluid motion, Ewen dropped to one knee, grabbed a rock, and hit the animal just above the left eye. The creature looked at Ewen for a moment, blood trickling down its fur, then turned and ran whimpering back through the woods.

"How dare you?" Lily spun to face him. "You are such a . . . a brute. These woods belong to him, not to us. Wolves don't hurt people. In fact, there are NO documented cases of a wolf hurting a person. Maybe it was a female and she . . . she had pups or something that she was trying to protect . . . thank God you didn't kill her!" In a visible attempt to rein in her temper, Lily added quietly, "You just can't do that. You can't go around trying to kill things like that . . ."

"Och, I can't?" Ewen asked with cocked brows. "Really lass, are you quite done?" His voice was measured and seemed all the more calm in contrast to Lily's spluttering.

"Contrary to your way of thinking, these are indeed my woods. Tell my crofters that the wolf poses no threat—to their land, to their stock, or to their very lives—and you can see how they treat that wee notion."

Ewen slowly examined the blade of his dirk then slipped it back into its sheath. "The wolf can change his coat but not his character, aye? Those who live with wolves learn to howl."

"Fine." Lily promptly cut him off. "Spare me the pithy sayings. Let's just go."

Mumbling to herself, Lily added, "Some son of the hound you are. I bet you don't even like dogs."

Chapter 11

Every morning, in the moments just before she opened her eyes, Lily dreamt she would awake to find that she had somehow been magically transported back to her own time. Or, better yet, that it had all been just a dream. But she'd been at the castle for days now, and her hopes dimmed with each passing hour. She'd felt optimistic at the start—not only had she helped vanquish actual redcoats, Ewen had sent his uncle Donald out to locate the labyrinth, even though they'd searched for it after Robert's arrival and had never been able to find it. Lily was crestfallen when the gruff old man returned two nights later, still out of luck and surly from what he'd considered a fool's errand.

Stretching, she felt the now-familiar scratch of the bed linens underneath her. She inhaled, and the smells of her seventeenth-century bedchamber filled her senses—the fur thrown over the bed for warmth, the remaining embers left in her fireplace, the general mustiness of the place. No, this was definitely not her San Francisco apartment.

She opened her eyes and waited for the morning routine to begin. Every day, just after dawn, the maid would come in the room with some hot tea, porridge, and fresh peat for the fire.

That was one thing she could get used to: Kat's daily ministra-
tions. By the time Lily left her bed each morning, the room
was warm, and fresh clothes for the day had been laid out.
Worming through her clothes hamper for a not-so-dirty pair of
jeans, or using a combination of shower steam and her hair
dryer to remove some of the more obvious wrinkles from a
shirt were a couple of twenty-first-century habits she definitely didn't miss.

Lily was struggling with her shirt when the door flung
open. She was momentarily taken aback. Her instinct was to
turn her back to shield herself from the eyes of the large Scot
standing there. But surprise turned to anger as she thought that
it was her room and she refused to cower in it in front of any
man. And besides, apart from tying off the laces on the linen
blouse, she was done dressing.

The laird couldn't help but smile as he took in the sight of
Lily in a woolen arisaid in a muted blue and red plaid. While
Kat was busily stitching her new clothes with a proper fit, Lily
had to make do with the largest women's clothing that could
be found. As a result, the skirt she wore skimmed above her
ankles and her shirt strained over her ample bosom. Ewen
cocked an approving eyebrow. "I see you finally decided to
rise from that bed, lass."

Lily caught his assessing look and her cheeks blazed red.
Pulling the tartan shawl tightly around her shoulders, she said,
"And I see you have no manners here in backwoods medieval
Scotland. Have you never heard of knocking?" Her pulse
quickened as her body responded to his gaze, making Lily
even more flustered.

Ewen chuckled at her quick temper. "Aye, it's my house
and I'll do as I please. And for an educated woman, you don't
appear to know much. You're a few hundred years too late for
medieval Scotland. Though, if you wish, we can go in search
of that labyrinth of yours. I'm sure some fourteenth-century
chieftain would be well pleased to get his hands on a fresh little lass like yourself."

"I know what medieval is," Lily grumbled. "That's called
sarcasm."

"Fine lass, you can explain it to me on the way."

"On the way where?"

He flashed her an amused glance. "You're going to work."

Lily did not appreciate the devilish gleam in his eyes. In fact, she was downright afraid. She barely knew this man, and wouldn't put it past him to get the better of her by employing her as a washerwoman, or scullery maid, or some other such dreadful job.

"Work where, may I ask? Or does a powerful laird such as yourself not even need to share such information with his subjects?"

While her other comments merely amused Ewen, the last remark somehow riled him, and the blue eyes that were carefree but a moment ago became suddenly steely. "A laird does not become truly powerful without compassion and understanding for his subjects. You'll not imply I do less than that."

His chiseled jaw clenched. Lily spied a subtle change in Ewen's stance as his muscles flexed slightly. He appeared suddenly as the warrior he was, making her heart pound with fear and more than a little admiration.

"You're right, of course, Ewen." Instinctively, she reached her hand out to touch his arm. The thick bicep beneath his shirt tensed into solid muscle, and Lily's legs grew weak beneath her.

Her modern mind clung to logic—she needed to find her way home at all costs, to leave this place where a woman's life was full of hardship, where girls were passed from father to husband with no rights of their own. Yet Lily's body kept barging in on those rational thoughts, announcing loud and clear that equal rights were one thing, but a body had its own demands. A primal physical want seared through Lily, her reason unable to govern her traitorous body. She stammered, "I-I'm sorry, I really do appreciate all you've done for me."

Their eyes locked as the suddenly intimate moment seemed suspended in time.

The effect he had on her utterly dumbfounded Lily. Here she was, cooped up with some ferocious Highlander, and instead of focusing single-mindedly on getting back to her own life, she was quick to apologize and appease, like some sort of crushed-out schoolgirl. Inhaling deeply, she removed her hand and vowed to keep more control of herself.

Ewen, caught off guard by her familiar gesture, seemed to

make the same internal declaration and was the first to break the strained silence. "As for work, if it pleases you, you'll be my son's teacher. Every governess in my employ has either been a severe old carlin for John to torture, or a malleable lassie straight from home to be managed by John rather than the other way round."

"So, I am halfway between a spinster and a trembling young girl? How pleasant," Lily muttered.

"This will go much more pleasantly in general if you spare me your insolence." The twinkle in the laird's eye belied his stern words.

She couldn't help but slip into these crackling exchanges with him. Was she losing it? What was she thinking becoming so comfortable with him? She had never had such an easy familiarity with a man in her life—how was it that she was suddenly at ease with some grim seventeenth-century warrior?

Ewen continued, "I haven't told John more than he needs to know. He thinks you're a distant relation from France, and the lad's not so keen with languages, so you'll not worry yourself on that account. If your conjugations aren't pretty, the lad won't catch you in the lie."

"My conjugations are just fine, thank you." Despite her tone, Lily was distracted. Fabricating a preposterous cover story was one thing, but putting voice to the lie somehow made her situation feel real. Up until that point, she had been overwhelmed by the surreal and nightmarish quality of her situation. But this was her life, and she needed to get control of it. As he led her down the dark and twisting hallway, she made a conscious effort to keep her eyes off the sight of his powerful back, a rippling triangle of lean muscles that led down to his belted kilt. Instead, she tried to note every twist and turn of the low-ceilinged stone corridor. If the varying sizes and types of stone were any indication, several additions had been made to the original castle and the result was a confusing warren of back passages and dark corners.

Lily was engrossed, counting how many of the dimly lit wall sconces they had passed when she felt a wall of cold air hit her leg and foot as she abstractedly wondered just where the floor went.

The laird spun in time to catch her by the elbows and swing

her up against a small rough-hewn doorway. She looked down to see a cavernous stairway winding down into blackness below.

Lily gasped at his touch. As he grabbed her, his hands had managed to push her sleeves up and they felt warm and powerful on her skin, yet his grip was gentle. He gave a quick squeeze, and Lily lifted her eyes to meet his. His features burned with a dark intensity, yet a mischievous hunger played at the corners of his smiling eyes. He wore a devilish grin, like a tiger eyeing prey that he planned to toy with before devouring.

A jolt of desire shot through Lily. She tried to fight it by crossing her arms purposefully across her chest. "Wh-what do you think you're doing?"

"Easy lass. I can't let you fall down the stairwell." Ewen wrapped his arm tightly around her for emphasis.

Cocking an eyebrow, he said, "Who knows where you'd end up this time, aye?"

Their eyes locked, and Ewen encircled her more snugly in his embrace.

"I think I know how to walk down the stairs," Lily managed breathily.

"I wouldn't be so sure, Lil'." His voice was dangerously low. If she lost control for a moment, Lily thought she could be seduced by its husky timbre alone.

She realized in a panic that she'd somehow become pinned snugly against the doorjamb with one of his iron-hard thighs trapped firmly between her legs.

Ewen slowly slid his hands down her arms and gently uncrossed them. Stroking his thumbs in her palms, he clasped her wrists and raised Lily's hands over her head. Standing this close, she could see the faint stubble of his beard, dusted like charcoal along the strong line of his jaw, and she felt it as it scraped along the tender inside of her arm as he brought his face to hers.

"These stairs . . ." Ewen began. Lily felt the brief, shallow whispers of his breath on her cheek, and it was as if by not fully exhaling, Ewen could keep in check an avid lust that had overtaken him. "These stairs . . . they're particularly treacherous."

"I . . . I can see that—" Lily's words broke off with a gasp as Ewen shifted his hips, inadvertently skimming his leg along the cleft between her thighs. The rough linen of her petticoat grazed her tender skin, and Lily felt the answering flush of desire with a wet ache between her legs and the sudden exquisite chafe of fabric across her tightened breasts.

Her intellect was putting up a valiant fight but she was starting to give in to the wanting of him that pulsed deep in her. In one last effort to suppress the clamoring of her heart and body, Lily stammered, "B-but, Ewen, don't you think—"

"Och, that's precisely it, lass," Ewen growled in a voice thick with desire. He became suddenly—frighteningly—still. Inhaling sharply, he rested his forehead on the damp stone above Lily's shoulder. He turned his head slightly, just short of nuzzling her neck and, like a wild animal, breathed in her scent for what seemed to Lily like an eternity.

Gathering himself, the laird lifted his head and, dropping her wrists, abruptly pulled away. "Aye, that's it lass, it seems I'm not thinking at all at the moment." His eyes were unable to meet hers and instead focused on some vague point below. "Shall we down the stairs then?"

The passion that had roiled within her only moments before just as violently flashed into anger. She was furious. Furious at her body for having such a traitorous reaction to the man. And furious at the man himself for bringing her to the brink of surrender only to pull back at the last moment. It had happened once before at the lake after she had injured her foot, and she vowed she would not let it happen again.

Lily glared at his profile and declared in the iciest and most clipped tone she could muster, "Yes. Let's do continue."

Ewen became the stoic Highland warrior once again and, with a curt nod, led Lily through the door.

"Is this how it is with you and all the women at this damned castle?" Lily uttered under her breath.

Swinging his head about, Ewen stared fiercely, "What did you say?"

"Nothing."

Ewen began to descend the stairs, but Lily stopped again, demanding, "You said you'd help me get home. I don't understand why I'm off to work now like it's no big deal."

The laird turned slowly. "I'm doing everything in my

power to precisely those ends," he told her in an even voice. "So until which time we can divine this maze, I ask that you live as a member of this household. A tractable member, aye?"

"Tractable?" she sputtered. "How's this for tractable? You find the maze and I'll get out of your hair. I don't understand how you can't find the thing. It was huge."

"If there were a labyrinth, root it out we would—"

"Are you saying there's no maze?"

"Och, lass"—the corner of his mouth twitched up, as if amused by her outburst—"heed my words." His gaze softened. Taking a deep breath, Ewen continued gently, "I understand there's a maze. What I can't understand, and what no man can, is the fickle way of the universe. Be it stars, or magic, I've no way to know. But I continue my search, lass. Meanwhile, I've also scouts looking for the witch woman. If there's anyone able, it is Gormshuil who'll lead us to the portal that will find you home."

Ewen gave her an encouraging nod. "I gave you my word, and my word I keep." Extending his arm toward the stairs, he added, "Now please come with me, Lil'."

She paused a moment. She supposed she had no choice but to trust the man. "Okay," she grumbled.

Lily ducked through the low doorway and momentarily forgot her indignation as she looked in amazement at the staircase below. It reminded her of something out of a horror movie. As they wound around and down the stairs, she had to steady herself with one hand along the gray walls, shivering at the clammy, damp stone underneath her fingertips. The passage was shrouded in darkness but for an eerie light that danced across the aged stone, emanating from the torch that Ewen had taken from one of the hallway sconces.

"This staircase is a part of the original castle keep," Ewen explained in an uncharacteristically reserved voice. Putting aside her anger, Lily had to admit she was thankful to have the laird by her side. This place gave her the creeps.

If only the sound of his voice didn't send such a shock of heat through her center.

"When it was first built, this was the maids' stair; they used it as a way to get from the kitchens to the main bedrooms. So they'd not have to traipse through the rest of the keep carrying tea or whatnot.

"There's also a passage to a wee dock off of Loch Linnhe, but that was sealed off by my grandmother when my own father was but a lad."

They reached a small landing. "Most of it has been closed off, but for the library, and"—Ewen opened the door to a flood of sunlight—"John's rooms." Lily gasped at the stark contrast between the dark passageway and the lovely room in front of her. Unlike the original castle, this room had walls of a rich, coffee-brown wood. Above the wainscoting were small paintings, hung atop swaths of a sunny yellow fabric. The paintings were all small oils, detailing landscapes, horses, the sea, and similar idyllic subjects. Lily was transported. It was what she imagined old England to look like—small, upholstered couches, a gaming table, chessboard by the fireplace. The only thing missing, Lily mused, was a pianoforte.

Then the tranquility was shattered by an inhuman shriek.

Lily turned in time to see the blur of a boy barreling his way into Ewen's legs. The laird bent down to grab him, but the child was too quick. He disappeared out of the room before she had a chance to register what was happening.

"Johhhhn!" Ewen bellowed his name, stretching it out into two syllables.

The boy skulked back into the room with his head hung low. Despite the tousled black mop of hair and the streaks of dirt on his clothing, the child was clearly a handsome one. Lily bit her lip when she saw how much John was the image of his father. And a total hell-raiser at that, struggling through that difficult age when he was no longer a young child, yet not fully an adolescent either.

"Aye, sir?" John was clearly trying as hard as he could to sound innocent.

"You're filthy."

Seeing his chance, the boy spun to escape, mumbling, "Sorry, sir, I'll just go now and clean myself—"

"Och, I've not given you leave!" Ewen was barely masking his frustration.

"Aye, Da, may I leave?"

"No. You'll meet your new governess." Ewen gestured to

Lily, and his son's eyes lit up. Cocking an eyebrow, the child smiled a challenge to her, and suddenly his utter resemblance to Ewen annoyed her.

"Pleased, ma'am." John nodded his head, not once losing the raffish smile. Lily got a feeling of dread in the pit of her stomach. The kid looked like a starving man eyeing a plate of meat. She shuddered to think what indignities the former nannies had suffered at his hands.

Surely, she thought, controlling this handsome child couldn't be as hard as managing a team of disgruntled Silicon Valley artists. Thinking the best approach would be to take the upper hand from the start, Lily proclaimed in the most commanding voice she could muster, "Your father is right. You are filthy. Please go wash up now."

She was quite pleased, congratulating herself that no boy would ever be a match for her twenty-first-century determination.

The boy, looking unimpressed, turned to his father and announced in an exaggeratedly thick brogue, "I didn't ken her meaning, Da."

Apprehension gnawed at her, and Lily realized she would prefer disgruntled to unruly any day.

"Well . . . you're going to have to try, aye?" Ewen turned on his heel and walked briskly out of the room. "And, Lily's right, go wash yourself. You look like the stable boy."

With that, Lily was left alone with John.

❈

Ewen felt a momentary pang of guilt at the beating he was giving poor Hamish. Normally a well-suited sparring partner, the youngster was getting the workout of his life. He let his guard down for a moment to brush a sweaty lock of long brown hair out of his eyes and the laird made him pay with a particularly violent slap of his sword to the torso.

"Och, sorry lad. I'd not intended to let at you so hard."

Coughing, Hamish replied, "Nay, nay, you needn't say sorry, Lochiel sir, 'tis me who's the sorry one. It's my honor to spar with the laird. The devil take me, I don't know what's the problem with my arm."

"Your arm is sound, lad, the problem is between my ears.

Though you might want to keep that cow's lick out of your eyes. You can't hit that what you can't see. Once again then, eh?"

The laird had at Hamish once again, this time moderating his attack. The intention was to practice with the lad, not kill him. Hamish was a talented swordsman, but once Ewen set his mind to dueling, it was a rare man who could best him. There was no reason the poor boy had to suffer the full, unmitigated blows of real combat just because Ewen's own preoccupied mind kept drifting. No matter how hard he tried, though, Ewen just couldn't get his mind off of that troublesome woman.

He didn't know what he was thinking, embracing her so in the hallway. He caught Lily before she tumbled down the dark stairs and his cursed male instincts took over. Holding her so close had awakened a need, primal and urgent, that had slumbered for a long time now.

Damn her but she was different. Lily spoke to him in a way that no one else would. She seemed unimpressed with his title. While others under his care treated him with almost unthinking obedience and loyalty, Lily challenged him. She had a mind as bright as the sun, and he found himself wondering throughout his day what she would think of one thing and another. He had to earn this woman's respect as she demanded acceptable explanations and reasons for the way he did things in his household. And he had to admit, for the first time in years he was finding himself circumspect about everything from how he raised his son to whether or not Kat was happy in his employ.

He had been able to restrain himself, though. He'd pretended he hadn't noticed the enticing cut of a Scots dress on her body, that he hadn't marked the flush in her cheeks and the sparkle in those intelligent eyes.

He had even been able to pretend that he didn't respond to the smell of her. He cursed himself for being no better than a feral dog, attuned as he was to her scent, a mingling of lavender from Kat's homemade soap and her woman's musk that always flirted on the edge of his senses to drive him to distraction.

But when he caught her on the stairs, all reason finally fled. She was so soft in his arms he couldn't resist daring that desire. Seeing what it would feel like. Whether she would respond.

And respond she did. He could feel it in the loosening of her hips against his legs. In her breath, increasingly deep and slow, in counterpart to the pounding of her heart. She was so open to him and immediately responsive to his touch, their verbal sparring seemed but a shadow of how well-matched they would be physically. He brought them to the brink of temptation, and he was the one to pull them back.

He feared she hated him for it.

"Och, and I hate myself for it too, lass," Ewen grumbled to himself.

"Eh, Lochiel, what . . . was . . . that you say?" Hamish could barely grunt the words out through his panting.

"Nothing of your concern." Ewen threw his practice sword to the dirt. "We're done today, lad."

The laird turned abruptly to go. What he really needed was a dip in the freezing loch, not to kill one of his better young swordsmen.

"And go find someone to cut that bloody hair for you."

Chapter 12

The razor hovered midway down his cheek as General George Monk paused to study himself in the mirror. Such a sizeable looking glass was an almost obscene luxury in a military encampment, but he was a big believer in the tenet that distinguished men must maintain their dignity, no matter how savage their circumstances. His eyes shifted to the reflection of the rugged wilderness looming just outside his tent. Yes, the general had indeed found the need for refinements particularly essential when camping amidst the uncivilized Highland natives. Living on the rough Scottish crags and moors, moral certitude challenged by his brutishly ferocious foes—no, there was no better time than the present to have a good, clean shave.

He had enjoyed his verbal jousting with the Cameron. Ewen might be a laird, but Monk considered him no more civilized than an ancient Gael chieftain.

One of the men in his party—the laird's surly uncle, he presumed—had managed to take papers from Monk's tent. Although it was an outdated manuscript, it detailed proposed movements and tactics of the British military and it vexed the general greatly that the brutes had been able to spirit it away somehow. He made a mental note not to underestimate the

Camerons again. He would have to keep a closer eye on them when next they met—who knew what tricks beside thievery they were capable of.

The general rubbed his smooth cheek. The flesh there was as soft as it had been when he was a boy. He attributed such a supple complexion to his impeccable grooming habits, helped along by regular use of a milk and rose water concoction, the recipe for which was handed down by his great-grandmother.

He carefully rinsed his blade in a small pewter bowl then rubbed his face vigorously with a linen towel. Stimulating the circulation was key to maintaining healthful skin and keeping the humors in balance. He pouted, admiring his appearance in the glass. It was a nuisance that this Highland laird was not going to be as easily bought as some of his peers. Monk wanted nothing more than to continue his military campaign, perhaps moving farther north to see how much more of this crude and rocky land and its Highland primitives were there to be requisitioned for England. Camping for so long in the bloody mist made him peevish, not to mention the damage it did to some of his finer coats.

If the Cameron wasn't tempted by the promise of lands or money, perhaps it was time to exert a little more pressure. Make it clearer to him and his people that they were not the true owners of that savage acreage known as Lochaber. He had taken a particular fancy to Inverlochy, a lovely loch-side tract that would afford his men precious timber and fishing, not to mention critical access via Loch Linnhe.

The Cameron would rue the day he refused Monk's generous offers. His spies had recently discovered that Ewen's men spoke of the laird as the "Deliverer of the Highland Army." Of all the preposterous notions. Rather, the laird would beg for quarter when he discovered the full might of the English army. The only place Clan Cameron would be delivered was into Monk's waiting hands.

It was becoming aggravatingly clear to the general that he needed to create more permanent holdings for his troops. A much larger fort, more durable lodgings, perhaps even a prison. A massive garrison at Inverlochy would hold the country in awe of British sovereignty as demonstrated by his own visionary leadership.

General Monk admired his profile in the mirror. His gaze shifted back to the trees reflected in the looking glass.

And smiling, he decided that Cameron's Lochaber timber would be just the thing to build it.

Chapter 13

Only a month had passed since she'd begun as John's governess, and already Lily was at her wits' end. The mouse that he hid in her sheets on the first night of her new job seemed like a charmingly naughty trick compared to some of the more elaborate pranks John was beginning to mastermind. She was practically nostalgic for that frightened little gray creature that had scurried up her leg. On her last trip to his rooms, John had snuffed out the stairwell's only torch when she was but a quarter of the way down, leaving her to navigate the steep stairs in pitch darkness with only the feel of the damp stone walls to guide her way. It had taken an hour for her heart to stop pounding after that bit of mischief.

To add to the challenge, Lily found herself in the position of teaching subjects she hadn't thought of in years. She had once cursed her high school Latin teacher but now found she was thankful that cruel old Mr. Crabtree had been so mercilessly thorough. She had no idea that all of those tedious Latin declensions were still in her brain after all those years. Geography, too, was a tough one. Not only did she have to familiarize herself with what countries were where in the seventeenth-century world, Lily also had to interpret the ornate and barely legible script that detailed Ewen's various globes and tattered nautical maps.

Aside from the obvious differences she would expect, like the roles of women, class structure, and so on, Lily was startled daily at the tremendous gulf between the world she had experienced as a child and John's reality. She clung to those differences in attempts to find some modicum of sympathy for the boy. The thought that this youngster, still shy of his eleventh birthday, would likely be sent to battle in the next five years sobered Lily and renewed her lagging reserves of patience. She wanted to do right by him, and for as long as she was trapped where she was, she would put her all into his schooling. Regardless of the fact that his wicked behavior had her fantasizing about taking a good old seventeenth-century switch to his rear end.

She announced her intentions to the boy that morning over breakfast. Ewen had gone out early, so she figured that even if the laird found some complaint or other about her leaving the Cameron keep, he wouldn't have the chance to voice it.

"John?" Lily inquired in a sweet but firm tone. She started every day off anew, willing herself to an even temper.

He sat silently, wolfing down his runny eggs. She could feel her patience wearing thin already.

Kat entered the dining room with a fresh pot of tea. She looked at the two of them, sitting across from each other at the enormous black oak dining table and gave Lily a sympathetic smile.

Feeling bolstered, Lily set her shoulders and tried again. "John."

Pretending not to hear her, the boy merely continued to mop up eggs with a wilted triangle of toast.

Telling herself that being a governess was not a democracy, she announced, "We will not be having lessons today."

That got his attention. Lily continued, "Instead, you will show me village life outside this castle."

She had awoken that sunny morning thinking a change of pace would do them good. A day spent walking through the village just outside the keep, which she learned was known as Tor Castle, might be a pleasant way to make some inroads with the boy and expend a bit of his abundant youthful energy to boot. Besides, it would give her a chance to scope out the lay of the land and maybe give some clue as to the location of the labyrinth. The days were flying by, and Ewen still hadn't tracked down this Gorm-whatever-her-name-was witch whom he said could help her return to her own time. Lily thought familiarizing herself with the surrounding countryside probably wouldn't help, but it couldn't hurt either.

"My da won't like me not having lessons today." He made the announcement gravely, as if to inspire fear of the dark laird in the heart of his governess. Lily was having none of it.

The great laird Cameron could just live with it, she thought. He wasn't the one who had to deal with this monstrous boy day in and day out.

Kat diffused the situation. "Oh lad, you're just being contrarian. You'll not tell me that you don't want to get out into the fresh air for the day. Aye, and you can point out the glen's plants and animals to our Miss Lily so the day's learning isn't wasted."

It was the most Lily had ever heard come out of Kat's mouth, and she gave her an eternally grateful look. "She's right, John. Today is about learning. Just not sums and Latin. Today we will study the flora and fauna of the surrounding environment."

John looked pained.

"I'm not so sure what those are," Kat interjected, continuing to manage the tense situation, "but I do ken that Glen Albyn is the most beautiful of Lochaber glens. Aye, with lochs all around and Ben Nevis looking down on the lot of us." The maid beamed and Lily realized how lovely she must have been before the years of tending the castle became etched so deeply on her kind face.

"Aye, give me but a moment and I'll pack some food for the pair of you explorers today."

John seemed to forget his contrary mood and was suddenly energized by the prospect of spending the day roaming. Pushing his chair out from the table with a loud screech, he raced out of the room mumbling something about getting a coat.

"Thank you," Lily sighed.

"For what lass? Don't be troubled by the lad. He's the image of his da at that age. Folk say wild geese don't lay tame eggs. Hellfire, our Lochiel was as a mite. And could charm the horns off the devil to boot. But mind you, the laird is a soft one deep down, and the son is no different."

Lily couldn't imagine what the maid could be referring to. *Soft* and *Ewen* were two words that she would never think to use in the same breath.

❀

John raced ahead of her, kicking rocks, swatting tree branches, and racing to and fro on the road. Lily enjoyed the opportunity to really take in the sights around her. She had only been outside the keep once, and, as she had been frantically trying to flee in the night, she hadn't really noted much of anything about the surroundings. Now, though, she found herself utterly charmed. The village wasn't large, yet the warmth and broad smiles of the people she encountered on the road made it feel as if it was humming with life.

The air was sweet, like rich earth and heather, and the contrast between the crisp breeze on her cheeks and uncharacteristically warm sun at her back invigorated Lily.

Small cottages dotted the countryside. They looked to be no larger than one-room shelters, the gray stone of their walls barely peeking out from thickly applied mortar, cheered by squat wooden doors painted in shades of yellow, red, or green. Lazy plumes of dark peat smoke rose from the small chimneys, dissipating over the thatched roofs.

Some of the homes were nestled in their own modest valleys, with clusters of sheep and cattle grazing on small tracts of lush, green grass. Others were separated by small moors, tangles of purple and brown and red creating makeshift fences between them. White and wine-colored heather dotted the land. Lily also spotted numerous clusters of bittersweet, and its sprawling vines put her in mind of the labyrinth. She made a mental note to keep her eyes peeled for a wall of those telltale black berries like the one from the maze.

"Hello?" Out of nowhere, a woman's voice purred from behind Lily, startling her.

"Oh!" Lily yelped.

"Oh my," the woman said, placing her hand on her heart to affect dismay. "Do accept my apologies for surprising you."

Her tone of voice suggested that some sort of minor victory had been won.

Lily turned to see a young woman, lips pressed into a regal smile, with the fragile beauty of a fairy-tale princess. Two flawless and impossibly yellow ringlets framed a creamy complexion. She wore a rose-colored dress, and her corset was drawn so tightly that her petite, perfectly rounded bosom seemed as though it would burst out at any moment. Not one speck of dust clung to her rose brocade skirt or to the yellow silk slippers that just happened to match exactly the color of her hair.

Lily quickly scanned her own clothes and noted in dismay that she was already somehow covered in a thin film of soot, even though they had left the castle but an hour past.

Lily stifled a grimace and thought that this was the kind of woman who got winded after an afternoon of too much embroidery.

"Rowena!" John suddenly appeared and threw his arms around the woman's surprisingly tiny waist.

"I didn't know you were coming! Why are you here? How long are you to stay? Can we go for a picnic?" John's barrage of questions elicited a prim grin from the china doll's face.

"Oh my, did your father not tell you I was coming?" She tsked and heaved an exaggerated sigh. "He can be so forgetful sometimes!" Rowena shot a proprietary look at Lily, and, despite her better judgment, Lily felt a pang of angry jealousy prickle down her spine.

"You, my handsome laddie, will have the pleasure of my company, staying in your very own keep!" Rowena tittered at her own merriness. "Isn't it grand?

"Oh! But where are my manners? Aren't you going to introduce me to your village friend?" If Lily thought at first sight that she wasn't going to like this woman, now she knew for certain. She recognized her type in an instant. Coy was unfortunately not limited to a particular century.

"Aye, her. No, she's not from the village. My da took her in. She's my new governess."

"Oh, how very pleasant for both of you!"

Lily grimaced at her false enthusiasm—especially when she could see the bemused glint in Rowena's eye. The woman was clearly tickled by the prospect of another one of John's victims, and likely relished it all the more since the boy plainly adored her.

Rowena stood for a moment in haughty silence, then announced impatiently, "Well, I am assuming your friend has a name other than just"—she turned to Lily and, with raised eyebrows and pursed lips, chirped—"governess?"

"Yes, of course." Lily nodded slightly, as if to shake off her distraction, and attempted a smile. "My name is Lily."

"Just Lily?" Rowena asked, with a playfulness that didn't entirely mask her mockery.

"Nooo," Lily spoke as if to a misbehaving child, "it's Lily . . ." She cursed herself for stumbling, then added with bravado, "Lily Cameron."

Rowena's imperious attitude cracked for a moment, revealing something wicked roiling beneath the surface. "Cameron?"

"Yes. I'm a distant cousin from France."

"France?" Scowling, Rowena assessed Lily from head to toe then asked with thinly veiled skepticism, "Really?" A venomous smile turned the corners of her mouth. "Well then, *enchanté.*"

John had tuned in at the mention of his surname. Ewen hadn't disclosed more than the barest of details about Lily's origins, and the boy was now looking puzzled. Lily quickly replied, "Yes, quite." She was anxious to change the subject. Rowena's eyes were intense, and Lily feared whatever machinations they might be hiding. She was obviously territorial when it came to the Cameron laird's family; that Lily was traipsing on Rowena's domain was about as evident as a cloud of stink from a skunk.

"And just where in France are you from?" Rowena's tone hinted that any place other than a cow pasture would come as a surprise.

"Oh . . ." Lily's mind raced for the most believable cover story, something that wouldn't have changed too much over the years. She had only traveled through France once, and her memories were dominated by sidewalk cafes and the Eurail. "Just a small village, you probably wouldn't have heard of it."

"Try me. The French countryside is so . . . *très charmant, n'est-ce pas?*" Rowena's gaze narrowed. "What's the name of your village?"

Dread unfurled in Lily's belly. She had to choose probably the one Francophile—and a nasty one at that—in all the Highlands to test her story on.

"Oh . . ." Panicking, Lily could only recall place names from art history class. French Impressionist images of lavender water lilies and golden hay bales flickered through her mind. Not entirely sure how to pronounce Giverny, she quickly said, "Arles." Lily hoped nobody pressed her for details because all she knew of Arles came from Van Gogh paintings.

"Arles." Rowena rolled it speculatively over her tongue. Lily tried not to look visibly relieved that the woman didn't seem to recognize the name.

"Yes. Arles," Lily replied with what she hoped was a tone of finality.

"Well." Silence hung for a moment between the two women, then a fan gracefully appeared in Rowena's hand and she flicked it open with a dramatic flourish. "I don't know how you stand this heat!"

Lily quietly exhaled at the topic change. She seemed to have survived round one of Rowena's interrogation.

The woman gave a coquettish tilt to her head and began fanning at her neck and breast. "I am myself not particularly accustomed to the outdoors but"—pursing her lips into a grin, she studied Lily's face—"I can tell from the . . . healthy color in your cheeks that you often find yourself alfresco."

Lily couldn't imagine what Ewen saw in this woman. Or rather, she could guess exactly what he must see in her. Flawlessly pretty, delicate, and, if the way she doted on John was any indication, she must have been downright fawning with his father.

"Yes," Lily replied, mustering all the grace she could manage. No longer able to bear being the sole focus of Rowena's inquiry, Lily looked to John for a little relief and asked the boy amiably, "We have a good time, don't we John?"

He merely scowled and, spotting a gang of kids down the road, ran off, managing to tromp on Lily's skirt in the process.

Lily glanced back at Rowena in time to catch her hissing a

barely audible "Savage" under her breath. Then just as swiftly as the cattiness had appeared, serenity bloomed on Rowena's features, a beatific smile washing over her face like a single wave smoothing a sandy shore.

Lily shivered and made a mental note to steer clear of this particular brand of poison in a corset.

Chapter 14

"Och, lass, you're like a wet cat trapped in a sack! Now stand yourself still while . . ."

Kat cinched Lily's corset a hair tighter, and Lily could've sworn she heard a rib crack. "Oh!" Lily exclaimed, then grumbled, "I don't understand why women do this."

"Surely, lass, you've corsets in France?"

"Yes, of course we do, I just meant . . ." Lily fumbled to change the topic. She was growing too friendly with the maid and needed to remember to guard her words. "It's just, please Kat, I appreciate the effort, but any more and my breasts are going to knock against my chin."

Kat's pale, freckled features flushed red and Lily was amazed at how the maid could speak so candidly about some topics yet positively quail at others.

Over the past month, Lily had used some of her old-fashioned American boldness to chisel away at the maid's timidity, and she was quite satisfied to discover a mutual appreciation there. Kat was very aware of propriety and her place in the household, but between Lily's mysterious origins and her function as child's governess, she existed, if not in the servant's class, in a peripheral role in the household. Each was unsure how to regard the other, and as a result they discovered a kind of amicable fellowship. Besides, Lily figured she needed all the kind faces she could get.

Kat had spent the better part of the afternoon combing, curling, tucking, and tugging at Lily, humming and muttering to herself all the while. It was giving Lily entirely too much time to think. Meeting Rowena on the road the other day had unsettled her, and she was surprised that she'd had such an intense reaction. There should be no logical reason for such a visceral response to Rowena's brand of femininity and, if Lily didn't know better, she'd call it jealousy.

Rowena gave the impression of a fine porcelain doll. Lovely to look at but cold to the touch. Lily thought with a flush that Ewen needed more woman than that. He was a large and powerful man with a body sculpted by the hard life of the Highlands. He needed someone with passion and strength, not perfectly crafted pin curls.

Crimson blossomed on Lily's cheeks. What the hell was she thinking? She needed Ewen to find this elusive Gormshuil so she could find her way home. The laird evaded her questions every time she pressed him on it, merely assuring Lily that the witch would only be found when she wished it. For now she just had to hold on to hope that she'd get out of this mess. The last thing she needed was to make more of one by getting all doe-eyed about some long-dead Scottish laird.

It was no wonder that Lily would feel a physical attraction to him. The man was all ripped muscles and husky Scots brogue, worn with the self-possession of a warrior and respected clan leader. But she refused to accept that she might actually be jealous of Rowena and whatever part the woman played in Ewen's life. Lily had considered the high school homecoming queen and her varsity football boyfriend the picture of perfection, but that hadn't meant Lily had wanted to be her.

She needed to focus now on getting back to where, and when, she came from. She paused, realizing that, in that moment, she hadn't thought of her time as "home." But modern America was what she knew, and logic told her she should want to return.

No, she insisted to herself, she should care less whom

Ewen chose to socialize with. Lily felt vulnerable enough without imagining some sort of catfight over a man whose place and time she needed to escape as soon as possible.

She had to chalk her strong feelings up to envy for something that she would never have. She had never mastered the frothy feminine wiles exuded so effortlessly by types like Rowena. In Lily's modern world, it was those women who never had to diet, whose makeup was always just so, and who could walk in high heels without teetering around like a drunken gorilla.

Besides, outright jealousy would imply that she had genuine feelings for the laird and she doubted that was the case. She needed to get back to her time, to reality, as quickly as possible. She made a mental note to nag Ewen yet again about whether he'd made any progress finding this witch of his.

"Come back to me, lassie!" Kat gave Lily's cheek a good-natured pinch.

"If I didn't know better, I'd think your mind was on my laird." Then, as if considering something, Kat pinched the other cheek, and this time not gently.

"Yeouch! What are you trying to do to me today, Kat?" Lily playfully stepped back. "And I am most certainly not thinking about your laird, I was just . . ."

Lily caught a glimpse of herself in the mirror and gasped. She looked like a Celtic princess. A stunningly gorgeous Celtic princess. It wasn't as if she had never been dressed up before. She did the usual dolling up for dates or after-work cocktail parties, but this was different. It was as if she had stepped off the pages of a fairy tale. Kat had unearthed a gown that once belonged to Ewen's mother and in no time worked a number of miracles on it. Lily had been skeptical. Not only did she doubt that anyone could wear the color green with any success, she was certain that her modern-day height would likely exceed that of any seventeenth-century Scottish lady.

Although the gown was indeed on the short side, Kat turned it to her advantage by putting a white lace-trimmed dress underneath the emerald green velvet bodice. As a result, a few inches of frothy lace peeked out from under the gown to delicately skirt the floor. The neck was so open as to be almost off the shoulder. A wide white collar encircled the top of the dress, lace billowing along its edges and sweeping over the tops of Lily's arms and suggestively atop her bosom. White cuffs folded up over the three-quarter length sleeves of the gown, matching the more elaborate pattern that was tatted along the collar.

What most surprised Lily was how the deep, vibrant color flattered her complexion. She had always assumed that she couldn't wear green or yellow. Though, come to think of it, she hadn't come to that conclusion from any experience. It was one of those inane beauty tips that you accumulate as a woman—something that she read somewhere or was told by her mother or a friend, like suck in your cheeks to apply blush, brush your hair a hundred strokes every night, and only redheads can get away with green. The rich emerald shade of the velvet, though, made her skin look creamy instead of pale, and the flush that Kat had pinched onto her cheeks was a rosy glow.

Lily felt tears sting the corners of her eyes. "Thank you, Kat."

She had been nervous about facing her first formal dinner at the laird's hall, particularly if that Rowena woman was to be their guest. But she felt like this elegant gown would be her own personal armor against the most malicious woman the country could conjure.

"I don't know how you did it."

"Och, lass"—Kat surprised Lily with a quick and clumsy hug—"you're the one who did it. I just ken how to find the beauty that you so like to hide."

Both of the women were startled by a throaty sound coming from the doorway. The laird stood there staring unabashedly at Lily. "I . . ."

Lily met his gaze and felt a jolt of electricity crackle between them, leaving her with a light-headed feeling that she tried to convince herself was merely the effects of the corset.

Kat bit the corner of her mouth to suppress a smile. "Now, Lochiel, you need to knock whilst the lady is in her dressing room."

The maid's good-natured scolding brought Ewen back to his senses. "Aye, I . . . I need to ready myself for dinner. Time seems to have gotten away from me."

That many unnecessary phrases was just short of rambling by the laird's standards, and Lily was beginning to feel a bit triumphant, though she didn't want to imagine why.

"I . . . that is, Lily, I wanted to request your presence in my study before dinner. Please."

Then, just as abruptly as he entered, Ewen turned on his heel and disappeared, the door slamming behind him.

Lily and Kat turned to each other and the tension and uncertainty and fear that Lily had felt in the past days erupted in a release of full-bellied laughter. As Kat joined in, Lily thought just how thankful she was to find such an unlikely friend in this timid maid who, Lily was discovering, was not short on surprises.

❀

Lily could barely hear her own knock on the immense door. This was her first visit to the laird's private rooms and all of the confidence she had felt earlier with Kat evaporated as she stood there with her heart hammering in her chest, waiting for Ewen to open the door.

When he finally did, it was her turn to feel speechless.

Dinner with the Cameron laird was no informal occasion, and in the space of an hour Ewen had transformed himself. His hair, still damp from his bath, was pulled back into a single warrior's queue. A white silk shirt replaced his usual coarse linen one. The hound brooch was pinned at his neck, over a short spill of lace that cascaded down the front panel of his shirt and ended just short of his formal black vest and waistcoat.

Lily couldn't help herself as her eyes roamed the rest of his figure. He wore black leather shoes with laces that wound their way up his calves and strained over muscles that couldn't be concealed even by the white hose that ended at his knees. Her gaze came to rest on his fur-tasseled sporran, and she was mortified to find that she was blushing.

She looked back up at the laird and was surprised to see a smile playing at the corner of his eyes. Ewen's smiles were rare and Lily found the effect disarming.

"Come in, Lil'." He stepped aside so that she could enter. Lily faltered for a fraction of an instant. No matter how many

times she heard him say it, Ewen shortening her name to Lil'
sent butterflies straight to her stomach. He sensed her hesita-
tion and instinctively placed his hand on her shoulder to usher
her in, which didn't exactly help with the whole butterfly situation.

"I'll escort you to dinner, but first I've something for you."
His deep voice was more subdued than usual and Lily was becoming uneasy. "I ken how hard it's been for you. John can be
a rascal and I've not been the most . . . well, you've not had
the most cordial of welcomes."

Lily had to concur, though was so shocked by his admission she was struck speechless. He looked intently at her, the
crackling of the fireplace the only sound in the room.

"The truth of it is, I'm obliged for all you do for John. And,
lass, I admire the courage you've shown."

The situation suddenly felt overwhelmingly intimate.
Standing there alone with him in his study, he with something
to give her. It seemed that no matter what either of them
vowed, merely being alone together always felt like an overly
private moment.

As if he could read her mind, he paused and, rubbing his
chin mumbled, "Och, I don't know where my mind has got to.
I think it's seeing that dress again. My mother wore it but
once . . ."

His voice trailed off, and Lily felt a surge of sympathy for
the man. He lost both parents so early in his life, had such responsibilities placed on his head at too young an age. Then
lost his wife and, no matter what his relationship with her was
like, it meant that he was left alone to raise his son. Lily wondered if she hadn't misjudged the man, that perhaps his
brusque manner was merely adopted as a way to mask some
deeper pain in his life.

He placed his hands on her shoulders and turned her to
face a mirror that hung on the dark-paneled walls. Goose
bumps shivered across her skin at the gentleness of his touch.
He produced a fine gold necklace out of his sporran and
draped it on her neck.

"I saw you earlier and remembered this. My father gave it
to my mam to wear with the dress. Seems a shame to part the
two."

He looked flustered for a moment and then continued, "You need to appear as any proper Cameron lady would, aye? My mother would not mind putting it to such use for a night. No one need know the origin of the piece."

He clasped the chain, adjusted it on her neck, then stepped back. Lily saw the entire necklace for the first time and gasped. It wasn't that it was an ostentatious piece. In fact, aside from the obvious value of the emerald that was its focus, the necklace itself was simply designed. In spite of its simplicity—and perhaps because of it—it was the most beautiful thing she had ever seen. The emerald was the exact color of her velvet gown and hung from an impossibly thin yellow gold chain. Small purple amethysts and yellow opals inlaid in gold filigree wove in a spiky pattern above the stone. The effect was an artfully abstract image of a thistle, with the emerald as the heart of the flower.

Lily didn't know much about antique jewelry, but it was clear that fine craftsmanship went into the creation of the piece.

"You look exquisite, lass." Ewen's husky voice cracked uncharacteristically.

She turned to thank him and was taken aback to discover that the laird had already left the room and was waiting, with his back turned to her, in the doorway.

"Well, thank you . . . Ewen." She paused, realizing how rarely she called him by his first name. "It's truly a lovely piece and means a lot to me that—"

Ewen cut her off with a curt nod. "Come lass, or we'll be late for supper."

Lily chided herself for feeling a momentary connection to the man. Her sympathies for him—not to mention the butterflies in her stomach—were squashed as she concluded that Ewen was the ill-mannered, uncivil, boorish old Neanderthal that she had first suspected.

She stormed behind him to the dining room, resolving to not be fooled again by the man.

❦

He hadn't intended for that meeting to go as it did. Though he did feel indebted to Lily for her efforts with his son and that lending her the necklace was an appropriate gesture, Ewen's intentions were also practical. He wished that any guest at his household be properly attired for formal dinners—particularly when outsiders were to be in attendance. He wanted Lily to blend in as any other woman of her station would.

But that had all changed when he saw her in Mam's gown. The green velvet was enough to recollect his mother's memory, yet the cut of the dress was so altered that it did not resemble his mother in the slightest. His mother had been no less regal for her smaller size. Hers was a commanding presence, with a quiet sinewy strength that'd been perfect for a laird's wife.

Lily, however, was an entirely different matter. Although no less commanding, her figure evoked a more passionate temperament with that rosy flush to her cheeks and a body that was all long lines and deep curves. Ewen was shocked to discover his heart in his throat upon seeing her so attired. Kat had clearly made some alterations, and though the result was not scandalous by any means, the strategically placed bits of lace did much to suggest what lay beneath.

He had immediately thought of the thistle necklace. His mother had worn it with that very gown. He only wanted to lend it to her for the evening so she would be no more nor less adorned than any of the other Highland ladies. His critical error was placing it on her neck himself. When his fingers brushed the creamy expanse of her throat, he longed to take her shoulders firmly in his hands and thought what it would be like to turn her toward him and take her mouth with his. It had been so long since Ewen had entertained any such thoughts, yet now desire clutched at his throat like the thirst of a dying man and refused to let loose.

He at times admired the cut of a woman's figure, or the sparkle of an eye, or the gleam of one's hair, but he was not tempted to do more than look since Mairi passed. She had taught him that lasses were more trouble than they were worth. And then some, in her case.

This one, though, was different. She was outspoken, yet not in the shrewish way that Mairi had been. Lily's temperament seemed to emanate from an inner strength and self-knowing rather than the immature and feline rebellion that was Mairi's way.

He hadn't intended the moment to feel so intimate. Clearly there was a deeper connection to the woman that allowed them to slip into such easy familiarity.

He would not allow it to happen again.

Chapter 15

Rowena caught a glimpse of Lily from the corner of her eye and moved closer to Ewen on the divan. She had requested an audience with the laird on the pretext that she hadn't known that he'd been in search of a governess for John. That he received her in a private sitting room had been an added and unexpected bonus.

She was determined to arrange a betrothal with Ewen by summer. If her cowardly father was unable to make it happen, then she would just take matters into her own hands. She would be the next lady of Clan Cameron and she hoped Ewen's blind bullheadedness didn't stand in the way of coming to an arrangement in the usual course. He was shockingly reserved, though, in his reactions to her feminine attractions, and she was not used to being so disregarded. Rowena had always been able to use her looks and her wiles to control the men around her. After all, she had spent her girlhood honing the arts of manipulation on her father.

If she couldn't win him over in the traditional way, she vowed to use other means. She had already made inroads with his monstrous child and had a few other designs at work. In the meantime, Rowena would fabricate as many pretenses as necessary to have private discussions with him.

She announced to Ewen that she would be able to do him the favor of offering her own governess services to his son, stating that she was, after all, at least as well-versed in the more sophisticated aspects of court culture than this woman from the French countryside. She had been surprised when the laird only glowered at her proposal, forcing Rowena to change strategy midway through the audience. No matter. Men, she found, were dumb sops manipulated easily enough with but a well-placed sigh, or "accidental" brush of the hand or knee.

She didn't like this newcomer Lily or what it implied for her plans that, up until this point, had been going so smoothly. John adored her. She commanded respect from the servants, and neither solicited nor required their admiration. All that was left was to secure once and for all the affections of the laird, which she supposed would be achieved easily enough. Talk about the keep was that he paid more attention to leading the clan than to dallying with women, but Rowena knew there was not a man in Scotland who wouldn't welcome a woman like herself to warm his bed.

And if the usual wiles did not prove sufficient, well, she could remedy that easily enough with a well-placed bit of hearsay. The impression of a dalliance would be just as acceptable to her plans as the dalliance itself, though she found she did honestly crave the latter. Ewen may have been coarser than the courtiers she was used to, but Rowena imagined that those rough, untamed ways of his would serve her purposes quite satisfactorily in the bedroom.

The lass who called herself Lily peeked through the door again, and Rowena was not about to let her meeting with the laird get cut short. She edged even closer to Ewen, trilling out a delighted laugh as she did so. The laird merely scowled in disgust, but that was no matter to Rowena. His back was to Lily; the wench couldn't read his face and would surmise that she was interrupting an intimate rendezvous.

Ewen stood abruptly, but by that time Lily had edged back out of the room, afraid to interrupt. That lass was proving to be a meek one and would be no match for her. Rowena smiled, undeterred by Ewen's sudden close to their discussion.

She relished the thought of besting this Lily almost as much as she anticipated bedding and wedding the laird.

Chapter 16

"Och, lass, did you think me that much a savage?" Ewen pitched his voice for Lily's ears alone as he topped off her glass of Bordeaux. She flushed crimson, as much from the husky intimacy of his whisper as from his words. He was right. She hadn't been expecting such a formal dinner and was thoroughly—and quite pleasantly—surprised. Had her skepticism been written so clearly on her face for all to see, or was he just that attuned to her? Looking at the others seated around the enormous dining table engrossed in their own conversations, she half hoped it might be the latter.

Lily had been afraid she would have to wrestle with haggis or blood pudding or some other food involving the entrails of some unlucky creature. Instead she was presented with crystal goblets of the finest wine, roast goose with mashed potatoes and turnips, and buttered bread still hot from the oven.

Dinner had been a painless enough affair. Although Lily had at first dreaded seeing Rowena, she grew to be almost thankful for her presence. The girl's endless prattling about this bit of gossip and that Edinburgh fashion meant that all Lily had to do was sit, nod politely, and dispatch as neatly as possible a meal that was surprisingly delicious.

The dining room was a cavernous one and part of one of the original wings of Tor Castle. Although impenetrable black shadows lurked in the corners, dozens of wall sconces and candelabras made the table dance with a warm yellow light. It put Lily in mind of the thrill she would feel as a child when the power went out and everyone gathered into a single room, safe and cozy amidst the eerily cast shadows.

Lily had been troubled to discover that she would be seated at the laird's right hand. She wasn't sure if she felt relief or disappointment to discover that the seating arrangements didn't indicate any sort of preference on Ewen's part. Rather, they enabled him to keep control over Lily's story and guide the conversation away from sensitive areas when necessary.

Lily did find some comfort being seated across from Robert, possibly the only person as out of place in this social situation as she was. His earnest attempts at conversation warmed her, though she did begin to tire of his endless Latin quotations. She had made the mistake of asking him about a particular declension that John was working on, and he'd been exclaiming pithy Latinate observations ever since. It took her halfway through the second course before she figured out that *bonum vinum laetificat cor hominis* was that good wine gladdens, not fertilizes, a person's heart.

She was also thankful that Rowena was seated toward the other end of the table holding court with her sister Tessa—a flighty creature with ash-brown ringlets and a brash, tittering laugh—and Tessa's beleaguered husband Archie. Lily's two-second appraisal of that relationship was that Tessa had been the young, comely bride to Archie's older and, Lily assumed, richer groom. Now the poor sop just sat there nursing his third glass of port, adjusting and readjusting a too-tight waistband, and trying his best to surreptitiously dab the sweat from his brow.

Ewen's Uncle Donald sat at the opposite head of the table, wearing a frank scowl on his face. Lily had to keep stifling the grin that threatened to spread across her face every time she spied the surly old warrior sitting trapped between Rowena and Tessa.

There was one young man in attendance whom Lily had never seen before, and she liked him immediately. Young Hamish had arrived conspicuously early, and Lily still had to gnaw the inside of her cheek every time she looked at him to keep from giggling at his raggedly short-cropped brown hair. Ewen caught her eyeing the poor boy, and winking at her asked, "Hamish lad, what damage have you wrought upon your poor head?"

Hamish's cheeks turned as crimson as the glass of wine in front of him. "You . . . I mean, sir, you instructed me to cut it."

"Och," Donald grumbled, "was it a plough you used for the cutting?"

The table fell silent as all eyes turned to Hamish, who was blushing more furiously by the minute. Despite Ewen's mild aggravation with the boy, Lily got the impression that young Hamish was a grudging favorite of the laird's. "Well, lad, so I did, so I did," Ewen said, coming to his rescue. "Though, next time, you're welcome to ask our Kat to cut your hair for you."

Hamish exclaimed, "Thank you, sir!" as if Ewen had just promised him a lairdship, rather than a simple haircut.

Anxious to change the subject for the awkward young man, Lily asked, "So, Hamish, do tell me about yourself."

"Myself? I, uh . . ."

Lily cursed herself. She thought she had lobbed him an easy opening, but he was clearly shy beyond measure. This time it was Donald who came to his aid. "Lad, tell them of General Middleton."

Hamish lit up. "Aye, I'm off to join General Middleton. He's our own Highland general. Lochiel says I'm ready to join the other men. Under the general, aye? I was having to help my da with the lands, but I'm to be married come Yule. Married to Bess, bonny Bess"—he paused, a near beatific smile spreading across his face—"her father finally gave us his blessing. And my own da says if I'm to be a man, really be a man true, 'tis time for me to find my own way of it and I've a way with the sword, so Lochiel tells me. We spar together, aye? Lochiel and me, and Lochiel says I've a way with the sword. And so I'm off. To join the General Middleton."

The news piqued Archie's interest. "General Middleton? Has he replaced Glencairn then as leader of our Highland armies?"

"Aye," Ewen said. "We've been to see General Monk and the British camp. Monk is getting reinforcements from

Cromwell by the score, and General Middleton has asked for able-bodied clansmen to join in the fight."

"There will be a fight?" Tessa nearly shrieked.

"Calm yourself, lass," Donald snapped. "We don't know what's to come, but Monk tried to bribe the laird and Lochiel had none of it. Of course, this nettled the greasy Monk to no end."

"And now I fear he's got Lochaber in his sights," Ewen added.

Archie exclaimed, "Why the blackguard is bringing his lobster-backed whoresons into the very bosom of our Highlands! I too will join the fight, yes sirrah, I will!"

"I thank you, Archie," Ewen hedged, "and will let you know when you're needed. For now, though, I'm sending just a score of eager lads like young Hamish here to help General Middleton keep an eye on Monk and his troops, until we ken what's what."

This silenced the table, and Lily looked around nervously. So far, the evening had gone off without a hitch and she didn't want that to change now. She mused that, at the moment, such lulls in conversation probably unnerved her as much as poor Hamish. A handful of the laird's tenants were also at dinner, and although they seemed friendly enough, Lily had studiously avoided conversation with them. She hated to appear rude, but not only could she barely make out their thick accents, she was terrified that she might say something to reveal she wasn't who she claimed to be. A visiting French relative was an exotic thing indeed and Lily wanted to avoid the questions that she would certainly be barraged with if given the chance. She had studied European history like any other high schooler, but the only knowledge of seventeenth-century France that she retained stopped at Louis XIV, Versailles, and Molière. And even then, she was very uncertain of exact dates. She didn't want to have to elaborate, especially considering the Bordeaux's pleasant warmth that was beginning to buzz through her body. Lily silently cursed Ewen for not preparing her more thoroughly. Beautiful clothing was all well and good, but what really mattered was knowing whether or not the Louvre had been built yet.

Rowena clinked the side of her wineglass with a spoon to

get the table's attention, and Lily quickly fantasized that getting cornered into a conversation about French politics would surely beat whatever was about to happen.

"If I may, my laird . . ." Rowena tilted her chin down and mustered her most dazzlingly coy smile. Lily could see from the dark look that flashed across his face that Ewen was less than pleased. Settling into her seat, Lily took a gulp of wine and thought this might prove amusing after all.

"As you all are surely aware, I have just returned from some time spent in Edinburgh where I stayed, of course, in Moray House itself . . ."

Rowena paused dramatically and expectantly, awaiting an awestruck response that the table did not provide, except for Tessa, who nodded and smiled so frantically that her ringlets were sent bobbing. The plain and faithful sister reminded Lily of a cocker spaniel, and she was so tickled by her own tipsy observations that she had to quickly turn an inadvertent laugh into a cough.

"Lily, you can go first."

Lily gathered herself after what turned into a real coughing fit only to find that all eyes were upon her.

"Um, I beg your pardon?"

"The game, silly." Rowena looked around the table as if seeking sympathy for having to deal with such a dimwit.

"As I was saying, everyone in court is mad about Forfeits. You do know the game?" Rowena was incredulous. She pressed, "Surely you have heard of it. I'm certain they must be mad for it in Paris. Though if it hasn't made it into the French countryside . . ."

Uncle Donald came to Lily's rescue and she could have kissed him for it. "Refresh an old man's memory, will you, lass? I don't spend myself on the fool pastimes of Lowland lassies and their dandies."

"Well." Rowena cleared her throat and made the word sound like a reproach. "To put it as simply as possible"—she gave a saucy nod directly to Donald, which seemed to anger Ewen yet merely amuse the older man—"one person leaves the room. Everyone places a personal token on the table. The person comes back in the room, selects something from the pile, and instructs the owner to do something."

"How do you know who the owner is?"

Rowena looked at Lily as if she were simpleminded. "That is the point. You do not know who the owner is." Rowena's disdain was obvious. "You've truly never played this game?"

"Oh, Miss Rowena." Robert took control of the situation, and Lily had to admire his courage. For him to face down Rowena was not unlike the mouse taking on the cat. "Not everyone has the luxury to spend their days enjoying such frivolity."

He matter-of-factly elaborated on the game as if making scientific observations about another culture. "The primary player returns to the room and selects an item. Then he announces something the owner of that item must do. If the item's owner does not perform said act, that person will lose the object they had placed in the pile."

Tessa exclaimed as if she had just realized something for the first time. "Forfeits! That is why it is called Forfeits!"

Donald muttered from underneath his linen napkin, "The lass is daft as a yett on a windy day."

Lily had to take a big gulp of wine in an effort to avoid laughing. She had no idea what a yett was but was thrilled that she wasn't the only one at the table mystified by Tessa's stupidity.

"The second player must do the first player's bidding or they forfeit their possession. If they refuse, the first player gets to keep it!" Tessa looked quite pleased with herself and Lily marveled at the fine line between endearingly flighty and just plain dim.

Rowena wrested the table's attention back to herself.

"As I said, Lily, you shall leave the room first." Rowena flashed her teeth in what was supposed to be a curt smile, and Lily's stomach turned with the suspicion that Rowena was only beginning to avenge that evening's seating arrangements.

Chapter 17

"Come, Lochiel, it's your turn, you must place something on the table!"

Ewen could only glare at Tessa in response. He had intended the evening to be no more than a simple meal. He would introduce Lily to a select number of his tenants and had assembled a benign selection of loyal clansmen who cared naught for any place outside the Highlands, much less France, and whom he knew would not ask too many questions. Then tomorrow's gossip would dispatch any lingering village speculation as to who Lily was or where she came from.

Ever since she returned from court, Rowena had been like a blasted midge buzzing for his attention. He had hoped that hosting her, the absurd creature she called a sister, and that poor simp Archie for a meal would put off her unwanted attentions for a while. He couldn't bear her company and didn't understand why she persisted with her flirtations. Ewen supposed she was the type of woman who would be incredulous to discover that there was actually a man in the world who found her wanting.

"Nephew," Donald growled, "as much as I'm enjoying this torture, if you don't put something on the table, I'll cross it and put something for you."

Robert raised his eyebrows encouragingly. "Yes, it would be pleasant to retire soon for the night."

Rowena was immune to the criticism and merely sat beaming as if everyone were clearly having the time of their life.

Sighing, the laird rifled through his sporran. He pulled out a small brown tooth and tossed it on the table. A curious look passed between Ewen and his uncle.

"Well, doesn't that look delightful?" Rowena's cheery exterior threatened to crack.

Robert peered down at the laird's offering. "Remains of some sort. An interesting choice."

"Interesting indeed." Rowena oozed sarcasm through her pinched smile. "You are full of surprises, Lochiel."

Heedless of Rowena's derision, Robert continued, "This is an odd specimen. Tiny. Possibly order Rodentia? Is it bone? Nay, I see it now. *Dentalis!* Yes, it looks to be some creature's old rotted tooth."

Undaunted, Rowena purred, "But Lochiel, what if you were to lose such a . . . treasure? Or is there nothing you wouldn't do?"

Donald pushed his chair out and stood. "Och, let's just get this fool game underway, aye?" He drove his dirk into the table with a suddenness that silenced even the girls' giggling.

Oddly, it was Archie who broke the momentary silence. "I suppose I can take a chance and place this in the pile." He unpinned a brooch from his cravat and placed it on the table with an exaggerated care that the slightly tarnished piece didn't at first seem to merit.

"You see it is a fine old piece of Celtic craftsmanship that has been in the MacLean family for generations. These fish indicate the bounty of Loch Linnhe that the clan has relied upon for centuries."

The pin was indeed a handsome little piece with stylized Celtic creatures intertwined with fish crafted in silver. Archie noted young Hamish looking closely at the piece and continued with an enthusiasm that was endearing, if not slightly pathetic. "You see, my family's holding is just on the other side of the loch. This is quite a dear brooch to me, so I guess you could say that there is nothing I would not do either!"

Archie guffawed at his own jest and, in answer to the

table's silence, felt compelled to qualify, "That is, just like our Master Ewen here! Nothing I would not do, no sirrah! I will not be forced to forfeit!"

Tessa appeared suddenly flustered. Turning her back on her husband, she fretted to Rowena, "I just do not know what I shall place on the table. I have a lovely embroidered handkerchief, but it was Mama's and I would be positively lost without it. I suppose I have these earrings, but I've always thought the blue stones do so much to pick up the color of my eyes."

She mistook the table's silence for rapt attention and continued, "I've got it! My comb! It's only ivory so I wouldn't be too sad to miss it, although Papa did bring it back for me from one of his travels. But, no, I won't have to miss it. I shall just have to persevere if forced to do something I do not want to do. But nobody here will make me do something I don't wish to, isn't that right, Lochiel?"

There was a protracted silence while Tessa awaited some sort of response.

"Och, lass, you could talk the hind legs off a donkey."

"Aye, empty barrels make the most noise, Lochiel."

"Lochiel! Donald! Don't be rude!" Rowena tried to playfully defuse their comments. Tessa tittered nervously and merely looked confused by the men's notice of her.

"I think your hair comb is a lovely idea, Tessie." A rebuke for Ewen was in Rowena's glance, but the laird was too busy refilling his wineglass to care.

"I know what I shall put on the table," Rowena continued. She shot Ewen a challenging look. "Though I wonder if your lady friend would even be interested in such a thing, since it is so uniquely Scottish. She doesn't seem to have much of the Highland blood in her, does she, our new friend Lily?"

Although Rowena hoped that would be an insult Ewen would understand, the laird merely scowled at her feline hostilities.

"Enough, lass," Ewen grumbled. "Put what it is you will onto the pile so we can call 'our' Lily back in."

"Well, Ewen, that's just it. I need some assistance, so if you would be so kind as to help a lady . . ." Rowena rose from her seat and sauntered down to Ewen's end of the table. She slowly lifted her skirts to reveal the handle of a small dagger tucked into her stocking just below the knee.

A serving woman who had been standing by the door gasped audibly. Ewen shot her a murderous glance and she scurried out of the room, cheeks aflame.

Donald nearly choked on his wine then finally manage to sputter, "What are you thinking, lass, carrying a *sgian dubh* in your hose like a lad?"

"Oh, Miss Rowena! Please have a care!" Hamish seemed genuinely alarmed. "You could harm yourself!"

"Nonsense! A woman does need to protect herself, does she not, Lochiel? I am a good Highland lass, why should I not have a *sgian dubh*? Now, would you please be so kind as to assist . . ." She wagged her calf in his general direction.

"How dare you behave so at my table, Rowena," Ewen spat. "If you can carry the blade, you can unsheathe it yourself. Now somebody please call Lily back so we can have this over with."

As Ewen turned his back on Rowena, Robert was the only one to notice the spark of anger that flashed through a crack in her otherwise meticulously cultivated visage.

❁

Rather than enjoying the moment's rare solitude, Lily spent her time in the hallway fretting over what she'd request as her part in the game. She had never been good at Truth or Dare either. The other kids always came up with provocative questions to ask or clever pranks to dare, but she always found that she just ended up dreading her turn. When Donald called her back into the room, she resolved to pick the smallest thing off the table and request a simple song from the owner. That seemed easy enough.

The items in the pile presented a stunning array of what would have been priceless antiques in her time. Lily mused for a moment that if she could bring any one of those things back with her through the labyrinth and sell it, she wouldn't have to work for a year. At this thought, a vague sense of anxiety washed over her.

Lily didn't understand why the thought of leaving the Camerons would make her stomach clench so—she was desperate to get back to her own life, wasn't she? Granted, she clearly felt a connection with the laird. How could any red-blooded woman not? With his gravelly voice and intense dark blue eyes, the man was sex personified. And then there was the loving appreciation that she'd seen flicker in his eyes, at the sight of his son, or even of Kat, or that monstrous horse of his.

Lily smiled, and recalled the way he carried himself through the halls of Tor Castle, with a purposeful stride that implied the future welfare of the Highlands rested on his shoulders alone. An image of him flashed in her mind, Ewen walking toward her earlier, his formal white shirt setting off the utter blackness of his hair, and his handsome waistcoat as it strained over the muscles in his arms and back. His eyes and mouth had been set in a determined line, even as he reached tenderly out for her, tracing the line of her neck with hands that, though strong and scarred, were capable of such gentleness.

Just the memory of that touch sent a rush of warmth through her belly, contracting the muscles at her very core.

She dared not confuse desire with true intimacy. Just because her body responded to him, to his touch, his voice, did not mean that there was any real connection there. Didn't he pull away every time there was even a suggestion of emotional intimacy? She felt a rush of dread, and wondered that maybe he even considered her coy, or a flirt. Lily quickly replayed their exchanges in her mind. No, she had seen the sexy sparkle in his eyes during some of their more playful banter. Yet he always pulled back. Clearly he knew what he wanted, and it wasn't some twenty-first-century woman with improper notions of femininity and equality.

She could only attribute the confusing sensation to too much wine and her nerves at having to participate in this preposterous game. Rolling her shoulders, Lily took a deep breath. She needed to get this evening on and over with. Mindful of her plan, she studied the table and was thankful that there was a small, seemingly worthless item for her to select.

"I choose this." She gingerly picked up the tiny brown tooth and studied it in her palm. A number of silent looks passed across the table, and Lily began to feel embarrassed, though she had no idea why.

"And I would like the owner to sing us a song."

There. She did it. Her turn was done, and if the owner didn't want to sing a song, then, all they would be out was a gross old tooth.

"Och, lad, did you really think to forfeit your badger tooth?"

"Uncle, I've not lost it yet."

Donald, looking positively grieved, was not satisfied with this answer so Ewen continued, " 'Twas the simplest thing I could think of."

"I . . . I'm sorry, did I pick the wrong thing? I'm happy to pick something else. Actually, please let me pick something else." Lily was growing annoyed that her simple strategy was backfiring and the one thing without value on the table ended up being of some sort of priceless emotional value to the Cameron clan.

Lily was touched to glimpse a moment's insecurity in Ewen and could suddenly and vividly imagine the boy he had been as he mumbled, "I thought nobody would want it, aye?"

"You see, Lily," Robert took it upon himself to let her in on the secret, "this item originally hails from a badger, and badgers are not without significance to the clan. Badgers are quick and clever fellows."

"Aye, and braw too."

"Thank you, Hamish, yes. And they are brave creatures too. They don't give up a fight easily, just like we Highlanders. Many men carry a badger tooth on their person to represent their own strength and endurance."

"My sporran has a badger's head on it, see?" One of Ewen's tenants thrust his soiled sporran toward Lily and flashed her an enthusiastic gap-toothed smile. "It's most common."

Ewen cut their exchange short. "It was a gift from my grandfather not so long before he died. He'd killed a badger with his own hands when he was just a mite and kept this with him all his life. It was a sort of luck charm for him. I carry it now."

"And may you live as long as he," Archie announced, "and

be as stout-hearted and fair a laird!" This led to a number of toasts and *slàinte* after *slàinte* wishing both past and future Camerons well.

It was beginning to look like the increasingly drunken table had forgotten about the game until Rowena chided, "And the song, Lochiel?"

"Och, a song?" Ewen was not immune to the effects of the wine and he was as expansive as she had ever seen him. "Lil', can you not have something simpler?"

"Would you have the lass ask for a swordfight?" Donald seemed to be enjoying his nephew's discomfort. "Now Ewen, let us hear your honeyed voice."

Ewen rose, scowling. "I've not sung in years . . . I'll . . ." He downed the contents of his glass in one gulp and grumbled, "I'll sing 'The Dowie Dens of Yarrow.' "

Lily expected some sort of rousing battle chant from the laird and was surprised when he began to sing a ballad. She had difficulty making out some of the language at first, but her ear became accustomed to the slow cadence. Like all good ballads it was a mournful tune of love and loss, but Ewen's rich, smoky voice invested it with a significance not imparted by the words alone. She was astonished at the quality of his voice. His deep vibrato echoed with a sorrow that Ewen himself seemed to feel as he sang of a woman who loved and lost a man, simple and good, who died defending their love.

Ewen shut his eyes, emotion threatening to overwhelm his voice, and sang in a near whisper,

> *"As she walked up yon high, high hill,*
> *And down the glen so narrow,*
> *'Twas there she found her true love John,*
> *Lying cold and dead on Yarrow."*

Ewen opened his eyes and looked at Lily with a directness and intensity that overpowered her. She had been transported by his husky voice and the way a sad song can be particularly disarming when sung by an otherwise unyielding man. It was the laird's rapt gaze, though, that made her feel as though she were frozen in her seat. She wanted desperately to look away, but couldn't take her eyes off him.

Lily became acutely aware of the rise and fall of his chest, the slight tilt of his chin as he sang, the single strand of hair that had unloosed from his queue. She began to tremble slightly as he sang the next verse.

> "She washed his face, she combed his hair,
> As she had done before o,
> And she kissed the blood from off his wounds,
> On the dowie dens of Yarrow.

> "O daughter dear, dry up your tears,
> And weep no more for sorrow.
> I'll wed you to a better man
> Than the ploughboy lad of Yarrow."

Ewen seemed to come back to himself and his voice returned to its normal pitch for the final verse.

> "O father dear, you've seven sons,
> You may wed them all tomorrow,
> But the fairest flower among them all,
> Was the lad I wooed on Yarrow."

Lily had been so entranced by the song, she was startled by the abrupt burst of applause from the table. Taking a deep breath, she discreetly dabbed the corner of her eye, making as if she had an itch rather than a tear there. Robert flashed her a proud grin, and, flustered, she looked down and busied herself with a bit of lace at her sleeve.

"My dear brother! You have truly shown us, *vinum et musica laetificant cor!*"

Lily had never seen the otherwise bookish Robert so effusive. She thought that, if wine and music did indeed gladden the heart, then any more of either and dear Robert would be under the table from his gladness.

"Might I have a turn to leave the room?" Robert turned to Rowena for her nod of approval.

Everyone had placed their trinkets on the table, and Lily was still wondering what she could offer. Everything she wore belonged to Ewen. She couldn't very well forfeit something that wasn't hers, nor was she entirely sure that she would be up for doing whatever it took to keep from surrendering her chosen item. Rowena had been eyeing Lily all evening, surely trying to devise the cruelest way to make her supposed rival squirm with embarrassment.

"Oh, please do hurry, Lily," Rowena snapped. "If you can't decide what to put on the table, why don't you offer up that darling . . . thing . . . you've got round your neck?"

Lily fingered the emerald necklace that Ewen had loaned her.

"What is that supposed to be, thistle? What a charming little trifle. My young niece has something similar. It's favored by young girls, is it not, Tessie?"

"Oh, I could never . . ." Lily stammered. Rowena could think what she liked, but Lily treasured the piece already. It was clearly no ordinary bauble.

"Aye, it's thistle." Ewen gave Rowena a dark look that made it clear to everyone at the table that she had gone too far this time. "It was a gift from my father to my mother and now 'tis a gift from me to Lily."

The admission silenced everyone at the table but for Rowena, whose audible breathing attested to her efforts at maintaining control at the laird's affront. By the scowl on Rowena's face, it was clear that she perceived this as an insult. And Lily knew then and there that she would be the one who would suffer for it.

Ewen rose from his chair and stood behind Lily to unclasp the necklace. The touch of his hands on her neck in such an intimate gesture made Lily light-headed. She was thankful that Ewen placed the thistle on the table for her, as she was certain she would be unable to stand on her own. Lily knew the gift was made in haste, and in anger. She didn't know what Ewen's relationship with his parents had been, but it was clear that Rowena had crossed a line to make him invoke their memory.

Or perhaps he meant to make Rowena jealous. Lily was unclear what the woman's involvement with the laird was, though if Rowena's relationship with John was any indication, perhaps Ewen was grooming her to become a part of the Cameron clan. Even though the laird had pronounced he'd never marry again, Rowena was a beautiful young thing, her nasty temperament aside. She'd make a lovely bride.

Regardless, she did not want to dwell on the fact that Ewen had staked the necklace and Lily would be forced to do whatever it took not to lose it.

"*O di immortals!* Why such melancholia? Dispatch your gloom that we might continue this delightful *divertissement!*" Lily hadn't noticed Robert's return. "Archie my man, please retrieve another bottle of the laird's splendid Bordeaux whilst I peruse these fine items."

Robert rifled through the pile. Lily breathed a sigh of relief as he passed over the necklace. He paused for a moment then, with a twinkle in his eye, swept his hand back and snatched the thistle up from the table.

"Nostalgia has seized me. I must claim this as the next stake in the game."

Ewen shot him a threatening look that only seemed to give Robert fresh resolve.

"And I dare say I know the porcelain neck upon which glittered this fine treasure." Robert turned to face Lily. "We have in our midst an unsung *artiste*. As Virgil instructed in his *Aeneid*, 'Inventas vitam iuvat excoluisse per artes.' Let us improve life through science and art! Lily, would you please ennoble our mortal coil through your pictorial arts and bless us with . . . with a sketch of our very own laird!"

Lily could have died on the spot. Ewen didn't seem any more pleased with the situation than she did. The rest of the table, though, erupted into pleased exclamations of how lucky they were to be in the company of an artist, and how stylish it was these days for women to sketch and paint, and wherever did she learn such a craft.

"I've already taken the liberty of having Kat fetch your pencils and paper from John's rooms." Robert promptly presented her with her supplies.

Lily sat frozen, feeling mortified at the prospect of such a public test of her skills.

Ewen sensed her dismay and, pouring her a fresh glass of wine, muttered under his breath, "You'll do fine, lass, a swig of this will help."

His sensitivity only made her feel all the more uncomfortable. She was uncertain, which made her more anxious, being forced to sketch—tipsy no less—in front of a group of strangers, or having to stare unabashedly at Ewen for as long as it would take her to study and record his features on paper.

"Just do as good as you can, Lil'," Ewen whispered in his maddeningly husky voice. "I'm sure you can make a right bonny little picture."

Lily's anxiety turned to anger at his last statement. How dare he patronize her? She was a talented artist, not some simpering female who dabbled in pretty pictures of flowers and horses. She suddenly felt she was up for the challenge.

Taking a sip of her wine, she looked Ewen directly in the eyes. "Sit still, Ewen." The use of his name in such a familiar way gave Lily a burst of confidence. She would show him.

"Ah!" Archie declared. "You two are like lightning to a tree!"

"Or the frost on Ben Nevis." Rowena hissed under her breath. Her comment was for Tessa's ears only, though Lily caught it.

"Ah, but who is the lightning and who the tree?" Robert speculated.

Ewen bristled, and Lily imagined that his foster brother would be in for some talking to after the guests departed. The laird's public gift to Lily, though, gave the table free rein to discuss the two of them as if some sort of relationship existed.

This time it was Lily who cut the charade short. "Please. I need silence to work."

The unfortunate result was that all eyes rested on her expectantly. All she could do was pour herself into her sketch.

She glanced at Ewen and quickly turned her eyes back to the paper in front of her. Overwhelmed by the man seated in front of her, Lily thought the best and only way to begin would be to do a rough outline of his figure. Capturing the essence of his face would be a difficult task; the set of his jaw, his unwavering gaze, and the innate power that Ewen exuded all seemed too much to reproduce with mere light and shadow.

So she set to work on the outline of his body. Lily had noticed how imposing a figure he cut, but it was only now, able to stare at Ewen so openly, that she saw just how broad his shoulders were. How the fine material of his waistcoat strained from the muscles of his arms and chest beneath. Lily the artist tried to visualize those arms and that chest so she could best represent them, but the woman in her shivered at the thought of what that body was capable of. Suppressing her body's response, she mindlessly began to scribble a few lines on her paper to bring herself back into the moment and try to get a little control over her wayward imagination.

She worked in silence for some time. At first, she had just wanted to prove her artistic talents to the skeptics at the table. Once into the sketch, though, she became obsessed that the end result be more than a mere lifelike rendering of his figure. She wanted to express Ewen's essential nature, what it was about him that at one glance conveyed his power, character, and spirit.

The drawing became a way for her to get to know Ewen. And the more she studied the subtle shifts of expression, his every line and crease, the more intrigued she grew with who she saw.

The materials at hand were beginning to frustrate Lily. She needed charcoals for this, not graphite. Charcoals to capture the deep black sheen of his hair, the shadows cast by his strong angular features, and the faint cast of whiskers that had already appeared even though he'd shaved that morning.

She caught herself staring into his eyes, marveling that she hadn't realized just how dark a blue they were, wondering how she would ever capture their intensity.

"Lil', the sketch?" His knowing smile was enough to tell her that he knew which direction her thoughts had been going.

She gave a small start. "Yes, it's just about finished." Lily used the edge of the blunted pencil to loosely dash off some background shadow, more as an excuse to collect herself than because the picture required it.

Any discomfort she felt vanished the instant she revealed the portrait. Lily couldn't explain why the look of quiet pride on Ewen's face filled her with such satisfaction. As for the rest of the table, everyone erupted into enthusiastic exclamations over the laird's likeness, Lily's talent, and when she would be available to do their own portrait.

Everyone except for Rowena, whose expressions ran the gamut from sulky, to indignant, to outright murderous.

❁

Ewen cursed himself. He had not intended to actually make a gift of the necklace. He'd just thought to loan it to Lily for the evening, as it and the gown were a pair.

And to reminisce publicly that it had been a gift from his father to his mother. The implication would be obvious to a blind man. He had spoken in a moment of anger and drawn a parallel between his parents and him and Lily. There was no taking it back now, though. At least not without seeming a fool.

He was furious with himself. The laird should always act with discretion and, most of all, with a clear head. There was something about Lily, though, that made him want to stand up in her defense. Something that made him act so without thinking.

Not to mention that he enjoyed leveling that mindless Rowena. She took far too many liberties. Ewen noticed that she'd done a tidy job of insinuating herself with John as well. He didn't know how or when that had happened, but he would need to talk with the lad about it. He didn't know what Rowena was up to, but he knew he didn't trust her. Perhaps he would have Robert keep an eye on her. He was such a curious one anyway, he could keep watch on her without garnering too much undue attention.

And what of Robert? What could his foster brother be thinking to bait him so? Requesting a sketch from Lily placed the two of them in an unacceptably intimate situation. Though Ewen had to admit, he enjoyed having her eyes wander over him so intently.

Her occasional flush of discomfort was more telling to him than any feminine wiles would ever be. That Ewen kept women at arm's length did not mean he didn't know how to read a lass. To the contrary. He could tell that this one was as drawn to him as he was to her. He knew her confused blushes spoke of an attraction to him.

And he knew a surge of desire in response.

Lily's drawing had given Ewen the opportunity to study her. She was forced to regard him openly, and he'd been unable to look away. Instead, he'd felt like a mischievous schoolboy eyeing her so unabashedly in turn.

He had recognized her appeal before, but tonight—dressed as she was and with the wine in her cheeks—it was clear just how lovely she really was.

And how unknowingly seductive. Engrossed in her sketch, Lily's tongue had played at the corner of her mouth and Ewen was forced to adjust his kilt several times as his body made its fervent response uncomfortably clear.

Most women played their strengths brazenly. Exposing a leg to dance, turning a cheek just so, or using fashion to display trim waists, full bosoms, or other assets. But Lily wore her beauty effortlessly, as if she had no idea what a beauty she was. And Ewen imagined she probably didn't, which is partly why he found her so appealing. He wanted her, and wanted to make her feel just how desirable she was.

Once she had finished her sketch, he had reclasped the necklace about her throat himself. As he had run his hand over her shoulders, a bolt of heat had run through him. He had to steel himself from looking at that neck again, at its creamy expanse underneath the gold of the necklace, at the fullness of her bosom just visible underneath the froth of lace at her chest. A body like that deserved more decoration than such humble jewelry.

Ewen chided himself. This was not the way a laird should be comporting himself. He had learned his lessons with Mairi. He had an heir and did not need the complications in his life that a woman would bring. No matter how genuine that woman seemed to be.

Nor how tempting.

Chapter 18

"I've been wondering if you'd recovered." Lily came upon Robert on her way back from the stables. The walk, not to mention patting a few horses, was always good to clear her mind. And she found herself needing to clear her mind more than usual.

"Hmm?"

"The other night. A little too much *veni vidi vino*, as I recall."

Robert blushed. "Yes, well . . . but what of you?" He quickly changed the subject.

"*Me?* I wasn't the one hitting the Bordeaux. In my time, there's a rule against something called 'drinking and dialing.' I think you discovered its seventeenth-century evil twin, 'drinking and discoursing.' "

"Dialing?"

"It's a phone thing. A phone, well a phone is . . ." Flustered, she said, "Oh never mind."

"I do know what a telephone is, Lily."

She looked at him as if she had just discovered a plasma TV on the wall of her castle bedroom. "You *do*?"

"Aye," he laughed. "I've been wondering why you've never

asked me about my time, knowing as you did that I too went through the labyrinth."

"Yes, I, well . . . it seemed too personal a thing to ask about."

"Wouldn't you say we're past that now?" Robert asked mischievously. He added in a comically thick Scots brogue, "I mean, you have seen me piss drunk off my rocker, aye?"

She laughed. Hearing such modern slang come out of his mouth was refreshing. It was a sudden rush of her own time, a reminder of its quirks and most of all its ease.

A pang of nostalgia for the modern world straightened her features. She said, "But when we spoke that first day, it didn't seem like you were from my time. And, well, you're always wearing those clothes."

"Ah, but you said the twenty-*first* century. I'm of the twentieth. As for my clothing, I confess, I enjoy walking about the keep feeling as if I were Copernicus occupied with my scholarly inquiries."

They laughed, but then Robert's smile faded. He looked for a moment into the distance, as if concentrating on a faraway place. "No, I hail from a more modern era. To be precise, 1916."

Lily stared at him, silently, expectantly, so he continued, "I told you that I was but fifteen when I found the maze."

"But where are you from?" Lily pressed. "What of your family?"

"They were . . . where to begin? I lived with my father, he was an archaeologist." A distant smile lit his face. "And you think me a bookish soul. If only you were acquainted with my father!"

"So, I take it we have him to blame for all of that Latin of yours?"

"Oh yes," he laughed with uncharacteristic ease, "but I have spared you my Greek, have I not? Though I've been meaning to dust it off and—"

"Just do continue," Lily interrupted. She'd had a lifetime's worth of Latin aphorisms already—she didn't need any Greek at the moment. "Your father?" She prompted.

"Ah yes, my father." He nodded. "I didn't have a mum, you see."

"Robert, everybody had a mother at some point," Lily chided. Now that he was speaking so freely, she couldn't help but pry a bit.

"You're a vexatious woman." He shot her a playfully annoyed look. "You speak truly. I did indeed have a mother, but she died when I was quite young."

Robert's voice became suddenly serious. "I have no recollection of her. I once had a photograph . . ." His voice trailed, and his smile faded into a look of regret. "I do wish I still had that." He shrugged. "We had lavatories, newspapers, medicines. But my pictures. I had but a few, yet they are what I truly miss." His voice was distant as he mused, "I was told I have her hair. But, you know, you can never really tell from a photograph, can you?"

"No." Lily paused. "I suppose you couldn't tell with the old black and whites, could you?" Puzzled, he looked at her for a moment, as if considering a different question.

A sudden shouting interrupted them, and they looked in the distance to see John attacking a lone tree with his wooden practice sword. The dull clack of wood striking wood echoed through the glen as the boy feinted, thrusted, and whirled about like a young berserker, hollering unintelligible, but clearly dire threats.

Lily laughed. "He is his father's son sometimes, isn't he?"

"You speak truly," Robert replied. "I feel a special tie to young John, you know."

Lily looked confused, so he explained, "Because of his mother. I also know what it is to live without a woman's presence."

He shut his book and placed it in the grass. "Most difficult was how my mother's loss defined my father. I see that too with Ewen.

"Mind you," he quickly clarified, "Ewen didn't care for that woman, Mairi. But still . . ." Robert became thoughtful. "I see it in him. That small part of a man left hollow from want of a woman."

Lily felt a quick spark of jealousy, and unwittingly let confusion and envy flash across her face. Robert added quickly, "Not from want of Mairi." He studied Lily as if noticing something for the first time. "But from want of a woman."

He sighed. "I sometimes fancy the different turns my own life would have taken, had my father remarried. I wonder the same of John." Robert hesitated for a moment, scrutinizing her reaction. "The boy would flourish under a woman's hand. Do you not agree?" His eyes twinkled as he added, "If only our bullheaded Lochiel would take himself a new bride."

Uncomfortable, Lily quickly redirected the conversation. "So what happened to your father then?"

"Well, he was quite broken up when my mother died. It was the typhus that got her. In Persia. He specialized in Persian prehistory, you see. My father never forgave himself."

Robert's voice was detached as he rattled off the rest. "So he trundled us back to Scotland, returned to his dig, and immersed himself in his work. He'd come back for holidays, otherwise it was just me, Gordon—he was my brother—and my uncle."

He gave a bitter laugh. "I had always thought, if I were good at my studies, perhaps I'd catch my father's eye."

"Were you and . . . Gordon, is it? Were you close?"

"Ha!" The dark look on Robert's face chilled her. "That's just it, Lily. We were *not* close. He was older than me, enough to remember my mother, aye? Gordy hated our father, blamed him. And so I hated Gordon." He snatched a tuft of grass and began twirling it in his hands.

"I can't imagine you hating anybody, Robert."

"Oh no," he countered dourly, "I despised him. He was such a strapping lad. Sports and lasses came with ease."

Robert added acidly, "And then the war broke out, and he couldn't sign up fast enough."

"Oh," Lily gasped, sensing what was to come. She shook her head, "World War I and the trenches . . . that was a horrible time. Historians came to call it the 'Great War.'"

"Great, eh?" Robert snarled in disgust, and Lily immediately regretted having interrupted him.

She quickly asked, "Where did he die?"

"In Picardy. France, aye?"

"Yes," Lily said quietly, "I know Picardy."

"And do you know what I found in his kit?" Grief thickened Robert's voice. "A picture of us as lads."

His voice grew louder as he elaborated, "No letter from some lass. Not some book. A photograph. Of him and me."

Robert was silent for a moment, and then added gravely, "I'm ashamed. I should have been with him."

"But you were too young!"

"No," Robert spat, "that didn't stop any number of other lads. I *could* have been with him, could have doctored my papers, passed for eighteen. The soldiers from the west, where we lived, aye? They formed what they called a 'pal's battalion,' so the Highland boys could fight together." A look of self-loathing twisted his features.

They were both silent for a moment. Lily wanted to cry out: *But you were only fifteen, there was nothing you could have done!* But she knew she couldn't convince him. She sat silently, waiting for Robert to finish.

"And it was that day that it happened. Traveling here, I mean. The day I found that photo of Gordy and me." He looked at her imploringly. "I had to walk it off, you see, that feeling. Like to betrayal it was."

He shook his head, "Dear braw, fool Gordon." He added distantly, "It had to have hurt, living all those years and no parent there but for the memories of our mum."

He sighed. "Walking that day, that's when I found the labyrinth. And . . . you know the rest."

Robert cleared his throat and, with that, his voice assumed its usual formal tone. "And so, fair Lily . . ."

Lily was startled back into the moment. "So what?"

"And so now it's your turn."

"My turn for what?"

"You must tell me," he tsked, "what of the future, then? Did we win the war?"

Lily smiled gently. Robert was the inquisitive scholar once again. "Yes, we won the war," she told him. "What else . . ." she thought aloud. "You obviously know about stuff like planes and cars." He nodded impatiently.

"This thing called the Internet was created. It's . . . how should I describe it?" She rubbed her forehead. "It's a world of pure information where you can search the text of millions of books and learn anything about most everything."

"A true wonder!" Robert's eyes were bright. "Do you mean to say, a man could lose himself for days in a world of thought?"

"Yea, a lot of weirdos do just that, actually," Lily laughed. She paused, and then added, "You know, I don't much miss it."

She put her chin in her hand. "Let's see, what else? What's a really good one?" She brightened suddenly. "Men walked on the moon."

"On the moon? Truly?"

Lily nodded.

"The moon." A beatific look softened his features. "Now that's a bonny, bonny thing."

Chapter 19

A subtle but noticeable shift had occurred in the Cameron household, and Lily wasn't sure if it was more a source of pride or aggravation. The staff was treating her less like a peer and more like a member of Ewen's inner circle, albeit an odd one. Everyone but Kat kept her at arm's length. Her performance with pencil and paper the night of the dinner party was the talk of the place, and although it garnered her respect, it made Lily stand out as that much more of a peculiarity in castle life.

She'd appeared out of nowhere and had held out hope that she could disappear back through the labyrinth with few being the wiser. But with Ewen's public show of gift giving and her sketch being passed surreptitiously among the staff, Lily was the favorite topic of hushed conversations.

The laird treated her even more stoically than before, and Donald took to nodding gravely at her whenever they saw each other in passing. She had been so startled by his attention at first—after all, a nod was downright ebullient for Ewen's uncle—she'd stopped in her tracks to try and think if there wasn't something she did or was supposed to be doing for him to acknowledge her so.

The only person immune to this new course of events was young Master John himself. He still tried her patience at every turn and didn't seem to care about Lily's new standing. If anything, he was developing the new and irritating habit of disappearing at every opportunity. Combing the entire keep all the while calling John's name brought Lily even more unwanted attention than she was already getting. She would find the rascal in the most banal of spots—sitting idly in front of the kitchen hearth, distributing apples to horses in the stable, pretending to pore over books in the library—always with an aggravatingly innocent look on his face. It was a burgeoning power struggle and she was quickly getting in over her head. Lily had to nip the new behavior in the bud and was not about to get Ewen involved.

"Feeling alright, lass?" Lily looked up to see Kat's concerned face hovering over her. She realized that she had been sitting in a daze, pushing her eggs and sausage around and around her plate while everyone else had left the table long ago to get on with their mornings.

"John is gone again."

"Ah. I ken the problem now." Heaving a knowing sigh, Kat pulled out a chair and plopped down next to Lily.

"The lad is too clever for you." The maid pressed on, despite Lily's skeptical glare. "Too clever for how you are now, at least. Look at yourself moaning over your good food.

"Mind me, lass." Kat's voice took on a conspiratorial tone. "His father were the same way as a lad. After breaking his fast of a morning, off like a spooked horse young Ewen was, and no sign of him for hours. He went through governess after governess; none could tame the likes of our laird when he was a mite. He missed so many lessons under one teacher, his uncle Donald was forced to take a switch to him."

"I can't beat John to make him stay for his lessons." Lily was aghast at the thought.

"Aye, but you can make it more lively for the lad. Perhaps—"

Lily interrupted, on the defensive, "Please, I do my best and—"

Kat touched her gently on the arm. "I was saying, perhaps if you made it more lively for the lad by doing a bit less sums and a wee more of that picture making that you do. When the laird was young, it took him a while till he found his passions. He's more the scholarly type, our Ewen. 'Twasn't till Donald and his grandda—God rest him—put him to reading different manner of books that the lad settled down. He had no use for Latin on a page, but put it in a book, why, there he could decipher for himself stories and history and such, and he became a different child entirely. Now, as I see it, our John has the same problem. A lad's got energy, aye? And this one hasn't any way to tire himself of it."

"But do you think he'd be interested? I mean, all I know how to do is draw and paint."

"Och, lass, what do I need do to make you see? It's not just the pictures you make, but the way you see the world around you. It's like this. I've seen John building simple things with rocks and sticks and the like when he thought nobody was looking. Of course, he just knocks them back down again. But you can show him how to really make something to be proud of."

A look of sad introspection crossed Kat's face. "Since John's mam died, 'twas like Ewen was done with everything to do with her." She lowered her voice to a whisper. "Sometimes including the boy, I fear."

Kat looked at Lily as if weighing her response then continued, "The son and heir was born, so he was done. Mairi had been no wife to Ewen, and he likes to push it out of his head. But I fear seeing his son sometimes puts him in mind of her. Any child would feel the distance from his da like that. 'Twould be good for the both of them if John found something that he could be proud of."

Lily stared thoughtfully at her plate for a moment then startled the maid with an abrupt hug. "Kat, you are positively a genius!"

❁

They sat side by side at his table. John tore apart the eleventh sheet of paper that day, frustrated over his attempts to sketch the still life that Lily had set up on the windowsill using a flower, some fruit, and a book. Lily scowled at all the wasted paper littering the floor and hoped that it wasn't too rare a commodity in seventeenth-century Scotland. For all she knew, she was wasting away the family fortune in art supplies alone.

She watched the boy in frustration from across the child-sized desk. His usually ruddy, boy-thin cheeks were smeared with charcoal, the dark streaks matching the black hair that rose up off of his head like the unruly mane of some wild animal. Lily thought she probably didn't look much better. Her own hair was a ratty mess from mindlessly twirling strand after strand in attempts to channel her aggravation.

She was getting as exasperated as John and decided to take a completely different tack altogether.

"Alright. Let's forget this."

The look of gratitude that beamed from the boy's face sparked new reserves of patience in Lily. The poor kid was trying hard; she couldn't let herself forget how difficult drawing could be when tried for the first time.

"Let's take a turn in the garden. I think I'm going to have you make a collage and you can gather items for it as we walk."

John looked confused. "Collage?"

"Don't worry." Lily scruffed the boy's hair, and for once he didn't shrink at her touch. "I'll explain as we go."

❁

Once they got outside, John bounded ahead, giving Lily the chance to think. She had discovered she quite enjoyed wandering through the overgrown garden. It was small and rarely used, shunned by the occupants of the keep in favor of a grand formal garden elsewhere on the castle grounds. Lily, though, much preferred the seclusion of this side yard.

She had stumbled upon it purely by accident. Having missed lunch one day in favor of preparing John's lessons, she begged a snack from the cook and went out a side door to eat in the cool, late afternoon air rather than bear the stuffy confines of the kitchen. She had been overjoyed to discover the rusted gate almost completely concealed beneath a dense thatch of myrtle. As it was only accessible from the servant's wing of the house, Lily deduced that she discovered what was once the cook's garden, and by the wild, untamed look of it, it was now long abandoned.

And now her own private haven. Not to mention the source of what she considered many of her finest sketches.

Lily especially loved the humble stone path that wound through the garden's dense plants and ragged flowers; she cherished the times she could escape from the goings-on of the keep to meander along it, so without purpose as it was. She paused in front of a particularly ragged plant that she loved as much for its happy yellow flowers as she did for its name. She had been so proud to recognize the species and pointed it out to John one morning as ragwort; he gleefully corrected her, saying its true name was stinking nanny and that the cook used it to treat burns and ulcers.

Lily had been unable to suppress her quite unladylike bark of laughter at that one. Now the old weed always cheered her no matter how dark her mood.

The smile still faint on her face, she began to ponder the boy wandering ahead of her, spindly and restless as a colt, swatting at leaves and kicking unseen rocks. Lily thought for a moment at how insecure John might really be. If it was true that his father couldn't spare much time for him, who else was there? Donald and Robert weren't likely to offer much solace, even despite Robert's admission of sympathy for him. No, Lily reflected, the life of a child was certainly dramatically different in the seventeenth century when compared to Lily's generation, weaned as it was on Dr. Spock and child psychology.

Kat had said there were many similarities between father and son. Lily wondered at what unplumbed depths were to be found in Ewen. She could see with her own eyes that, unlike his son, the man had not a shred of insecurity in him. But she did believe that his seemingly impermeable exterior had to be masking some hidden pain. On the surface, he seemed to be just donning the stern formality of his role as laird. Lily, though, sensed something deeper flashing in his eyes, and she was beginning to suspect that what she saw was the ache of loneliness.

She shook her head at the direction her thoughts were taking. The laird and his inner life had to be of no concern to her.

The son's feelings, however, all of a sudden were. If nobody at the keep was going to take an active interest in John,

well, she certainly would. She caught up to John on the garden
path, resolved to be as patient and as loving a tutor as she possibly could be.

That is, until the time was right for her to go.

❈

She was brimming with pride at the sight of John working intently over his collage, arranging and rearranging feathers,
leaves, and a good number of mysterious scraps mined from
their garden excursion. Lily had never seen him so silent for
nearly so long before.

She had remembered a few tips from a crafts course she
took in college where students were taught to make things like
paper, glue, and dye without relying on modern materials. At
the time, Lily had thought it a waste of time. Some of her
peers had loved steeping themselves in obscure craft-related
arts like bookbinding, paper making, or encaustic painting using just wax and pure pigments. She had not been one of
them, however. Lily had wanted to be a painter using the usual
techniques and she figured she would rely on her local art supply store for whatever she needed, just as she always had.

Lily had experienced a moment of panic remembering that
there was no Elmer's in seventeenth-century Scotland. Glue
was as old as the Egyptians, though, and she was so thankful to
her alma mater that what she had thought of as Artinsanity 101
instead of Artisanship 101 had been a core course on the way
to her degree. John had loved their fishing expedition to Loch
Linnhe, but even more he loved that the goop he made from
boiling their catch would actually make things stick to paper.

Considering the extracurricular fishing, the whole enterprise took three days. Though she would never admit it to
John, Lily had been delighted to have a few glorious days with
no Latin, sums, or geography to speak of. John had even
shocked her by requesting they stay up late together after supper to complete his masterpiece.

"Done." The glee that had been clearly writ on John's face
during the past days was now muted. Lily sensed some trepidation on his part at revealing his finished artwork. She could
understand, though. After all, she was the one with a closet
full of canvases at home that she'd never shown to anybody.

"I would love to see it, if you're ready to show me." Remembering more than a few public humiliations during art department critiques, Lily tried her best to be gentle.

John screwed up his face, visibly mustering his courage, and silently placed his artwork on the table in front of Lily. She had been prepared to feign appreciation for the thing, but what she saw startled her. She exclaimed with total sincerity, "It's wonderful!" She was amazed at his sense of composition; bits of garden refuse were arranged on the page in an abstract—though clearly visible—seascape. Lily was also impressed by his creative use of materials. She had been uneasy to discover that he had stolen a handful of flour from the kitchens, but all of her concern disappeared to see it put to use so ingeniously spattered in the corner and across the picture as the sun and its reflection on the water.

"Truly, John, this is beautiful."

The anxiety on his face melted and the boy just beamed. Lily was overwhelmed. It thrilled her to have such an impact on him with something so simple. John had finally discovered something that interested him and that he was good at. Even if he dabbled in the arts for just a couple of months, it would be a perfect opportunity for him to learn more focus when approaching his tasks. Lily was already thinking of ways she could integrate other lesson plans based on the arts—calligraphy instead of penmanship, dye making instead of ecology. And best of all, they were all things that involved getting their hands dirty. She was no professional, but Lily knew dirt was something every boy loved.

"Let's go show your father!"

Anxiety appeared anew in John's furrowed brow. He seemed afraid of Ewen. Or rather, afraid of disappointing him. Well it was no surprise, she thought with a swell of anger. The laird could be impossible sometimes: he was a formidable man, powerful clan leader, and, from what she gathered, a fierce warrior. In other words, not the most approachable dad.

Lily, feeling like an angry bear protecting her cub, was determined to see Ewen forge a loving and open relationship with his son. Something more than just the laird and his heir. Ire prickled through her as she considered the dangerously narrow "fearsome sons of the hound" attitude. Every kid needed the nurturing support of their family, even if that kid is the future Lochiel of Clan Cameron.

❁

As it turned out, Ewen was nowhere to be found and the late hour forced John back to his rooms. He had worked himself up to see his father that evening, going from room to room, anxiety growing at every turn, and it seemed as if they kept just missing the elusive laird. They never could find him, and by bedtime, the poor boy was still tense from the missed encounter.

John jumped at the sound of a light rapping on his door. "Da?"

"Nay, just me, lad." The door creaked open to reveal Kat's face. She turned to Lily and added, "I've come to settle the boy into bed."

Deflated, John sank onto the side of his bed, and without thinking, Lily placed her hand on his back to comfort him. The thought of parting with the boy now left her feeling empty and she surprised herself by saying, "No, Kat, I've got this one."

A startled grin shone on John's face, and Lily knew she had made the right decision. "I'd like to see him into bed tonight." She wrapped her arm around his shoulder and laughed. "I think we can handle it, don't you think, John?"

"Aye, lass"—Kat paused, a slow smile warming her face— "I think you've more than the handle of it. Goodnight then to you both." The maid nodded meaningfully and, just before pulling the door shut, added, "And I thank you, Lily."

Lily wanted to tuck him into bed and give him the kind of soothing bedtime ritual that her Gram used to give her. John never knew his mother and probably the only female nurturing he had ever experienced was at the hands of a household employee.

"So, then."

"So?" John asked timidly.

"So what do we do to get you into bed? You must have jammies or something."

"I don't know jammies, but I've a flannel gown I wear for sleeping." A look of mischief lit his eyes. "And once in bed, I'm told many stories."

"Many stories, huh?"

"Aye." He nodded gravely. "Dozens of them. Yarns about knights and fighting and such."

"Oh really?"

"Aye, mum."

"Alright, young man, get into that gown and into bed with you."

John scampered off to retrieve his dressing gown, and as he dressed, Lily was lost in thought. She found herself fighting back an inexplicable wave of melancholy. That her relationship with John had found such ease should have cheered her, but instead their bond grieved Lily. She dashed away a tear at the thought that she would have to leave this boy who had somehow sidled into her heart.

He ran into the room and dove under his covers, shy to show himself in his pajamas.

Lily couldn't help but beam at him. "No stories tonight," she announced.

"No?" John looked crestfallen.

"No." She leaned over and ruffled his hair in what was fast becoming an easy gesture between the two of them. "And don't fret. We're doing something different. I'm going to sing you a song."

The boy snuggled deep under his quilts, looking hopeful but a little uncertain.

"My Gram used to sing to me on nights I couldn't fall asleep, and I think it's time we add a little history of music to your curriculum."

He hesitated for a moment, suddenly uneasy at being treated like the child he was instead of the laird's almost-grown son. Lily also thought she read a trace of the skepticism he felt at being treated with such outright affection.

"I never knew my mam."

"Yes, I know that. I'm sorry."

"Seems my da didn't fancy her overmuch." He looked distant for a moment then focused his intent gaze on her. "You said your Gram. Didn't you have a mam neither?"

"Well"—Lily was taken aback at first at the frankly personal question—"I did have a mother. Or, I still do, I guess. She left when I was very young, though."

John looked eager for the connection that she was offering and Lily found herself willing to share. "Even though my Gram raised me and I loved her very, very much, I never got over feeling mad at my Mom."

John looked relieved. "I ken your meaning. I get mad at my own mam sometimes too, though I never knew her."

"Yea . . . my mom found some new man to marry." Lily was quiet for a moment then added, "I felt very lonely for a long time."

"A bit like me, aye?"

"I suppose you're right. I never thought of it that way."

"Do you still feel it? The lonely part, I mean?" The boy looked desperate for a magic answer, and, after truly considering her solitude for the first time in many years, she realized she couldn't give him one.

She didn't know why she was being so honest with him. Perhaps it was the culmination of an emotional day: watching him pour himself so completely into his project; sensing all the buried anxieties around his father; or seeing him—normally just a young troublemaker—so vulnerable for the first time.

"Yes, John." Sighing, she sat down on the edge of his bed and found she had to look away for a moment. "I do still feel lonely. A lot."

John's eyes met hers and he gave her a warm, albeit unreadable, smile. He snuggled deeper into the four-poster bed and Lily tucked him tightly under his heavy quilts.

She waited to make sure John was finished asking questions. Lily knew she was probably done answering them. She hadn't thought about her own situation in some time. Work had been so crazy up until the end, she'd never considered her solitude much. Lily dated like the other single women in the city and tried not to admit the fact that she could see somebody every night of the week and still feel acutely alone. John's question forced her to ponder why it was she had forgotten about her loneliness of late. Since she had arrived in Ewen's household to be precise.

She tried to stop that line of thought and asked abruptly, "Hmm . . . which song?" Lily began to stroke his head, and the boy closed his eyes. Her voice faltered as she realized she didn't know if her sudden emotion was because she missed home or because she was finally there.

She couldn't remember all of the words to the lullaby she sang, and repeated the same verse a few times, even after it had become clear that John had drifted off. Lily watched as the boy's face became slack, mouth parted in the deep sleep of a child, and she wondered at the will of the universe to send her here. And was struck that, for the first time in a long while, she felt a real connection.

She just didn't know if she was supposed to embrace it, or simply learn from it and walk away.

❊

Ewen was almost through the doorway when he heard the sound of her voice. Kat had told the laird that Lily and John spent most of the evening searching for him, so he came looking for them in John's room to see what the matter was. But now Ewen pulled back into the shadows, listening to Lily. Her singing was strong and, although not perfect, sweet to his ears, her voice hesitating with an emotion that she was clearly trying to stifle. He wondered for a moment if anything had happened—perhaps her feelings had something to do with why they had been searching for him so frantically.

But the bedtime scene he spied on was a peaceful one. Maternal even.

The laird had held his own mother dear to his heart. For the little while he'd known her, his mother's love had guided him, buttressed him as the small keystone supports the whole. John did not have such a mother. All John did have was Ewen.

His throat clutched with grief. He didn't pay much mind to his son, above and beyond the required tutelage and guidance. Seeing John solely as heir and successor had been a way for Ewen to distance himself from his former wife. Seeing him as a son had long been too painful a reminder of the mother.

Ewen's heart broke to realize that he had pushed away his own child. His child whom he loved more preciously than his own life.

When Lily began with John, the boy had responded like a plant to sunlight. Subtle changes unseen to others glared obvious to Ewen. He hadn't realized that the boy fought insecurities until he saw the lad bloom with a newfound self-assurance. His demeanor, even his stride had been different in the past days. And, curse him if John didn't remind Ewen of himself when he was a lad. The boy had boundless energy with curiosity that burned like a hot coal. It was not uncommon for the laird to discipline his son only to turn around, privately thrilled by the boy's cleverness and spirit.

He resolved to be more than just an instructor to his son. He would truly be a father.

Ewen leaned his head and shoulders against the door and listened, mesmerized by the sound of Lily's voice.

Chapter 20

Picking her way along the path, Lily fingered the carrots tucked in the pocket of her skirt and wondered if Morag had dropped her foal in the night. She had pilfered the treat for her new favorite horse when cook's back was turned. Lily wondered if she would soon notice how her carrot supply was slowly diminishing. She hoped not. Not only did the stunning brown and black mare have a penchant for them, but the cook seemed a surly sort and Lily didn't want to see what would happen if she crossed her. In fact, Lily was so cowed by the woman that she hadn't even had the nerve to introduce herself yet—she just continued to refer to her as "cook." She was just as Lily would imagine a castle cook to be: as thick as her cast-iron soup pot, with doughy jowls and a permanent scowl that made her seem as if she had always just come from cutting a bushel of onions.

She'd just have to trust that her luck would hold, and maybe see if cook had a supply of apples lying about as well. Morag would definitely love an apple. Lily snapped the tip off one of the carrots and started to munch, thinking she probably shouldn't hold her breath on the whole fruit thing. Though always a fan of meat and starch, Lily thought if she had to face yet another meaty stew, slab of meat, or meat pie, she'd cry. Granted, she realized what a luxury it was to be so well fed, and she appreciated all Ewen had done for her, but she longed for some good, fresh produce. A salad, some melon, maybe a little sparkling water to go with them. She sighed. She had thought to find the horse some apples when, at this point, a sweet and juicy hunk of fruit felt like nothing short of the Holy Grail.

Lily discovered the stables in her second month at Tor Castle and had come back almost every morning since. It was unlike her to rise at dawn—back home she didn't become human until she choked down at least two cups of coffee. But she found the chill Highland mornings invigorating, their serenity bolstering her more than any caffeine. While the rest of the household buzzed with the day's preparations, the stables at dawn were a haven of calm. Animals chuffed peacefully in their stalls, dust motes hung lazily in the air, and sunlight shone through the slats of the ancient barn, cutting dramatic angles on the hay-strewn floor.

Surprisingly, it had been Ewen who had encouraged her to explore the stables. He had blurted out one evening that she should see the pregnant mare, and Lily couldn't resist the offer. Besides, she didn't want to risk offending the laird just in case what she understood to be a suggestion was actually some kind of order. He could be impossible to read sometimes.

She had been nervous on her first visit but was made to feel immediately at home by Lennox, the effusively kind—if somewhat dim—stable hand. He was a short man of indeterminate years, his age blurred by a lifetime of whisky and a hard life outdoors. As far as Lily could tell, he could be anywhere between thirty and fifty years old. His hair was light, and again Lily couldn't tell if the color was a product of sunshine or age. But Lennox's most telling features were the deep creases etched at the corners of his eyes by the permanent grin affixed to his face.

He wasted no time introducing her to Ewen's prized bay mare, thick with her first foal. Lennox cooed and chatted to Morag as if she were his truest confidante and continually doted on her with tiny gestures—brushing her forelock out of her eyes, shooing flies, discussing the braw foal that she'd drop any day, and otherwise encouraging her in an exaggeratedly slow turn around the paddock.

Lennox's love for the animal immediately endeared him to Lily. His affection was so sincere and without guile, she found him an easy person to trust. Since then Lily felt free to come and go as she wished. She could wander through the stables in near silence and murmur to the animals—scratching behind ears and stroking velvety muzzles—and in turn was greeted only by Lennox's ready grin and the occasional whinny.

Like many girls, Lily had taken riding lessons when she was young, and visiting the stables had been a balm to her soul. There was something about stables that she found reassuring. The rhythm of the day was the same wherever—or whenever—you went: horses up to be fed and watered at dawn, exercised in the late morning, tack cleaned in the early afternoon, horses fed and watered again in the late afternoon. Never an exception nor alteration in schedule. Some people found barns unpleasant, perceiving only manure and dampness. Lily, though, loved the rich animal scents that greeted her whenever she entered; they were so distinct and universal—a mingling of horses, hay, and leather that brought her back to her childhood with an immediacy that only the sense of smell could do.

She was in a particularly expansive mood that morning despite the gray thunderheads that made it seem more like 7 p.m. than 7 a.m. It was going to storm; she could smell the moisture thick in the air. Lily smiled to herself and thought she was becoming a true Highlander to find the bleak sky overhead so exhilarating.

"Morning, Lenny!"

She had used the nickname playfully one morning and Lennox seemed so thrilled by her familiarity that she decided to keep it.

"Mornin', mum." The stable hand pulled his threadbare bonnet off his head and clutched it to his chest.

Lily looked round in confusion at the barn full of empty stalls.

"No horses here today, mum, except for our Morag. All's gone down to the picnic, left at sunrise to make a day of it."

"What do you mean, picnic? Don't be ridiculous, it's about to storm."

Lennox looked crestfallen, as if somehow he were at fault.

"No, not that you're ridiculous, Lenny. I mean . . . who's idea was it to go out on a day like this?"

"Mistress Rowena, mum. She's with young master John, and her sister, and some of the crofter's wives too, mum. But it's Mistress Rowena that's who's leading the party. Yestreen she came down here and said as she wanted enough horses for a small group of folk and they were going to meet up with the laird's hunting party that's gone out the day before stalking deer. The laird, he spotted a fine roe buck, near the Witch's Pool, aye?"

"Witch's Pool?"

"Aye, long ago the Camerons they chased a witch over the edge of the falls after she put a curse on their cattle."

This information was met by a blank stare from Lily. "What does that have to do with the picnic?"

"You ken the Caig River?"

"John has told me about it," she said impatiently, "but I haven't been up that way yet."

"Aye, well, the river can get angry, especially when the rain's been heavy like in the past fortnight."

Lily supposed the weather had been gloomy in the last couple of weeks. The path down to the stables had been particularly mucky in the mornings. She had become so accustomed to the bleak Highland weather, though, she hadn't really given it much thought.

She exclaimed, "And that's where she took John?" Lily couldn't imagine trekking near river rapids in such threatening weather. "What is Rowena thinking?"

Lennox hunched his shoulders as if bracing against a blow. She quickly amended, "No, don't worry, maybe I've just misunderstood. Please do continue, Lenny."

"T'weren't easy to get her as the witch she had changed herself into a cat, but the Cameron laird wasn't fooled. They chased her over the falls. 'Tis why they call it the Witch's Pool."

"No, I mean, tell me more about the river itself—they actually are going to have a picnic there? Is that where everyone went?"

"Aye, mum. Trying to catch up with the laird and his men."

Lily was getting more furious by the minute. Not only was Rowena endangering young John by leading him on a trek in such inclement weather, but she was undermining Lily's authority. She'd had a lesson planned for him that day—she had been threatening for weeks to quiz him on sums and today was to be the day. It was unacceptable for Rowena to swoop in and take him away without consulting anybody. Unless she had asked Ewen. Maybe he had given his consent and just not informed Lily.

She felt a surge of anger. "How fitting that the witch herself chooses to picnic near the Witch's Pool," Lily hissed.

Lennox's eyes widened in shock and confusion.

"Sorry, Lenny. I'd just like to retrieve John. Can you lead me there? To the river, I mean."

"Aye, I reckon so, but all the mounts are gone."

A breeze stole under Lily's skirts and chilled her. Leaning out the barn door, she looked up and felt suddenly tiny underneath the ominous sky. An enormous cloud was cresting the mountain in the distance. It dwarfed the gray wisps of cumulus that skittered beneath it, oppressing the valley below beneath a slab of shadow. Watching the thunderhead make its ponderous glide across the sky, leaching color from its wake, Lily realized an urgent need to get John. She didn't trust Rowena with John's safety, and she shivered at the thought of what a swift downpour would do to an already swollen and raging river.

"What about the ponies?"

There were a couple of shaggy old Highland ponies permanently put out to pasture. She had seen children from the keep challenging each other to catch and ride them bareback, but that was the extent of their use around the castle.

"The old ponies, mum?" Lennox began to guffaw, but was silenced by an icy stare from Lily.

"Yes, we need to get the laird's son." Lily assumed her most imperious voice. She hated to do that with dear Lenny, but she was starting to get frantic. "Please saddle up the ponies."

"Those ponies don't have saddles. Nobody rides them."

"Well, throw a blanket on their backs or something. Just do

what you have to do to get us out of here. Now." For the first time since her arrival, Lily was feeling nostalgic for a car. A nice four-wheel drive Range Rover perhaps.

Lennox had two ponies harnessed and ready to go in a surprisingly short amount of time. Lily looked with dread at the ancient and most certainly flea-infested blankets that were to serve as saddles. She hoped she remembered enough of her childhood riding skills to manage not killing herself. The ponies themselves didn't look much better than the blankets. They stood glassy-eyed, twitching their tails lazily at unseen insects.

"Here goes nothing." Lily grabbed the halter of a shaggy white pony, jumped up over its back, and swung her leg over with a grace that surprised both her and Lenny. She saw that the pony's legs were covered in mud from the rain-soaked paddock and felt even more urgently that she had to get to John as soon as possible.

From what she remembered about bareback riding, it was all about bruising her bottom while trying desperately not to fall off. She hoped her out-of-shape leg muscles were up to the challenge. The shorter gait of the ponies would be no help—she was certain she would get her brain rattled once they started with a brisk trot. Lenny mounted his pony and they were off, kicking madly at the sluggish beasts who were shocked that they were being asked to do anything but graze.

After riding for what seemed like an eternity, they reached Rowena's party. Lily's head pounded from clenching her teeth in an effort to avoid having her jaw repeatedly clack shut from the rapid-fire gait of her mount's short legs. Her hands and nails were filthy from twining in her pony's mane and her thighs burned from holding on for dear life.

In another circumstance, Lily would have felt a flush of shame at the amused looks that she and Lennox received upon their arrival. She supposed they did look a sight as they burst into the clearing, bouncing frantically on the backs of the old ponies. Rowena meanwhile looked particularly pleased with herself, crisp, rosy, and well put together, gloating over an adoring clutch of women that Lily was pleased not to recognize. But Lily didn't care about appearances or her rapidly waning dignity just then. It was John she was concerned with, and he was nowhere in sight.

She looked around. The picnic party was nestled in a grassy clearing overlooking the river. Lily spotted a steep path that wound down to the water's edge and was shocked by the violence of the white-capped waves that churned inexorably toward distant falls and the Witch's Pool far below. The contrast between Rowena's pastoral party and the roiling water they overlooked was absurd. The roar of the rapids filled her head, yet Rowena's friends sat on small quilted squares, blithely nibbling on bread and cheeses served from small baskets, trying to make their inane chatter audible over the thundering river.

"Where is John?"

"Well look who has come to join us! Welcome, Lily. The laird will be so pleased to see you."

Rowena's friends tittered behind lace hankies.

"I've got no time for this, Rowena. Where did John go?"

"Oh, did he not do his schoolwork?" a simpering friend of Rowena's called out in a high-pitched voice that matched her pert, upturned nose.

Lily answered with a satisfyingly withering look. She was doing all she could to keep her temper in check. She needed a cool head for this situation, even though what she really wanted was to assault these biddies with a flurry of well-chosen expletives.

The chirping of Rowena's friends suddenly ceased and she heard it. The thin strains of a tiny voice trying to rise above the crash of the river. A cold knot of dread settling in her stomach, Lily turned to look at the cluster of picnicking women. Half smiles still frozen on their faces, they now watched the rapids below. She followed their line of sight until she saw him. The dread in the pit of her stomach turned to nausea as she recognized the small, flailing figure. It was John. He must have slid from the muddy riverbank and been swept in by the strength of the rapids. Now he was barely keeping above water.

Lily screamed, "John! Swim, John!"

A few of the women glanced her way with looks of curiosity and some distaste. They probably found her shrieking ill-mannered, but she couldn't care. John needed help, and she didn't understand why nobody was doing anything.

Something made her look up. She noticed Ewen's hunting party standing high on a rise in the distance, mingling with their guns and hounds. They were too far off to do anything— even if they had noticed the drama below, none of them would be able to get there in time. She turned again to study the group of women and was shocked as it became clear that although they were now amply alarmed, they weren't doing anything to save the boy. They were merely spectators to the unfolding horror. Lily pushed back the wall of pure fury that rose in her as she told herself that she had to do something.

Time slowed to a crawl as Lily became intensely aware of everything around her. Suddenly she felt the burdensome weight of her clothes. The long heavy skirts, the linen shirt and vest, the thick wool of the plaid arisaid tied around her shoulders. If she had any hope of saving John and not drowning herself, she would have to strip. Her fingers were shaking as she tore off her shawl and raced to unlace her vest. She heard yelling coming from the hills above. The men must have noticed what was happening by now. Well, she figured, they would all get a show. She ran down the path to the riverbank, feet skittering on slick rocks and tree roots as she tore off her remaining clothes, all but the thin shift she wore in lieu of a modern bra and panties. That, she thought, would have to do for a bathing suit. She was thankful that she was already barefoot as she reached the bottom of the path and felt her feet hit the cold, slick mud of the bank. She had a split-second feeling of total freedom. Running as fast as she could, barely clothed, mud squishing between her toes. The act of pulling off some item of clothing or other had loosened her hair and she shivered at the feel of the wind whipping through her long mane. Her scalp never did like it when her hair was bound up, yet she had been wearing it in a variety of prim fashions since her arrival.

The second her feet hit the river, the moment rushed back to her, the freezing water jarring her senses back to reality. John was barely staying afloat now. Lily had to act quickly if she was going to save him. She battled the pull of the rapids and hiked her shift high above her knees, clumsily leaping from rock to rock, trying desperately not to slip into the river and get swept away from John.

She couldn't bring herself to think about the cloud of mist

on the edge of her vision where she knew the rapids crashed over the edge of the falls. To the Witch's Pool that Lenny had told her about. What had happened to Lennox, anyhow? He'd shrunk from the judgmental glares of Rowena and her friends then simply vanished into the trees. She couldn't think about that now either. Lily's only focus now was to get to John. She became dimly aware that the women had congregated on the riverbank. She could hear them talking excitedly, hollow sounds on the edge of her hearing.

Jagged rocks off to Lily's left cut the river into a whirlpool of waves, roiling savagely between her and John. She inhaled deeply and, bracing herself, dove straight into the current. Her only hope was that she could cut across the rapids and get to the boy before he was swept any farther downriver. The water hit Lily's head and back with a frigid slap, pummeling her into the rocky river floor. Immediately the undercurrent began sucking at her feet, pulling her down. She tried not to panic, knowing that it would surely do her in, and instead let herself get swept along, grabbing hold of tree stumps and slick razor-sharp rocks, moving herself across and down the river as quickly as she dared.

She lost sight of John momentarily then spotted him, clinging desperately to a tree stump much farther downriver. Time was running out. His arms flailed above the water as he was sucked back under, and his head began to surface with less and less frequency. When he managed to break above the surface of the river for a gulp of air, the look of terror on the child's face made her forget her own fear. She swam slowly and steadily toward him, and hoped that they would both make it out of the water alive.

Lily was gasping in pain now at the ice-cold water. She embraced the pain, though, using it to intensify her focus for she knew that perhaps more dangerous than the relentless pull of the current was the frigid temperature of the water. She didn't know how long it took to become hypothermic, but her forearms were already numb. Her feet no longer hurt from the cold and she could feel a paralyzing numbness creeping up her calves.

Lily was slowing. Her body was responding to the cold water and was trying to conserve energy. She disregarded every cue her limbs gave her and slowly counted, forcing a regular pattern to her strokes. She had crossed the midpoint of the river, and there was no going back now. She swam with everything she had. Memories of an eleventh-grade summer spent lifeguarding: swim steadily, across the current, keep your head above water, eyes locked on the victim. John slipped under, spurring Lily to surge forward with even greater strength. She could no longer see him. Taking a deep breath, she went under, her arms flailing in front of her in a desperate attempt to make contact with the boy. Her fingers brushed over a bit of fabric, floating oddly peacefully in the water. She made one last desperate kick and knocked headlong into the boy. Lily grabbed him across his chest, settled him under her left arm, and began to sidestroke frantically back to the riverbank.

Her palms were bloodied and nails shredded from grasping at whatever holds she could find. She had to make her way back across the river and not let the increasingly violent pull of the current sweep them over the edge of the falls. Every time she let go of a rock or stump, they were swept closer to the precipice. She concentrated on the people along the shore. She spied Ewen racing down the hillside, still too far from the riverbank to help. Some men from his hunting party had made it down to the water's edge and jogged clumsily along, tracking her and John's progress downriver. A few of the men were trying to fashion a long pole to hold out to her, but the rotted branches would not reach out far enough. They all seemed so small and far away. She could tell they were yelling for her, but the only sound that filled Lily's head was the thundering crash of water. Someone—Ewen, she was almost certain—was stripping down now, but the layers of clothing and weaponry were too much of a hindrance; he would never make it into the water in time. Lily needed to get John to safety and get some air in his lungs immediately. She too needed to get to safety immediately—her arms were trembling with the effort of paddling while clutching the boy to her side, and it was becoming increasingly possible that they would get carried over the edge of the falls. She felt a deep pang of loss. That Ewen would lose his only son, that maybe there was something she could have done differently. And she was stunned to feel a keen sense of regret that she hadn't spent more time with Ewen. It suddenly seemed so important to know him, and for him to have a true understanding of who she was.

Her body was almost completely numb now, the rigor of her chilled muscles the only thing keeping John at her side. She thought of the people on the riverbank—how they weren't of her time. How they wouldn't miss her if she were to succumb to the seductive pull of the river and careen to the pool below. Her head buzzed and a warm rush coursed through her veins, beckoning her muscles to let go. She thought again of Ewen. The people by the side of the river might mean nothing to her, but she was saving Ewen's son, and adrenalin spiked through her exhausted body at the thought. It took all she had to concentrate on those figures standing on the muddy shore to continue her deliberate and measured paddling toward them.

Her respect and love of water served Lily well as she relied on patterns in the rapids—not to mention a calm head—to get back to shore. Rather than fighting each distinct current, Lily swam across them, using their force to propel her and John back to safety.

In moments, her feet made contact with the slick mud of the riverbank. Cradling John in her arms, she raced out of the water and placed him on the ground. She didn't have much time. The surrounding onlookers were silent.

A couple of the clansmen approached to intervene. Lily hissed, "You will not touch this boy." The crowd started to buzz. One man silenced the others. Lily thought it might be Ewen, but she didn't give it any thought as she tipped John's neck in her hand and began mouth-to-mouth resuscitation. Lily hadn't thought about the finer points of CPR in years, much less how to resuscitate a ten-year-old, but it came back to her like clockwork—two breaths, fifteen compressions, two breaths, fifteen compressions.

In moments, John began to cough. Lily leaned him onto his side as he spewed foamy water from his lungs and belly. A collective sound of wonder rippled through the crowd as John was immediately surrounded by bodies, wrapping him in blankets, petting his head, cooing, and finally spiriting him up onto a horse where he was carried at full speed back to the Cameron keep.

Lily swayed to her feet. She was aware of numerous pairs of

eyes focusing on her. Not with hostility, but with apprehension and a kind of awe. Then Lily's cheeks flamed as she realized her relative state of undress. She looked down to see her shift was soaked and completely translucent, the thin fabric hugging every curve of her body. She could make out a triangular shadow between her legs and could see the pink of her breasts showing through the linen as two light brown halos. Her nipples were taut with cold, pointing erect under the clingy fabric.

Shaking, Lily looked around until she spotted her clothes in a trail toward the water's edge. She tried to conceal her body as best she could with her hands. As she turned to gather her clothes someone rushed up from behind and covered her with a thick tartan. She looked up to see the hard edges of Ewen's face looking down on her. Her knees buckled but his grip around her only tightened. The world began to buzz. Lily mused for a brief moment how odd it was that she wasn't surprised to see Ewen by her side. Everything went dark as she collapsed.

❁

When he was certain that his son would be all right, Ewen's eyes sought out Lily. She was still in the same spot on the riverbank, knees dripping black mud, staring blankly after the horse and rider who were rushing John back to the Cameron estate. A fierce sense of protection overcame him, seeing her trembling and forgotten amidst the crowd of people. He ran to her and wrapped her in the warmth of his tartan, sweeping her into his arms as she began to fall to the mud.

Ewen had never seen such a courageous act from a woman. Many men had lost their lives in this water. He knew hardened fishermen who would face down a field of redcoats before braving these rain-swollen rapids.

Fury roiled through him. Someone would be held responsible for putting his son in harm's way, and he thought he knew who that someone was. Ever since her arrival, Rowena had been sneaking about the keep with a wicked gleam in her eyes that belied her coquettish façade. Picnicking beneath storm-darkened skies wasn't merely the frivolous notion she'd have everyone believe. The woman was up to something. In the beginning, Ewen had thought she meant only to win his affections—it was no secret that she would have herself as the next mistress of his household. To put his son in mortal peril, though, spoke to a more insidious scheme.

He had left the day before, ostensibly with a hunting party, but only a fool would stalk deer on rain-soaked paths. The true errand had been to shed light on rumors of a redcoat incursion near Cameron lands. And curse it, but the talk was true. Ewen hadn't accepted Monk's overtures and the popinjay had responded by digging his heels into Lochaber and was already at work cutting Cameron timber to build himself a wee fort. Rather than being discouraged, though, Ewen thought he'd enjoy teaching Monk a lesson. He'd show the general that establishing himself on Cameron lands was no light matter.

When he returned that day and spied John in the water, Ewen was too far away to save him. It was Lily alone who took action. He had no idea what she was doing at first, stripping off all her clothes like that.

He remembered the sight of her, racing down the ravine in her sheer shift. She had put some more meat on her bones in her time under his roof, a fact that gave him a rush of satisfaction. Her body, though still lean, now had more rounded edges. The shift had clung to her body as she entered the water, outlining the curve of her hips and the graceful power of her legs. Most women he knew were shorter, but Lily was long, lithe. Strong, but undeniably feminine.

All the greatest warriors could swim, but with her powerful, sure strokes, he was certain she could keep up with the best of them. The strangest part for him was, once he was sure that John was fine, he was stricken with fear that Lily would die from the chill. Although the air was warmed by the early summer that was just around the corner, both the lochs and the rivers were icier than ever. The laird had seen seasoned men die from less exposure.

Ewen put his lips to her ear and whispered, "Hang on, lass," but Lily had already slipped into unconsciousness. He lifted her seemingly weightless body high into his arms and raced up the cliffside ravine to get back to Ares and to the castle.

❈

Gormshuil rubbed her hands together over the boiling water. The dried wood sorrel scratched and crumbled against her palms, releasing a smell like hay into the chill night air. The plant was a simple sour clover, but its tea always helped to soothe her stomach and nerves.

The kindling popped and settled, and the old witch used her walking stick to adjust the pot more steadily over the fire. She scowled. The cast-iron cauldron was a cruel mockery of her beloved china. Though small, it was a heavy thing, its bottom scorched deep black from decades of standing three-legged, directly in the cook fire. Gormshuil had left her home in the night, carrying the pot hung from a stick at her back, the other side counterweighted with a satchel of those belongings she'd need to survive in the woods for she knew not how long. She'd brought blankets thick enough to shield old bones from the relentless cold of the forest floor, her herbs, dried oats, clay pipe, a small roll of tobacco.

And her charts. She turned and spread them on the ground in front of her, relishing the warmth of the fire at her back. Red embers escaped from the crackling wood to spiral frantically heavenward before winking out. She dare not let the ancient papers get too close.

Gormshuil looked up, feeling the charged white light of the moon on her face, and studied the stars in the sky. She looked down to arrange the papers, and back up then down again, ordering the charts just so.

Dropping a page from her hand, the old woman froze. She canted her head, her face a still mask. The witch's unfocused eyes turned sightlessly to the black woods around her.

"Ah!" A small gasp of surprise escaped her.

"I see now, lass," she said. A knowing smile eased over her features, creasing her aged skin, thin like parchment. "And so it is."

Chapter 21

Lily slowly became aware of the world around her. She was in a bed. Securely bound in sheets or restrained somehow, yet she was oddly comfortable. Cozy even. She nestled deeper and remembered the river. Her hair was still damp but she was now blessedly warmer. Almost hot, in fact. She slowly opened her eyes and looked around. She was in a room that was not her own. It was large, with a row of glorious stained glass lining the upper wall. She was transfixed by the light shining through the windows, casting fragmented patches of green, blue, red, and orange light across the floor and along the surface of the bed. In that fog between sleep and waking, her eyes filled inexplicably with tears—it was the most beautiful thing she had seen in a very long time.

Her senses began to clear, and she was startled to find that she wasn't restrained at all. She was lying on her side and there was a large muscled arm wrapped snugly around her shoulders. She tried to shift, but the owner of the arm pulled her more closely along his body, pushing an iron-hard leg between hers to come to rest atop her own, much smaller one. She felt the tickle of short, coarse hairs and realized in shock that both the leg and the owner were naked.

"Let go of me!"

Lily heard a chuckle as he nestled in even closer. She paused for a moment to savor the heat emanating from him into her once-chilled body and then, with a start, felt a slight movement along the small of her back.

She knew she had to get out of this man's bed and his sudden hardness clinched it for her. "What do you think you're doing?" she yelled as she tore herself out of her warm cocoon. She turned to see Ewen lying there, face dangerously still.

"I'm saving your life, lass. You might thank me."

"Thank you? Thank you for, for . . ." Lily glanced down in horror at the recognition that she too was completely naked.

She pulled the sheet up under her chin and felt her temper rumbling like a volcano about to go. "I'll thank you to get out of here is what I'll thank you for. What the hell do you think you're doing anyway? Or do you enjoy taking advantage of unconscious women?"

A dark cloud passed over Ewen's face. He spoke quietly and deliberately as if he were trying to explain something to an unruly child. "You were freezing to death. If you don't remember correctly, you fainted on the riverbank, lass. You rather I'd left you to die, is it? I brought you here and heating water for a tub would have taken too long. You'd no time to spare, and the fastest way to restore your body heat was with my own."

"Well . . . well . . . ," she stammered. He had a point. She had been dangerously chilled by the time she got out of the water. It was a wonder she'd had the energy to revive John.

"How chivalrous of you to take this burden on yourself instead of having some woman revive me."

Ewen glared at her. "Would you rather I had one of the maids strip down to warm you? Aye, they could have done the job well, though you might have been infested with a few wee fleas afterward."

She had seen some of the scullery maids about the castle and supposed he might have a point.

"Besides, your shift isn't the most seemly thing, and I spied an odd mark on your back. I thought best to hide it from the slack-jawed servants about the keep."

"What? Oh, you mean my tattoo." Lily chuckled. She had

forgotten about that. A small, colorful butterfly in the small of her back leftover from her college days. Because she couldn't see it herself and it felt like years since a man had gotten close enough to notice the thing, she had all but forgotten it was there.

"A, what did you call it, tattoo, eh? I'd see it."

Before she could protest, two strong hands deftly manipulated her shoulder and hip and she was lying on her stomach. A mischievous light came into Ewen's eyes, giving Lily butterflies in more places than just her tattoo. He dragged the sheet lightly down her back and folded it over her buttocks. Lily wasn't sure if she hated this or loved it, so she just lay there silently, mesmerized, curious as to just what Ewen would do next.

His hand traced gently up and down her back then came to rest on her tattoo. "Aye, it's a beauty, it is. I've seen sailors with crude marks on their skin, but none so fine as this." He traced around and around the wings of the butterfly. "So, this is what they learn to do so many years hence? And do all women get them? Is it a mark of your family?"

Lily felt a slow throbbing begin between her legs and stammered, "Um, yes, they have machines that do this. They can do very delicate work with many colors. Not many people get them. Well, men have always gotten them, but only recently have women started to get them. It's fashionable for college kids especially. The butterfly doesn't have anything to do with my family. It doesn't mean anything really, I just liked the image that's all."

Lily was rambling in a way that she only did when she was nervous around a man.

He began stroking her back again, only this time his hand began to reach both higher and lower along her back. Up to her shoulders, down to the small of her back. Up to Lily's neck, down to just beneath the sheet. Up to tangle lightly in Lily's hair, then ever so slowly down, beneath the sheet. Ewen's hand ran lightly along the velvety soft skin, his thumb barely grazing along the line of her bottom, his hand pausing to gently cup the round flesh there.

Lily swallowed hard. This really was completely unacceptable, but she was frozen to the spot. She forced herself to speak. "You really need to get out of here now. I do thank you for heating, I mean, saving me, but I would like to be alone now to dress."

Ewen had a devilish smirk on his face that was making Lily more flustered by the second.

"Really, please get out of bed now. This isn't proper at all." Lily was getting nervous. She was in way over her head. She wasn't about to surrender to him for a third time. God only knew what he would decide to do—or not do—at the last moment, and Lily did have some semblance of pride to uphold.

"Out of bed?" Ewen smiled outright. "Well all right lassie, if that's what you want."

He swung his legs over the side of the bed, and Lily finally got Ewen's little joke. He rose up like a panther, turned, and stood towering over the bed, body tensed as if ready to pounce. He was fully erect, extending out of the tangle of black hair at his groin.

The delicious ache that Lily had felt earlier was nothing compared to the yearning that pounded between her legs, tightening her belly, making her breasts taut with need.

Ewen's naked form was like nothing Lily had ever laid eyes on. His dark hair fell loosely across his shoulders. His body rippled with power and the muscles earned from years of fighting for his life, training day in, day out along the unforgiving Highland terrain, swinging an immense claymore over his head as if it were no more than a kitchen knife.

He used his body to protect his people, and Lily found herself devouring every inch with her eyes. The smooth, broad chest. The silvery webs of scars from old battles that marked his right breast, his abdomen, his left forearm. She wanted to trace them, to run her tongue lightly along each one as if she could somehow absorb the pain of wounds past.

She looked up at Ewen. His face lost all humor as he looked down at her gravely, the desire clear in his eyes.

This had gone way too far now. "No," she forced the word out in a whisper. "I need you to leave. Now."

Ewen's voice was surprisingly gentle considering the driven look in his eyes and his otherwise rigid state. As he murmured to her, his Scottish brogue became even more pronounced, more sensual as he let the words roll slowly from his mouth. "Lass, you see I want you. And I think you want me. I've never wanted a woman like this and I'll fight it no longer."

He sat on the edge of the bed and tangled his fingers in her hair. His voice lowered to a husky whisper. "I'd give you anything, lass. I'll bring you all of Scotland. But please just say yes to me, sweet Lil'."

This seduction was more than she could take. Ewen was supposed to be helping her find her way back. To surrender to him now had a feeling of finality, as if she'd be turning her back for good on the place she came from. His words sounded so beautiful. She wanted him. Of course she did. But she was suddenly unsure.

Flares of panic alarmed her. Who was this man who killed his enemies with ease? Who might even have a little romance going with that nasty Rowena. Whose words of love tumbled easily from his mouth.

"No. Please just get out."

"Just tell me why, Lil'."

It had been so long since she'd made herself vulnerable to another. It made her afraid now, and uncertain. Not knowing what else to do, Lily found herself lashing out.

"Don't call me that," she snapped. Ewen looked as if he had been slapped. "I don't trust you, Master Cameron. You or your flowery words."

"Trust?" He looked bewildered. "Och, what have I done to fail your trust?"

"Seducing women seems far too easy for you, Ewen." She wasn't sure where she was going, but Lily plowed ahead anyway. "You should think less about carnal matters and more about . . . well, about other things."

Ewen looked at her in disbelief. "Seducing women? I haven't spoken so to a woman since I was a lad, and then I was but trying on the words of a man, not giving voice to my heart."

His gaze grew gentle again. "Who are these women you're so intent on, Lil'?"

Lily didn't know why she said what she said just then. She just knew she had never felt so susceptible to a man, and her panic to protect herself at all costs made her speak without thinking.

"Well, there's Rowena first off."

"Rowena?" Ewen's face got very still, his eyes glinting cold with anger. "That cursed lass spills lies like a horse dealer. I thought her a mere nuisance, but now it seems she's a mind for treachery where John is concerned." He scrubbed his hand over his face. "To take the lad off like that. If you hadn't been there, he'd be, well," he added quietly, "I'm grateful you were there."

Outrage clouded his blue eyes. "I'll discover the truth of her deceit"—he pierced Lily with a dark look—"and henceforth you'll not speak her name to me."

"I . . . ," Lily stammered. "I'm sorry. You're right." She forced out a small laugh to break the tension. "She is a horrible creature, huh?"

Confused, he asked, "Well then why would you say such a wicked thing?"

"Well, I guess I meant, you know, maybe you preferred women like her . . ."

"I've naught but contempt for such women." His gravelly voice was hushed as he added, "You don't know me one bit if you think my head is turned by one such as her."

She felt her heart break to see the hurt written openly on his face. "What else have I done to deserve your judgment in this way, Lily?"

The use of her full name was not lost on her—she had gotten used to his affectionately referring to her as "Lil'." She lashed out again. "There's your son. You never give him any attention. Do you really love him? You would do well to take a lesson from your brother, Robert, I think."

The rage that came over him was palpable. "Robert? You want me to take a lesson from Robert? Tell me you've not eyes for Robbie. I love the lad like he's my own blood, but what has he done to gain your steady heart? Has he risked the welfare of his family by taking you in? Has he entrusted the care of his only son to you? Has he done everything in his power to ensure your comfort and safety?"

He turned, a look of disgust on his face. Ewen angrily donned his kilt and, shirt in hand, stormed to the door. He didn't look back at Lily when he spat, "I thought you a woman, with need of a man, but you may keep your young Robbie instead."

Ewen was halfway out of the room when he stopped. Lily was just beginning to feel frightened when finally he turned to look at her, grief etched clearly on his face. "As for what you said about my John, well, aye, you do have something there. I love him more than life, but I've failed if the lad doesn't see it clear."

The door clicked quietly shut, and Lily crumpled on the bed. She much preferred seeing Ewen angry than in pain. She didn't know what she had been thinking to say such things. The desire that tore through her at the sight of him had left her feeling exposed, confused. She didn't know how to handle it and instead railed blindly at him, injuring him for making her want him so.

He had been right. Why did she fight the attraction? For that's what she knew she was feeling and she couldn't explain it. Cerebral, modern, urban Lily, whose most recent boyfriend had been a computer geek, heartsick over some grim Scottish warrior who literally had seventeenth-century notions of women's equality. But there it was. The relief that washed over her to discover that there was nothing between Ewen and Rowena had rocked her. Lily had felt her attraction to him slowly building from the moment she'd arrived and hadn't fully admitted it to herself until Ewen spoke the words.

She didn't understand how, but she had somehow come to know the stoic laird. Known precisely what to say to inflict the most acute injury. To accuse him of not loving his son enough was unforgivable. But then to bring up Robert, of all people. She especially didn't know where that had come from. She was fond of Robert, but he clearly was not made of the same mettle as his foster brother. The thought that she might be attracted to him was preposterous.

She curled up tightly on the bed and pulled the heavy quilt up to her ears. Warmth still radiated from the deep impression his body left on the mattress, yet Lily found she still could not get warm enough. She couldn't help but inhale his scent. The subtle mix of peat, leather, and man that she had come to recognize as his own filled her senses. Her heart sank to realize that she had kicked Ewen out of his own room. The oversized bed, dark furnishings, books on the bedside, and claymore perched in the corner all mocked her.

She thought how she should scamper back to her own room but the shame, anguish, and hurt pride were too much for her. She fell into a fitful sleep, wondering how she would ever be able to face Ewen again.

Chapter 22

Ewen didn't understand why she didn't trust his words, and despite himself, it cut him to the heart. He hadn't opened himself up to a woman that much since, well, perhaps ever. Even with Mairi, he had kept a large part of himself walled off from any undue emotions. It had been a suitable and politic match, no more. There was something about Lily, though, and it was beginning to aggravate him. He couldn't believe the nonsense that flowed out of his mouth after the incident at the river and was thankful that it hadn't gone any further than it had between them. He could only attribute it to a heightened mental state after fearing for his son so. Regardless, what was done was done. She was a part of his household—at least until they could figure out how to dispatch her back to her own world—and he needed to make amends. He had become too contented where she was concerned; there were even moments when he thought that perhaps she was sent to him for some greater purpose. After their last encounter, though, he resolved to put such nonsense out of his mind. He would find this mysterious maze and get her back through it as soon as possible.

He knew just who could help. After days of searching, his scouts finally tracked down the elusive Gormshuil. The old woman would never have been found had she not wanted to be, and Ewen feared what tidings she might have for him. Many believed she should have been outcast—or worse— long ago for witchcraft. He couldn't bring himself to cross her, and although he liked to think it was to honor his grandfather, who had sought Gormshuil's counsel, a part of him wondered if he actually feared the old woman.

They desperately needed to understand the key to this labyrinth, and the laird hoped that Gormshuil would be able to offer counsel. The mystery had long frustrated Ewen, who generally considered himself a man of science. He suspected Robert's and Lily's journeys through time had to do with the alignment of the planets and stars, but he had no more to go on than that. After one too many drams of whisky, his uncle Donald would speculate that the fairy folk had a hand in the matter, but Ewen dismissed this as nonsense such like the Irish would believe.

So, until he could talk to Gormshuil and track down the maze, he was left with this peculiar woman from some distant future. He wanted to atone for his loss of control and thought to offer her a token of peace and friendship, of the platonic variety. Ewen ruled out giving her any jewelry; he had done a poor job presenting her with the necklace, and besides, he was beginning to see Lily as a woman not easily swayed by the usual feminine baubles.

Inspiration had come to him in the most outlandish place. He would give her a gift that, though heartfelt, didn't speak of courtship. It hadn't been too difficult tracking down the mutt; he knew of a widower farmer living on the outskirts of Lochaber who took up husbandry as a pastime to while away the lonely hours once his five daughters were wedded off. Although the old man's primary focus was hog breeding, he had a particular fondness for hounds, and Ewen counted himself lucky that the farmer's prize wolfhound bitch had recently dropped a litter. If he was to take some mongrel canine into the keep, he vowed it would be a pup that could be trained. Lily had shown an unreasonable connection to the wolf that day in the woods and he figured a spirited canine would be just the thing to occupy her. As if John weren't spirited enough.

He'd wanted her that day in his bed, and thought he saw that desire mirrored in her own eyes. More perilous, though, had been sensing Lily's ability to hurt him. Her words had left an ache in his heart no less shocking than his first sword wound. Ewen was convinced that the solution to the problem was simple enough. If they both occupied their minds with other pursuits, the beckoning of the flesh would soon be forgotten as a momentary lapse of weakness. Giving Lily a hound would be a token of apology for any loss of control, without really having to say the words. Besides, John had been clamoring for a dog for years, and this would be a way for Ewen to earn a sorely needed victory with both of them.

Lily was in her garden hideaway when Ewen finally tracked her down.

"What can you see in this wee tangled corner? We've a much grander garden for your strolls."

She turned, ready to strike, but the irritation that had been written clearly on her features immediately dissolved when she glimpsed the mass of gray fur and tartan wriggling in his arms.

Her curiosity getting the better of her, Lily forgot for a moment that she was supposed to be mad at the laird. "What have you got?"

"Nay, lass, it's what you've got." An uncharacteristically broad grin broke across Ewen's face and just as quickly disappeared. "It's an offering of peace after, well, you know the mistake I'm talking about."

Lily recoiled as if slapped. Even though she had been berating herself, running the scene in the bedroom over and over in her mind, cursing whatever weakness had gotten her into that situation, for him to express his own remorse stung.

"You seem overly fond of wolves, and though I'll not abide such a creature near my keep, I'd not mind a canine."

Ewen unwrapped the frayed blanket that had been concealing his treasure, and a gangly puppy sprang out and bounded straight for Lily. She couldn't help her delighted squeals as she wrestled with the enthusiastic pup. Looking up at Ewen with gratitude in her eyes, Lily once again spotted that elusive but heartfelt smile that played at the corners of his mouth, warming his normally stern features.

"It seems he's chosen you," he said. "But you'll need a name for him."

Lily patted his wiry fur, a steel gray the color of the Highland sky, while he teetered on overlong legs like a newborn colt. The pup gently swatted her on the shoulder with enormous paws that spoke to the huge size he'd one day grow to be.

As if reading her mind, Ewen marveled, "Aye, those feet are like wee boats. He'll be a braw one, this lad. But don't mistake his playfulness—these animals will kill to protect their own."

Ewen squatted down to pat the dog roughly on the side of his belly, and their hands accidentally brushed. Lily jerked her arm back to her side, pretending that she suddenly had to make herself more comfortable on the cold, stony ground. She was annoyingly aware of Ewen's proximity and vowed that her mind would keep control over the sensations that once again rushed through her traitorous body.

"It looks like an Irish wolfhound to me," she said in a voice that wavered more than she would have liked.

"Aye, that sounds right. I'm told the mutt's grandsire hailed from Ireland and was used to track and kill wolves. The Irish haven't been able to eradicate the pests as we Highlanders have."

Though Lily flinched, she decided not to make an issue of it. Ewen was clearly trying to make amends, so she would do the same and not mar her first wonderful moments with her new puppy. She steered the subject in another direction. "How did you guess I'd want a puppy? I've always wanted a dog named Finn. Doesn't he look like a Finn?"

"Och, Finn? 'Tis bad enough to have a beast that hails from Ireland, but to name him thus? Why not Angus or Fergal or some other braw Scots name?"

Lily looked directly at him and, without thinking, raised her eyebrows and shot, "Get over yourself, Ewen."

Lily didn't know who was more startled by the staccato burst of laughter that erupted from the laird, her or the puppy.

"You're a curious lass, Lil'. I'll be going for some time now—I trust you'll have no troubles minding both the pup and my son while I'm away." The tease in his eyes told Lily that this was his effort at matching her sarcasm.

She didn't know what game they were playing, but she found herself joining along. "Mmhmm"—the words were out of her mouth before she could think about them—"and I'll need to keep an eye on Robert too, I suppose."

"Robbie can mind himself." Ewen's lighthearted tone turned suddenly serious. "Don't be troubling with him. You'll have troubles enough keeping your eyes open for Rowena. The wench hasn't been spotted since that accursed picnic of hers."

"I didn't mean *keep an eye on Robert*, I meant . . . ," she mumbled. "I . . . I don't know what I meant. And of course, I'm on the lookout for Rowena."

"Aye then. I'll see you when I return."

"Wait! I mean, wait. Where are you going?"

"It's not of your concern, lass." A dark cloud swept over Lily's face. "Och, woman," Ewen amended, "I've a wee bit of spying to attend to. The redcoats are up to mischief on the clan's own borders."

He regarded Lily for a moment then added, "And I've a person to see on the way home."

Before she could ask any questions, Ewen instructed, "I'll be home by nightfall. Mind yourself while I'm away." He turned abruptly and stalked out of the gardens before Lily could even register his comment.

"Mind myself?" Exasperated, she muttered to her new confidante, "Mind myself. How dare he? Mind myself indeed . . . bullheaded man."

Finn merely looked on with liquid brown eyes and a gleefully lolling tongue.

❄

"I'd say you were heartsick, lad."

Ewen merely glared at his uncle, then wordlessly kicked Ares into a canter. Donald's laughter boomed through the valley, the sound echoing off the rocks and hills all around. His uncle knew him too well, and his laughter was a mocking challenge to the laird to get ahold of himself. Ewen had vowed never again to get caught up in the wiles of womenfolk, yet here he was, acting the heartsick boy.

Something about Lily set him off balance. Giving her the mutt had started well enough. Then, before he could master the situation, it devolved into wordplay that crackled like dry kindling set to flame. Like a fool, Ewen had purposely grazed his hand against hers just to feel once more the touch of her skin and the shock it sent through his loins. He couldn't help himself where she was concerned—his desire for her heard suggestion in her every word, read it in every glance.

She had offhandedly mentioned Robert and he'd lost his wits. His accursed foster brother was enamored of her intellect, and Ewen had seen the lad's eye rove over the rest of her one too many times as well. The thought of her possibly returning his interest agitated him.

Of all the people under his care, Lily and Robert were two who vexed him most, and on a regular basis. Encouraging a friendship—or more—between them would not only get them out of his hair, it might banish the undue attraction that was growing between himself and Lily.

But damned if the notion of Lily and Robert together didn't gall him. The thought was ludicrous, but it had still haunted the laird ever since Lily had mentioned Robert while lying in his bed. He couldn't believe that she'd want a lad like Robbie, for that is how Ewen considered him. An overearnest, insufferably pedantic, at times arrogant, but admittedly well-meaning lad. But perhaps that's what women wanted where Lily hailed from. Men who lived in their heads, not their bodies.

But Lily, who fought like the wolf she so stubbornly protected, who survived the labyrinth without losing her life or her sanity, who worked with her hands in that ridiculous garden of hers. He didn't credit that she would choose one such as Robert, but then perhaps that is what all women craved. Well-groomed men who wielded their words with more skill than they did their swords.

"Lad, you'll slow that beast down now." Donald had ridden up beside Ewen, catching him unawares. "I'll not abide you riding a perfectly good mount into the dirt." Laughter gone, his tone admonished Ewen, treating him like an ill-behaved nephew rather than the laird that he was.

Ewen bit his tongue. He wouldn't lash out at his uncle, nor should he be taking his frustrations out on Ares, who gamely kept up with the unnecessary pace that Ewen was setting for him.

"Aye, you're right, of course." Gripping his thighs against the horse, Ewen eased his gait down to a trot and eventually a brisk walk.

"That's better, lad. Now you'll tell me what's got you in such a fankle."

Ewen didn't answer, so Donald continued to press. "I'll venture your problem has a bonny tangle of curls on its head, eh?"

"You venture wrongly, uncle," Ewen snarled.

"You'll not fool me, Ewen Cameron. I can see the lass writ clear on your face. Deny it and I'll redden your seat with my stave just as I did when you were a wee lad."

Distant birdsong and the skittering of gravel under the horses' hooves were the only things filling the silence that stretched between the two men. Donald watched the feelings that warred on the laird's face, and just when it seemed his comment would go unanswered, Ewen replied in a voice hoarse with emotion, "Aye, I suppose the lass does get under my skin."

"Aye, I do suppose," Donald muttered in a whisper thick with sarcasm.

Not looking at his uncle, Ewen continued, "I've sworn off the lasses. With John as my heir, there's no need for me to take another wife."

"So lassies are just for breeding then, is it?"

"Och, don't fash me, man. You know what it is I'm saying to you."

"Make it clearer for an old man such as myself, aye?"

Ewen pulled Ares to an abrupt halt and turned to face Donald. "I'll not discuss this more than need be. You know my marriage to Mairi was a farce. John will be Lochiel after me and so I'm not in want of another wife." He kicked his horse back into an easy trot.

Donald called out to Ewen's back, "You're just marking the clan's needs. What of the needs of the laird himself?"

Donald took the laird's silence as an invitation to continue. "Soon the day will dawn when you look in the mirror and see an old man looking back. Don't be like me, lad—a lonely old bull with naught to show for a life of hard work."

"Uncle, you're a feared warrior and an indispensable part of this clan. I'll not have you speaking so—"

Donald interrupted gruffly, "Don't be daft. Warrior, farmer, tinker, I don't care what I am, lad. What I really want is a plump lass to warm my bed, with a smile on her face and a kind word at the ready. And if you've not yet realized that's what it comes to, then you're greener than I took you for."

Ewen didn't respond. Donald barked, "Are you listening, boy, or am I just gathering wool?"

"I hear, uncle. Now mind me. The lass doesn't belong to this time or this place." His voice dropped to a dangerous whisper. "I'll wager that what she truly wants isn't a man such as is bred by the Highlands."

"Then you've no eyes in your head, lad. Lily looks at you with a spark in her eye, like she's drowning and you're a gulp of air."

Ewen muttered angrily to himself, "I'm the one who's drowning, man."

The laird cleared his throat then continued in a tone that left no doubt as to whether or not the subject was changed. "It's time to stop nattering like a bunch of lassies and discuss what we're on for."

Donald paused a moment and decided to allow his nephew the abrupt change in conversation. In a garrulous tone that belied the more sensitive subject matter, he asked, "So our fool general friend found he couldn't grease your palms so now he's building a wee fort nigh to Cameron lands, eh?"

"Aye, uncle, I don't yet know what the man's about, but reports have it he's building more than a wee fort. Scouts say he's putting up an entire bloody garrison. He found I wouldn't abide his pretty words nor his dirty bribes so he reckons constructing it with my own timber might make me repent."

"And our General Monk will find it no easy task to finish this wee outpost of his?"

"Aye. That's precisely the plan, uncle." Ewen kicked his horse into an easy canter and added with a husky laugh, "That's it precisely."

Chapter 23

Lily sat at Ewen's desk, mustering her courage. She'd spent the morning racing around the keep in an effort to sort out her new puppy, and had quickly realized that dog ownership was much more than long walks and games of fetch. Even the most basic task of feeding posed a challenge. Convincing the cook that a mere animal merited scraps of meat from the laird's table had been no small feat.

Before she knew it, the day was half over and she had yet to begin John's lessons. She had decided to make her absence up to him with a special art project, but had yet again found that, in this century, the easiest tasks became formidable. Lily thought nothing could be simpler than helping John with a pen and ink drawing—or quill and ink as she was calling it—but she was having trouble tracking down something as meager as a pot of ink.

And so she sat, frozen. Lily knew that the laird sat at his desk to write letters, and she assumed that somewhere within its hulking mass there was ink to be found, but she was nonetheless nervous about the prospect of poking through his things.

The desk was a solid, well-built piece, made of a glossy,

reddish brown wood Lily guessed to be mahogany. She had smiled at the apples in the corner, resting in a dainty ceramic bowl that looked out of place on such a masculine piece of furniture. So much for her gripe, she thought, that there was no fresh produce in old Scotland.

Ewen's tidiness surprised her. A candle, a small sheaf of papers, and a few gray feathers resting in a simple silver quill holder were the only other things to adorn the desk's surface.

She helped herself to one of the tiny red and yellow apples and, puckering at the sour taste, considered which drawer to open first. Three of them flanked her on either side, sturdy and squat atop fearsome clawed feet. A long thin drawer was in the center, a bronze key still in its latch.

She reached out to open a side drawer and balked, struck by last-minute panic. Perhaps she was crossing a line here. She had looked for Robert—he'd surely have some ink to lend her—but he had been nowhere to be found. Tapping her fingers on the bronze drawer knob, she hesitated. If Ewen left the desk's only key in the latch, she thought, how sensitive could its contents be? The ink was for his son, and he surely had some in here somewhere.

Convincing herself that the laird wouldn't grudge her, she opened the top drawer and was surprised to see the collage John had made of the seashore. Shuffling it to the side, Lily stared in disbelief. The drawer was stacked full with John's artwork. She had often wondered what became of all of his creations. She always made certain to display her favorites, and had just assumed it was Kat who whisked away the rest during one of her many cleaning binges. Lily hadn't considered that Ewen might be squirreling away his son's projects. In fact, she hadn't even realized he'd been paying attention.

But now, rifling through page after page of John's earnest drawings and collages, Lily's throat clenched. The laird obviously loved his son, but it was unexpected to see how he treasured him so.

What else didn't she know about Ewen? Compelled to discover more, she opened the next drawer, and the next. It felt like such an intimate look at the man, and seeing the things that he cherished fascinated her.

She gently leafed through a stack of yellowed letters, tied

up with string, addressed to Ewen's father. They had been written long ago in a woman's hand. His mother's hand, Lily deduced.

Amusement lit her eyes as she opened the next drawer, so orderly, and full of clean parchment that was stacked neatly and arranged in two piles according to size.

The next drawer held a small stack of essays, each bound with a leather cord and dense with black script. They looked to be obscure treatises on science and nature.

Lily was utterly enthralled, now hungry for what other secrets she might uncover, for other glimpses of the man. Ewen's doings, his pursuits, his heart.

She opened the top middle drawer to find a gorgeous walnut box nestled perfectly inside. It had a leather lid attached by delicate brass hasps, and bore a gilt hound medallion at its center. The sharp smell of pitch filled her senses as she slowly opened the box. A grid of small compartments neatly organized several pots of ink, blotting sand, a nib cutter, a beautiful seal made of turned wood, and red sealing wax.

She had her ink. She should go.

But Lily couldn't stop herself. There was one drawer to go, on the bottom right. Surely just an inconsequential drawer, she thought, easy to walk away from, yet she couldn't fight the compulsion. Not giving herself a chance to think twice, she leaned over and pulled.

It was empty but for a small leather-bound volume. Lily picked the book up and studied it. A floral design was stamped in an oval around the title, written in an elaborate gilt script. *Poems* by someone named William Drummond of Hawthornden. A bewildered smile warmed her face. She wouldn't have thought the laird to be a man of verse. Captivated, she opened the book and began to peruse its pages of sonnets, some lovely, some florid, alternating Scottish imagery with abstruse references to Greek mythology.

As she read, Lily noticed a spot toward the middle of the book that kept separating, as if the binding had been broken and wanted to return to a well-read page. She placed the book flat on the desk and flipped to the spot, marked, she saw, with a small scrap of paper.

As she turned the bookmark in her hands, a current of

energy snapped along Lily's body. She knew this little scrap of paper well. It was a quick, she thought inferior, sketch she'd dashed off in the gardens one evening. She had tried to capture the dramatic fall of late-afternoon light on an herb bed and, unsatisfied and frustrated, she'd set the drawing aside and promptly forgot it.

Baffled, she turned to the poem that Ewen had marked. As she read, fire crackled through her, as if she had to will herself whole or she would fragment, dissolving into a wisp of smoke and air.

> *Then is she gone? O fool and coward I!*
> *O good occasion lost, ne'er to be found!*
> *What fatal chains have my dull senses bound,*
> *When best they may, that they not fortune try?*

It was a poem of regret. Of a chance not taken. Of denying the will of fortune, that same fickle instrument which had sent her to Ewen.

Why would he have such a poem? In her mind, she heard his voice, rich and deep, calling *"Lil'."* Her recollection of him was vivid, as though, despite a great distance, she could sense his summoning. Vertigo, like the earth suddenly falling from her body, dizzied Lily, and she felt something inside her answer. And a thought, radiant and clear, rang through her head. To suspect Ewen's love for her and feel this elation could only be possible if she loved him in return.

Comprehension came to her like the sun through parting clouds. Lily understood that although she came from another time, her heart belonged to Ewen, and here, in this poem, she read the glimmer of his own desire.

Her mind raced with the possibility of leaving the world of the future behind forever. Could she stay? Would he even want her to? Though the prospect didn't scare her, neither did she know if she'd be ready to say good-bye to modern America forever. Lily had always assumed that someday she'd mend ways with her mother; to close that door now was something to be considered.

She may not know what her own future held, but she knew what she would have of her present. The past months had been physically challenging—a dizzying, sometimes violent struggle. And yet, as she read and reread the stanza, something clicked into place, as if her body and heart and mind were, at long last, grounded and in harmony.

The poet had written that only in following the impulse of the heart did one avoid ruin. And now, hopeful that Ewen might dare try his destiny, Lily felt the freedom to pursue her own heart's desire.

❁

"'Tis about time, fool lad." Smoke from Gormshuil's pipe curled about the old woman's head, filling the small cave with the sweet smells of cherry and bark. "What, are you not well? Come in with you. Sit, sit, boy, that's it, down by the fire mind you, or you'll catch your death."

Ewen moved to sit down across from the old witch, and after all these years found he still had to force himself to meet the intensity of her watery blue gaze. Gormshuil clicked the clay pipe between her teeth and shot Ewen an arch grin that made him feel like a boy of ten rather than a man full grown.

"Aye, that's the way lad. I've waited for you nigh on one moon now."

Ewen could find no words, and Gormshuil's cackle broke the silence. "You're gaping like a dead fish, you are. I hope you use prettier manners on your new lassie than with an old *cailleach* like myself."

"You've my apologies." Ewen's deep voice resonated off the cramped stone walls. "Though I don't ken your meaning. I've no lassie. Or rather, there's a lass, but she's not mine. I've come merely to find her way home."

Gormshuil once again laughed. "No lassie, eh? So say you, boy." She took a couple shallow, distracted pulls on her pipe, and the thick coils of smoke made her eyes half-lidded and teary. Just as it seemed she had forgotten his presence in the cave, the old woman's voice cracked into song.

"*Came a lass to Alba,*
To her an ancient shore.
She traveled along the star road,
Come seeking a hero of yore.

Leaves of deadly nightshade,
The white Lily pricked red,
When she braved the road to Alba,
Her fate, a hero long dead.

"Nay lassie indeed." She barked another laugh, and clarity abruptly replaced the distant gaze in her rheumy eyes as if emerging from a trance.

The laird cleared his throat. "Respectfully, Gormshuil, I'd have you speak your mind. I've no head for songs clothed in riddles and rhymes. You know my plight. Aye, there's a lass, you've the truth of it there. But you don't know the weight of it. I'm in want of your help if I'm to return her to her rightful home, so I beg you brew the tea leaves or do what it is you do to see the way of it for me."

Ewen fought to mind his tongue with the old woman, but his patience was wearing thin. His grandfather once told him wise women spoke in mysterious riddles so that people not touched with the sight would be made to choose their own way. "Son," he'd told Ewen long ago, "the witch woman is but a torch on fate's dark path. Though she'll not guide the fall of your feet, she will light your step."

More than once she had favorably advised the lairds of his clan, and he knew the great risk it would be to ignore her words, but singing a song and insisting Lily was somehow his was not the sort of wisdom he sought from the old witch.

"My Lochiel"—the gravity in her voice roused Ewen from his thoughts—"'tis you who doesn't ken the weight of it. The star road lets but a few pass. Mind me, boy." The sternness of her words brought his eyes back to hers. "You neglect its signs at your peril."

"Are you saying"—Ewen hesitated—"that she's meant to stay?"

"I'll not say one thing or t'other." She paused to consider her next thought. "Tell your lass, a person has but one present and best she open her eyes to it."

Ewen stared into the fire. He had just assumed Lily would return to her own time. That she could choose to stay suddenly seemed so simple, so obvious, but was nonetheless a revelation to the laird. In that moment, he experienced a flash of relief so profound, Ewen realized how his feelings for Lily had deepened. To hear Gormshuil tell it, those feelings might actually be ordained by a greater force that, in bringing Lily across time to him, played destiny's own hand.

But then Gormshuil added in a voice once again thinned by age, "If you've not the heart, boy, here's her path home." She thrust a soiled sheet toward the laird. The paper was ancient, its creases nearly disintegrated from generations of folding and unfolding. He held it gently up to the firelight, studying the series of lines and points, surrounded by an ancient runic pattern. It was a crudely rendered star chart that Ewen recognized as integral to returning Lily to her own time.

"You ken Donald Dubh, aye?" Gormshuil asked, nodding toward the old parchment.

"And what Cameron doesn't ken their first laird? Black Donald led the clan over two hundred years ago. And what has he to do with this business?"

"Patience, lad," Gormshuil chastised, stabbing the stem of her pipe toward Ewen, "that's my story, if you'll give me the telling of it."

Exaggeratedly taking her time, the old woman settled her skirts, touched a stick to the fire to relight her pipe, took a few thoughtful puffs, then began, "There's always been bickering betwixt Highlanders, oft times full war. And the earliest days of Clan Cameron saw no different. They'd the usual skirmishes over cattle and lands, and one day the chief Donald Dubh Cameron saw a friend become his enemy.

"Now"—Gormshuil paused to suck rapidly at the dying pipe as she considered—"it isn't like a Cameron laird to shrink from battle, but for whatever reason, the Black Donald fled to Ireland."

Ewen interjected, "And Donald's enemy took Cameron clan lands as his own."

"Aye, lad, but something happened to Donald Dubh when he was in Ireland. Say what you will of the Irish"—she cackled softly—"an Irishman may fritter the day, nose in the trees on the hunt for elves, but they're a canny bunch. They've one foot in the world of the fae, and Donald Dubh Cameron, he returned from Ireland with tales of skiffling through the stars to other times."

"He returned with force," Ewen said, "taking his lands back, and beating his enemy handily. Woman," he chuckled, "are you meaning to tell me that Black Donald returned from Ireland with a fairy's star chart and marshaled heroes of old to help him win his lands back?"

Anger glinted in the old woman's eyes and she snatched the paper from the laird's hand. She spat, "Those are your words, boy. I know not what transpired with the man, just that he returned with a bit of fae lore about the traveling through time." Her voice calmed, and she mused, "I don't ken what manner of bargain the Donald struck, but this chart seems to have the good of the clan at its heart. You've seen with your own eyes that the maze pulls people through, who knows what for."

"Och," Ewen interrupted, "Robert came through and it isn't as though his role is clear as crystal."

"Mmh," she grunted, chomping on the stem of her pipe, "and now it's the lass, your Lily, who's some purpose now."

Gormshuil gave an inscrutable shrug to her shoulders and handed Ewen the star chart.

"But what use are any of your papers, woman, when we can't even find this maze?"

"The maze?" Gormshuil grinned, pipe clenched between her teeth. "Of course you can't find the maze, lad, it's not yet built, aye? 'Twill be built by one who comes later than you, who seeks retreat from his fate."

Ewen stared in impatient confusion.

"Worry not about the labyrinth, boy. It's but a chimera concealing the true heart that lies beating within. The pattern, the lay of lines and symbols, that is the power." She waved dismissively to the paper in his hand. "Your lass will recognize the shapes, she'll ken what to do. You only need to puzzle the when of it."

He stared at the chart, then looked at her, brow furrowed.

Gormshuil tsked. "Don't put on the sour face with me, lad. For the nonce, the lass isn't the only affair to vex you. You've ample troubles to come. Don't be like that Irishman mooning at a tree, without eyes for the forest around you. Cromwell waits in England to set flame to tinder, and the hand he reaches into the Highlands is that coxcomb general. The man will soon bedevil you plenty, and right on your doorstep."

"Aye," Ewen sighed, "that would be Monk."

Gormshuil nodded. "He's got it in for you, boy, for some reason." She hooted suddenly with laughter, cut short by a racking cough. The woman spat into the fire and continued in graver tones, "Lochiel, you must heed the warning of one whose days grow short, who kens the pain of losing all to cowards in English coats. Don't be mistaken, this Monk may be soft as uncooked pork, but he's tough as a withy. And he's taken a notion to you and that lovely spit of paradise you call Inverlochy."

Chapter 24

Ewen sat at his desk, absentmindedly twirling his *uisge* around the heavy glass snifter. He wasn't a big drinker, but there was nothing like a dram of good, peaty malt to collect a man's thoughts. He knew that first and foremost he should pay heed to her portentous prophesies about General Monk and his plans for Clan Cameron, but the laird couldn't get Gormshuil's words about Lily out of his mind.

Ignoring the sidelong looks of the castle staff, he'd foregone dinner and went straight to his rooms upon his return. He didn't know what to make of the visit with the witch. She seemed to say one thing and then another. Or rather, sing one thing and then another. He knew she wouldn't tell him the path he was to take, but it certainly seemed as if she was trying to give him a hint. He just couldn't believe it to be true. Ewen hadn't considered that keeping Lily, truly keeping her with him for always, could be an option.

He looked down once again at the wee scrap the old woman had tucked into his hand with the star chart. She wrote in an aggravatingly elaborate hand, but her instructions were clear enough.

"When her today becomes tomorrow,
When the hunter looks east in the sky's dark dome
Where the jewel of the night rises bonny bright,
Then can she return to yestreen's home."

Many men might not have understood Gormshuil's in-structions, but she chose her words well for one such as Ewen, priding himself as he did on his knowledge of the sciences. With but a moment's thought, he easily deciphered just what—and when—it was that the old witch directed. When today becomes tomorrow he readily understood to mean mid-night. The sky's braw hunter could be none other than Orion, the constellation named for the great hunter from Greek mythology. And, though they may not know it by name, many a Highlander would recognize their sky's bonny jewel as the bright morning planet Jupiter.

And it was Jupiter that ruled the skies just now. From what he could tell by his last night spent under the stars, the planet was steadily closing in on Orion from the east. Which meant that Lily would soon be able to traverse what Gormshuil had called the star road to return to her own time. Her real home.

Ewen raked his fingers through his tousled black hair and once more played Gormshuil's words through his head.

"Her fate, a hero long dead."

Was she not advising that Lily's true place was by Ewen's side? Or was that merely the wishful thinking of a besotted wretch, for that is what he was beginning to fear of himself.

The door to his study suddenly swung open and slammed against the wall with a force that belied its heavy weight.

Lily stood in the doorway looking startled to see him. "What are you doing here?"

Pensive as he was from his current reading materials, Ewen's tone was gently playful. "Well, 'tis my room, lass."

"I know that." She began to get flustered. "I . . . it's just . . . I can't find Finn and I thought he might be in here. But I guess not, thanks."

Lily began to edge her way back out the door but was stopped by an unusually talkative Ewen. "So you've lost the mongrel, is it?"

Despite herself, Lily couldn't help but slip into their flirtatious repartee. "No, merely . . . misplaced."

Ewen grinned outright and the effect on Lily was like that of standing in front of a blazing hearth on a gloomy day. "Well, lass, shall we have a look then?"

She was taken aback by his sudden effusiveness, but before she had a chance to respond the laird was up on his feet, looking behind curtains, under tables, and behind chairs.

"Really, Ewen, I appreciate this, but I think if Finn were in here he would've heard me and greeted me by now."

"Don't doubt how much of a fancy your wee mutt has taken to me, Lil'." The rakish glint in his eyes was disarmingly out of character for the usually stoic warrior and, against her better judgment, Lily found herself relaxing.

Ewen and Lily suddenly froze at precisely the same moment, their eyes meeting as both became aware of the sound of a light thumping coming from beneath Ewen's desk.

The dog had been at his feet under the desk the whole time.

"Aye, you see now, lass. Your Finn may have an Irish name, but he's a braw Scotsman who kens his laird."

"Mmhmm." Lily turned to leave. "Come on, traitor, let's get out of here and let the laird get back to his critically important business."

"Stop. I mean . . . Lil' . . . will you not bide a wee moment with me?"

Lily was now completely disarmed by Ewen's erratic, almost tender, behavior. She heard her heart say the word before her head knew what she was about. The word that, at that moment, had became invested with so much more weight that its three letters implied. That answered so many more questions than merely the one he'd just asked.

"Yes."

Ewen nodded slowly, his gaze never leaving hers, and it was as if they were both assenting to something that had become much larger than themselves. Lily felt her spirit soar at the rightness of it all. And the recklessness. It felt unlike her, unlike the Lily who had always done the right things, the responsible things. Who had denied herself a life as an artist in favor of stock options and a mortgage. Who had dated responsible men. Never the dangerous ones. And Ewen was nothing if not dangerous. Yet with the realization that she loved him came a sense of joyous completion.

"I know how you can return home, Lil'."

She heard him speak the words but she had to replay them over in her mind before she could make sense of them. It was the last thing she had expected. She damned herself bitterly. She felt like a foolish girl who had been caught doodling Mrs. Lily Cameron on her schoolbooks.

The air rushed out of Lily's lungs and she wondered for a moment if her body had forgotten how to inhale. How dare he, yet again . . .

Ewen chuckled, and Lily felt the tears sting her eyes at his dismissal.

"Nay, nay, lass, don't fret so." Ewen rushed to her side, embracing her without thinking, as if it were the most natural thing in the world for the two of them to do. "I see the thunderheads on that bonny face of yours. I was saying, the witch Gormshuil showed me your way home." He pulled away and, keeping one arm cinched tightly around her, tilted her chin up so that her reddened eyes could meet his. "But right now, Lil', all I truly know is that I want you, need you, here with me."

Smiling through her tears Lily nodded once, giving Ewen the only assent he needed. Still gingerly cupping her chin, the laird brought his mouth down to hers so slowly Lily felt her heart break and mend again a thousand times.

Finally his lips brushed hers, whispering over her mouth as tenderly as if it were his breath itself. He gently deepened the kiss, and Lily's body responded like a blossom unfurling in the sun. The measured cadence of his breathing was the only indication of the great control Ewen exerted over his body, now taut with desire. She opened her mouth to him and pressed her body against his with an urgency that swept them both away from any thought of place or time, save for one exclusively their own.

Their hands roved each other's bodies, fingers touching and exploring as if their senses had been long deprived of form and texture, hands holding fast to the solidity of the other as a drowning man would the shore. Ewen's hand found her breast, chafing it into a rigid peak beneath the coarse linen of her dress.

The intensity of her response brought tears to Lily's eyes. She had long denied herself the pleasures of her body and had forgotten just how much she needed to be held. And Ewen was doing so much more than just holding her. His touch was skillful, as if he lived to serve her body alone, anticipated its every want, mastered its every need. He was awakening in her a violent current of desire that coursed with a depth and power that she didn't know she possessed.

The newfound pure and joyful lust of her body brought with it a newer and even headier sensation. She wanted him. But with that wanting came a glimpse of something even larger and more frightening than the intensity of desire alone. Lily began to grasp just how deeply she had fallen in love with him.

Her breath came in ragged gasps as she tried to get closer and closer still to Ewen, wrapping her leg around his, rubbing herself along the entirety of his body, all coiled muscle, every inch of him stiff with his need for her. Just as Lily began to feel almost angry that she couldn't be any closer, the laird lifted her effortlessly and carried her before the hearth. With a flick of his wrist, his tartan billowed out and fluttered to the ground to protect them from the hard, cold stone of the floor.

In one fluid motion, he lifted her dress up and over her head as he laid her gently down. Pulling off his own coarse tunic, he lay next to her, and Lily gasped at the beauty of him, fully erect, with the rippling muscles of a warrior gilt in the dancing firelight.

Ewen caught her assessing gaze and the intensity of the moment found some release as he chuckled knowingly, for he recognized her hunger for him writ clear on Lily's face. He silenced her astonished grumble of protest with a hungry kiss then abruptly pulled away.

"Lil'." Ewen's voice was choked with emotion. "My Lil' . . ." He slowly traced out her long, pale curls into a halo around her head. "You're as brilliant as the sun and bonnier than the flower you were named for."

He swung his leg over her and pinned her hands lightly beneath his. "And I'll have you now."

Lily wasn't sure if he was being playful or serious and she didn't care. She savored the feeling of living truly, heeding her most heartfelt of desires, with mind, heart, and body in accord. She realized that all she wanted—all she had ever wanted—was this moment. This single moment that, looking back, everything in her life seemed to lead to. Suddenly everything about her confused, lost, and lonely existence made sense as necessary steps to this coming together. That indeed the universe had even conspired to bring her together with this one man.

She felt as if she were parched earth and Ewen the rain. She wanted not just to have him, but to absorb him with her very being. And, as the wishes of her heart, thoughts of her mind, and longing of her body became one, everything fell away and all that was left was the aching need of the flesh.

Lily felt the sudden and insistent craving to taste his mouth and clawed at his back to bring him to her. All gentleness fled as she nipped on his lips and tongue, the need to savor every part of him consuming her. She wrapped her legs about his waist seeking out his hardness, and he rubbed easily against the slickness between her legs. Rather than quenching her desire, the feel of him so close to her just kindled it to a fever pitch and she moaned with her need for him.

Ewen had never experienced such unchecked desire and growled in response, tearing his mouth away from hers to take her breast, suckling her between teeth and tongue. Lily thought her heart would burst to have one more moment without him inside of her.

Taking his head between her hands, she pulled his face up and pierced him with her gaze. "Then take me," she snarled, the intensity of her want giving edge to her voice.

The laird obliged.

In a single movement their mouths and bodies collided and Ewen drove into her like a wave crashing on the beach, moving with inexorable force and intent, yet soft too, as the water sweeps over the sand in the crash and whisper of the tides' ebb and flow.

Lily thought she would shatter into a thousand pieces as all control was lost to her. No longer conscious of the separateness of their bodies, they moved with a singular impulse, one moment all slow tenderness, the next fiercely carnal.

Her heart pounded, blood thrumming just beneath the surface of her skin. Lily's body felt insubstantial, as if she would drift away were it not for the man over her, inside her. She wrapped her arms tightly around him, clutching him to her until she felt the give of his skin under her nails, and heard his responding moan deep in his throat. Want of him consumed her, and she took Ewen ever deeper until they climaxed in effortless unison.

She knew at that moment that she had been changed forever. Belonged to Ewen forever.

It was Ewen who roused first. He chafed the cool, pebbled skin of Lily's arm, kissed one eyelid then the other, and rose to dress.

"You won't get very far without this." Smiling, Lily gestured to the tartan that lay tangled between her legs.

"I thought you were still resting, lass."

"No, I'm just this side of comatose, but how could I sleep after that?"

A satisfied—and quite proprietary—look spread across the laird's features. "Then come with me. I've something to say to the men and I'd have you by my side."

Something about the possessiveness of his tone made Lily smile so broadly she felt like a foolish schoolgirl until she saw Ewen's features break into an equally adoring grin.

"Are you saying that we have to get up?" Stroking her hands along his kneeling legs, Lily reached up for the laird and pulled him back down to her.

"Och, woman, you'll be the death of me." Ewen pinned her legs with his, and bent to taste Lily's neck. He whispered in her ear, "But I'll die a happy man."

A sudden pounding at the door startled them. They shared a conspiratorial look and ignored it. Instead, Ewen leaned down and kissed her deeply. Rocking his hips into hers, he began to tease his thumb around Lily's nipple, tracing slowly from breast to belly.

"Lochiel!" The urgency of Donald's shout was finally enough to tear Ewen away from her.

"The keep itself best be afire, old man," he growled. "What's—"

"Ewen, it's Hamish . . . the redcoats, man. Ewen, the lad's been killed."

The laird sprang off the floor and wrapped himself in his

tartan in a single motion. He looked at Lily for a long moment, getting strength from this woman whom he could tell, from the anguish on her face, was probably one of the only people who would know how deep this loss would cut him.

"Ewen, I'm so sorry," Lily whispered. "What can I do?"

"There's naught you can do, Lil', but just stay by me."

Chapter 25

Lily was given more than a few curious glances when they joined Ewen's men already assembled and waiting in the common room.

Donald cocked an eyebrow, and Ewen shot, "The lass stays with me, aye?" His words may have been posed as a question, but Ewen's tone brooked no response from his uncle.

"Aye, Lochiel." Had Ewen not already been so preoccupied, he might have noticed the flicker of understanding in his uncle's eye. Rallying the clan together in time of battle was a private matter reserved for Cameron family members only. And, with the possible exception of the laird's wife herself, men were generally the only ones in attendance.

Ewen stood at the head of the long oak table, and his presence alone was enough to silence the room full of men. He turned to Donald. "Now give me a full accounting, man."

"Lochiel"—Donald recited the events in an uncharacteristically dispirited voice—"General Middleton and about three score of men were surprised by two regiments of Cromwell troops near Loch Garry. All the Highlanders were slain, some mayhaps dispersed. But most slain." He sighed. "We don't yet know the full count from Clan Cameron, but young Hamish fell." The old man rubbed his face vigorously and added with a grim smile, "And I'll wager the lad gave those redcoat bastards a fight. His was a braw sword arm."

"Aye." Ewen visibly fought to gather himself. "I'd wager that as well, uncle." He cleared his throat and addressed the room. "So it is, men. If this Monk has a yen for a fight, the Camerons are happy to oblige. We ride on the morrow."

The room erupted into a chorus of whoops and cries, and the gathering of clansmen transformed into a troop of battle-hungry warriors.

"Silence." Ewen's voice was dangerously quiet. As much as he craved a fight with the British, he never took bloodshed lightly.

"We ride for Achdalieu at first light and have much to prepare before then. We've but few ready clansmen to face an unknown number of redcoat regiments. So we'll just make our numbers an advantage, aye?" Ewen quieted a new round of enthusiastic shouts. "If Monk was last at Loch Garry, Achdalieu gives us the best possible position. We'll need provisions for a small company of men for as long as a fortnight. Donald will see to supplies, but you'll need to ready your own mounts and gear.

"General Monk tried to buy our allegiance and found that Clan Cameron is not for the selling." Another round of cheers exploded among the gathered men, silenced just as quickly by a steely look from their laird.

"Laird, may I?"

"Aye, uncle."

"The lad who brought the news spied Cromwell ships coming from the open sea and up Loch Linnhe like flies creeping along a horse's arse."

"Well, men," Ewen replied, "we're the whip that's going to flick these bloody flies back to where they came from."

While his men shouted and clapped their approval, Ewen walked to a side table and poured himself a snifter of whisky from a decanter sitting there. When they finally quieted, the laird continued, "That confirms other intelligence we've gathered on the matter." Ewen didn't share that Gormshuil's prophecy was his intelligence. "Monk's come equipped with more than enough supplies and men to build himself a wee fort where he can rest his red tails awhile."

A chorus of voices erupted once again and a redheaded clansman shouted over the din, "I say we give him a proper Highland welcome!"

"Aye, that we will, Malcolm." Ewen couldn't help but smile, the fellow had such incongruous freckles for his weathered, middle-aged face. Malcolm was a good family man, and the laird was proud to have roused one such as he to battle.

"It seems," Ewen pronounced, "that our enemy has offered us their throats to be cut."

"Aye," Donald shouted, "the redcoats won't be able to step from their wee fort without the Camerons taking a bite!"

"We ride for Achdalieu on the morrow." Ewen glanced at Lily as he continued, "And will wait for the bastards on the north side of Loch Eli."

He could see the anxiety etched plainly on her face, but there was nothing to do for it. He couldn't merely sit by while Monk erected a fort on his property, felling Cameron men and Cameron timber in order to do so.

"This won't sit well, but I'm to send some of you home." He continued over the grumbling, "Aye, I ken you'll all want to . . . express your grievances to Monk and his men, but you need to secure your livestock, your homes. We don't know how long this will take, or how much it will take from us, aye?" His men nodded, understanding his implication. They not only would need provisions assembled for the coming days, but there was a sizable chance that they would need healthy, whole men in reserve as well.

"I'll be taking thirty-two of you, meaning there'll be more than a few redcoats for every one of us." Ewen paused for effect. "And I reckon the redcoats still won't like the odds."

The men roared their approval, but this time the laird didn't interrupt their carrying on. Despite his jesting, the odds were actually decidedly not in the Highlanders' favor. Ewen had misgivings about taking so few men with him, but ultimately decided that a lean and swiftly moving party would be their best strategy.

"Then gentlemen, it's as simple as camping in the woods for a wee spell while we await our chance."

Lily had been growing increasingly pale during Ewen's speech and he thought he'd best cut the meeting short, lest he have an even more dangerous battle on his hands.

"Now off with you," he concluded abruptly. "Donald will give orders to you individually."

❀

Lily sat in disbelief. She had finally surrendered her body and soul to a man, and not only was he standing there blithely making jokes about cutting throats, he was riding off to face a well-armed regiment of what was likely to be over one hundred British soldiers and his almost certain death.

"You're a beauty when you look so fashed, Lil'." Ewen came up from behind her and began rubbing her shoulders.

"Fashed, nothing. I can't believe just when I decide to be with you, you choose to ride off into the sunset like some tragic hero. I'm familiar with the history of Scotland, Ewen." The laird's hands stilled at her words. "I don't know exactly what happens when, but I do know that you don't exactly have the greatest odds here on your little glory ride."

"Aye, well"—his voice was unusually serene—"I do what I must. Don't worry yourself so." He turned her chair around to kneel between her legs. "I've no intention to leave you now, after it's taken me so long to find you. And I will do all in my power to ride back to you. But if I live my life in fear of its ending"—he cupped her chin in his hand—"och, Lil', I'm no good to either of us. I'll not live my life as half a man. That's the certain death. Do you understand, lass?"

Lily had to admit that she did. It was precisely those qualities that she had fallen in love with—Ewen's courage, strength, integrity—that now drove him to ride out to protect his land and his people.

"Yes, I know. You have to go." Lily managed a smile, her voice hoarse from unshed tears. "But I don't have to like it."

❀

"I'll be what?" Robert was livid.

"Mind your tone, lad. You'll not run off with us when I need you here." Although Ewen was distractedly cleaning and readying the various weapons arranged along the edge of his bed, there was no doubt in his tone as to who was in charge of the conversation.

"I may, in general, prefer the company of books to swords, Ewen, but I will remind you that I and mine are under siege also. I was as fond of Master Hamish as you, or did you not realize? *Nemo me impune lacessit!* The kings of Scotland themselves thus proclaim. No one provokes me with impunity, Lochiel! I'm no less a man than your battle-hungry crofters, and I dare say I would have some value on a field of battle. If you would ever try me."

Ewen studied his foster brother. He had taken Robert for granted, assuming his love of books merely hid a disdain for the world of the warrior's arts in which Ewen steeped himself. A fierce sense of pride welled in the laird as he realized that Robert yearned for vengeance as much as any other clansman.

"Or is it that you would have me stay behind to watch your woman for you, Ewen? Is that it?"

The laird paused to inhale deeply as if collecting his temper then pinned his foster brother with a steely glare. "Take heed, Robert. You'd be wise not to test me."

Ewen sat, resting his elbows on his thighs in an unusually resigned posture. "Listen, lad—" Robert grumbled a protest that Ewen immediately silenced. "Och, that's what you are to me. A lad yet. Now hear me. You've seen skirmishes and done more than enough to prove yourself a man of this clan. You'll see the wrong end of a redcoat musket soon enough."

Ewen's tone softened as he continued, "But you know as well as I, Robbie, that I need you here. The clan needs you here. Aye, you tell it true, I do think of your mind before I think of your sword arm. But it's your mind that I need now. A thoughtful mind about the keep. We've no way to know what—or who—could happen to the heart of Cameron lands with so many clansmen away."

Robert's angry expression began to slacken and he flopped down into a chair at Ewen's bedside. The laird added, "At any rate, 'twill be hard enough to leave Lil' without your histrionics."

Their eyes met and they shared a subdued laugh, the tension in the room palpably relieved. "Yes, Ewen, I know, I know. I see the right of it. But it does not mean I wouldn't relish riding to Achdalieu by your side, brother."

Ewen leaned forward to clap Robert on the back, then fastening a firm grip on his shoulder, he added gravely, "Protect her, Robert."

"I will at that, Lochiel, with all that I have at my disposal. Should any misadventure come our way, you can consider me a man prepared: *In omnia paratus!*" Ewen looked skeptical and Robert shot him a reassuring smile. "Dear Ewen. Don't you know? I would proffer my life, if it came to that."

❁

There was one more person the laird had to see before leaving. His son John might be the youngest member of the household, but it made the visit no less daunting. Ewen had never known his own father well and that was a loss he felt keenly. The lad might only be ten, but in fewer summers than Ewen cared to count, John would be a man and ready to bear arms in a field like Achdalieu. The laird vowed to be a better father to the boy, and if he didn't return from the upcoming battle, he wanted his son to have some meaningful memory of him.

It took some tracking to finally hunt him down. It seemed to be common knowledge to everyone but the laird that the kitchen gardens had become John's favorite haunt, and he had to smile at that. Ewen knew that Lily treasured the garden as her own special refuge and it warmed him that John felt the same. He wouldn't have figured the boy for such contemplative pursuits and he hoped it was a sign of the favorable effect Lily was having on the boy's life. Ewen smiled mischievously. He certainly knew *he* found Lily's effect to be favorable.

"There you are, lad. I was beginning to think you'd gone and hid yourself in Donald's saddlebags."

John looked up at his father with some trepidation. Many times these brief exchanges were less paternal than disciplinary.

"Och, lad, be at ease." Ewen studied the collection of leaves and flowers John had compiled. "Are you to make another of your wee pictures?"

John swept his hand out, quickly tousling the neat piles of greenery.

"Nay, lad, don't doubt yourself. You're not to be ashamed

of those pictures. You've a good eye. Lily's been showing me your best works."

"She . . . she has?"

"Aye, lad, she has, and you've the makings of a fine artist. Your collages are very striking. I like them."

"You . . . you do?"

"John, lad"—Ewen sighed and sat next to his son—"truly, be at your ease. I know we've not been the thickest of mates, but I'm vowed to change that. You're my only son, and I love you more than my life, lad. I don't always show it and for that you've my apologies." Ewen cuffed the boy playfully then grabbed him into a rough hug. "But you're to be laird after me. Someone needs to make a man of you, aye?"

John laughed and returned his father's hug, furtively wiping the tears from his eyes on Ewen's shirt.

"I'm away, and I'd give you a small token before I leave. You'll be a man soon and 'tis best you start acting like one. I've left Robert in charge, but no mistake, you're his close second, aye? I'll have you keep an eye on Lil' and the goings on at the keep."

"Aye, sir," John replied gravely.

"That's not the whole of it. My father . . . well, you ken my pin." Ewen pulled his brooch out of his sporran and studied the Celtic hounds crafted in silver. "My da gave it to me before his last battle." John gasped.

"Och, this will not my last battle, lad, so you can clear those storm clouds from over your head." Ewen placed the brooch in his son's hand.

"But I'd have you take this for your own, just the same. You've a notion of it's meaning?"

"Aye, sir. A Cameron clansman will be on no man's leash. We're sons of the hound."

"You speak truly, lad." Ewen beamed. "There's something else, though, which you may not yet know. We Cameron men, we've a war cry, aye? My hope is you've a few more summers yet to pass before you hear this for yourself. But a Cameron man into battle has but one thing in his heart and on his lips."

Ewen rose and, placing his hand on his son's head, told him, "*Chlanna nan con thigibh a so's gheibh sibh feoil.*"

"Sons of the hound"—the boy nodded solemnly—"come and get flesh."

Ewen smiled. "Remember those words well, lad." Ewen turned abruptly to leave, then paused, facing his son from the garden entrance. "You're a Cameron man. You'll grow to be a braw warrior and fine laird some day."

He studied his son, holding his gaze with the tenderness in his voice. "It doesn't mean you cannot also make fine pictures or write fine words. Don't be ashamed of the things you create, and you'll be more the man for it. And lad, you're also never to be ashamed to find tears in your eyes. A real man never is. 'Tis a stout heart that's made braver when touched by grief."

Chapter 26

Lily paused to arch backward over her heels, her fists massaging the small of her back. She had been aggressively weeding the small kitchen garden all afternoon, and her body was starting to rebel. Not to mention the fact she had a sneaking suspicion she had moved on from the weeds and was attacking some of the more legitimate herbs in the garden.

She reached out and distractedly patted Finn on the head. His tail thumped the ground and he rolled over to offer his belly for the same treatment. The poor mutt had been so faithful in the past days, and as if sensing her gloomy mood, he hadn't left her side since Ewen's departure.

The laird had left the day before and Lily had found herself hopelessly useless. She couldn't focus on John's lessons, was too distracted to draw, had no appetite to speak of, and certainly couldn't sleep. She decided to try working in the garden, that secret haven where she had found so much solace since her arrival at the castle. Lily had thought that the physical exertion and mindless rhythm of hoeing dirt and pulling weeds would clear her head of the horrible scenarios that played themselves over and over in her mind's eye.

Ewen getting ambushed. Ewen in a sword battle. Ewen getting shot. Ewen facing down a bayonet.

Lily was finding that she could be remarkably imaginative when it came to morbid scenarios involving Ewen and the wrong side of danger.

But sweat, dirt, and aching muscles did nothing to ease her. No matter what task she set herself to, Lily was unable to get his face out of her mind. The face that only she got to see, the tender side of him with a ready smile and eyes full of love.

"Lily!" John's shout tore her out of her daze.

She quickly turned her back to the boy to surreptitiously blot tears that she hadn't realized had fallen.

"I'm very sorry, Lil'."

She was surprised that John's use of Ewen's nickname for her cheered Lily rather than sinking her deeper into her melancholy.

"I can come back if it's a bother to you."

She opened her arms to him and mustered a smile. "No, no, sweetie, not at all. What's the matter?"

"Well . . ." John's voice drifted and the usually garrulous boy for once seemed at a loss for words.

"Do you miss your father?"

"No. I mean, aye, I do miss him, but that's not why I came to you." He screwed up his courage and continued, "I saw something. I didn't mean to see it. I mean, I wasn't spying. Well, maybe I was doing a wee bit of spying, but I saw something that I wasn't supposed to see, but I think I . . . I think you need to hear it. And Robert too. I think we need to tell Robert. Da says he's in charge. But you were the first one who I found. I mean, I didn't have to tell Robert first, I just . . ."

"No, no, I understand." John didn't usually concern himself with the comings and goings of the castle or with anything outside of his immediate circle. For him to be so alarmed over something he saw had Lily more than a little worried. "Now don't worry—we'll discuss the spying thing later. First just tell me what's got you so spooked."

"I thought I'd bide a wee in the hall." A pointed look from Lily inspired the boy to elaborate. "Och . . . I set myself up in the hall outside Rowena's door. I heard tell from my da that all the keep folk are to be keeping watch for her. Well, there's a dusty old hanging on the wall nigh to her door where you can stand and not be seen."

Lily glared at that bit of information and John quickly hedged, "I only know because, well, it's only that I heard . . . I heard . . .'twas another lad, aye, what said her maid sometimes opens the door wide with Rowena strutting about in just her petticoats plain as the nose on your face, for all to see."

"Mmhmm. Plain for all who are hiding in the dark hallway to see. We'll definitely be discussing that bit later. Now tell me what it is you saw exactly. Surely Rowena wouldn't do us the favor of just showing up in her room."

"Aye, well, I was in my spot when the door opened. I peeked out thinking to see Rowena, and I saw a man instead."

"Ugh." Lily put her hand up. "I don't know that I want to be hearing this."

"Nay, you're not understanding. The man's plaid were fastened with a MacKintosh brooch."

"You didn't like the man's pin?" Lily asked incredulously.

"Nay, Lil', it isn't that I didn't like his pin. Och, the brooch, it's a cat. You ken Da's hound pin, aye? What it means to him? Well the MacKintosh clan, their battle animal is a cat."

She recalled Ewen telling her of the infamous bad blood between Clans Cameron and MacKintosh. If what John was saying were true, it would be a serious accusation indeed.

A chill shuddered through Lily to think that a man from an enemy clan had made his way into Tor Castle while most of the Cameron clansmen were no longer under its roof. She didn't know the nature of their feuding but this could only have serious—and downright frightening—implications.

"Are you positive, John? It was dark after all."

"Aye, it was as plain as porridge, it was. I looked close thinking it could be an ill-made hound. So I looked till I knew for certain, and it were the MacKintosh cat alright."

"Okay." Lily gathered herself. If anything disastrous were to happen with Ewen out of the castle it would be up to her and Robert to get John to safety. She didn't know much about Scottish history but she did know that clan feuds often went beyond merely stealing cattle to all-out bloodbaths. "Tell me anything else you saw or heard, John. This is very important."

"Well there you two rascals are!" Robert sauntered into the garden. "I've been searching high and low to see what all the fuss is—" He stopped short at the grim expressions on Lily's and John's faces.

"What's this then?"

"I'm glad you're here, Robert." Lily was deeply relieved that Ewen had had the foresight to leave his foster brother behind. She was feeling much more at home of late, but dealing with a clash between two Highland clans was not something she felt prepared to face alone. "John was just telling me how he saw someone from the MacKintosh clan in the castle."

"Aye, and coming out of Rowena's rooms as bold as brass."

"As Virgil has it, *latet anguis in herba*. A snake lies in the grass, lad." Robert's brow furrowed. "But how can you be certain?"

"He'd a cat brooch." John looked at them accusingly. "I may be a lad but I'm not daft, I ken the MacKintosh token."

Robert visibly deflated as he sank to the ground. He paused to give Lily a meaningful look that did more to unsettle her than allay any of her quickly escalating fears.

"Ah, yes, the MacKintosh clan and that infernal cat." Robert turned to Lily to explain, "They've a motto, 'Touch Not the Cat Bot a Glove.'"

Lily looked perplexed so Robert clarified, "The MacKintosh symbol is a cat-a-mountain, their warning is that you're not to touch the cat without a glove." He paused, but Lily still didn't look satisfied. "Peculiar it may be, but Cameron's are hounds, MacKintosh's are cats, and the lairds have been at odds since Ewen's grandfather was Lochiel. Clan MacKintosh is disposed toward feuding over the same parcel of Cameron lands. And we've a saying here in the Highlands: Those that board with cats may count on scratches!" He muttered, "I suppose that is applicable to our fair Rowena as well. Feline indeed, that one was, but no matter. I don't know where she's got off to, but to have given him access to her rooms . . ." He gave Lily a somber look. "She's clearly in league with the MacKintosh."

Robert's voice then took on a gravity that would have surprised Lily had she not otherwise been so grateful to have him by her side to face the situation. "John, listen to us. This is very important, lad. Did he see you?"

"Nay, sir. I'm never seen if I don't want to be."

"Good. There's a clever boy."

"Robert," Lily interrupted, "what could someone from Clan MacKintosh want? Do you think we're in danger?"

"I fear it's our laird who faces the most danger." Robert paused for a moment, then added, "I never did trust that lass. I say the best course will be to keep our peace about this matter until we've the truth of it. With the men of the clan gone, there's no need to fley the castle staff with news of a MacKintosh underfoot."

Lily stilled. Ewen. The MacKintosh man would be on the hunt for him. The sudden knot of fear felt like a physical thing in her gut, and Lily choked it down, knowing she needed to be levelheaded if she were to get John out and to safety. If the MacKintosh clan wanted the laird dead, they'd surely have an eye to his heir as well. Lily felt adrenaline explode through her veins, like some additional sense firing to life.

Robert steadied her with a stoic smile, and she nodded her own resolve. He added, "No, we'll not stir the pot by betraying to the MacKintosh that we know of his involvement."

Lily was struck by a depth in Robert that she usually overlooked amidst all the proverbs and pedantry. She thought how he'd mature into a fine man, especially with Ewen's sage guidance and impeccable character as an example.

Ewen. If only he were here to help them. John's safety was foremost in her mind, and Lily was determined that she would give her own life to protect his. She only hoped that she would know the right course of action so that it wouldn't come to that.

An idea flashed into her mind and she startled them by suddenly blurting, "I've got it! The west wing of the house!"

Although John stared at her as if she'd lost her mind, Lily was touched by a reassuring look from Robert. "Yes, Lily, what have you in mind?"

"Assuming this mystery man is somehow a threat—and I think it wise to assume the worst—I think we need . . . I need to get John out of here and to safety immediately."

"I'm not leaving! I'm near a man grown and—" John was silenced by two withering looks.

Lily continued, "The back passageway that leads to the

western wing of the house. Ewen told me that the stairs continue down to a hidden doorway that leads out to the Loch."

"Yes. Yes, that there is. The door is likely covered by brush by now, so you must hack your way out, but once freed from the copious verdure there's a wee path that will lead your intrepid selves directly down to Loch Linnhe."

"Do you think you could arrange for a boat to meet John and me?"

"I can do better than that, dear Lily, there's an old dinghy already there. There's a stream that links the Lochs Arkaig and Linnhe where Donald likes to fish for salmon. Eddies along the shore slow the fish, making for easy prey, you see. She won't withstand any tidal surges, but the boat will get you down water a ways. That will have to do until I can get to Lochiel to warn him."

Instantly, panic skewered Lily, and words began to repeat rapid-fire, looping over and over in her head. *He was a fey lad and not so old. With hair spun from rings of gold.* She felt a stabbing in her heart, as fear hammered each painful beat. *One day tragedy learnt his name. In a skirmish with men in coats of flame.*

The song. She had neglected the song. She'd been so involved with John, preoccupied with Ewen, absorbed in her own concerns, her newfound contentment had held her spellbound. *On a bonny hill the lad met his ruin. When he took a bullet meant for Sir Ewen.* How could she have forgotten Robert?

"Be careful," she said, voice cracking. "I'm worried you're walking right into danger." Forcing her voice to be strong, she added, "Don't be a hero, Robert."

He looked at her somberly, as if already comprehending some forgone truth. "Sometimes a man needs to be a hero, Lil'."

Robert tilted his head, and, eyes creased with affection, he considered her. He added lightly, "Now don't you fret, lass, I'll find you once we sort this affair out."

Taking his cue, she made as if to buoy her attitude. "That's all well and good, but what if you don't 'sort it out'? And what am I supposed to do in the meantime?" Lily affected a disgruntled air. "I'm no Girl Scout, you know."

"No, Lily, I do not know." That smile lit Robert's face again, and if Lily didn't know better she'd suspect the bookish young man was actually enjoying this. "But that's where young John will prove himself a man. Won't you, lad?"

John puffed with the indirect praise. "Aye, I could live on the land for a year, if it comes to it."

Robert interjected, "*Qualis pater talis filius!*"

"Don't tell me . . . like father, like son?"

"Brava, dear Lily! Each passing day finds you a more capable Latinist."

John had been ignoring the exchange, his shoulders suddenly slouched and brows scrunched in an attitude of young concern. "But"—he looked to Lily for reassurance—"let's hope then it won't be as much as a year, aye?"

"Yes," Lily had to concur, "let's."

And the words continued relentless, boiling to the surface of her consciousness. *A MacMartin hero in Cameron plaid.*

Chapter 27

The sun cast long shadows in the dawn light, promising an un-characteristically warm Highland morning. Ewen rubbed his brow, the dirt of the previous day's hard ride still etched deeply in the lines of his hand, each nail outlined with a thick brown halo. There would likely be no bathing until their return back to Tor Castle—which, if Ewen had his way, would be as soon as humanly possible. He was eager to purge his lands of the redcoat vermin and get back to Lily. His scouts had spotted General Monk and about 140 British soldiers settled outside the village of Achdalieu, and they were now merrily pissing on his land, pillaging his people's homes, and reiving poultry and cattle enough to fill their coward's bellies.

His uncle advised caution. He encouraged the laird to bide his time, size up his enemy, enlist reinforcements if it seemed prudent. They numbered less than two score of Cameron men after all. But watching the sun rise on that early spring morning, Ewen knew in his heart that he could not squander the element of surprise. Besides, Cromwell himself could rain one thousand men down on his Highlands and they'd still be no match for the warriors of Clan Cameron.

No, he would strike today. For perhaps the biggest incentive of all was that his Lily waited for him. He wasn't keen on the thought of her alone at the keep, with just Robert, John, and a few servants at her back. More importantly, Ewen now knew with certainty that he would make Lily his, and that conviction drove him. He would have his people safe and his land under his control, and not loiter overlong fretting about the most opportune moment to strike. The sun was rising on a cloudless Highland morning, his men, though few, were braw and ready, and he would heed his instinct and attack on the heels of daybreak.

"Hear me, men!" Ewen's baritone rang through their makeshift camp and the laird was at once surrounded by his clansmen, with grim resolve and an almost childlike eagerness for the battle ahead warring on their faces.

"We will strike this very morning, before the sun rises too high overhead." Ewen silenced the muffled cheers of his men. "Silence, lads. Mark me. Some men fear to fight with England and her troops. But we are not those men." The men nodded forcefully, a chorus of "nay's" sounding through the camp. Ewen continued, his voice intensifying, "Some spy a redcoat and see a shining musket and the might of Cromwell's coin. But a Cameron man sees different. A Cameron man sees only another man." The laird finished with a shout, "And this morning we will see that man, with sleep still fogging his brain and morning's hunger gnawing at his belly. A man with breeches about his ankles and his morning bannock still in his throat. Just a man."

Ewen let the sentiment resonate and resumed, his voice low with subdued intensity, "But you are not just men. You're Cameron men. And today we bear the words of our clan. The words that formed us when we were but knots in our mothers' bellies. They were our lullaby when we were wrinkled bairns wrapped tight in bunting. The words that drove us as we cut our second teeth on cattle raids and wooden swords. The words that made each and every one of us a man, and more than a man."

"*Chlanna nan con thigibh a so's gheibh sibh feoil!*" he roared. His men cheered wildly, then were silenced as their laird continued in a dangerously quiet voice.

"These are the same words that we declare today, they are

the lullaby we'll sing to Monk as we send his soldiers to their own very long sleep.

"Sons of the hounds . . . come here and get flesh."

❀

Although prudence dictated the men should march slowly and stealthily through the woods on their way to engage the enemy, the Cameron warriors jogged quickly through the brush, eager to rid their land of its unwanted vermin in red coats.

The laird could tell by the sound of the man's panting that it wasn't one of his more battle-weathered clansmen who ran up alongside. "Ew– . . . Ewen!"

Dread knotted his stomach as the laird turned to see Robert, face reddened and chest heaving, standing by his side.

"We rest here," Ewen barked, as he grabbed his foster brother's arm and pulled him out of earshot.

"What are you thinking, fool? I gave you but one task, and it wasn't to come chasing after us like a wounded pup."

Robert did look wounded but stood tall, despite his wheezing. "Are you so hasty to judge, Lochiel? I am no wounded pup. Though I am feeling a bit of the wounded comrade with such an accusation." Raising his chin high, Robert announced, "I gave my oath that I would protect Lily and John, and I am bound by my word, sir. *Meum pactum dictum!* But I've risked travel through the night upon horseback, forced to seek your counsel forthwith, and finally have I found you. I've grave tidings to deliver about the state of Tor Castle and the threat espied within its confines."

Impatient to return to his attack, Ewen snapped, "Stop your prattling, lad, and spit out the news."

Robert proceeded with his report. "A MacKintosh is within the castle walls, spied in the apartments of none other than the mistress Rowena—I never have trusted that woman, *maior risus, acrior ensis*, you know. The bigger the smile, the sharper the knife. But that is—"

"You what?!" Ewen growled. "Are you daft? You spied a threat and instead of fighting you capered down to find me here, leaving Lily and John to make do with the MacKintosh about? What were you thinking, Robbie?"

"I . . . Lochiel . . . ," Robert stammered.

"Losh, man!" Ewen exclaimed. "The MacKintosh is an ill-bred skellum who'd barter his sister if he thought he could claim a spit more land in the bargain." Ewen rubbed his forehead. "But a Cameron, och, he'd slit a Cameron throat in a crack for just a glimpse of the Loch Arkaig."

"There is no need to jump to such an ill-informed conclusion. Lily and I have formulated a plan. She and John have snuck out of the castle to spirit themselves out of harm's way in a boat concealed in a cove off Loch Linnhe."

Incredulous, Ewen asked, "You sent them off in a wee boat?"

"I did." Robert looked proud of himself.

"Did you put them in this boat yourself?"

"I did not, but I trust that Lily is more than competent in that regard."

"Aye." Ewen gave a quick nod. "The lass is more than competent. But did you give a thought as to where they might be headed in your dinghy? Or are they simply to float about the loch until this MacKintosh becomes bored and decides to go on his way?"

"I . . . well . . ."

"Och, lad," Ewen growled, "keep it." The laird inhaled sharply and looked toward some distant spot for a moment. "You've done what you think best, I see that." Resigned, he raked his hand through his hair and concluded, "That what's done is done, aye? We've a task at hand, we've no choice now but to finish what we've begun and hope Lily and John are safe and away in your wee boat. John's an industrious lad, he'll know where to land." The laird nodded as if saying a thing could make it true.

"We're about to break our fast with some redcoats, and I'll not have you blundering through the woods and betraying our position." The laird looked to a distant point in the trees uncharacteristic agitation knotting his brow. "Och, I don't like it, but you'll follow with us, lad. Stay behind and well away from the fight. Then I'll send some men back to the keep with you." Ewen clapped his foster brother on the shoulder, his anxiety fading into bluster. "The men will make easy work of it, aye? You'll be back to Tor in short order." He abruptly gripped Robert's shoulder with a small shake as he added, "And you'll do naught but find and keep Lily and John."

Robert could only nod in answer.

Ewen sprinted back to the impatient cluster of High-landers. "We're off, men. We've wasted enough of the morning." Once again the Highland warrior, he looked slowly from man to man then thundered, "There's bonny weans in red frocks who'd hear a Cameron lullaby."

❦

It was but a slight rustling of bushes that announced the approaching Highlanders, then a sudden wave of tartan-clad Camerons burst from the woods surrounding Monk's encampment. A young, towheaded officer spied them first, and his tin mug hit the dirt, splattering silty coffee all over the white breeches of his redcoat uniform.

The comrades by his side were not so stunned. A few of the British soldiers managed to fire off a round at close range, felling a Cameron clansman as he emerged from the trees. The crofter jerked backward and fell, his body hitting the ground with a final bucking spasm.

So it begins, Ewen thought grimly. He shook his head and with a roar raised his claymore high.

The initial surprise spent, it was time to charge, voices howling, swords brandished wildly. Their berserk ferocity belied the expert precision of what was a typical Highland attack: startling, loud, violently short.

Terrified by such an assault on what had promised to be a serene blue-sky morning, many of the Englishmen made the single most critical—and fatal—error that a soldier can make when wielding a firearm against sword and targe. A knot of young redcoats fired their muskets far too soon to find vulnerable flesh amongst the Highland warriors. Before they could reload, the Camerons were upon them.

"Cameron men! *Aonaibh ri cheille!*" Ewen's call to unite thundered over the din. Swords cleaved through guns made pathetically useless by their empty barrels; metal clattered as shaking hands attempted in vain to reload; and one sound endured like a sickening drone in the ears, the suck and dull thud of flesh as it hit the ground lifeless.

"Lochiel!" Ewen turned at the sound of his uncle's voice. "To Malcolm!" Donald shouted. "Away to Malcolm, lad!"

The laird quickly scanned the field and spotted the red-headed clansman. Cornered by two redcoats, Malcolm had sustained a belly wound and a deep gash to his sword arm, and the man's strength was flagging.

Ewen hastened to Malcolm's side, darting between tangles of fighting men and bounding over the bodies of fallen soldiers. A redcoat sprang in front of him, and the laird barely slowed his pace as he smashed the soldier's firearm away with his claymore then slashed across the man's suddenly exposed torso.

He closed in on Malcolm. Approaching his clansman's attackers quickly from behind, Ewen skewered one with his tremendous sword. He placed his foot on the back of the downed redcoat, and retrieved his claymore. The action took only a moment, but looking up, Ewen realized in horror that he had been too late. Malcolm sunk to his knees, a redcoat bayonet in his chest.

Savage rage consumed the laird. He swung his claymore down and sheared easily through the redcoat's collarbone, killing him instantly.

"What bloody nuisance these redcoats are, aye?" Malcolm smiled weakly, his eyes gentle even in death. "You'll take care of them for me, Lochiel? My lassies?" A spasm in his belly doubled the clansman, and he collapsed onto his back. "My sweet Una has a house full of mouths to feed."

"Och, Malcolm"—grief ripped through the laird, and made his voice hoarse—"your family will not go hungry."

Ewen clasped Malcolm's hand firmly in his. "I'll tell them how proud you made me, man. You fought well. And you die a hero's death."

Malcolm stilled, his features serene, green eyes gazing into an unseen distance.

"*Guidh soirbheachadh Dhé le*, Malcolm." Ewen's voice cracked as he pulled his clansman's bonnet over those vivid eyes and his ruddy, freckled face. "Godspeed."

"Cameron men!" Ewen rose to his feet, renewed fury in his voice. "*A' slàraigeadh!*"

The camp fell into chaos as the clansmen methodically split small clusters of redcoats apart from the larger group like stripping boughs from a tree, and all the while the raging

Highlanders darted in and out of the woods, appearing more like one hundred men than their meager thirty-two.

When reaching the end of a battle frenzy, Ewen never knew if a quarter of an hour or a quarter of a day had passed. As he watched the tails of no less than fifty redcoats flee through the trees and away from the onslaught of his men, a grim smile chiseled into his stilled, clenched features.

"Uncle, to me!" The laird's smile faded when he caught sight of Donald and the reddish brown blood smudged across his cheek and staining the entire left shoulder of his shirt.

Donald laughed off his concern. "Och, lad, 'twas only a scratch on my cheek. I'm thankful too, aye? I needed a braw shave this morning."

He clapped his nephew on the shoulder. "It'll take more than a young redcoat to fell me." Donald's laughter boomed and in his voice erupted an unmistakable note of relief, sounding a release from the single-minded gravity of combat. "Though, the clever laddie did miss my neck by a whisker."

"You're like a lad after his first kiss, uncle. I'm glad of it." Affection shown clearly in Ewen's eyes. "Our work's not yet done, but you shouldn't find it too wearisome. A bald head is soon shaved, aye?" They shared a quick laugh, the tension of battle still needing an outlet. The laird continued, "Tell the men to root out what remains of our wee red squirrels and round them together for me."

"Aye," Donald said, "I spied some what thought to get to the sea and leave the way they came. I'll give them chase, you see to the woods. A few got away through the trees like ewes afraid of a shearing."

Ewen was picking his way through the forest, hunting for the last of the retreating redcoats when he heard a familiar voice.

"Greetings, Lochiel."

He turned and recognized his enemy at once. Despite his stocky build, Monk had an effortless elegance, and appeared all the more so for his pristine uniform. The general smiled and shook his head at Ewen as if he had caught the laird in some naughty prank.

"Och," Ewen spat, "I see you chose to wear a uniform this morn, instead of that bonny blue topper you donned when last we met. Tell me, Monk, it that what makes your men call you general? You've the coat for it?"

Monk ignored his comment and said genially, "Shan't we settle this like gentlemen over a brandy? It's not too late, Lochiel. You can save your clansmen."

A man emerged from the trees and glowered dramatically at Ewen. Though his tartan and bonnet proclaimed him a Scotsman, he stood—legs apart and hand poised over sword hilt—directly behind Monk, in a manner that announced his true allegiance.

Ewen inclined his head toward the man. "A MacKintosh, is it?" Shaking his head, the laird looked to Monk and mused, "I see the way of it, then. You've men to cook for you, men to bow to you, and you're also a coward who'd hire men to die for you?"

"I'll not soil myself with your savage blood." Monk laughed. "This man goes willingly to fight for me. But to die for me? That is not necessary. No, Ewen, you are the only one who will be dying today."

Monk turned and appraised the man behind him. The Scotsman grabbed his sword hilt and gave Ewen an exaggerated scowl, bearing a set of uneven and much-decayed teeth.

The general chuckled. "Ah, Ewen, do not imply I send my man to his death. Do you really think I'd waste a youngster on such an enterprise as this? To kill the laird of Clan Cameron— what a magnificent trophy! No, I rely on only the best to kill you."

"Now, sirrah?" the Scotsman hissed.

"Yes, and do let me know when you've dispensed with the Cameron. I'll make certain your Lauchlan MacKintosh knows that I am well pleased with your efforts." Monk examined Ewen thoughtfully, a slight smile on the edge of his lips. "Good day to you, Lochiel. It is a shame you neglected to do business with me." The general made a slight bow and disappeared back into the trees.

"I ken you, man." Ewen spat by his feet. "You go by Allen, aye? Word is, your laird sent one of his men to the Cameron keep, but your pursuit's in vain. Once I'm done with you, I'm back home to kill your kinsman."

"Nay in vain, Ewen." Allen's voice was a hoarse whisper, as if his throat had never recovered from a long-ago injury.

"'Tis my laird himself in your keep, and by now Lauchlan has killed your boy and taken your woman." He gave a toss to his tangled mat of mud brown hair. "I'm not knowing if he'll keep her or not. Depends on how much she pleases him, aye?" The man sucked on his teeth a moment, then asked, "What say you, Ewen? Is she pleasing? 'Tis a shame she's not here to see you die like a dog." Allen MacKintosh began to circle the laird. "She might could save her own skin if she pleases Lauchlan. He's done dallying with that Rowena. The yellow-haired wench thought to wed you, Cameron." He barked out a laugh. "Now there's a lark." Allen began passing his sword from hand to hand, continuing to crouch and circle the laird. "I've a thought to give Rowena a ride myself. But maybe I won't waste my time on a used parcel like her and save myself for your Lily. That's her name, aye?"

The laird stepped forward and strolled almost lazily toward the man. Allen baited, "Some distant French relation, is she? Curious lass, I hear. But no matter. I'll just keep her in a vase like, in my rooms, and none the wiser for her peculiar ways."

Ewen exploded in a forward dash, the blur of his claymore startling his opponent, despite his readied posture. The metal of their swords crashed and sang through the air and crashed again, hammering a furious beat. The two Scotsmen were evenly matched, and Ewen's nonchalance rapidly morphed into acute focus.

Though somewhat shorter, the MacKintosh man was built like a bull, and his barrel-chest and arms like small trees slammed his sword down upon Ewen's again and again in an avalanche of hatred and vengeance.

Allen's attack was unrelenting. Ewen fought for calm, hoping to gain the upper hand. "Why would you do it, Allen?" he asked in a voice as casual as he could muster. "Why would you play traitor to the Highlands?"

"You don't see the way of it, do you, Cameron?" The man was big but slow, and the rapidity with which Ewen countered his attack was beginning to wind Allen. He huffed, "The MacKintosh clan will play hired sword if it means getting our lands back." Although he thrust his sword with renewed effort, Allen's shortness of breath betrayed increasing fatigue. "Lands . . . rightfully . . . MacKintosh."

"Ah, is that what this is about then!" the laird exclaimed. He saw his opportunity. Lacking Allen's girth, Ewen was the more agile of the two and used that to his advantage by making his opponent come to him, all the while carrying on with the conversation. "Your laird saddles up with Monk, the general helps your clan slay me and my son, and the MacKintosh takes my lands neat as a pin, is it?"

"That's our lands, Cameron!"

The laird forced a smile, never wavering in his attack. "So the MacKintosh has said all these years. And his father, and his father's father." Ewen's feet were moving more quickly now. "But it matters not how many Cameron men your clan may kill"—the laird dashed around to Allen's side, momentarily confusing him—"you'll never be able to take what is ours." In the split second that he had gained, the laird flicked Allen's sword from his hand.

"You've joined the redcoats," Ewen shouted, as his opponent's sword clattered across the craggy hillside, "and sullied your soul for naught!"

Allen bellowed, "My soul's not done yet, Cameron bastard!" and charged Ewen, barreling him to the ground. Ewen's sword was flung from his hand as the men plunged backward, tumbling down a small ravine into a dry riverbed. They wrestled for dominance, ignoring the sharp stones and stinging nettles that had found purchase beside the dry bank.

The MacKintosh clansman heaved his enormous weight and flung himself atop the laird, pummeling Ewen's head into the rocks, briefly stunning him. Seizing his advantage, Allen braced Ewen's throat with his forearm and snatched a dagger from his belt, but they were too close and the laird struggling too violently for the man's weapon to do more than graze flesh. Allen shifted his weight to better leverage his knife arm and, arching his back, separated the men just enough to strike a death blow.

Ewen's vision dimmed as he labored for what small breaths of air he could. In that instant the laird's fate flashed before him. Rage and a violent desire to survive boiled in him, and for less than the span of a heartbeat he saw his opponent as defenseless, torso and arm fully extended for the dagger thrust. It was in that desperate moment that Ewen struck. Grabbing Allen's collar in his hand, Ewen pulled himself up, and using the only weapon left to him, sank his teeth into the MacKintosh kinsman's throat.

Ewen flung the man aside, and rolled into a squat. Allen stared with wild eyes at the laird, his jaw snapping at the air as he labored in vain for breath. He went rigid, with legs splayed, heels hammering the ground and fingers clawing the dirt. The MacKintosh clansman suddenly stilled. A final exhale rattled from his body, a panicked grimace frozen on his face.

Using the tail of his own tartan to wipe the blood off of his face, Ewen looked up to see his uncle standing at the top of the gully appearing delighted.

"You bloody savage!" Donald's voice boomed across the walls of the ravine.

"The tree doesn't always fall with the first stroke, aye?" Ewen nodded back. "But 'twas the sweetest bite I ever had."

"Ewen . . ." Robert stood by Donald's side, disgust threatening to overtake the look of shock plain on his features. "You, well . . ." He mustered an appropriately encouraging tone. "*Vae victis*, Lochiel. Your foe had not a chance. Fighting as you did with . . . with the primitive ruthlessness attributed to our ancient Pictish forefathers."

"What else would you have me do, Robbie?" Ewen stared at his foster brother a moment, intense thoughtfulness wrinkling the corners of his eyes. "But I thank you the same. Come men"—he gave a nod—"it seems the battle's not yet over."

Ewen scrambled up the side of the ravine and collected his lost sword. "Where've the others got to?"

Donald gestured toward an overgrown trail. "They've made off for those redcoat cowards who ran into the woods."

Ewen took off at a dash, leaping over small logs and ducking to avoid branches. Donald and Robert struggled to match his pace until they came upon a small clearing. Alder trees reached like enormous columns into the sky, shading a couple dozen redcoats who were on their knees and surrounded by a knot of angry Cameron men.

"Stop." Ewen's voice was steady. A quick glance told him that the situation before him was escalating and his men were preparing to dispatch the last of Monk's soldiers. "Give me but a moment, aye?" The laird calmed the Highlanders. "We'll not slaughter these men."

He looked at the subdued and frightened redcoats, his gaze resting on each one. "I offer you quarter. Each and every one of you." Ewen circled the knot of men. "You may live by the ways of Cromwell, but we do not. 'Twould be craven to butcher near two score of boys, scared and on their knees. Nay, quarter you shall have, and all that I ask—"

A rustle and click is all that betrayed the British soldier. A lanky redcoat no older than twenty had hidden a pistol tucked at the small of his back and he held it now, shaking, and pointing directly at Ewen.

"You think to offer me mercy"—the boy's composure was at odds with his trembling hands—"but I will not accept charity from a barbarian. You may call yourself leader of these men, but you are just a feral dog"—he fumbled to cock his weapon—"leading a pack of animals."

A deafening crack echoed through the trees as he discharged his gun. Ewen snarled and leaned in toward the boy, ready in his final moment to embrace death like a warrior. But it wasn't Ewen's flesh that the bullet found.

Robert had leapt in front of his foster brother, offering his life to save Ewen's.

The group plunged into chaos. The Highlanders turned upon the cluster of redcoats, mad lust for vengeance distorting their features.

Ewen stood apart from the melee and roared at the sky as he held the body of his brother, limp but for the slow wheezing of his chest up and down as he struggled for breath.

Donald appeared at his side and said, "I'll take the lad to the keep. He'll need attention." He placed his hand on Robert's head, and in an uncharacteristically tranquil voice, asked, "Can you make the ride, lad?"

"Do not worry for me . . . Oh, *pallida mors*!" His body convulsed with a brief fit of coughing.

"Och," Donald erupted, "ever with the Latin. I'll nick your other shoulder, lad, if I hear any Latin on the road home, aye?" He turned to Ewen. "I say the lad'll be fine. There's always life in a living man."

"Aye, he will." Ewen's brow furrowed. "The bullet looks to have bit below his shoulder. Just send up a prayer that it's not nicked the lung."

"I'll take him now." Donald reached for Robert with a tenderness that belied his gruff voice. "Come away now lad. You'll ride astride before me."

By the time Ewen turned his attention back to his men, it was clear that there would be no prisoners after all. Those redcoats who didn't fall at the hands of the Camerons had fled into the trees.

"Men," he announced in a tight voice, "we'll be celebrating this night under our own roof." Despite the upbeat message, the Highlanders recognized the solemnity on their laird's face and remained silent. "There's a beck not fifty paces off where you can take a quick wash. Then we're off."

The men started to disperse when Ewen added, "One final thing." The shadow of a smile momentarily lightened his features. "I'd send a few of you seaward. Stick to the trees and make a racket as you go. What few redcoats slipped through our fingers, well, I'd have them turning tail back to their boats with the notion that Cameron broadswords grow on trees."

Chapter 28

"Ouch!" Lily grumbled, "I need my Nikes not bare feet for this, not to mention . . . ow!!" She slipped again, catching herself before falling on her backside for what would be the third time, and tried not to think about just what the thick slime was that coated each step and was now soaking through the seat of her skirts.

One of the secrets of Tor Castle, the old passageway was more akin to a tunnel than any stairway. They had been laboriously descending for well over an hour, and Lily was beginning to wonder if they were ever going to make their way out of the keep to Loch Linnhe. John had promised that the long-forgotten staircase led to an old doorway, now concealed from the outside by the tangle of hedges and undergrowth that shrouded the base of the castle like a thick ring of hair encircling a bald man's head.

Her torch threw uneven shadows in the otherwise pitch-black stairwell, throwing off what little remained of her depth perception that hadn't already been confounded by the irregularly spaced stairs. "What were they thinking, I mean, make these things real, bona fide stairs or don't, but these long shallow steps, who walks like th—dammit!"

John stopped and looked back at Lily with a mix of astonishment and delight upon hearing such a word cross her lips.

"And you, young man"—Lily shot him her best outraged adult glare—"you can spare me any attitude."

"I didn't say anything! I don't mean to rush you so fast, do you need to rest a spell?"

"I'm not infirm, John," Lily scolded, "I'm just finding my stride—"

"*Ist!*" John hissed.

Shocked, Lily opened her mouth to give the boy what for, but was stopped short by the startlingly intense look on his face. "Please, hush." He pinned her with his eyes. "Did you hear that?"

Her heart pounded in her chest as she strained to listen. There it was, the incongruous whisper of satin against stone. Lily looked around frantically. "What was—"

A sudden rustling was their only warning. Rowena materialized from one of the hallway's many niches just two steps below John. Although she was the taller of the two, standing below the boy on the stairwell they were the same height. Her usually dainty features were drawn into an ugly sneer, lips parted to bare her teeth like some feral animal.

Then Lily saw it. Rowena's arm was cocked at her side, holding a large pewter tankard, knuckles white from her frantic grip on the mug's handle.

Lily felt as if she were moving underwater; every second was agonizingly long and yet she couldn't make herself move any faster. Rowena's surreal appearance—absurdly brandishing an old beer stein, her face a menacing rictus—overwhelmed Lily's senses, already unbearably piqued from navigating the dank stairs for so long. And all the while a faint tap-tapping played at the edges of her consciousness, like the soundtrack to a nightmare.

Her eyes caught it and connected sound to movement. Rowena's arm was shaking convulsively, the barest of trembling, but enough to cause the lid of the tankard to rap gently on its lip, where she clenched it hovered in the air, now just over the boy's head.

Lily's dreamlike fog lifted and reality jolted back into place.

But she was too late.

Rowena swung her arm with a hysterical shriek and the pewter tankard struck the side of John's head with a horrific crunch. The dull sound of ringing metal echoed over the stone walls as the boy crumpled to the ground.

"He's dead! That'll do for you, you wee *luch*. I killed him, you see?" Laughter exploded out of Rowena, and her grimace transformed into a look of deranged glee, the calculated polish of her voice replaced by a coarse burr. "I shown him, I did, bloody *abaisd*, like a wee mouse he was, skittering and spying through the halls. Snot-faced chit, I'll learn you to cross Rowena Margaret Irene MacPherson."

Lily fell at once to her knees by John's side, leaning her torch against the stairs to illuminate his wounds. Blood soaked the side of his head, matting his hair and forming a ghastly pool that was already dripping slowly down onto the next step. "Why . . . why would you?" Though momentarily paralyzed by shock, Lily felt it simmering into a very reassuring rage.

"You don't see? I thought you were the brilliant Lily, but you don't ken the way of it?" Rowena began methodically wiping the blood from the tankard with an embroidered handkerchief. "If our precious Ewen hasn't an heir, then he'll be wanting a new wife, aye? A laird can't be without a son to take his place." Her voice was manic, the edges of her accent continuing to bloom into a barely comprehensible brogue. "And who'll be there to comfort the grieving father?" Her shoulders shuddered with a fit of shrill giggling.

Lily darted her eyes about the tunnel in search of something she could use to overpower Rowena, who was now using the stein to admire her reflection. Lily imagined she was likely also strategizing about which of Lily's own body parts to pummel with it. She tried to stall. "And you are the new wife in question, I suppose?"

"Aye." Rowena turned the full force of her gaze onto Lily, and beamed with a look of self-satisfaction. "There you go, *Lil'*, there's the clever cat who bewitched Lochiel. I'm to be the new wife." An eerily serene smile smoothed her features. "Once I rid myself of the cat, aye?"

Lily smiled back, and it was a true smile. She had felt a pulse on John's neck, strong and steady, and spied his eyelashes beginning to flutter. She suddenly saw Rowena for what she was. A weak, conniving brat whose petulance had deteriorated into something evil.

She sent up a silent thank-you for all those miserable years of step aerobics and kick boxing at the local Y. Lily had gone to the gym more out of guilt than pleasure, but she now realized that with so many years of those accursed Nautilus machines to gird her, she could eat a peevish little monster like Rowena for breakfast.

"Rid of . . . me?" Lily stood and her smile became radiant. "I don't think so."

Uncertainty flickered in Rowena's eyes, fueling Lily's burgeoning confidence. But first Lily had to satisfy her curiosity. She understood why the girl might want John dead, but that didn't explain the man spotted in her rooms.

"Before you have at me with your cup, Rowena, please do tell me, what was a MacKintosh doing in the castle?"

She was momentarily taken aback. "You've seen the MacKintosh in my rooms, eh? Your wee spy, I suppose." Rowena kicked John with her slippered foot, and with a toss of her blonde ringlets asserted, "The MacKintosh is long fled from the castle. If you or Robert or any other of your wee warriors had hoped to capture him, you're too late."

"But what on earth could the MacKintosh man have to do with your plot?"

"He's as well served by the boy's death as I. Though he's eager to spill the blood of the father besides. He reckons some Cameron lands to be his own. If the son turns up dead, and the father too, then what bedlam, aye? Whilst the clan sorts itself out, the MacKintosh will take what land he will." Then she trilled, "Easy as you please."

Lily had to laugh. "You're a dim bulb, aren't you Rowena?" Wickedly conniving was one thing, but recklessly stupid was more than she could bear. The fury that had been rolling in her steadied, and her anger attained a levelheaded focus. "I mean, your plan goes out the window if your husband-to-be is murdered by your coconspirator. Or am I missing something?"

"Oh," Rowena purred, "the MacKintosh has vowed to make any such . . . inconvenience worth my time."

She had always felt cowed by girls like this, with their effortless prettiness and blithe flirtations. She studied Rowena, and it struck Lily that she had something those types of females never had to rely on. Self-reliance was Lily's currency. This freshly realized confidence summoned an otherworldly strength in her, and before her head knew what her body was doing, she launched herself over John's limp figure and hurtled into Rowena.

The blonde went down like a rag doll. She was thin but her body lacked muscle tone, and her doughy midsection expelled a clipped, satisfyingly high-pitched wheeze like a collapsed bellows as she hit the stone stairs. This time Lily moved quickly, and she at once pinned Rowena's arms and squeezed her wrists until the pewter tankard slipped from her grip, clattering down the steps and disappearing into the darkness below.

"*A nighean na galla*!" Rowena hissed. "You'll nay get the better of me. The MacKintosh has a man after Lochiel even now. He's likely dead, and you're soon to follow. If Ewen's not to be mine, then he'll belong to no one."

"You know as well as I, Rowena"—Lily dug in her nails for emphasis—"that nobody gets the best of Ewen. And besides," she added through clenched teeth, "it looks as if I've already gotten the best of—"

Wrenching her torso, Rowena yanked an arm free and jabbed her elbow into Lily's ribs. She cried out, her arms instinctively recoiling, and lost her grip on Rowena, who quickly rolled out from under her and scuttled down the steps, fumbling under her skirts as she went. Lily sprang to give chase, leaving the torch perched along the stairs in her haste.

The women stumbled recklessly down into the increasingly impermeable darkness. Very quickly it became impossible to see, but Lily's eyes still instinctively opened wide, searching for some glimmer of light. She was forced to rely on her other senses, and could tell from the rustle of Rowena's skirts that she was gaining on her.

They hit the bottom of the stairs at the same time and stumbled, legs adjusting to the pitch of the floor that their eyes were now completely blind to. Lily stepped on the hem of Rowena's dress and the woman grunted, hitting the wall.

She sensed Rowena's arm stabbing empty space with her

tiny *sgian dubh*. Lily flailed in the blackness, grasping a handful of Rowena's skirts, her fingers and nails struggling for purchase on the slippery satin, when she felt the slice of a blade along her forearm. For a brief, shocked moment, there was a strange absence of feeling, instantly replaced by a sizzling pain and the warm feel of blood seeping along her arm.

The sensation focused Lily, and she pulled her opponent toward her, clamping an arm around her tiny waist. So close, she could smell the scent of rose in Rowena's hair and the tang of sweat soaking the satin of her dress, straining now over her panting chest. Wrestling for control of the woman's knife arm, Lily's nails found the back of Rowena's hand, clawing her viciously. The ping of the blade hitting the floor echoed off the damp stone walls, and Rowena began to thrash like a wild creature in Lily's grip, slamming them into the wall of the landing.

Lily barked out a curse as her hip struck a sharp protrusion, then she grinned in the darkness, realizing she had just found the doorknob. Still clutching the struggling Rowena, she reached around and fumbled with the handle, encouraged by the sounds of Loch Linnhe, lapping on the other side of the door. The knob was jammed tight with rust from years of neglect and moisture, and when Lily finally managed to turn it, the door swung open through a tangle of undergrowth, flinging both women through the biting shrubbery into the muck along the lake, the shore of which lay much closer to the edge of Tor Castle than Lily had realized.

It took Rowena a moment to understand what had happened. Lily pressed her advantage and wrestled her down into the mud, straddling her and pinning her arms at her back.

"Och," Rowena spat, "you're a braw coo, aren't you?"

"A coo? What's a . . . a cow?" Lily leaned hard into Rowena. "Did you just call me a cow?"

"Aye, I always thought you a shaggy coo with that mop of hair." Rowena thrashed under Lily's weight. "Och, what is that infernal stench?"

"A cow, huh?" Lily laughed. "Well, if we're talking farm animals here, I'd have to say you're a sheep." She leaned down and, ignoring the brown halo of grunge along the edge of Rowena's skirts, tore into the fabric with her teeth.

"*A ghalla*! What are you doing to me skirts?"

"Or would it be a lamb? No, no, too innocent. I'd say you're most like a sheep because, my dear"—Lily rent the fabric of Rowena's skirts up the middle—"you are about to get shorn." She began methodically ripping strip after strip off from the hem, all the while keeping the now frenzied Rowena pinned between her knees.

"*Dé an diabhal a . . .*" Rowena screeched. "Bloody hell, fool! What are you doing? Och, hell, bitch, you let me go." She bucked and screamed, struggling to get Lily off of her back. "I'll see you dead, *a shiùrsach*!"

"Let you go?" Lily was having fun now. "I'll let you go in one moment." Anchoring Rowena's arms with her own, Lily deftly wound the strips of fabric around the blonde's wrists. "Just. About. Done. There, now I'll let you go."

Lily stood over Rowena, hogtied, howling, and raging, almost completely immobilized in the muck.

"Oh, you asked about the stench? I'm surprised you don't recognize it." Lily began dusting herself off, and exaggeratedly adjusting her clothing. "Though, I suppose you've always had servants to deal with these sorts of things for you. Not for long, once Ewen gets wind of what you've done. Anyhoo, that smell? It's the aroma of chamber pots. They must empty them out this side of the castle." Lily looked around with an exaggerated thoughtfulness. "Makes sense. It's so remote back here, and right by the lake too."

Lily began to make her way back to the door. "Get used to it, because you'll be smelling it until someone finds you. *If* anyone finds you." Lily cleared the brush aside and opened the door. She turned once more to look at Rowena, who was now hysterical and rolling on her belly in the mud, arms and legs writhing like a flipped turtle.

"So"—Lily smiled—"gardyloo, honey, because if one of those pots gets dumped on you . . . well, you'll never get the stain out."

❀

"Don't upset yourself, Lily. The laddie'll be right as rain come morning." Kat tucked the quilt snugly around John's shoulders. "Though how you managed to get him up the stairs all on your lonesome is no small miracle. A big and braw one John is, just as his da was at this age."

Lily sat on the bedside, stroking John's hair. He had regained consciousness then quickly slipped back into a deep sleep with the help of a dram of whisky insisted upon by Kat. Getting the boy back up all those stairs actually hadn't been as hard as she would've thought. Between her brawl with Rowena and fear for John's life, adrenaline had been coursing through Lily. She'd just knotted her skirts at the knees and, heaving the boy into a fireman's carry across her shoulders, did what she had to do. She barely recalled the long trot back up the stairwell. Panicked thoughts of John's safety had pushed all else out of her mind.

"Lass?"

"Hmm? Oh, sorry, did you say something?"

"Och, I told you not to fret so. Now up you get, there's still work to be done and I'd do it while the lad sleeps." Kat rustled the overstuffed pocket of her green striped apron. "I've some sugar; I'll be needing to pack up his head tight."

"Sugar?"

"Aye, sugar, and what else?" Kat stared incredulously. "You don't use sugar where you're from?"

"Are you sure that's an okay thing to do?"

"'Tis the only thing to do." Kat shooed her off the bed. "The sugar halts the bleeding and keeps the wound clean."

Lily had been relieved to find that, once cleaned up, the boy's injuries weren't as dire as they had originally seemed. The alarming amount of blood aside, the gash on John's head was shallow and only a few inches long, a small half-moon in his scalp echoing the lip of the tankard that struck him.

Kat set to work drizzling spoonfuls of sugar into the gash and wrapping it tight with strips of linen. "*A bhobain!*" the maid mumbled. "You wee rascal, I kent you'd look trouble in the eye one of these days. But who'd figure that trouble would appear in a kirtle and petticoat? Och, that girl." She knotted the bandage emphatically and wiped her hands on her apron. "That girl! And to clout the lad on his head with a tappit hen? Losh! I kent from the start that girl wasn't right. But she came round to curry favor with the Lochiel. He'd have nothing of her, aye? He's no time for the jillets who try to catch his eye with flattery and their sighs and pouts. But he saw how the lad took a notion to her so Ewen opened his doors. But give a beggar a bed and he'll pay you with a louse. Aye it's true," Kat responded to Lily's widened eyes, "and that Rowena is a beggar if I've seen a one. But what can't be helped must be endured, and I did endure that lass and her mischief for long enough."

John moaned and shifted in his sleep. "Och, I'm riling the lad." Kat gently pushed the hair away from his face. She whispered, "You sleep now, Johnnie, *caidil gu math* my darling. Sleep and I'll be here when you wake."

"Come lass, we've things to discuss." The maid whisked her into the hallway. Lily began to follow dutifully behind, but what she had to say couldn't wait. She grabbed the maid's arm. "Kat"—Lily's voice threatened to crack—"I've made a total mess of things."

Kat turned and studied her for a moment. "Oh, you sweet, *gypit* girl. How've you made a mess? You saved the lad's life is what you've done. And proud you should be. As I am. And as the laird will be when he hears tell of it."

"But that's just it, Kat. Ewen's in trouble, and Robert too probably. Rowena said the MacKintosh man has fled the castle, and he's surely on his way to find Ewen. MacKintosh wants him dead"—Lily felt her chin start to tremble—"if the redcoats don't get to him first." She vowed not to cry. The strangeness and intensity of her situation suddenly overwhelmed her. Lily took a deep breath to gather herself. "I just . . . what should I do, Kat?"

"Lily," Kat tsked, "you've a stouter heart than this, aye? What you'll do now is what you've been doing since you set foot in Tor Castle." Kat cradled Lily's face in her calloused hands. "You'll be the braw lass I ken you to be. You'll fight for those you love. As you did for John. And as you will for your Ewen." Kat tightened her grip and smiled. "Aye, lass, don't look from me now. I ken that you love our laird. Just as he loves you. And love you he does. I can see it in his way, how he looks at you, speaks with you. Och, the man can be as stubborn as a mule but I've kent him since he was a wee laddie and I can tell you true, Lily, I've never seen it and never thought to see it, but you've our Ewen's heart."

"Thanks, Kat." Lily beamed, and was filled with the feeling that she could conquer anything in her path. Redcoats or mysterious clan enemies, bring them on. "With the MacKintosh gone," she added, "you and John should be safest here. Now, I think I've got me a laird to save."

❊

"Why, Mistress Rowena!" Lennox swayed easily in the saddle, a look of befuddlement spreading across his worn face. "Is that you?"

The stableman flung down his rusted pitchfork and it landed prong-first into the muck. Swinging his leg over the side of a disinterested old mare, he babbled cheerfully, "Miss Kat wanted that I should muck some of the larger bits into yon burn. So it can wash away like. The midden has got quite sour, aye?"

He laughed knowingly, as if privy to some precious inside knowledge. "Lochiel himself says a feckful stench has been blowing in the windows."

Rowena shot him a withering look. She had managed to roll onto her side, but had been unable to loosen her ties.

Lennox warily approached her. "Just what are you about out here, mum?" Concern filled his voice. "Were you for another picnic, is it?"

Confounded, he studied her. The front of her dress was sodden with filth, but her bound hands and feet remained obscured by her shredded clothing and the sludge that she had been rolling in. "Don't you know you're in the middens, mum? You'd best watch that the muck-fleas don't get you. Them's worse than midges."

"*Ist!*" Rowena struggled to release her wrists but only soiled herself further. She jeered, "You bloody *tumfie*, don't stand there dumb." She flipped onto her belly and bucked her legs, revealing the bonds on her filthy calf. "Help me out of this!"

"Och, mum." Panicked, Lennox circled around Rowena's prostrate figure. He mumbled, "I cannot, mum."

"What?" she shrieked.

Lennox cleared his throat, and his usual merriment was replaced by dread, which now paralyzed his features. He warbled uneasily, "But your legs, mum." He added in a whisper, "I can see your legs. It's not proper like."

"You'll be seeing the bottom of the loch if you don't get me untied, you worthless nit!"

"Aye, mum." Lennox scuttled quickly to Rowena's side and began worrying the knot. "Yes, mum."

Minutes had passed when the stableman hesitated. "The knot's in a snarl, mum, I can't get it unstuck." He added hopefully, "But I might could unstick it with the prong of my dung fork."

"Don't you dare touch me with that thing," Rowena hissed. "Haven't you a knife, you imbecile? Get a bloody blade and cut me loose! Or," she added in an ominously low voice, "I'll fell you like a lame horse."

Obediently, Lennox knelt and removed a small dagger from his belt. "I ken it's not of my concern, but who was it to tie you up so?" The stableman set to work shearing through her restraints, looking as if he would cry, so dismayed at the impropriety of handling Rowena's legs.

"Don't be fashed, mum," he said weakly, "just a blink now and you'll be freed."

He continued, "You should tell the laird, mum, and I'll wager he'll tan who's done this to you. Lochiel's a good man, he is, you'll see. He'll not let this pass, aye?"

Rowena flailed her arms and legs free from the last of her bonds. Kicking herself away from Lennox, she spat, "You're right, fool, it's not of your concern."

She stood and spent a moment visibly collecting herself, then shook her arms and stomped her legs back to life. Gathering her skirts in her hands, Rowena slipped and stumbled away from Lennox toward the trees on the far edge of the loch.

"Mum!" he shouted, alarm in his voice. "Where're you off to? What should I tell the laird of you?"

She sped into a run. "You can tell your cursed laird anything you like, you daft *amadan*."

Halting at the forest's edge, Rowena turned back to Lennox and shrilled, "Nay, tell him this. Tell your Lochiel to tread in fear." She cackled gleefully. "The MacKintosh comes even now to claim vengeance."

She spun, and disappeared into the woods.

Chapter 29

"Salve! Salve!" Robert's voice pierced the silence, startling Lily. She stopped and leaned down in the saddle, as if getting closer to the ground would improve her hearing.

After the incident with John, she had abandoned the notion of taking a boat anywhere, frantic to find Ewen and his foster brother, and see with her own eyes that they were safe. And now she was hallucinating Robert's voice. In Latin, no less.

She'd been riding for just over a mile now, carefully picking her way along the shores of Loch Linnhe. It was a rarely used route away from the keep, secluded by forested Lochaber land on one side and the glassy lake on the other.

Lennox had been mysteriously absent from the stables, and she regretted her choice of mounts. The gray mare seemed docile and large enough for a smooth gait—she'd vowed never again to sit one of the smaller ponies—but the old nag was plodding too slowly for Lily's patience to bear.

She strained to hear, the sounds of nature growing loud in her ears as she focused, the chirrup of birds, rustle of trees in the breeze, and the gentle sloshing of the lake against the rocky muck of its shores. It had been a long day, but surely she was not yet fatigued enough to hallucinate Robert's voice among them, no matter how badly she wished he were with her.

"Haloo!" There it was again, clearer now, and definitely Robert. "Just here, Lily!" She scanned the horizon and imagined every large shrub and small rock, all uniformly gray in the distance, to be Robert. Hope swelled in her chest. The burst of courage she had felt with Kat had started to waver with each lonely step, and she would have loved to have a friendly face with her as she traipsed through the countryside, alone and unarmed, into the lap of redcoats, a rival clan, and who knew what else.

"Just here, lass," Donald's voice barked unexpectedly close and Lily jumped, turning in time to see the pair emerge from the surrounding woods not three feet behind her. They rode astride a single horse, the gruff older man supporting Robert between his arms. Both were covered in a film of grime and spattered, blackened blood, but it was Robert who nursed a ghastly wound that still appeared to be oozing fresh blood from his shoulder.

"*Salve*, Lily." Robert delivered his greeting in a theatrically weakened voice with the bravado of a Roman warrior.

"What on earth . . ." She swung her leg over the saddle and leapt down. Horror curdled her stomach. She was terrified that Gram's song was coming true, that she'd done nothing to stop it. And now Ewen was in grave danger, without his family by his side.

"What happened?" Lily fixed Donald with a distressed look. "Where's Ewen?" Her heart pounded in her ears and adrenaline cascaded through her system enough to make the edges of her vision waver.

"Lily," Robert said feebly, "*quem di diligunt, adolescens moritur* . . . whom the gods love," he coughed with finality, "die young."

"Calm yourself, lass," Donald soothed. "And Robbie." He turned an exasperated look to his charge and scolded, "You fool lad, you've had my hackles up with all your philosophizing since we crossed the ben side of the woods. Keep the proverbs to yourself, aye? Nobody's listening anyhow, and he that speaks to himself is speaking to a fool. How's that for philosophy?"

Donald looked down at Lily with a matter-of-fact impatience that she might have found reassuring had she not been choking down full-fledged panic since spotting the two men. "It's but his shoulder that's been nicked," he said dismissively. "The lad will be fine by the morrow, and I left your laird not but three hours past, braw as ever he was."

"That's what Kat said about John." Lily added through gritted teeth, "If one other person proclaims that someone close to me will be fine by tomorrow, I'm going to scream. What is going on?"

"What news have you?" Concern broke Donald's otherwise stoic features. "Is John hurt then?"

Robert gasped and Lily quickly replied, "No, no, he'll be fine. Rowena got it in her head that she wanted the boy dead, but I took care of her. Kat said he'll be back to normal in no time."

"Took care of things, did you? Good work, lass. Rowena, eh?" The two men exchanged a charged look. Donald added, "I kent that lass for fasherie from the moment I clapped eyes on her." He thought for a moment then added, "I see the MacKintosh's hand in this devil's work."

Lily looked at Robert. "You told him about the man in Rowena's rooms?"

"Yes, I reported the whole of it."

"Och," Donald grumbled, "we've had time enough to talk, aye?"

"Rowena told me that MacKintosh wanted Ewen dead . . ."

"Aye, lass," Donald considered, "I can see it clear. There's a spit of land, by Loch Arkaig."

"A spit of land," Robert continued, "that has been the cause of a long and bloody dispute between Clans MacKintosh and Cameron." He thought for a moment then added, "I can only but surmise that if both John and Ewen were to turn up dead, the absence of an obvious laird could throw the clan into temporary disarray, affording Lauchlan MacKintosh the opportunity he needs to seize the lands in question."

Robert grew alarmed. "We must warn Lochiel! He knows the MacKintosh threatens, but to hazard John's life so . . . the scoundrel has put into play something greater than a mere foray for lands. He has designs on utter ruination. We must alert Ewen to prepare for the mortal perils facing him and his."

"And what do you think it is I'm doing?" Lily asked. "I'm not exactly out on a trail ride here."

"Aye, of course, lass"—Donald glared at Robert—"if she can manage yon hellcat Rowena, I reckon she can manage stumbling into the laird on his way back to the keep to give him warning.

"Though, lass," Donald scolded, "next time you unseat your mount, you'd best tie her to a tree. You're chancie she's such an old hack or you'd be away to the laird by your own two feet."

Robert sighed. "I would that I could accompany you on your quest, fair Lily." He grimaced as Donald adjusted his hold on him. "But as you see, I have a grave injury that needs tending."

"You'll be fine, lad, so stop your mumping. Though you did a braw thing when you took the bullet for Lochiel as you did."

"What did you say?" Lily's head began to buzz.

"I said a braw lad our Robbie is, he took the bullet for Lochiel." The old man beamed. "Jumped like a stag betwixt Ewen and a redcoat pistol."

Lily's vision dimmed as Gram's voice filled her head.

"To protect the laird whom he called his brother,
He gave a gift he could give no other.
On a bonny hill the lad met his ruin,
When he took a bullet meant for Sir Ewen.

A sidhe lad
In red and green plaid
Died before he was old."

It was the song, it was coming true. She looked in horror at the tartan he'd worn that day in lieu of his usual jacket and breeches, the pattern Ewen's own favored red and green. "Donald!" Lily nearly shrieked. "You've got to get him to the castle immediately. Please! Go now!"

"Calm yourself, lass! What's come over you? I'm off for

Tor Castle presently. Or what else is it you think *I'm* fixing to do? You're the one's keeping me here cracking like some tawpie lassie."

"Right, right." Lily's heart hammered in her chest as she suddenly found it hard to catch her breath. She needed Ewen. She felt her fear for Robert like a physical symptom, pulsing through her veins, chilling her limbs and making her body tremble, and it only intensified her anxiety. She needed to see for herself that Ewen was unharmed.

She realized in that moment how he had become her rock. Lily had never needed to rely on another person for strength or courage, but she found she needed Ewen now. She had felt alone all of her life, braving difficult decisions, enduring both the sad and the happy times on her own, yet rather than feeling lonely her spirit had craved the serenity that solitude provided.

But she had met Ewen and something fundamental within her had shifted. Ewen, his bravery, his integrity, even his ferocity, and the depths of his devotion, for clan, for his Highlands, and now for her, had become Lily's touchstone. All she knew was that she needed to find him, that he was the only one who could help make it right.

Lily snatched her horse's reins and, clutching her skirts high in one hand, clumsily remounted. Turning the animal roughly on the path, she shouted, "I'm going to find Ewen and will meet you back at the keep." Lily kicked into an abrupt canter, the sounds of Donald's bewildered murmuring quickly fading in the distance.

She had hoped that riding hard down the uneven path would jar the panicked thoughts from her head, but it didn't seem to be working. Feelings of dread about Robert clutched at her gut. Lily refused to accept that his fate was somehow etched in stone. Simply because she grew up listening to a lullaby that praised his deeds and mourned his death, didn't mean she couldn't try to change what was about to happen at this moment in time. The song had been written in what would be the future, years after Robert's death. Her present was now, and she had to live in it as if she knew no other.

Robert wasn't dead yet. Donald said he'd get him safely back to Tor Castle, that Robert's wound wasn't that dire.

There was no reason for him to have to die. Who knew? Maybe Lily had been sent back for precisely that reason, to somehow prevent Robert's death. A weak laugh escaped her as Lily refused to contemplate the laws of nature she'd violate if she could just prevail upon the fates to change time's course of events.

"*Latha math dhut.* A good day to you, lassie." Lily inhaled sharply, nearly running into the horse and rider who suddenly blocked her path. She stared, dumbfounded. She had been so intent on her worries, she hadn't heard him gaining behind her.

He dismounted and was suddenly by her side, hand on her leg. "Let's discuss as civilized folk would, aye? I'd have you down where I can look at you."

One firm tug and Lily slid down the side of her saddle to the ground. "Ah, you're even bonnier than they say." The man's eyes roamed over her body, pausing overlong at her breasts. "Though it's Rowena who's doing the telling, and one lass isn't likely to paint a bonny picture of another, aye?"

Lily felt strangely unafraid. Her single-minded focus was on tracking down Ewen. She had gone through so much already that this man felt to her like just one more in a series of interlopers who stood in her way.

She studied the stranger in front of her. He was of a height with the laird, but where Ewen was brawny muscle, this man was sinewy and lean, the length of him exaggerated by his long face and pointed, hawkish features.

She eyed the brooch on his bonnet. A gold cat with eyes of dull, pocked amber. The MacKintosh cat. "You're Lauchlan, aren't you?"

He gave a quick smack to the rump of each horse and they bolted off through the trees. Lily cursed that she hadn't been more wary and could hear Donald scolding her now.

"Bonny *and* bright, I see." He grabbed her arms and gave them a sharp squeeze. "You'll make fine spoils indeed. Loch Arkaig and a new birdie for my nest."

Lauchlan leaned down as if to kiss her but Lily ducked, and twisting her arms loose, she broke away and raced toward the trees.

"Donald!" Lily screamed. She hoped her voice would

carry over the lake's silent tranquility. Their paths might not have diverged too much, they might not be too far away. She turned and bolted away from Lauchlan. "Donald!"

"Your Donald isn't coming, I felled the crabbit old bull but a moment ago," he laughed. Lauchlan loped effortlessly behind her, enjoying the chase as if it were something to whet the appetite, as a wolf would toy with a doe. "The redcoats are come calling and here he is out for a wee stroll in the woods. The fool was looking about not minding me, and he dropped, easy as a wink."

Lily sprinted for the tree line. If he thought Donald had been alone, Robert was out there somewhere. If they had heard the MacKintosh coming, maybe Robert had been able to ride away. She just hoped he was not too injured to make it safely back to the keep.

She could hear Lauchlan panting behind her, and it wasn't exertion that she heard so much as the sound of lust. A chill shivered up Lily's spine. It would be impossible to outrun his long, easy gait with speed alone. If she used her smaller size to her advantage, she had a chance of losing him in a dash through the dense brambles and scrub that carpeted the Lochaber woods. She believed she could escape him, she just needed to keep her wits about her. Darting between the saplings that grew along the forest's edge, she lunged for a spindly branch and snatched it in her hand, its young fibrous bark slicing through her palm as it dragged across her skin, leaving a sticky track of sap in its wake. She let go and heard a satisfyingly loud crack as the branch smacked Lauchlan across the bridge of his nose.

"Bloody hell, you *fremmit* whore," he raged. "You'll be sorry. Aye, sorry you'll be to have vexed a MacKintosh." He growled and Lily felt his hand swipe at her sleeve. "I'd thought to take you soft, but now I've a new mind of it." He bobbed through the trees, arms flailing, trying to grab hold of Lily.

"Get here, *galla ileach*!" Lily felt the tug at her skirt and heard the fabric tear. She managed to pull away from Lauchlan's grip but it had thrown her off balance, and she was sent tumbling onto the damp mulch of the forest floor.

"I generally appreciate when the lassies give me a wee

chase"—Lauchlan was astride her in an instant—"but this is over much. Och, a hellcat you are." He struggled to flip her onto her back. "Face me. Or is it you prefer it like a dog?"

The rich smell of decayed leaves filled her senses as she struggled to stay on her belly, legs clenched tight, digging through the loamy soil feeling for something, anything to help her. Her hands found a rotted log and she grabbed hold, trying to pull and wriggle her way out from under him, but it crumbled into sodden dust.

Lauchlan abandoned his attempts to turn Lily and began to tear at her skirts instead. His grunts became soft laughter as the crisp sound of ripping fabric resounded through the trees. A blast of cool air hit Lily's legs. She heard the jingle of Lauchlan's buckle as he tossed aside his sword and began to fumble with his sporran and kilt, and she cried out, finally breaking, a rush of hot tears spilling out, muddying the filth on her face.

She perceived a faint growling. It wasn't until she felt Lauchlan pause that she realized the sound didn't emanate from him. His hands, once fumbling, bruising, trying to part her legs, were suddenly still. "*Dé an diabhal a . . .*," he muttered.

Lily wrenched her head up in time to glimpse a blur of fur leaping over her head, aimed straight for Lauchlan's throat. "You bloody cur!" he shouted, and rolled off her back, fumbling for the *sgian dubh* tucked in his sock while his other arm guarded his neck.

Lily scuttled away on her knees and her heart soared at the sight of Finn worrying the front of Lauchlan's shirt, snapping desperately for a taste of flesh. He cuffed the dog and Finn let out a brief whimper before attacking with renewed ferocity.

The man stood at his full height now, kicking at the dog. "Don't rusk at me, you accursed rat." Lauchlan snatched at the scruff of Finn's neck, his other hand closing around the dagger at his calf. Lily swayed as terror erupted in her anew, quickening her breath and weakening her legs. She looked around desperately for anything to stop him.

His arm was poised now over the dog's neck, mouth quirked into a sinister half grin, his dagger glinting in the forest's dappled sunlight. And poor Finn fought so bravely. He had no idea what was about to happen, that his efforts were to be in vain.

Lily stepped toward him and stumbled. She glanced down and there she saw it, a large rock in her path, inexplicably clean and perfectly formed amidst the debris on the forest floor. She bent and took its smooth, cool weight in her hand.

Lily caressed the stone. It fit snugly, reassuringly in her palm. She looked from Finn to Lauchlan, and hatred of this man who would torture innocents out of spite roiled in her. A violent sneer distorted his features and a red stain blossomed on his shirt, now wet and sticking to his side. Good, then, she thought, Finn had drawn blood.

She stared at Lauchlan for a moment more. Then, just as he was stabbing down, she wound back and threw with all her strength. The rock struck Lauchlan on the forearm with enough force to make his hand falter. The knife slipped from his grasp at the last moment, grazing Finn's shoulder rather than delivering a killing blow.

The dog fell onto his side, panting heavily, his long gray legs floundering, at once trying to rise, then trying to reach his wound with his tongue. "Good boy, Finn," Lily soothed, the sight of his struggle unbearable, "it's okay, boy."

Lauchlan's soft laughter echoed through the trees once again. "You're a witch, you are, Lily. Now I ken what the Cameron saw in you. You'd best be worth the trouble."

A rock sailed inexplicably from the trees, striking the man on his leg. "Christ! What the bloody hell now?" He gaped as Robert emerged, limping, from the trees. "Och, woman, do you and your friends have a mind to fash me to death?"

"Let her be!" Robert announced heroically.

"What's next, have you a wee badger army too, with wee pistols what shoot scree instead of bullets?" Lauchlan turned to Robert, "Lad, you speak like you fancy yourself smart as Solomon. You've too many brains in your head. But I'll tend to that, aye, when I knock them all back out for you."

The MacKintosh spat. "And when I'm done"—he snatched a fistful of Lily's blonde curls—"I'll rid myself of this besom. And what a waste it will be." He dug his face in her hair, nosing it with an exaggerated sniff.

"Don't I have a say in this?" Lily swung her elbow up and back, smashing Lauchlan's beaklike nose with a wet crunch.

At once blood flowed down his lips and chin, his nose set at a sickeningly skewed angle.

Lauchlan dragged his sleeve across his face, leaving one side a crusted mask of reddish brown. "You're dead, woman," he said in a barely comprehendible whisper.

"Not yet." Robert's voice rang clearly, and Lily felt a surge of pride. She was certain there was a desk out there where Robbie would have rather been seated, yet here he was instead, by her side, death a very real possibility for both of them.

Robert leaned down and in a single movement, grabbed Lauchlan's *sgian dubh* from the leaves and hurled it toward her. The small dagger landed blade first in Lily's hand and she gasped from the shock of cold metal slicing through the flesh of her palm. She tossed the weapon up gently to catch it handle first and swung blindly back, hacking the taut muscle of Lauchlan's bicep. Unlike soft flesh, the tissue didn't yield easily, and Lily had to pull the blade out from where it had cleaved him.

Lauchlan roared and struck Lily with his good arm, smashing the side of her head. A shrill ringing filled her skull and she stumbled, choking down bile as her system began to retch from the shock. She caught herself, digging one hand into the dank leaves of the forest floor to keep from falling on her stomach.

Lily looked up. The MacKintosh stood above her, legs astride, predatory want darkening his eyes. He had retrieved his sword from the leaves and held it aloft, hand twitching with fury. Lily's palm was damp and hot where she still clutched the leather handle of the dagger. As Lauchlan slowly reached his bloodied arm over her, Lily summoned a desperate strength into her trembling legs and sprang up to meet him, raking the knife along the inside of his thigh as she rose.

The only sound he made was a clipped grunt, and the near silence terrified Lily more than any of his bellowing had. Eyes burning into her and a vicious hunger snarling the edges of his mouth, Lauchlan threw his sword, driving it into the ground blade first. He grabbed Lily's hand and pinned her to his leg, his coarse tartan chafing her face where she crouched awkwardly in front of him. The sour odor of mildew assailed her.

His hand was slick with his own blood, which oozed from between his clenched fingers onto Lily, drizzling down her arm. His grip tightened suddenly, the bones in her hand sounding a sickening crunch as he secured her tightly to him. In that instant, Lauchlan rammed his knee in her abdomen with violence enough to tear her hand from his.

Lily slammed into the dirt bottom first, and at once began frantically scrambling away from Lauchlan, her throat rasping and burning with the need to get air into her lungs. The man quietly stalked her, hands flexing, a grim smile betraying his intent. Unable to tear her eyes from Lauchlan, she heard Robert crawling between the trees, mumbling hysterical curses as he rifled his hands through the leaves.

Robert gasped and rose shakily to his feet. All of the movement had aggravated his gunshot wound, dislodging the dressing, and now a black and gruesome maw stared out through a tear in his shirt, shimmering crimson from the fresh blood that pulsed unchecked down his chest. He had retrieved the *sgian dubh* from the forest floor and now stood, gripping the weapon, and looked at Lily. A tranquil resolve softened his gaze, courage stilling his features.

He walked with painful deliberation toward the MacKintosh, whose eyes were still fixed only on Lily. Robert's body convulsed and he lunged forward, stabbing Lauchlan's neck before the MacKintosh knew to look behind him.

"Robbie, no!" Lily cried, as Robert crumpled to the ground. Lauchlan stumbled backward, disappearing into the trees, clawing for the hilt of the knife where Robert had planted it deep into the meat between shoulder and neck.

Lily rushed to Robert where he lay limp in the leaves, his stomach rising and falling as he pulled each breath in with a wheezing effort. A look of serenity hid what must've been tremendous suffering, and gave his face the calm innocence of a child's.

"Robbie, I'm so sorry," she whispered. "There was a song . . . I knew you were in danger." He looked at her quizzically, and she continued, "I could have warned you . . . should've warned you."

"Och, hush . . ." Robert coughed, and a small trickle of blood pooled at the corner of his mouth, proof that the redcoat bullet had pierced his lung. Robert's tranquil blue eyes studied Lily where she knelt, cradling his cheek in her hand.

"Hush, lass. This is how I'd have it." A trembling smile warmed his face.

He coughed again, face red with effort. Lily wiped the blood from his cheek, anguish twisting her features. "It truly is alright, lass." Robert smiled. "I believe it's why I'm here, why the maze brought me. I couldn't protect my own brother"—Robert looked away, a tear slowly spilling down his cheek—"but I could protect our laird."

He turned and fixed an intent gaze on Lily. "Dear Ewen. He loves you, you know. Tell him . . . ," he added in a tight whisper, "tell him I proved myself worthy of the clan."

Goose bumps shivered up Lily's arms upon hearing words that so eerily echoed the lyrics of Gram's lullaby.

"I will Robert." Lily's chin quivered, but her voice was strong and clear. "He loves you too; everyone will know the hero you are."

She stroked her fingers through his sweat-dampened hair, and sang.

> "He was a fey lad and not so old
> With hair spun from rings of gold.
> Upon Letterfinlay soil he did land,
> Claiming he came from a future grand.
> A MacMartin lad who knew no fear,
> Clan Cameron took and held him dear.
>
> "A sidhe lad
> In red and green plaid
> And charming to behold.
>
> "One day tragedy learnt his name
> In a skirmish with men in coats of flame.
> To protect the laird whom he called his brother,
> He gave a gift he could give no other.
> On a bonny hill the lad met his ruin,
> When he took a bullet meant for Sir Ewen.
>
> "A sidhe lad
> In red and green plaid
> Died before he was old.

"The fearsome laird and his hounds did forgive
Any trespasses the fey lad did give.
For known as but a lettered young man,
He proved himself worthy of clan.
Honored is he until this day,
For a most precious price he did pay.

"Lochaber lasses still grieve for the lad,
A MacMartin hero in Cameron plaid."

A shudder coursed through Robert, and his features became at ease, limbs heavy and body still, as he seemed to reach a point beyond pain. He licked his lips, and he looked at Lily for one last time, eyes roving avidly over her face as if he would memorize her. He whispered, "Thank you."

A last breath sighed from his body, and Lily laid her hand gently on his cheek, awed by the peace that smoothed his features, and the knowing smile that curved the edges of his lips.

It was then that she heard Finn trying to rouse himself, and his agonized whimpers shattered the last shred of nerves holding Lily together. She wept mutely, and the throbbing pain in her belly swelled into a grief that suffused her, dulled her mind, making her body sluggish, reluctant to move or draw breath.

A flicker of movement brought Lily to her senses and terror skewered her, as she realized it had been a mistake to put Lauchlan at her back.

She rose slowly, unable to face the MacKintosh, and watched with horror the shadows that played on the forest floor. Lauchlan loomed behind her, his silhouette black in the late afternoon light. Lily stood, frozen, staring at the approaching shadow. Thoughts hurtled through her mind, yet she was powerless to seize on a single strategy for escaping this man one more time. She watched as the shadow enveloped her head, and a deafening crack reverberated through every muscle in her body until she became that darkness.

Chapter 30

Sensations slowly pierced her consciousness. Gentle murmuring and the light touch of fingers on her brow. Water with the bitter cold taste of a Highland lake soothing her parched lips. The reassuring smells of musk and leather. Something licking her hand.

Lily's eyes opened with a start. She gasped and promptly shut them again. Pain thrummed through her head with a keen-edged agony that made her jaw clench and her eyes tear. She needed to surface more slowly. Hesitantly, she opened her eyes again. White specks crackled and danced across her vision in stark contrast to the muted twilight.

The dark blur overhead resolved into Ewen. He smiled down at her, and relief flooded over Lily. That smile unraveled the knot of anxiety and fear that she had felt like a suffocating pressure on her chest.

"Ewen," she whispered, smiling back at him. Lily glanced down and laughed at the sight of Finn studiously licking her hand. "Oh . . . my head." The throbbing in her skull cut her laughter short. She was relieved to see the dog alive. Although his gray fur was matted black with blood, he seemed undaunted and preoccupied only with the soaking of Lily's extremities.

"There you are, Lil'. You came back to me." The evening's half light gilded Ewen's cheeks, lighting the tracks of recently shed tears.

Laughing, he abruptly bent down to kiss her eyes, her cheeks, her mouth. "What am I to do with you? I keep finding you knocked insensible."

"Lauchlan?" Panic shattered the contentment on Lily's face. "Where is he? Did you kill him?"

A forbidding look unknown to her darkened Ewen's brow. "Nay, lass. The MacKintosh is gone from here."

He turned her head and carefully arranged her hair, its paleness now the dun color of dirt and blood. Ewen sucked in a breath. "Och, Lil', he gave quite the clout to your head before turning tail through the woods."

The laird sat erect, his mind withdrawing for a moment to a more pragmatic place. "There was much blood spilled. Yont those trees"—Ewen nodded behind him—"the leaves are soaked through. It looks like someone struck a dire blow to the MacKintosh." His eyes turned back to Lily and he added gravely, "You're lucky he left you for dead, lass."

"Yes." Lily's voice was tight with sorrow. "I know. It was Robert who injured him. He stabbed him, near his neck."

"Ah." Ewen nodded. "The MacKintosh would've fled before the blood loss came too dear."

"Robert." Lily's voice cracked with anguish. "He saved me." A sob choked her. "Robbie is dead, Ewen."

"Quiet yourself, Lil'. I know. I saw young Robbie. Donald is away to take him back to the keep."

"Donald?" Hope momentarily brightened her voice. "Donald's alive?"

"Aye, the old man is harder to kill than that. His head is even harder than yours, lass, if such like is possible."

"But Lauchlan said . . ."

"Och, I'm sure I ken what the MacKintosh said. I say my uncle's a hoary old Highlander who's been left for dead more times than I can recall. 'Tis Lauchlan who'll be wanting to watch his health. Donald won't rest until he's seen young

Robbie avenged. He's raving with anger at himself for letting the MacKintosh best him. I dare say it won't happen twice."

"I'm sorry." Grief smothered Lily's voice, barely discernable above the rustling trees. "I'm so sorry, I feel like it's my fault, like . . ."

"My Lil'." Ewen took her face in his hands. "I ken how you feel." Fury rippled through his voice. "I ken where the fault lies, and it's not with you, nor me." Serenity quieted his features, pride clear in his eyes. "Our Robbie is a hero. You say the lad saved you, but I tell you true, the lad saved us both."

"He said . . ." Lily faltered as fresh tears threatened to fall.

"Tell me, lass."

"He was . . . it was like he was happy at the end. At peace. He said it's why he was sent back." Conviction bolstered her. "To save you."

Lily absentmindedly rubbed the dirt from her hands, a faraway look in her eyes. "I just wonder . . ." She met Ewen's intent gaze, and finished, "I wonder why I was sent. I mean, if Robert was originally a MacMartin, and my Gram was a MacMartin"—Lily let out a humorless laugh—"that would make us distant relatives, right? Is that why we were both chosen?"

"Och, Lil'," Ewen said tenderly, "I know why it was you were sent back." Lily's eyes studied him silently for the answer. He continued, "You've saved my life too, aye? And that's why you went through the maze." He took her hands in his. "You were sent back for me."

"What is that?" Lily's voice cracked as the laird retrieved a folded paper from his sporran. Even as she asked, Lily knew it was the star chart.

"This, lass?" Ewen spread the paper between them, the lines and points faded gray in the dying light. "This is everything and nothing, my love. And I'd destroy it if you'd let me."

Lily studied the chart. A series of patterns drawn on a ragged slip of paper, and the only thing with the power to take her back. Without it, she would never see San Francisco again. No more modern medicine. Never again pizza or movies or hot showers. If there was a chance she could ever mend ways with her mother, it lay with this single piece of paper. She considered it, the memory of those lines and points burning in her fingers.

And then her eyes shifted slightly, considering the hands that held the chart. Ewen's hands, strong, male, bearing scars, and soiled with the day, with horse and leather and dirt. Lily felt something in her soul shatter at the thought of never seeing this man again. Never feeling these hands on her body. Never again hearing the deep burr of his voice. She would have seen the last of his rare and wonderful smiles. Would never again see him magnificent in tartan and sword, brave and honor-bound.

It was as if she stood at the edge of a precipice, the black void at her feet a life without Ewen, as if choosing to leave him would swallow her into that vast emptiness. Lily knew then she would never leave him. Could never leave him, if she wanted to be whole.

She took those hands in hers and whispered, "Yes." Emotion clutched at her throat and joy overwhelmed her as it became clear to Lily, perfect and uncomplicated, that her place was at Ewen's side. That Ewen too would have it no other way. "Destroy it." She smiled.

"Then I've a question for you," Ewen said, hoarse with emotion. "Marry me, Lil'? Be my bride?"

"I will." Lily beamed. "I would love nothing more than to marry you, Ewen Cameron."

He laughed, and joy softened his features, the handsome man a flare of light bursting through his usual warrior's mien.

"But there's one thing," he said with mock severity. "A laird's wife has certain duties, aye?"

"Really now?"

Suddenly serious, his voice thick with desire, Ewen replied, "Oh, aye." He took Lily into his arms, his hands already roving hungrily over her body, eyes glinting like dark blue steel as they devoured her. "You're to give yourself to your laird."

"Oh, aye," Lily murmured, and she gave her whole self.

Epilogue

She moaned, feeling the babe inside her turn and kick again. Lily shifted her weight. The plush furs on Ewen's bed had been divine before she became pregnant, but now, no matter what Lily did, she couldn't get comfortable.

"He's a braw one, aye?" Ewen whispered, rubbing her belly, tugging her even closer to him. He thought that falling asleep only to wake the next day with Lily by his side was heaven on earth. But to wrap his hand around and feel the movement of his babe inside her was more than a man could dream of.

"A little too braw, for my tastes. I don't get why this kid is such a night owl."

Ewen's drowsy laugh was a husky, languid sound that never ceased to shoot a tremor of desire up through her legs, into her core.

"Go on, ha ha." Lily playfully kicked her feet against his hard-muscled legs. "You're not the one who's getting a tap dance on his insides."

"He'll give you a run for it, as wee John has."

"John isn't so wee anymore, by the way, and have you noticed how excited he is about the baby?"

"Aye," he laughed proudly, "I'll have to sell a parcel of land to keep that boy in paper."

"I know, I've created a monster, haven't I? There's no more space left on the nursery walls from all of his artworks."

"Not a monster at all, Lil'." Ewen's tone was suddenly serious. "You've done a fine job with the lad. He'll be laird some day, and mark me, he'll make Clan Cameron proud."

"Oh!" Lily startled, as Finn leapt onto the bed, turned in circles by her feet, and plopped down with a loud groan. "The gang's all here now." Despite Lily's grumbling, there was laughter in her voice.

Ewen caressed Lily's side, trying to soothe her restlessness. They had been married a mere handful of months when the bairn had quickened in her belly. Now her stomach was rounded and tight under her swollen breasts. She had never looked more beautiful to him.

They had held their wedding ceremony almost right away. Initially they'd wanted to wait until Donald made a full recovery, but the old man had protested heartily—and colorfully. Lily finally agreed they should exchange vows immediately, despite the grievous wounds of their best man, if only to stop his increasingly ribald exclamations that, as far as she could understand, had something to do with Ewen yoking himself to her.

"And by the way, *da*, you keep saying 'he,' but he could be a she. There is a fifty-fifty chance, you know."

"Aye." Ewen patted her stomach possessively. "And a bonny lass she'd be. Wee bonny Roberta."

"Yes." Lily grinned at what sounded to her ears as a very adult name for a baby girl. "Or a young Master Robert."

They lay in silence for a while, letting the memory of Robert hang in the room. "Quiet yourself, love," Ewen rasped, tangling his fingers in her hair. "I can feel you thinking."

"I know," Lily admitted. They hadn't been married long and he already had the uncanny ability to read her thoughts. "It's just . . . I feel guilty. About Robert. I feel I should've warned him more, that maybe I could've saved him, changed the outcome somehow."

"Och, lass, there's no changing what must be." Ewen turned her face to look at him. "I see history like a road we travel, aye? And you've no choice but to stay the course, as a wagon wheel along a rut in a well-worn path."

Stroking her hair, he leaned in to kiss her on the forehead. "I can't fathom the ways of the maze, why it called to Robbie, or to you. If it serves only Clan Cameron, or if it only has regard for those of your bloodline. I do ken that it sent you here, to me, and it's here with me that you'll stay."

Lily kissed him lightly, silently, in response. She'd never know if she could've saved Robert, as he gave his own life to save theirs. But Lily could hope that her own appearance had helped spare the laird, and maybe his son, from a worse fate.

Ewen snuggled her close, massaging his hand along her side, and Lily could feel by the slowing of his touch that he was falling back asleep. She was fidgety, though, and refused to let him go yet. It was impossible to sleep with the baby turning leisurely somersaults and elbow salutes in her belly, and she'd have just a little more company in the wee hours. Thinking to rouse him, Lily asked, "Is it true what I hear about Monk?"

"You mean his wife?" Ewen chuckled. Rumors abounded of a hasty marriage between Monk and his reputedly homely mistress. "Aye, so I gather. The claver about the castle is that she's beneath him."

The laird knew his wife well and, feeling her bristle at his last comment, quickly added, "I mean to say she's . . . a lady of low extraction, aye? She's not of Monk's circles."

"But you didn't see her when you met with him last week?"

"There was nary a sign of the woman. But," Ewen added derisively, "I wasn't exactly there to tour the sights, aye? Just because I've a truce with the man, doesn't mean I'll take tea with him. And besides, he showed me the MacKintosh petition and my appetite quit me. I wanted in, then out of his camp."

"I can't believe the MacKintosh is now trying to convince Monk that he should have your lands."

"Aye." Ewen chuckled. "Fool thing, that. Though as long as he stays away from you and that bonny head of yours, Lauchlan can write to Cromwell himself and welcome to it. No MacKintosh will ever take Cameron lands." He gave a meaningful pause, then added, "Though he is welcome to that lass, Rowena."

"And won't they have some interesting offspring?"

"Indeed," he laughed. "I imagine she was sore put to discover just where her new home would be. The MacKintosh installed her in the clan castle, on a gloomy spit of land in the middle of Loch Moy. I'm certain Miss Rowena fancied herself holding court at Moy Hall instead, their estate outside Inverness."

Lily's laughter joined his, her melancholy put aside. It was difficult to stay sad when she was with Ewen, especially since he'd started showing her a lighthearted side that never failed to surprise her.

"So, are you relieved?" she asked, bringing the subject back around. "About the truce, I mean?"

"With a bonny new bride and a bairn on the way? How could I not be? Truly, lass, I will never accept a Monk or a Cromwell on my Highlands. But I'm a peaceable man, aye? So long as I can keep my clansmen in arms, I'll give my word of honor that I'll not pick fights with the redcoats."

"What if they start the fight?" Lily asked, already knowing the answer.

"Then," Ewen spoke definitively, "they'll suffer their actions."

Lily was silent.

"Och," he soothed her, "don't trouble yourself over the likes of Monk. I've handled him well and tidily before and will do so again if needs be. You're fretting enough between our son and our babe." He combed his fingers through her hair, the thick curls massed on the pillow above her head ashen in the darkness of their room. "So hush lass. Be calm."

Ewen's hand paused longer between each stroke. "What a sweet dream you are, Lil'," he said drowsily. "I never know if I'm waking or sleeping when I'm by your side."

She heard her husband's breath deepen into a slow rhythm. Smiling, she muttered, "Well, if you don't know I'll tell you, you're now sleeping, Mr. Cameron." Lily took his hand, and entwining their fingers, placed it over her belly. When he relaxed, the man could drift off anywhere.

Ewen's warm touch and steady breathing lulled Lily into drowsiness. Lying in their bed, tucked in his arms, she felt sheltered, as though she'd traveled through time to find the safe haven of family with this very man. She only wished her grandmother could have met him. Lily smiled, hearing Gram in her head exclaiming, *What a braw lad, your Ewen!*

Heavy-lidded, she watched as thin streaks of light slowly cut their way over the thick drapes, now glowing crimson from the sun creeping up the dawn sky.

With daybreak came the sounds of birdsong, growing louder outside the castle windows. Lily began to hum her own tune as thoughts of her grandmother brought a tightness to her throat. She began to sing softly, her voice trembling as it always did when she sang of the uncle her babe would be named for, and yet would never know.

> *"He was a fey lad and not so old*
> *With hair spun from rings of gold.*
> *Upon Letterfinlay soil he did land,*
> *Claiming he came from a future grand.*
> *A MacMartin lad who knew no fear,*
> *Clan Cameron took and held him dear.*
>
> *Lochaber lasses still grieve for the lad,*
> *A MacMartin hero in Cameron plaid."*

Author's Note

I've altered a number of facts and dates surrounding the life of Ewen Cameron of Lochiel, seventeenth chief of his clan, also known as *Ewen Dubh M'Ian V'Allan*, *Eoghain Dubh*, Ewen the Black, and "Ulysses of the Highlands." A great many details, however, were plucked straight from the pages of history.

Ewen was indeed a famously noble, loyal, and gracious leader whose great skill and imposing size also made him a fearsome enemy. He became clan chief around the age of eighteen, fighting in the Battle of Achdalieu at a much younger age than that I've portrayed. He was indeed fostered by his uncle, about whom there's not much written, though I can't imagine the gruff old Donald to be too far off the mark. The wise and wizened Gormshuil, certain events surrounding Robert, particulars around Ewen's great deeds in battle, and even General Monk's choice of bride are rooted in fact, and the laird's well-told lore is recounted in poems and songs, and was even the inspiration for a scene in Sir Walter Scott's "Lady of the Lake."

The real Ewen lived to the ripe age of ninety, and married three times, reportedly fathering no less than twenty-three children.

Be sure to meet the sixteen-year-old Ewen in my second book, *Sword of the Highlands*.

To discover other ways in which *Master of the Highlands* echoes true Cameron clan history, please visit my web site at www.veronicawolff.com.

Turn the page for a preview of the next
historical romance by Veronica Wolff

Sword of the Highlands

Coming June 2008 from Berkley Sensation!

The immense sign mocked her. Even though Magda's taxi was still a couple blocks from the Met, she could see the advertisement fluttering high above the museum's entrance. FINDING ARCADIA: PASTORAL PAINTINGS OF THE SEVENTEENTH CENTURY.

"You can stop here." She grabbed a crumpled ten out of her purse and thrust it at the cabbie. "I'll walk the rest of the way."

Clutching her toolbox and the now-mashed bread, she marched down Fifth Avenue, her irritation with Walter dissolving into a growing feeling of dismay. Magda hadn't really had anything else going on that weekend and she found she looked forward to having something to do, even if it was for her job.

Her wealthy childhood had afforded her the luxury of studying fine art, but she'd bristled at the cliché. Magda had resolved to be more than the little rich girl who knew her way around pricey antiques, and made sure she gave nobody the excuse to think her any less than a rigorous academic.

When she was first hired as assistant curator of European art, a few of her co-workers had looked down their noses at the girl who'd been hired for her last name. What museum in their

right mind would turn down a member of one of Manhattan's
more philanthropic society families? And so Magdalen Dea-
con had made it her mission to be the best of the best when it
came to identifying, cleaning, and restoring old paintings.

She entered a side door to avoid the typical throng of
Saturday-morning tourists. The heat of Manhattan in summer
was claustrophobic enough; given a choice, Magda would
avoid a crowded, enclosed space every time. Savoring the
sweet blast of air-conditioning, she flicked on a single light
switch and walked down a flight of stairs to an antiseptic hallway. Door after door of restoration offices lined a hall that,
during the week, had the feel of a busy hive, its workers
buzzing around independently and with intense focus. Empty,
though, it was like a tunnel. The tiles that glared white during
work hours now were a shimmering gray under the single row
of buzzing fluorescent tubes.

She had been amazed the first time she visited the
employee-only area. Dozens of rooms lined the bowels of the
museum. A number of them housed mismatched sculpture
like a millionaire's garage sale, while others felt like bank
vaults, with temperature-controlled facilities housing drawer
after drawer of prints and drawings. Her favorite, though, was
the painting storage, where hundreds of priceless works hung
on panels that she could flip through, much like browsing
posters in the museum shop.

"Thanks, kid."

Walter's voice startled Magda and she smiled at herself.
She always had a tendency to get a bit fanciful whenever she
was among so much art. The empty rooms and dim lights only
intensified it.

"No problem," she said, realizing that it was true. Now that
she was there, it really wasn't a problem. Magda was actually
quite curious about the paintings that would drive Walter to
call her for such a fast and loose clean-up job for a ready-to-
go exhibition.

"They're in here." He rattled through the dozens of keys
hanging from his belt, surprising for a curator. Generally a
tweedy set, they weren't inclined to janitorial-grade key
chains. "They arrived by courier late last night, anonymous
bequeathal. All Scottish pieces, which is unusual."

Walter fumbled along the wall for the light, continuing, "Frankly my dear, I don't give a damn what their provenance is, they're a perfect fit for the exhibit. We've got Flemish paintings coming out of our ears, but we're short on Britain. I even see some Scottish Highlands landscapes here, which is unheard of for this time period."

The lights flickered on and Magda drew in her breath. The table was cluttered with dozens of miniature landscapes, each bearing some romantic vista on a small scale: seascapes under bright blue-saturated skies, idyllic farmlands dotted with sheep, storm-clouded castles, purple heather-tangled moors, and emerald green rain-drenched glens.

"Don't have a cardiac, kid, I don't want you to clean the lot of them. There are just two that I have to have. The rest is gravy.

"Besides," he added, picking up one of the small paintings, "they look like they were restored not too long ago." He held the piece horizontally up to his eyes, shifting it under the light, scanning the surface for imperfections. "You should get these under the UV, see what's what. Otherwise, they should tidy right up with a superficial cleaning."

But Magda wasn't listening. Nor had it been the number of paintings that had made her gasp. It was the portrait that held her attention, looming so incongruously alive among the pool of formal landscapes. Leaning askew against the rear wall was a life-size painting of a man, pictured from the waist up, against a background of dense, impermeable black. Only the man's face was illuminated with color, and his features seemed to emerge from the darkness. White paint slashed dramatically across his left breast, as if he'd been lit from below and a flickering candle cut through the shadows.

He was handsome, but not too perfect. His features were fine, except for his nose, which was just a fraction too large and gave his face a strong, masculine appearance. Brown hair hung in loose waves to his shoulders, making him appear somewhat more disheveled than these sorts of portraits usually depicted, as if the painter had just caught his subject in mid action. His black eyes stared, and they were painted with such vitality the man seemed about to break into a wicked grin, charisma pulling Madga toward the canvas like a magnet.

"You hungry or something?"

Magda jumped, and looked at Walter as if seeing him for the first time. "Huh?"

"You really are an absent-minded professor, kid." He nodded toward the loaf of bread being crushed under her arm. "You on an all-carb kick or something?"

"This?" Magda looked down and seemed to come back to earth. "Oh, yea, we're so short on time, I thought I'd bring out one of my favorite cheats."

"You're on a diet?"

"What? No, of course not. It's a trick I use, for the painting. Dough can clean better than any solvent. You just wad it up, and . . ."

"Okay, whatever, I get the picture. Now just get to work. And get your eyes off Mister Universe over there. You're only interested in these two." Walter pointed to a small matched pair of landscapes depicting the same Highland glen at different times of day. "You don't see that kind of thing a lot, at least not before the Impressionists came along."

"Walter, wait." Magda stopped her boss just as he was walking out the door.

"Who is that guy anyway?" she asked, staring again at the portrait.

He huffed an exasperated sigh, and asked, "I take it you're not going to concentrate until you know, huh?"

"Hm?" She looked at him distractedly. "What was that?"

"Mag," he grumbled, shaking his head, "the things I do." Putting his briefcase down, Walter shuffled through a stack of papers. "Aha. That is"—he took out a small, yellowed note card and read—"James Graham, First Marquis of Montrose."

"They had marquis in Scotland?"

"Yea, I guess so." He saw from her expression that she wasn't going to let him go without more information so, scanning the paper, Walter enumerated the pertinent facts to Magda. "Let's see . . . seventeenth-century nobleman . . . Scottish . . . started some group called the Covenanters . . . something about the king and religion . . . ah . . ." Walter was silent for a moment.

"What?" she asked impatiently. "Ah what, Walter?"

"Looks like the guy switched sides . . . led a bunch of Highlanders to battle . . . that must've been a sight, huh?"

Magda glared.

"Okay, let's see . . . ech." He finished quickly, "Captured, imprisoned, and hanged in Edinburgh."

"That's hideous!" Magda exclaimed.

Walter looked up at Magda. "Yea, I'd say. So much for your Mister Universe. Glad you don't live in seventeenth-century Scotland, huh?" Closing his briefcase, Walter demanded, "Now, take your Wonderbread, or whatever that is, and clean my paintings."

The door whispered shut behind him.

❀

She'd thought to spend Sunday catching up on rest and errands, but dreams of the mysterious man in the portrait had haunted her sleep. That roguish face, captured on canvas, came alive in a dream to break into a mischievous smile. And in another, the silk of his shining brown hair was wavy and soft under her fingertips. And, what had startled her awake over and over through the night, witnessing the flint in his eyes dampen to a flat black stare, as he stood to face his fate on the gallows.

Now Magda was compelled to spend some time with that curious portrait before Walter bumped it to the bottom of her workload. And so she was off to her basement workroom, by way of the library for a book on Scottish history, to pay a visit to the brown-haired Mister Universe.

She flipped through the pages as she walked and was surprised to find that James Graham was actually a famous figure. He had been a man of wealth and status when he sacrificed everything to fight for Scotland. He'd fancied himself a poet, and Magda pored over lines he'd written that now felt tragically prescient.

> *But how to conquer an eternal name:*
> *So, great attempts, heroic ventures shall*
> *Advance my fortune or renown my fall.*

❀

Her skin shivered and chest tightened with the unnerving intimacy as she examined the portrait in her windowless workroom where she looked at everything under an ultraviolet light. She didn't know why a painting of a man long dead would be different from any other work of art, but, hand trembling over the remaining light switch, she felt vulnerable sharing such a small, dark space with him gazing at her unblinking.

She shook her head, then flicked the light off and the UV wand on. The painting buzzed to life in an eerie, Technicolor glow. Immediately engrossed, Magda slipped off her sandals, and squinting her eyes, leaned in to study the bright hum of light wavering across the painting's surface.

She scanned for signs of tears, punctures, or even old repairs but, remarkably, there were no telltale dark purple blotches under the ultraviolet light. What she did see were centuries of grime and soot that had discolored the varnish and now glowed in a pale greenish yellow UV haze. Dust, visible as small bullets of electric blue, jangled across the surface.

"Where have you been? All these years"—switching off the UV wand, her eyes roved the surface of the portrait—"and not a single bit of harm done to you."

Magda studied his face, and her cheeks flushed at the strange feeling that those black, almond-shaped eyes stared back. Though his brown hair waved to his shoulders, it wasn't styled in the way she imagined court fashions required, falling loosely around his face and tousled over his brow. Magda studied his mouth intently and fought the sensation that, if she stared hard enough, his lips would curve into a slow smile.

Without thinking, she broke a cardinal rule of museum work as she extended her ungloved hand to touch the utter blackness of the portrait's background. Gasping, Magda pulled back as if stung.

The painting was cold.

Maybe she was just chilled, she thought, as she chafed her hands together. Although cool to the touch, paintings definitely did not generate their own temperature.

Magda slowly lowered her palms to the portrait, one on either side of the man's face, and she drew in her breath with the shock of it.

The portrait's black background wasn't just chilled, it was a raw, dead sort of cold. An ache creaked up Magda's forearms as she tried to puzzle out the growing impression of damp paint under her fingertips. Easing her hands along the surface, she marveled at the absence of the typical hard peaks and valleys of any oil painting. Magda had the sensation that her hands would sink into the paint if she let them.

The fluorescent tube overhead began to flicker, echoing the dull hum that had begun in the back of her head.

Once again she pulled her hands back, but slowly this time, and her eyes met those of the man in the portrait. The urge to touch him overwhelmed her; she had to feel the smoothness of his cheek, trace the light arc of his eyebrow beneath the muss of hair that rested on his brow. Magda flexed her hands, and mesmerized, reached out, her hand hovering just over the painting's surface.

The drone in her head became a loud buzzing as she stretched a single fingertip out to brush his face. A breathy sigh escaped her. Magda had known, somehow, that it would be warm. That he would be warm.

Dizziness nagged the edges of her consciousness but her compulsion drove her, and she fought to focus on the painting. Magda gently cupped the side of his face with her palm, and again, it wasn't like touching dried paint on canvas. But unlike the cold black of the background, his face felt as if it had been heated by that candle's glow, and was soft like velvet under her palm.

The dizziness burst through her awareness, consuming her, and Magda flung both hands out to steady herself on the painting.

Vertigo whirred in her skull like a fan's blade, and Magda felt herself falling through the cold blackness.

Enter the rich world of historical romance with Berkley Books.

Lynn Kurland

Patricia Potter

Betina Krahn

Jodi Thomas

Anne Gracie

Love is timeless.